TREASURE COAST

A CRIME THRILLER BY

JAMES FOLEY

Black Rose Writing | Texas

ISBN: 978-1-68513-555-3
PUBLISHED BY BLACK ROSE WRITING
www.blackrosewriting.com

Printed in the United States of America
Suggested Retail Price (SRP) $22.95

Treasure Coast is printed in Garamond Premier Pro

*As a planet-friendly publisher, Black Rose Writing does its best to eliminate unnecessary waste to reduce paper usage and energy costs, while never compromising the reading experience. As a result, the final word count vs. page count may not meet common expectations.

PRAISE FOR TREASURE COAST

"**A strong start to what could be an entertaining series featuring a well-developed, sympathetic cop protagonist.** Numerous noteworthy elements fuel Foley's narrative, including an impressively diverse cast of secondary characters, including a politician with twisted sexual proclivities, a naïve marine biologist, and a sleazy realtor. They effectively flesh out the multilayered mystery, and the author also explores environmental issues, such as global warming and marine plastic pollution, with subtlety and compassion. Infrequent moments of social commentary add brass-knuckle impact..."
–Kirkus Reviews

"*Treasure Coast* **is everything you'd want in a thriller**: action, intrigue, high stakes and even some heart. James Foley has splashed onto the crime writing scene with a promising debut! Bravo!"
–Matt Coyle, best-selling author of the award-winning *Rick Cahill* crime series

"**An engrossing, character-driven crime thriller** that thoughtfully explores grief, atonement and post-loss romance alongside gritty police work. Recommended for Karin Slaughter fans."
–BestThrillers.com

"**James Foley's talent in penning twists, tension, and interleaving dark secrets, makes for a brisk paced read that's impossible to put down.** Fans of David Baldacci's bestselling Atlee Pine series will love this one! Five stars!"
–Cam Torrens, author of the *Tyler Zahn* thriller series

"**James Foley has written us a bloodstained postcard from Florida.** You'll never look at the Sunshine State the same way. Treasure Coast has all the makings of an outstanding series. I can't wait to find out what's next for Lisa Owens."
–Holly Kammier, author of *Lost Girl, A Shelby Day Novel*

"**Unforgettable.** A hair-raising crime thriller that will keep you off the beach at night."
–Cat Ross, **award-winning author of** *City of Storms*

For Suzanne
With you, everything good seems possible.

TREASURE
COAST

FOREWORD

At two o'clock in the morning on July 31, 1715, eleven galleons carrying a cargo of silver, gold, and precious gemstones crashed into the treacherous reefs that lie beneath the waves, just off what is now known as Florida's Treasure Coast. Named for the treasure they carried from the New World, and blown off course by a powerful hurricane as they headed home to Spain, the ships of the Spanish Plate Fleet were on a mission to provide funding for a King whose greed for power had caused his country to fall into desperate financial straits.

Three hundred years after its sinking, the Spanish Plate Fleet, and the hundreds of other shipwrecks that followed, continue to deliver bounty to treasure hunters, SCUBA divers, and snorkelers searching the area's turquoise waters.

Throughout the years, pirates, smugglers, bootleggers, and outlaws have all played a part in the storied history of the Treasure Coast. A history that continues to be tainted by greed, though no longer driven by a Spanish King. Real estate developers make huge profits by bulldozing quaint seaside cottages and tropical savannas, overcrowding the area with oceanfront mansions, golf courses and condominiums. Clearing the way for those projects are politicians who approve loopholes and variances to building ordinances in return for alliances that keep them in power. To ensure those dream home purchases go through without a hitch, a bevy of realtors, mortgage brokers, financial planners, lawyers, and insurance conglomerates have settled into the area.

Of the many opportunities to get rich on the Treasure Coast, one of the most lucrative is the illegal drug trade. The practice of smuggling in the area goes back to the days of prohibition and the rumrunners of that era. But it wasn't until the rise in the international marijuana and cocaine trade in the 1970s that smuggling in Florida reached its peak. Now, on any given day, patrol boats and aircraft from the Customs Service, Coast Guard, and local police departments patrol the waters off the east coast of Florida under the coordination of a master radar center in Miami.

CHAPTER 1

Tuesday, July 6 - 9:00 p.m.

The boat pulled away from Grand Bahama Island, its destination a small barrier island on the coast of Florida, two hours north of Miami. If all went well, it would arrive around midnight. The sky and ocean were the same pitch-black, creating a blank space that allowed the fast boat to disappear, save for its telltale frothy wake. A highly skilled mariner steered the powerful vessel away from the island's shallows and into the Atlantic. On board with him, two young men and four duffle bags of cocaine, its street value in the millions.

As the boat departed, Lisa Owens, a senior homicide investigator for the City of Miami Police Department, sat alone at the steel desk in her glass-enclosed office, three computer screens glowing in front of her. On the desk was an opened bag of fried pork rinds, a bottle of hot sauce and a small, framed photograph of a young man she'd planned to marry before he was taken from her; a murder victim whose case hadn't been solved because the police had dropped the ball.

To avenge her fiancé's death or at least to make some meaning of it, Lisa had trained for a career in law enforcement, dedicating herself to bringing justice to the families and loved ones of murder victims so they wouldn't have to endure the unimaginable pain of not knowing. A pain she knew all too well. Although she'd solved hundreds of cases, her work hadn't made up for the loss she felt, and she still carried a mistrust that caused her to do the heavy lifting on her cases by herself. A workaholic, she was at the top of her game professionally and at rock bottom in her personal life.

Stretching her arms over her head, Lisa yawned. She was carrying a full caseload and planned to work for a few more hours. Her cell phone buzzed on her desk and, seeing the caller ID, her face lit up. "Dorothy, it's so good to hear from you. How are things on Stypman Island?" Dorothy Jensen had been Lisa's teacher in middle school. Now a close friend for many years, Lisa thought of her as a grandmother and her best friend.

"Hello, dear. Have I called at a bad time?"

"Work is crazy, and I'm up to my ears, but I always have time for you." She added hot sauce to a pork rind, popped it into her mouth, and bit down.

"I hear crunching. Tell me you're not eating pork rinds for supper again."

Lisa laughed. "Blame Scott, he got me hooked, and the hot sauce... you've got to have the hot sauce. How's everything with you? Still giving those polluters hell?"

"It seems our lawsuit may finally move forward. Maybe this time those greedy bastards will have to pay for what they've done. The politicians haven't helped, so we're hoping the courts will. Other than that, things are quiet here at Coquina Reef now that the snowbirds have gone back north. The few of us year rounders have the whole place to ourselves. It's heaven."

"I miss you. Are you still up for lunch in two weeks? I have someplace nice planned, my treat." The talk of food made Lisa's stomach grumble, and she eyed the bag of pork rinds.

"I'm looking forward to it. Umm... why don't you plan on staying the night when you come up here? You could leave early the next morning and be back in Miami in time for work. We'll have more time to talk that way."

Leaving Dorothy's suggestion hanging in the air, Lisa suspected there was more to it. *Something's up with her. I'm the one who always suggests a longer visit. She never pushes for it because she doesn't want to impose.*

"I'll even make those banana pancakes you like so much. We'll have breakfast before you head back."

A knowing smile crossed Lisa's face. *And that is how you close a deal, Dorothy.* "I'm in," she replied. "I'm obsessed with those pancakes of yours."

"Wonderful. Banana pancakes, it is. It's always nice to have someone to cook for."

Lisa could hear her friend take a breath and steady herself for whatever it was she was about to ask. After the brief hesitation, Dorothy began, "Lisa, there's something..."

"Hold on a second, Dorothy."

A member of Lisa's team stuck his head in her office. "You need to get downstairs. The guy you like for the Sylvester murder was just picked up. They're bringing him in now."

She nodded at him, then said into the phone, "Dorothy, it's work. I've got to run. See you in two weeks. Love you."

· · ·

Wednesday, July 7 - 12:00 a.m.

Josephine Paulsen couldn't sleep. She glanced at the clock next to her bed, saw the time and whispered to herself, "A new day... one day closer."

About to turn eighty, this birthday was a milestone she wasn't eager to reach. She stared at the empty space on the left side of the bed. "Eighty, Michael," she spoke to a man who was no longer there, "we were supposed to do this aging thing together."

A longtime resident at Coquina Reef, Josephine had moved to Stypman Island with her husband. Their first year there was a happy one, but then he dropped dead from a massive heart attack on the golf course. Now Josephine spent most of her time alone in her top floor condo - an oceanfront corner unit that afforded her a bird's-eye view of the beach, the ocean, the pool, and most of the community in which she lived. Lonely and armed with binoculars, she found a new purpose and took command, watching everything and everyone and reporting what she saw to the community's property manager or the police.

Rather than lay awake in her bed fretting about her birthday, Josephine got up, put on a long robe, and switched on the lights in her living room. It was a balmy, humid night, and a soft sea breeze wafted through the sliding glass doors when she opened them a bit to take a better look at the sliver of moon glistening across the surface of the water. Taking in the sight,

Josephine's thoughts turned to her husband and a faint smile came to her face.

"What's that?" she asked herself. The tranquility of the moment was interrupted by the distinctive hum of a boat's motor and the sound of muffled voices, both unexpected given the late hour. Curious, Josephine fetched her binoculars, put them to her eyes and focused the lenses. Spotting a boat rocking in the water a few feet from shore, she whispered, "there's something going on over there." Gripped by what was unfolding, she watched as two figures, who stood knee deep in the water, unloaded what looked to be some bulky items.

"What are they up to?" she muttered to herself. "I think they're headed this way." Josephine saw the figures dart up the beach toward the small footbridge that crossed the dunes and led onto the condominium grounds. The boat motor started up again, and she could see the craft's expanding wake as it picked up speed before disappearing into the darkness. With her binoculars trained on the two figures who now made their way across the footbridge, Josephine gasped when they headed directly below her window.

"How strange... two men in dark clothing, and they're carrying what appear to be heavy bags." Josephine spoke to herself, a habit she'd picked up since living alone. "Let's see if we can get a better look." She opened her sliding doors further and bright interior light spilled out of her condo, catching the attention of the men. They glanced up at her. Through her binoculars, Josephine studied their youthful faces and short-cropped hair. They spoke a few words to each other. "I think that's Spanish," she whispered.

Just then, a dog barked. The two men sprinted to the exit of the condominium complex, onto the island's main road, and beyond Josephine's sight. Wasting no time, she picked up her phone.

"Police Department, how may I help you?"

"This is Josephine Paulsen. I want to report the suspicious activity I've just observed."

Hearing it was Josephine, the officer on duty rolled his eyes and whispered to his partner, "It's her again." After hearing her out and asking a few questions, the officer noted the call in the online log and placed a copy of his incident report along with a yellow sticky note on his boss's desk.

· · ·

12:05 a.m.

Unable to sleep since her conversation with Lisa a few hours earlier, Dorothy Jensen stared up at the ceiling from her bed until the sound of a barking dog broke the silence. Sitting up, she reached for her phone. *I've got to tell her before it's too late.*

She dialed Lisa's number. No answer. When the call went to voicemail, she left a message. "Lisa, it's Dorothy, call me. There's something you should know."

· · ·

12:15 a.m.

"Over there!" the young man pointed, then sprinted toward the waiting car. The heavy bags he carried bounced against his sandy, wet jeans and his running shoes squished with seawater. The other man followed. No sooner had they jumped into the backseat of a black Range Rover, than the car pulled away.

A few minutes into the silent drive, the exhausted men dozed off. "Wake up!" the driver commanded in Spanish. Their eyes popped open, and they sat up straight. Reaching back, the driver waved a cell phone in their faces. "One of you, take it and press the call button."

One of the young men did as he was instructed, and a man's voice demanded in Spanish, "Do you have the delivery?"

"Si señor."

"Good. Did everything go as planned?"

"Si."

"Were you observed by anyone?"

"Someone saw us as we were leaving the beach on our way to the car."

"You have done well. I will see you soon."

Thirty minutes later, the Range Rover pulled up to a Spanish-style villa that stood behind thick, white stone walls with a massive gate made of ornate black iron. Bright pink bougainvillea covered the walls, adding drama to the magnificent estate. In front of the large house, a lighted fountain pumped streams of water around a brass sculpture of a jumping sailfish.

The driver used the cell phone. "I'm here."

The young men peered out from tinted windows as the iron gates pulled back, allowing the Range Rover to pass through. Recruited from the impoverished streets of a small, rural town in Colombia, they hadn't seen any place else in their eighteen years. Eyes wide and mouths open, they stared at a magnificent house in America and wondered if their luck had changed.

"Follow me and bring the bags," the driver instructed. As they reached the front door, a man with a long scar on his face and a rifle in his hand appeared at the doorway. He motioned for them to enter and led them down a long, dimly lit hallway lined with exotic wood paneling. Several potted palms stood along the walls, leading to a carved mahogany door at the end of the corridor. Sand from their wet shoes fell onto the richly colored stone flooring and crunched under their feet. Hearing the sound, the man with the scar looked down at the sand and shook his head in disgust.

Noticing the mess they'd made on the floor, the young men mumbled, "Forgive us, señor." The man didn't acknowledge the apology and tapped his knuckles on the door before opening it. He motioned with his gun for the three to enter.

Light from a single desk lamp revealed the room served as an office. Behind the desk, in an overstuffed leather chair, sat a man with eyes so black they betrayed nothing of his humanity and everything about his dark past. Shaded by heavy brows, the man's eyes focused on the two young men but conveyed little interest in them and what they'd been through tonight. The young men knew that look. Their only purpose was to serve this man and, unless they could be of service to him again, they no longer mattered.

"I am your employer; my name is Ricardo DesFuentes." He didn't ask their names; they weren't that important. Rather, his attention was on the duffel bags hanging from their hands. "Now, what have you brought me?"

They lifted the heavy bags to show him. "Leave those here. You have done well to bring this shipment to me. I need to ask you something, though. Who observed you on your trip here? Where were you seen?"

The young men looked at each other, then one of them answered. "An old woman was looking out her window. She saw us leaving the beach after we arrived onshore."

"Did this woman see your faces?" DesFuentes leaned forward in his chair, his dark eyes fixated on the young men.

"Yes, I think she could see us. We were under her window when we looked up at her. She had binoculars."

"Where can I find this woman? Be precise."

"She was on the top floor in a corner apartment, facing the beach."

"That is unfortunate, but I will take care of it." DesFuentes shrugged it off, waving his hand to show there was nothing to worry about. "You must be thirsty and hungry after your journey." The young men nodded their heads.

"Angel," he said to the driver, "make sure they are appropriately rewarded."

The young men thanked their employer and followed their driver outside to a manicured garden surrounded by thick trees, leafy plants, and flowering hibiscus bushes. In the center of the garden was a rectangular swimming pool, softly illuminated and glowing in the tropical night.

Gesturing to a table set up near the pool, the man they now knew was called Angel directed them to sit. "The beer is for you; food is coming." They made their way to the table. As they settled into their chairs, they eyed the bottles and salivated. Beads of moisture dripped down the sides of the bottles, enticing them. Reaching for the beer, their shoulders dropped, and both sighed with relief.

"We made it," one of them whispered to the other. They shared a brief grin and put the cold bottles to their thirsty mouths just as a single bullet slammed into each of their heads, splattering blood and brain matter on the pristine white pool deck. The bottles dropped and shattered on the cement and beer foam mixed with blood. Angel stuffed a .22 caliber pistol back into his pocket. Taking out his phone, he pressed the call button.

"It's done."

"Good. Those idiots got what they deserved. Alex will help you drag them to the river. I'll meet you there." DesFuentes ended the call.

Two splashes sounded as the remains of the young men were tossed into the wide stretch of river that ran behind the villa. Ricardo DesFuentes clapped in amusement and Angel gasped when, minutes later, two massive, fifteen-foot alligators, DesFuentes referred to as '*Uno* and *Dos*' broke the surface of the water. Both animals weighed just under eight hundred pounds. Regular feedings kept them in the area. Watching in delight as the beasts' thrashing tails smacked the water and their powerful jaws clamped down on the bodies, DesFuentes stood laughing at the water's edge until the boys' remains were dragged deep below the surface to be ripped apart and devoured.

When the alligators had disappeared, DesFuentes walked back to the house with Angel, his arm around the killer's shoulders. "I trust you enjoyed that as much as I did."

Angel shrugged his shoulders. "You can't see that in New York, but I would have liked to have seen them eaten alive."

DesFuentes raised his eyebrows. "Perhaps another time. I have another assignment for you. You must complete it tonight."

"Who's the target, and where do I find him?"

"It's not a him."

. . .

3:45 a.m.

By the time he arrived at the Coquina Reef beachside condominiums, the twin buildings were dark and barely illuminated by the fading moon. Having been sent here to fix a problem that others had created, Angel didn't expect the task would be difficult. His target was an old lady. She'd be his third kill on this new day, and it was still a few hours until dawn. Angel liked to stay busy.

Although he preferred a gun, he opted for a Ka-Bar blade designed for Marine combat use. He was no Marine, but it would be quieter that way. He parked the black Range Rover in the darkest section of the parking area. After pulling on a pair of tight-fitting black leather gloves, he picked up the knife. Out of habit, he checked his appearance in the rearview mirror. Liking what he saw, he smiled at his reflection. *I look like a killer.*

It was cooler now; the long night having worked its magic on the tropical heat, but the air remained thick with humidity. Without any breeze, the tall palm trees surrounding the condominium buildings stood motionless. Taking in the buildings on either side of him, Angel paused for a minute before moving through the parking area toward the building on his left. He entered through the open courtyard and took the stairs, his rubber-soled shoes assuring a silent climb to the top floor. Exiting the stairwell onto an open walkway that surrounded the spacious courtyard, he grinned when he saw all the windows on the floor were dark. *Too fucking easy.* Angel grinned again.

He headed to the condo in the north corner of the building, facing the beach. Pulling a small tool from his pocket, he picked the old lock, corroded from years of exposure to the salty environment. He stepped inside and listened. Hearing nothing, he turned left into a bedroom and found it empty. He swiped at the beads of sweat dotting his forehead with the back of his gloved hand and whispered to himself, "So damned hot in here. There's always something to ruin my fun."

He walked through a spacious living room area surrounded by large windows that looked out onto a black sea, the stars in the dark sky providing the only light. As his eyes adjusted, he paused and listened again before he entered a second bedroom.

"Ahhh... she *is* here," Angel whispered. Anticipating what would come next, a venomous sneer came to his face. On impulse, he decided to do something he'd learned years ago. Something that would horrify the unlucky soul who found her. Angel wrinkled his nose and raised his upper lip, recalling the mess it made.

Without making a sound, he leaned over the old woman and gently pressed his knife against her pale, wrinkled throat. Where the razor-sharp blade touched her skin, a thin line of what he knew to be red formed. In the darkness, it looked black.

She awakened with a start, groggy and confused. As her eyes focused, they widened, her confusion giving way to terror. Covering her mouth with his gloved hand, he muffled her weak screams for help that would not arrive. Her pale blue eyes pleaded with him. He moved in closer. Angel's face—the last thing she would ever see—hovered in front of hers, filling her field of vision.

Leaning in even further, he whispered in her ear, "This is what happens to old ladies who don't mind their own business."

. . .

3:45 a.m.

Fast asleep in her Miami apartment, Lisa Owens jerked awake. She sat up in bed, her instincts screaming. She turned on a lamp and looked around her bedroom. Seeing nothing unusual, she got up to check the rest of her small apartment. Careful, methodical steps, waiting, listening, then moving forward. Lisa checked the bathroom, the closets, the main living area, and the kitchen. She looked out on her eighteenth-floor balcony, hoping not to find whatever or whoever might be there. Empty.

"Weird," she said to herself, "I'd bet my life someone just touched my shoulder and woke me up." She couldn't shake the feeling that something had just happened. Something bad. She shook her head. "I've got to lay off the junk food," she muttered and headed back to bed.

CHAPTER 2

Wednesday, July 7 - 7 a.m.

A few hours ago, she'd heard a noise from the condo above and had been awake ever since. Fully alert, she sensed something new had occupied the room. At first, she caught only the slightest whiff, but now it filled her nose and commanded her attention. She looked up to see dark liquid dripping from the ceiling fan, which turned above the bed, creating the soft breeze she enjoyed so much. A droplet fell on the pale blue cotton blanket next to her. It had an interesting smell. She leaned over to examine it and decided to taste it. Human blood.

Outside the bedroom windows, the Atlantic was calm, resembling a lake more than a majestic ocean. Without the usual rhythmic sound of breaking waves, the room remained quiet except for the sound of steady breathing. Still asleep, Jason was on her left, nearest to the windows. Clara slept on the right, closer to the bathroom. She slept between them because she felt safe there and could keep an eye on them.

More drops fell on the bed and around her. As they hit the blades of the ceiling fan, they spattered about the room. Excitement suffused her. A droplet hit Clara's cheek. She tried to lick it off her, but Clara rolled away and quietly said, "Not now, Marley, it's too early to go out."

More blood splattered throughout the bedroom, crimson drops now everywhere. On the walls, on the silver-framed photos Clara kept on her dresser. On the clothes Jason had worn yesterday and left on the chair when he came to bed last night. Marley wanted Clara and Jason to see what was happening and started barking. Jolted from their sleep, they sat up and looked at the dog standing on the bed between them.

"What is it, girl?" Jason asked, his voice groggy from sleep.

Clara touched her face and noticed the bloody smear on her hand. Her eyes focused, and she looked around the room. And then she screamed.

Jason glanced up at the ceiling fan and a droplet fell into his eye. "What the hell?"

This wasn't just another day in paradise.

. . .

While Marley alerted her owners to the hellish scene in their bedroom, Mary Dillard, a resident in the adjacent condominium building at Coquina Reef, slipped off her terry-cloth robe and draped it over a lounge chair just as she did every day. At this early hour, she always had the pool to herself. She'd left her phone and hearing aids at home, not expecting any conversations so early in the morning. The pool area was next to the beach and included a small bathhouse with ladies' and men's bathrooms, changing areas, and showers. Large bushes of sea grape kept it private. Mary looked around and smiled, happy to have it all to herself.

Thin and just under five feet, her paste-white skin contrasted against her navy-blue bathing suit. Once in the warm pool, she pushed off and swam her version of a slow breaststroke, making her way back and forth and counting each lap until reaching twenty.

After her swim, Mary entered the changing area in the ladies' room, turned on the shower, and removed her swimsuit. She always showered at the pool because it kept her own bathroom cleaner. Not that it mattered. She paid someone to take care of her cleaning.

Under the flow of warm water, she closed her eyes while rinsing the shampoo suds from her hair. As they ran down her face, she had an uneasy feeling she was being watched, and a slight shiver ran over her. She shrugged it off.

When she finished, Mary opened the shower door and slid her wet feet into her flip-flops. Stepping forward, her left foot slid from beneath her. "Oh, my word!" she cried out as she struggled to balance herself. Then her right foot slipped, and she fell backward, hitting her head against the tiled wall. Dazed and in pain, she managed, "Please, someone help me."

Through blurry eyes, she could see someone standing over her and could feel her body being lifted by fingers pressing into her tender armpits. She thought she'd be okay until a forceful shove sent her crashing back onto the unforgiving tile. A cracking sound filled the otherwise quiet room when the back of her skull smacked against the floor. A crimson trickle ran from her right ear, turning pink as it mixed with the water on the wet white tiles. The life in her face faded and her eyes rolled back. Mary Dillard took her last breath.

· · ·

7:10 a.m.

Lights flashing and siren blasting, the black and white police cruiser raced down the two-lane road that ran the length of Stypman Island. A favored spot of snowbirds looking to get away from the cold winters of the north while avoiding the crowds in Miami, Ft. Lauderdale, and Boca Raton; the narrow barrier island was at the southern tip of Florida's Treasure Coast. The majestic Atlantic Ocean to its east and the Intracoastal Waterway on its west, a two-lane bridge connected the island to the mainland.

"We're coming up on it in just a minute, Dan," said the driver, Kim Witherspoon, to her partner, who chewed on his thumbnail. Both were in their twenties and only a few years into their careers. Palm trees, live oaks, and tropical plants flew by. Without any traffic, they were reaching speeds of seventy-five miles per hour.

"I don't know what we're in for. I've never answered a call like this," Dan Collins said.

"Me neither. There's supposed to be a lot of blood. That can't be good," Kim answered, her eyes locked in on the road ahead.

Collins continued to bite his nails. A self-described man's man, he'd come to Stypman Island from St. Augustine, where he'd worked as a bar back, hauling boxes of liquor and kegs of beer at a grungy bar favored by local kids for cheap drinks and a blind eye toward their fake ID's. When he impregnated a seventeen-year-old high school prom queen, Dan hightailed it out of town. In need of a new job, he entered the police training academy, scraping by and barely graduating. Now, on his way to what could be his first serious crime scene, he was nervous and insecure—something he didn't want to admit to his partner. He excelled at following orders, doing whatever his boss asked of him without question. Today, he'd have to make decisions without his boss. Collins hoped he wouldn't screw up.

The road on which they traveled was the island's primary thoroughfare. Passing by secondary roads that led to bars and restaurants, Collins wished they could turn off on one of them. "I could use a drink right about now," he said before realizing he'd voiced the words aloud.

Kim Witherspoon glanced at her partner. "What did you just say?"

"Nothing. I just want to find out what this is all about."

"Well, I wish I was out on one of those," Kim said, referring to the boats floating in the glimpses of blue ocean that flashed between the buildings as they flew by. Fishing, snorkeling, kite surfing, and scuba diving were favored activities in the area, although the once famous coral reefs of Florida were now largely dead, the result of warming ocean temperatures and acidity. What climate change didn't kill on the reefs, fertilizer and chemical runoff did.

"Gorgeous day to be on the water," she said, trying to make conversation. Collins ignored her.

"We're here," Kim announced as she made the turn into Coquina Reef, a small beachside condominium community built in the 1970s. Two twin stucco-covered buildings stood before them, both painted in an unusual color that made Kim think of cream of tomato soup. Terracotta barrel tiles covered the roofs and bright white trim accented the buildings' architectural features. Stypman Island had a wisely designed building ordinance limiting structures to no more than five stories to prevent the ghastly high-rises and overcrowding that defined most of the Florida coastline. "Pretty sweet place," Kim said to Collins as she exited the police cruiser.

"Yeah, nice spot, a real-life Garden of Eden," remarked Collins, taking in the heavily planted grounds. Adjacent to the beach, he could see a rectangular swimming pool. Next to it, a wooden footbridge crossed over the dunes. "How many units?"

"Looks like eight on each of the four floors," responded Kim. She'd counted the thirty-two doors, wondering how many of them she'd be knocking on today. "Covered parking and the courtyard on the ground floor," she said to her partner while making a mental note for the report she'd be writing later. She glanced around the paved courtyard, noticing the tall palmetto palms and the collection of tropical flowers growing in the center. "Let's go. I see a man waving at us."

The police cruiser had pulled up about fifteen minutes after Jason Anders had called, yelling into the phone, "We're in the Coquina Reef community, the building on the left, third floor. And hurry, please hurry." Marley heard the siren long before the cruiser arrived, first picking up the sound shortly after it left the police station. Her ears were hurting from the siren's piercing wail by the time it arrived. She jumped up on the sofa next to Clara and buried her head in her lap. Understanding that Marley didn't like loud noises, Clara placed her shaking hands over the dog's floppy ears and stroked her head.

Jason went outside to wave at the officers and help them locate the right unit. "Use the stairs. They're over there and faster than the elevator. We're on the third floor." The officers shook their heads to show they understood and met him outside his front door.

"Mr. Anders?" Kim asked, her mouth hung open in disbelief. Dan Collins swallowed, pushing down the bile rising in his throat and wincing at the burn. Now that they were closer to him, they could see what they hadn't been able to see before. Jason Anders' white t-shirt was spattered with blood, it clung to his body and his wrinkled, gray pajama bottoms were in a similar condition. His feet were bare. On his forehead was a smear of deep red. Waving his hand, Jason motioned for the officers to come inside.

"Ma'am," said the female officer, acknowledging Clara upon entering the couple's home and seeing she was crying. "I'm Officer Witherspoon, and this is my partner, Officer Collins. Can we please have your names?"

"I'm Jason Anders, and this is my wife, Clara." Shaken, Jason's voice cracked when he spoke.

The Anders were in their early sixties. Tanned and healthy, they both looked like hell. On Clara's pale blue nightgown were deep red splotches. Bare feet, light brown hair tied in a loose ponytail, she wore no make-up. Her brown eyes were bloodshot and swollen from crying. Her husband glanced at her and struggled to keep his composure. The nightmare of what was happening had become more real with the arrival of the police.

The officers tried their best to hide their concern as they got their first look at Jason, Clara, and their small brown dog, all doused with bloody drops, drips, and smears.

"We thought we shouldn't clean ourselves in case that would tamper with evidence, and we didn't want to ruin the sofa," explained Jason, noticing Officer Witherspoon glancing at the towels on the sofa.

"We appreciate that, Mr. Anders," she responded.

Officer Witherspoon studied the scarlet foot and paw prints on the otherwise spotless, shiny marble floor. Outdoorsy and athletic looking, she was perspiring from her run up the stairs. Her tan uniform was snug and looked uncomfortable. She smelled of deodorant soap and sunscreen. Nose in the air, Marley was taking it all in.

Collins was perspiring, too. Fit and muscular, he was a few years younger than his partner. On his right biceps, a tattoo of a black shark peeked out from under his short-sleeved uniform when he moved his arm. He'd pushed back his wavy black hair with his mirrored aviator sunglasses when he'd entered the condo.

Marley directed her attention toward Collins and cocked her head, picking up a scent she recognized - Axe body spray. Jason had once tried it, and Clara made him throw it away because it made her nauseous. There was something else in the room, something much stronger and more prevalent than Axe body spray and Officer Witherspoon's deodorant soap and sunscreen. Fear. Sensing it, Marley stood rigid and alert, her long tail pointing up.

Struck by the incredible ocean view before them, Witherspoon and Collins looked around the condo. Inspired by the colors outside, the place was decorated in shades of turquoise. Turning her back to the Anders,

Officer Witherspoon whispered to her partner, "For such a peaceful place, I'm not feeling the Zen."

Collins nodded in agreement. "Feels more like Freddy Krueger's house."

Motioning for the officers to follow him, Jason led them to the primary bedroom and opened the door. Witherspoon's mouth dropped open. "What the heck?"

Blood still dripped from the ceiling fan, although Jason had turned it off, stopping the splatter. An ugly, deep red stain had spread on the white cotton sheets of the unmade bed. Curious, Marley jumped off Clara's lap and poked her head into the bedroom, her eyes focused on the growing stain that was in the very spot where she liked to sleep.

Collins' face went pale, and he looked like he might pass out. Collecting himself, he asked, "Mr. Anders, can you please tell me the names of the people who live above you?"

"It's only one person. Her name is Dorothy Jensen."

"We're going upstairs to check on Ms. Jensen."

"Please wait for us here," added Officer Witherspoon as she and her partner left and made their way to the staircase outside.

While the two officers climbed to the fourth floor, Jason stood by his front door wondering if Marley already knew whose blood this was. He thought back to a particular the morning when he and Clara learned their dog had some remarkable attributes.

Half toy poodle and half golden retriever, Marley, a mini-goldendoodle, had taken off to chase a group of sanderling birds on the beach. Frantic that the dog was lost, Clara called for her, but she disappeared. When Marley finally returned, happy, panting, and tired from her run, Clara was so upset she wouldn't talk to the dog until Jason convinced her she was being ridiculous.

After that incident, they hired a local dog trainer and veterinary student at the University of Florida who happened to be researching the sense of smell and hearing in domestic canines. Marley became a subject in a research study that determined her olfactory senses were off the charts.

As he stood listening by his front door, Jason recalled the trainer's words, "Dogs have a sense of smell that is far beyond that of humans and

Marley's sense of smell is well-beyond what we normally find. It's her superpower." The trainer had explained that although Clara couldn't see her when she chased the birds, Marley knew where Clara was because she could smell her. And with her large, sensitive ears, she could hear her too.

Jason looked at his dog from the doorway and wondered. He understood she learned a lot more from her nose than she did from her eyes or ears, and that she could smell and sense all kinds of things even when she couldn't see them. He remembered being surprised to learn she could smell things humans don't recognize as having a smell to them, like fear, aggression, and even danger. *She's getting a nose full today*, he thought.

The dog trainer had explained how Marley took everything in, processing it in a big brain that came from the poodle side of her family. He'd assured Jason and Clara that their dog recognized everyone in the condominium building. "No doubt she's taken a good long whiff of each of them," he'd said. "And standing on the ground floor, she can tell who's coming down the elevator long before they get here. Bottom line, her nose is remarkable."

Jason looked at his dog sitting quietly next to Clara.

She knows whose blood it is; she knows.

. . .

7:35 a.m.

Witherspoon and Collins reached the fourth floor, cautiously making their way toward Dorothy Jensen's condominium. Reaching her door, the officers pulled out their guns, something they'd never had to do before.

Witherspoon took a deep breath, knocked, and announced herself. "Ms. Jensen, this is the police. Please open the door."

No reply.

Listening at their doorway one floor below, Jason held his breath as the knocking continued. He glanced at Clara, who's grip on Marley tightened. The dog squirmed, trying to jump from her arms. Clara held her even tighter, as if somehow the hug might improve this unimaginable situation.

Officer Witherspoon tried the doorknob. "Unlocked, Dan. Get ready."

As she opened the door, she announced herself once again before the two crept forward into the condominium. It was noticeably warm and quiet. Nothing looked disturbed.

"Kitchen is clear," said Collins as he joined his partner in the main living area.

"So was the second bedroom," said Witherspoon.

Dreading their next step, they headed toward a bedroom located above the Anders' primary bedroom. "Get ready for Freddy," Dan whispered.

Witherspoon called out one final time. Silence. She opened the bedroom door and looked away. "Holy shit!" she gasped. Hearing a gagging sound and a splatter, she turned to see her partner bent over and coughing, having thrown up his breakfast.

The scene was like none either of the rookie cops had ever witnessed or imagined. Bar fights were one thing, this was something altogether different. What had once been Dorothy Jensen was lying on the queen-sized bed. Her torso, dressed in a bloody nightgown, hung down over one side of the bed. Seemingly, all the blood that had once circulated through her body had poured onto the floor. Her severed head was also on the floor, having rolled a few feet away from her body before settling next to an antique chest of drawers. Her eyeballs had been pulled from her head. Bloody, they now looked up from where they rested on a nightstand next to a glass of water, reading glasses, and a paperback book. Upon a closer look, Witherspoon could see the woman's tongue had been cut from her mouth. The same tongue her partner had slipped on when he entered the bedroom, causing him to lose his breakfast.

· · ·

7:35 a.m.

Lisa Owens put her phone to her ear and listened to the message from Dorothy as she walked down a hallway at Miami Police Headquarters. When she returned the call it went unanswered. "Dorothy, just calling you back. Talk soon."

Her supervisor, Greg 'Mac' Mackenzie, had asked to see her first thing this morning. The team of detectives she led had experienced a breakthrough on a high-profile case that had been eating up their time in recent weeks. Lisa had been the one to crack it. An arrest had been made, and the prosecutor expressed confidence about a conviction. Standing in the doorway of Mac's office, she wondered if it was bad news. Maybe something had gone wrong.

"Lisa, come on in. It's another hot one today." Mac was signing paperwork and didn't look up. He'd relocated to Miami from up north for this job. Years later, he still hadn't adjusted to the local climate and probably never would.

"Hey, Mac, what's up?" she asked with a cheerful smile intended to hide her concern. Like always, she dressed in dark slacks and a white button-down blouse. Her credentials hung from a blue lanyard around her neck. She settled in a chair, waiting for her boss to finish with the stack of documents in front of him.

Mac pushed a pair of reading glasses from his face and perched them on top of his balding head. Even in the air-conditioned office, he looked sweaty. "First, very nice work on the Sylvester case. That was a tough one. The boss asked me to convey his thanks to you and the team. Getting that put to bed takes some of the pressure off." He took a breath and swallowed hard. "Now, I've been meaning to talk with you about something. You're incredibly valuable to us, Lisa, but I'm worried about you."

Looking over the paper coffee cup she sipped on, Lisa leaned forward; her large brown eyes focused on her boss. "Is it what the perp said when we charged him with the Sylvester murder? That I'd pay for putting him in jail. Mac, no need to be concerned about that. I've had worse threats."

Mac leaned back in his chair, putting as much distance as he could between himself and the woman seated in front of him. He knew Lisa well enough to see that things were about to go downhill. "It's not the threat."

"I don't understand. What are you saying?" Lisa set aside her coffee and folded her arms.

The expression on Mac's face said he didn't want to have this conversation. The HR Department had put him up to it.

"Lisa, I'm always after you to take better care of yourself, and you don't listen. You're here until all hours, and then you're back at the crack of dawn the next day. You forget to eat and when you do, it's crap from a vending machine. I can see how exhausted you are; you're going to burn out. I don't want that for either of us. Look, I know you. You're thirty now, and more than just a cop. It's time you get a life outside of this place."

Mac folded his hands and waited for the fallout. Everyone, including Lisa, knew he hated this part of his job; moving up hadn't been all he'd expected. Instead of being on the ground solving crimes, he was stuck in an office, signing purchase requisitions for office supplies. Awkward HR conversations like this one just weren't his thing.

Still, Lisa felt sucker punched. *Did he just say that to me? Be cool, Lisa. Be cool.*

"Mac, you know this job better than most. It requires long hours. I doubt your boss would call you with his thanks if I didn't make the sacrifice and, by the way, it sure would help if more people in the department did the same." She felt her face getting hot and knew it was turning red. *I can already see my next performance review, DOES NOT ACCEPT FEEDBACK WELL.*

"Lisa don't take what I said the wrong way. I care about you." Mac's voice was getting louder, his frustration with the situation now apparent. "I looked at your PTO records just before you came in, you haven't used any vacation or even a sick day in over two years. You've got close to eight hundred unused personal hours on the books!"

"So what, Mac? I'm doing my job damned well, if I do say so myself. Who cares if I don't take time off?"

Mac's tone softened, "Well, I care. So do me a favor and pull back a bit. Please?"

She didn't answer and looked down at her feet. "Mac, I explained myself two years ago when you took over this role. This work is more than just a job to me. It's my purpose. What happened to my fiancé drove me to this profession, and going all in, well, it's the only way I can do this."

"I get that, I really do. But you've got to make some changes."

Anger flashed in Lisa's eyes. *This is such bullshit.*

Instead of speaking her mind, she looked at Mac, took a breath and folded her hands on her lap. "I hear what you're saying, and I'll think about it. That's all I can promise."

"Fair enough, you're the best detective I have. I'll fly cover with HR, but please work on taking better care of yourself. Your guy would have wanted that for you, more than whatever it is you think you need to do for him."

Lisa's eyes welled up at the mention of Scott. *It's time to get out of here.*

"Thanks for the chat, boss. Now, if it's okay with you, there are a lot more bad guys to catch."

CHAPTER 3

Wednesday, July 7 - 8:00 a.m.

Beauford Jackson had been Chief of Police on Stypman Island for ten years. His eyes darted across the only incident report from the previous evening. Concentrating, he put his hand in his dark, curly hair and scratched his head. He glanced at the yellow sticky note attached to the report.

Might require follow-up. R.W.

The chief crumpled the report and tossed it in the trash can. Accessing the online log, he found the electronic version of the report, and pressed the delete key on his computer. "Just like it never happened," he muttered. Reaching down from his chair, he put a key into the lock on the bottom left-hand drawer of his desk, took out a burner phone, and pressed a number.

"I believe your employees were observed last night."

"I am aware," came the reply.

"Are you taking care of it, or do you need my assistance?"

"It's been handled." The call disconnected.

Having moved to Florida from a sad, little town in Georgia that offered high unemployment and low opportunity, Chief Jackson was now fifty-two years of age. A good 'ole boy who oozed southern charm, the locals on Stypman Island took to him right away.

Jackson was of the mind that it was a dog-eat-dog world. Everyone was out for themselves, and he was no exception. The law, in his view, had little to do with justice and everything to do with how much money you had, who you knew, and in his case, whose secrets you knew. With no political ambition and no actual interest in advancing his career, the chief considered himself fortunate to have made it as far as he had. Rather than chase the next job up the ladder, he settled in and found other ways to capitalize on his position.

Jackson's police force employed five officers besides himself. Their work involved patrolling the island's beaches, dealing with drunks, investigating minor thefts and shoplifting complaints, along with an occasional domestic dispute. Speeding and parking tickets were off-limits. It wasn't good business to piss off the tourists. Although the police work was basic at best, the chief had changed out every officer in the department, but for one, replacing them with his own hand-picked people. And the one he hadn't been able to change out, the thorn in his side, he kept on beach patrol where he was out of the way and wouldn't see or hear something he shouldn't.

CHAPTER 4

Wednesday, July 7 - 9:30 a.m.

"What the hell happened to that old lady?" demanded Chief Jackson, who sat behind his gray metal desk. On the wall behind him was a framed photograph of him shaking hands with the governor, both smiling broadly, the Florida state flag draped in the background.

Looking despondent, Officers Witherspoon and Collins stood before the chief.

"Shit," muttered Collins, glancing down at the brown smear of vomit on his shirt.

Witherspoon held her head up and stood straight. Portraying confidence, she cleared her throat and looked at her boss. "The victim is an eighty-four-year-old female named Dorothy Jensen. From what we observed at the scene, sir, the murder is likely gang-related."

"What did you say her name is?" asked the chief, looking up at Witherspoon with a start.

"Dorothy Jensen."

"That's what I thought you said." *I need her off this case right now.*

"And you think the murder was gang-related? Witherspoon, are you a moron? You just told me the lady was in her eighties."

Kim Witherspoon was a hiring mistake the chief regretted. When he recruited her, he was looking for an easy lay and someone he could push around. Kim was tall and attractive; he took one look at her when she applied for the job and didn't ask many questions. Soon after she started work, he learned she was batting for the other team and not interested in him. Worse than being gay, she proved to be whip smart. She wasn't a pushover either. The department's only female, the chief knew she'd be difficult to fire. She needed a nudge out the door, so he made her time on the force difficult and unpleasant. Anyone else would have packed up and left a long time ago, but Kim Witherspoon seemed determined to stay.

"Yes, sir, I'm aware of her age, but the way it looks, the victim was executed in the same way that gangs kill police informants."

The chief held up his hand to stop her from continuing. "Witherspoon, I'm not interested in your 'expert' opinion about how things look. Spare me your Cagney and Lacey routine and stick to the facts."

Determined to maintain her composure, Kim Witherspoon took a deep breath. She stuck her hands in her pockets to dry her sweaty palms.

"Chief, the victim's head was severed from her body, her eyes were removed, and her tongue was cut out. It was a messy kill, to say the least." Kim stopped, looking uncertain if she should continue. Annoyed at her delay, the chief waved his hand to indicate she should get on with it.

"The victim's torso was hanging over the side of the bed. She bled out on the floor. That probably helped to keep most of the mess off the killer. The blood made its way to the condo below, which is why we got the call."

"Witherspoon!" Chief Jackson exploded. "I'm losing patience with your theories about things you know nothing about. I said just the facts, and I meant it." He knew the rebuke would get to her. He looked at Dan. "I'm heading over there now. I need a steady hand on this. Collins, you're coming with me." The chief walked toward Collins stopping in front of him, a disgusted look on his face. "Fuck, Collins, you puked on yourself. Change your damned uniform."

"I'd like to go back to the crime scene with you, if that's okay?" Kim asked.

"This is above your pay grade. To be honest, honey, I don't think you're cut out for this kind of situation. I want you to work with Officer Whitefeather on a slip and fall. Another death in the same damned community. Shit, these old geezers are dropping right and left."

"A slip and fall?" asked Witherspoon. "Chief, I'd like to stay on the murder if that's okay."

"No, Witherspoon, it's not okay." Annoyed, the chief pointed his finger at her. "Some old broad fell in the shower at the pool at Coquina Reef and died early this morning. A little girl visiting her grandmother found her. The kid hasn't stopped wailing since and not because she saw a dead body. The brat is carrying on because we closed the damned pool!"

Jackson then directed his attention to Collins. "What the hell is wrong with people these days, Dan?" Turning back to Witherspoon, he continued, "The death was unattended, so we have an investigation to do, and you, Witherspoon, will do it. Now, stop whining, partner up with Whitefeather, and get out there and get it done." He smirked. *Done, she's off the case. After that smack down, she'll be sending out resumes tonight.*

After the officers left his office, Chief Jackson unlocked the bottom right-hand drawer of his desk and removed the burner phone for the second time. He placed his hand over the mouthpiece and whispered, "There's been a fuck up... a big fuck up."

CHAPTER 5

Wednesday, July 7 - 1:00 p.m.

Dorothy Jensen's body was removed from her condo on a gurney, the cause of her death was obvious. The reason for it was not. Her condominium was roped off with yellow crime tape and Chief Jackson, accompanied by Dan Collins and the coroner, came and went throughout the day.

Jackson and Collins visited Jason and Clara Anders several times. Each time, they asked the same questions, and each time, the couple provided the same answers.

"Once again, Mr. and Mrs. Anders, what do you recall from last night? Did you hear or see anything suspicious or unusual, anything at all?" asked Collins. Looking exhausted and overwhelmed, he sat at the Anders' kitchen table, a notebook in front of him and a pencil in his hand. Jason handed him a mug of coffee, which he accepted.

"As we explained," said Jason, "Clara and I take our dog out for a quick walk every night before bedtime, right around eleven o'clock. Last night, we were binge-watching a series on Netflix and stayed up later than normal. I think it was about midnight by the time we took Marley outside." He took a steadying breath. It was the seventh time he'd given the same statement. "We always walk down the stairs rather than waiting for the elevator because it's faster. It's very dark here at night," he explained to the officer, who was looking into his coffee and not taking any notes. "There isn't any light pollution, and because we live on the beach, the outside lighting in our community is amber, so it doesn't disorient sea turtle hatchlings as they make their way to the ocean."

Clara added, "Even though it's difficult to see, we know our dog hears and smells things we don't. As we left the stairway and headed onto the sidewalk, Marley was on high alert."

"That's interesting, Mrs. Anders, but I need to know what *you* heard or saw, not your dog."

"Well, you asked if there was anything unusual last night," objected Clara. "Marley pulled back on her leash and tried to prevent us from going around the corner of the building on our usual route. She was barking loudly and was out of control. That never happens. I think she sensed something that alarmed her."

"And that was around midnight, correct?" Collins looked bored. He took a last sip of coffee and set the mug down.

"Yes."

"Thank you, this has been very helpful." Collins left without making a single note. "What a fucking waste of time," he muttered under his breath.

Although Marley couldn't tell them, she'd smelled the men coming off the beach, an unfamiliar combination of sweat, boat fuel, and cigarettes. The dog knew that whoever these people were, they weren't from the community. She heard them breathing as they labored with the bags they carried. As their footsteps came closer, she could tell they were just around the corner of the building although a large hibiscus bush blocked them from view.

Protecting Clara and Jason, she'd pulled back on her leash, preventing them from running directly into the strangers. She'd barked to keep the men away, even as her owners scolded her for waking up the neighbors. When Jason and Clara bent down to quiet her, their backs were to the approaching men. Although her owners were unaware they were there, Marley saw the two men go by. Moving fast, they heard her barking but never looked back.

· · ·

4:30 p.m.

Jason and Clara checked into the Azure Beachfront Hotel and Resort not far from their home. They would stay there while the ceiling drywall in their primary bedroom was replaced, and the room was cleaned, disinfected, and painted. Their mattress and bedding had been removed and replacements were on order. Exhausted, they'd just laid down on the bed, with Marley between them, when Jason's phone rang.

"Mr. Anders, this is Chief Jackson."

Jason sat up and put the phone on speaker. "I don't have much time to talk, but I wanted to check in with you. Where are you staying? It's been quite a day, huh?"

"I appreciate that, Chief. What the hell happened up there?"

A few seconds of silence passed before the Chief spoke. "As you know, your neighbor, Dorothy Jensen, died last night. Because this is an active investigation, I'm not at liberty to share any details."

"I get that, but we woke up covered in blood, can you at least tell us how that happened? We can't even stay in our own home now, Chief. What happened to poor Dorothy?" Jason was riled up and the Chief of Police wasn't helping.

"Okay, okay, calm down, Mr. Anders," the chief raised his voice, making his irritation apparent. "Here's what I'm able to tell you. Ms. Jensen died in a bedroom that is located above yours. She lost a lot of blood. The blood found its way through an electrical outlet in her floor to openings in your bedroom ceiling where the wiring that powers your ceiling fan is housed. The blood did what liquid always does when gravity comes into play, it dripped down and made one hell of a mess in your place. We've contained the problem, and I can assure you that you won't be affected any further. Now, where are you staying, Mr. Anders? I need to know where I can reach you."

"Not affected any further?" Jason interrupted, his voice raised and his hands shaking. "We are very much affected, Chief. Are we safe? What are you doing about finding Dorothy's killer?"

"Mr. Anders, please just answer my question."

"We're at the Azure Beachfront Hotel, room 220."

The chief scribbled the hotel name and room number on a note pad.

"Thank you for your cooperation, Mr. Anders. Have a good evening."

"Well, doesn't he win the award for the most empathy ever?" said Clara. She'd been digging through the minibar and handed Jason a glass of whiskey.

"He sure does. Something's way off with that guy." Jason tossed back the whiskey, "Is there any more of this?"

"Well, I never cared for him." She poured another drink. "I've met him on several occasions around town, there's something I find unsettling about him. Marley doesn't seem to like him, either, which is really saying something. She likes everyone."

Looking over at Marley, Jason couldn't help but smile. The dog, freshly bathed and exhausted from the day's ordeal, slept on her back with her paws in the air. "Well, if Marley doesn't like him, neither do I."

. . .

The chief looked at his notepad and muttered, "Thank you for saving me time, Mr. and Mrs. Anders. Now I know where to find you if I need to get rid of you too."

CHAPTER 6

Wednesday, July 7 - 4:40 p.m.

Summoned by his employer, Angelo Scarella stood in the very spot where he'd shot two men less than twenty-four hours earlier. He looked down at the pool deck for signs of the killing. There were none.

Standing chest-deep in water, DesFuentes pushed himself up out of the pool, a white speedo seemed to glow against his tanned skin. *A fucking speedo?* Scarella squirmed inside, uncomfortable seeing his employer like this.

"You made a mistake last night," said DesFuentes, his expression hidden behind dark Gucci sunglasses.

What the hell is he talking about? A mistake? Angel's cocky grin left his face. He'd been expecting a reward for completing his assignment. Now, he was unsettled, and it wasn't just the sight of his boss in a speedo that was making him feel that way. This man did not tolerate mistakes.

"Because of your error, I have a problem on my hands." Water dripped from DesFuentes' body, puddling around his feet. "The woman who saw our two recently deceased friends is still alive."

"I don't understand." Nervous sweat dripped from Scarella's armpits, forming dark patches on his pale green designer polo shirt. "My target was a nosey old lady living on the top floor, corner apartment facing the beach and looking north. I found her and cut her up."

"You went to the wrong building and killed the wrong old lady." DesFuentes toweled off and stretched out on a chaise lounge. He adjusted his sunglasses and turned his head toward Scarella.

First confusion, then shock, and then dread registered on Scarella's face. He wanted to run, but there was no place for him to go. "No one told me there were two buildings there. The target was looking north out of her window, so I figured it had to be the building to the left." He stammered. "I-I-I mean, our guys, they wouldn't have walked between the buildings when they got off the boat, would they? There would have been too many eyes on them." Scarella was desperate. "I'll fix it, boss. Let me take care of this."

"You've done enough, I'll handle this." DesFuentes spoke quietly, something he'd learned to do years ago. It made others pay attention to every word he said.

Scarella wanted to keep his distance but leaned closer, trying to hear. "Boss, please let me do this for you. I promise, I won't let you down."

"Just do as I say. I want you to leave right now. Go back to Brooklyn. I'll call you with further instructions. You cannot be here. This situation requires a different approach."

Scarella didn't need to be told twice. Resisting the urge to run, he headed out without looking back.

. . .

DesFuentes picked up his phone and made a call. A woman answered. "Hello, Bethany. How is my beautiful daughter?"

"She's fine, Ricardo. Would you like to see her? I can bring her to you."

"That won't be necessary, it's you I want to see. There's something I need you to do for me."

"I can be there in an hour." Bethany's stomach was doing flips. *Oh God, what does he want from me?* Her head swirled, thinking of the possibilities, none of them good.

"Excellent," replied DesFuentes, lying back on the chaise lounge and closing his eyes. Like a cold-blooded reptile, he warmed his body in the sun.

. . .

Behind the wheel of her BMW sedan and on her way to meet DesFuentes, Bethany was sick with worry. Although grateful for his generosity to her and their daughter, DesFuentes terrified her. *I should never have left Iowa*, she thought. *I should have done what they expected me to do, get married, have kids and live a boring life in the middle of nowhere.*

A natural beauty with deep blue eyes and shiny long, blonde hair, she resembled her mother, who'd been a depressed housewife. Her father, a car mechanic who drank too much, had routinely slapped her mother around.

Bethany was eighteen when her mother found the courage to flee her husband, leaving her daughter behind with a monster. Her father's attention soon turned to Bethany, and two black eyes later, she'd had enough and hit back, striking him in the head with a heavy steel wrench she'd found in his garage. With her father unconscious on the kitchen floor, she'd left the only home she'd ever known, carrying a small beat-up suitcase packed with second-hand clothing.

Frightened but determined, Bethany traveled by bus. For days, she lived on two peanut butter sandwiches and an apple before arriving in Fort Lauderdale. With little money and no place to live, she stashed her suitcase in a locker at the bus station and went looking for work.

That was the day I met him, she thought. Her fingers nervously drummed on the steering wheel and her mind went back to the moment her life changed. It was after her first, and only, job interview in Florida. She could still see the manager of the Hotel Américan as she said, "I'm sorry, Miss Goodson, we cannot offer you a position on our hotel's housekeeping staff. We require someone who speaks Spanish."

Bethany recalled her brief response, "I see." It was all she could manage. Although she'd tried to hold them back, tears escaped down her cheeks while the manager sat behind her desk, looking at her as if she'd wasted the woman's time.

"That's when he showed up," she whispered to herself as she envisioned the handsome, well-dressed man, who sat next to her on the leather couch in the hotel lobby. He'd offered her a handkerchief and asked in accented English, "What is the matter, my beauty?"

I was so naïve, she thought. *I thought I saw kindness when I looked into his eyes.* Those same eyes looked very different to her now. She remembered how intently he'd listened when she told him her story, and how he'd bought her lunch and a margarita at the hotel's restaurant; her first meal since leaving Iowa, her first margarita ever.

After lunch, she followed him to his penthouse room, the most luxurious room she'd ever been in. She recalled the moment he kissed her and when he took her to his bed. It was the first time she had made love to a man. She played the scene back in her mind, as she had done hundreds of times before. *What was I thinking?*

As she thought about the sex, she could see Ricardo's face in her mind. *He'd been so pleased to discover I was a virgin.* Without the slightest hesitation or any sense of modesty, he'd educated her about what he wanted her to do to him in bed. *And I did it, all of it. Just like a whore.* Bethany shook her head in disgust. She recalled the moment he told her he was taking her to his home. *I didn't have any say in the matter, did I? I became his girlfriend, no, his property. I never even went back to the bus station to pick up that shitty, old suitcase.*

Not long after she moved in with Ricardo, Bethany became pregnant. When the baby was born she had the presence of mind to ask him what he would name her. He named the child Luciana, after his mother. *That sweet baby sealed my fate. She saved my life, too.* Elevated from a dispensable girlfriend to a family member, Bethany became the mother of Ricardo's baby daughter, whom they called Lucy. Looking at her reflection in the rearview mirror, Bethany exploded with emotion. "How could I be so fucking stupid?"

Fuck it, she thought, *it hasn't been all bad.* She was talking to herself now, justifying things. "He set us up in a beautiful house, he pays the bills, provides everything we need. He even asks to see Lucy sometimes." She gave it more thought and continued. Speaking the words aloud made her feel better. "Back in Iowa, you daydreamed of living in a tropical place near the ocean. Hell, you'd never even seen the ocean. Well, now you're living your dream, baby."

The positive self-talk stopped as the villa came into sight and she became queasy. This was no dream; it was a nightmare.

. . .

Wednesday, 5:45 p.m.

Parking in front of the villa, she took a deep breath and made her way to the door. The Valium she'd taken before leaving home was kicking in, and her anxiety lessened. Back in Iowa, she could never have imagined seeing such a beautiful place, let alone having a relationship with the man who owned it. Looking down at the small gold cross that hung from her neck, a gift from

Ricardo when he first learned she was pregnant, Bethany whispered a prayer. "Dear God in heaven, protect me."

DeFuentes met her in his living room—massively large, expensively decorated, and three-story high ceilings. A soccer game was on television, Colombia vs. Brazil. The sportscaster was calling the game in Spanish. Colombia was winning. *Good, that should help with his mood*, Bethany hoped.

"Thank you for coming on short notice, my love." Ricardo leaned in to kiss her cheek, pulling her toward him. Even the smell of him frightened her; she could feel goosebumps on her arms.

"I'm so happy to see you," Bethany replied with as big of a smile as she could manage. A tremor of anxiety moved through her, but she didn't run.

"I would like you to do me a favor, something very simple. Would you do that for me?" He stood in front of her, his hands on her shoulders.

She shuddered as she nodded. "Of course."

Aware that the father of her child was a powerful drug lord and a ruthless murderer, Bethany panicked when Ricardo asked her for a favor. He could demand anything of her, and she'd have no choice but to do it. And yet, all he'd asked her to do was deliver a gift to an old lady. She couldn't believe her luck.

CHAPTER 7

Thursday, July 8 - 8:00 a.m.

Jason sat on the edge of the bed, squinting. Bright sunlight streamed through the window of the hotel room. "Did you get any sleep?" asked Clara. She was already up and dressed.

"A little, I guess. You?" She knew he was lying to her. He was trying to keep her calm by downplaying how he actually felt. She'd watched him toss and turn for hours before getting up to sit hunched over in a chair with his head in his hands. He'd come back to bed around 4:30 a.m.

"I didn't sleep," she answered. "I got up around five. Here, I went to the hotel cafe." Clara handed him a mug of coffee. "I picked up a Danish for you. It's on the desk. Marley got eggs; we forgot to bring dog food."

"Lucky Marley."

Clara paced the room, "I was awake most of the night," she admitted, "wondering if all this really happened. When I think about it, I just can't accept it. I mean, poor, sweet Dorothy. Who'd want to kill her? There has to be an explanation, but for the life of me, I just can't..."

"I know." Jason stood and went to his wife, embracing her. A calm moment before the nightmare continued.

Jason broke the silence and the embrace. "We need to get to our place by 9:00. The restoration crew is supposed to show up then. I can't relax until that mess is gone and things are back to normal. Well, as normal as they can be." As he headed toward the bathroom, he added, "The mattress place said they can deliver tomorrow morning, so if things go well today, we could be back home tomorrow night."

Clara's entire body shook when he said the words "back home." It was the place where a nightmare had been unleashed, she wasn't sure she wanted to go back.

"I've got to calm down or I'll never make it through this," she said to herself before settling in an easy chair. She leaned over to pet Marley, who'd come over to sit next to her.

With a trembling hand, she reached for a glass of water on the marble side table next to where she sat. She accidentally knocked it over spilling water on Marley's head. The dog didn't seem to care, but the spill was triggering for Clara. Her mind flashed back. Twenty-four hours ago, there'd been another spill. Not just water. Someone's blood. And she'd been covered in it.

. . .

10:00 a.m.

Dressed in a blue polo shirt with a stitched rainbow emblem that read 'Spread the Sunshine,' a short white skirt, and tennis shoes, Bethany Goodson drove her BMW over the bridge and onto Stypman Island. She followed her GPS until the entrance sign to Coquina Reef confirmed she was in the right place. She picked up her phone, "I'm here."

"Good. Do you remember which building it is?"

"I do." The call ended.

She clipped on a name badge that identified her as 'Marcie' and removed a gift-wrapped box with a large pink bow from the trunk of her car. She took a moment to study the twin buildings ahead of her before putting a pair of cheap, purple-framed sunglasses on her face.

"It's the one on the right, he was very specific about that," she said under her breath. Taking the elevator to the top floor, she encountered an elderly man carrying groceries. He gave her the once over. *He's only interested in my short skirt, he doesn't care what I'm doing,* she told herself. She located the condo she was looking for and took a deep breath to calm herself before knocking on the door.

"Good morning, ma'am. I have a special delivery for Josephine Paulsen," she said when the woman answered. Bethany flashed the brightest smile she could muster.

"What a pleasant surprise," Josephine gushed in delight.

"You're welcome, ma'am. Have a sunshiny day." Bethany turned away from the door, briskly making her way back toward the elevator. Noticing an entrance to a stairway, she thought, *screw the elevator, anything could be in that box.* She bolted down the stairs and sprinted to her car.

Tearing away the wrapping paper, Josephine opened her gift. "Oh, how lovely, a bottle of Bombay Sapphire, my favorite!"

The accompanying note read: 'Cheers to you, Josephine! Happy Birthday!'

"Well, isn't that something?" she muttered. "I wonder who it's from. There's no name? I bet it's from Benji, it would be just like him to forget to add his name to the gift note, and he knows how much I enjoy martinis."

. . .

11:30 a.m.
Having returned from the hotel, Clara and Jason took Marley for a walk on the condominium grounds. Several neighbors stopped them.

"What happened to Dorothy?"

"Did you hear about Mary?"

"What do the police have to say?"

"Where are you staying?"

"Are you coming back or selling?"

The questions kept coming. Clara and Jason looked at each other, wondering if peace would ever return.

"For the first time in my life, I was hoping we'd run into Josephine Paulsen," Jason yelled above the music. "She'd be all over this situation." He and Clara had just entered their condo, the work crew was there and 'Gin and Juice' blasted from somebody's portable speaker.

"I heard today is her birthday, and she's out to lunch," Clara held her hands to her mouth directing her voice toward Jason.

"She's out to lunch alright…"

Clara ignored the comment and peeked in the bedroom, "It's coming along nicely," she said to a guy in a white t-shirt spattered with paint. He turned down the volume. "Could you please do me a favor and seal up the hole where the ceiling fan was. I won't be replacing that."

"Sure, lady, okay if we play music?"

"No problem, I'm down with Snoop," Clara replied, surprising him.

"Hey, you're pretty dope, lady." He grinned at her and went back to his work.

Clara smiled for the first time since everything started. It was short-lived. "I can't wrap my head around it, Jason. The two of them, gone on the same day, it's just unbelievable. It makes me wonder who's next."

"I'll tell you what's unbelievable, Clara, our ballsy neighbors. Asking if we knew who to contact about the sale of those units. Those ladies just died yesterday, both tragically. They even asked if *we're* selling!"

"Maybe we should," Clara answered quietly so Jason wouldn't hear.

"I've tried calling Chief Jackson several times today to see if there's any update on what happened upstairs. He isn't getting back to me, and that worthless Officer Collins has shut us out. We're being kept in the dark. I don't like it one bit."

"Remember Officer Witherspoon, she seemed very empathetic. She gave us her card yesterday; I have it here in my bag." Clara pulled the business card from her handbag and made the call.

"Hello, Officer Witherspoon? This is Clara Anders. We met the other day when you were at my home."

"Yes, Mrs. Anders, how are you and your husband? You had quite a shock. I was planning to call and check on you. It seems you've beaten me to it. Are you in a bar? I hear music." Kim Witherspoon was at police headquarters. Bored, she'd been looking at paddleboards online when Clara's call came in.

"Your concern is much appreciated, and no, we're not at a bar. We're at home. The restoration team is here, they have their music playing."

"What can I do for you, Mrs. Anders? And please call me Kim."

"We're hoping you might be able to share something, anything, about Dorothy Jensen's murder. We haven't received any information about what happened. The chief isn't even returning our calls."

Kim lowered her voice to a whisper. "Mrs. Anders, there is more you should know. It would be best if we could meet somewhere in private and not in your condo. I can't be seen there. My boss wouldn't be happy to learn I'm talking with you about this."

Twenty minutes later, the three of them huddled together in the Anders' hotel room. Clara and Jason sat on the bed. Kim used the room's only easy chair, her hands on her knees. Marley was on the floor next to her, sniffing at her ankles.

"I can't thank you enough for trusting us, Kim," said Clara. "And I want to assure you that whatever you have to tell us, we'll keep it to ourselves."

"I don't understand why this hasn't been shared with you already," said Kim, "but I need to warn you, it's very disturbing."

Kim described the way Dorothy had been killed and what she saw in Dorothy's bedroom. "The beheading and dismemberment indicate gang involvement," explained Kim. "When a victim is murdered in the fashion Dorothy was, it often means they were a snitch or a police informant."

Clara paled. Jason looked at Kim as if he'd misunderstood. "Did you just say that Dorothy Jensen was murdered by a gang?"

• • •

5:00 p.m.

After suffering through a boring birthday lunch with a friend who really wasn't a friend, Josephine Paulsen was looking forward to 5:00. She opened the bottle of gin she'd received earlier in the day and poured a healthy amount into a cocktail shaker with ice. She added a smidgen of dry vermouth and vigorously shook the concoction. *I just love that sound*, she thought.

Josephine poured the clear, cold liquid into a martini glass. Tiny slivers of ice floated on the surface. *Just the way I like it.* She added a twist of lemon and carried the treat to her favorite spot, a comfortable chair that provided an amazing view of the ocean. "Happy birthday to me," she sang to herself and raised her glass before taking her first sip. She did her best to enjoy the cocktail slowly but before she knew it, her glass was drained. Giddy and feeling the drink, she said to no one, "Well, would you look at that? Already empty."

Josephine trotted back into the kitchen and re-filled her glass. After settling back in her chair and taking another sip, she began to feel unwell. *I can't seem to get a breath.* Gasping for air, she closed her eyes and prayed that whatever this was would pass. Her heart pounded, and her head felt like it was about to explode. Panic set in. Needing to call 911, she tried to stand but couldn't.

"Oh, my God!" Josephine gasped and struggled to breathe.

Dizzy, the room swirled around her. The martini glass dropped from her hand, shattering on the floor. Clutching her chest and fighting for air, her bloodshot eyes bulged. Unable to help herself and in terrible pain, she took one last look at the turquoise sea. Her body convulsed and jackknifed, and then it was over.

. . .

7:30 p.m.

Chief Jackson called Josephine's telephone number several times that evening. She didn't pick up. He got in his cruiser and made the drive to Coquina Reef. If asked, the excuse he'd use for his visit was that he was making a wellness check having become concerned when Josephine didn't answer her telephone.

No need to knock, he thought, arriving at Josephine's door. Sliding a credit card between the door and the strike plate, he was inside.

The chief turned on the kitchen light, pulled on latex gloves and went to work. He pulled the gift box and its wrapping from the trashcan and put it, along with the gift note, cocktail shaker, and the bottle of gin, in a plastic trash bag he'd brought with him. Next, he walked to the chair where Josephine's body lay slumped over and touched her. *Still warm and soft, no rigor, it just happened.* He cleaned up the broken martini glass and placed it in the trash bag. The spilled cocktail was also wiped away so that no remnant of the poisonous liquid remained.

The chief left the condominium, taking the trash bag with him and placing it in the trunk of his squad car. Then he called for an ambulance. While he waited, he took the burner phone from his pocket and made one more call. "Your gift was received and enjoyed."

. . .

9:00 p.m.
With Josephine's body on the way to the morgue, the chief worked quickly. After garnering the name and contact information for Josephine's next of kin from the condominium property manager, he called her daughter in Chicago.

"Hello, this is Chief Beauford Jackson of the Stypman Island Police Department. I'm trying to reach Rochelle Bryant. It's regarding her mother, Josephine Paulsen."

"This is Rochelle. Is my mother okay?" Her timid voice wobbled.

Good, she sounds like a pushover, nothing like her mother.

Chief Jackson spoke louder than necessary, exuding authority, and assuming control. "I'm sorry to have to relay this news, Ms. Bryant, but your mother passed away sometime earlier today." Rochelle did not respond, so he continued, "She went peacefully, Ms. Bryant. We found her body at her home in a chair facing the ocean. Hopefully, there's some comfort for you in that."

"I-I-I've been trying to call her, it's her birthday," Rochelle stammered. "Was she ill? She didn't tell me she was ill." The daughter's initial shock gave way to confusion.

"It appears to have been a heart attack."

Rochelle had been through this before. She whispered more to herself than the man on the phone. "Just like Dad."

"Judging from the look of it," said the chief, "she fell asleep and never woke up. Not a bad way to go, if you ask me. Look, Rochelle, can I call you Rochelle?"

"Y-Yes, that's fine," she stammered then broke down and wept.

Tears, this is going well; time to close the deal. Chief Jackson moved in for the kill, the real reason for his call.

"I want to ask you something very important," Jackson continued, "Because your mother died alone, there's usually a need for an autopsy. In this case, I don't think there's any reason to put you through that invasiveness. I can talk to the medical examiner if you'd like."

"Yes, that would be better," responded Rochelle. "My mother insisted we avoid that when my father died." Her sniffling and periodic sobs grew louder.

The chief breathed a sigh of relief but remained stoic. Smiles don't need to be seen; they can be heard over the phone, he reminded himself. "Well then, all I need is for you to sign a document that I can email to you. It states that it's your wish that your mother's body is not autopsied, and we can avoid that unpleasant step."

Rochelle blew her nose. "I'll sign it as soon as I receive it and scan it back to you. Would that be alright?"

"That will do it. In the meantime, I'll put in the directive on your behalf. Your mother's body will be at the county morgue. I'll send you the phone number, and you can make whatever arrangements you'd like from there." Then, he swung for the fences. "Hey, given that you're out of town, the simplest thing would be to have the body cremated locally, the ashes can be sent to you."

"No, I'll bury her here in Chicago, next to my father, but thank you for the suggestion."

Well, it would have been cleaner with a cremation, but at least the damned body will be out of here before long. That'll have to be good enough. Chief Jackson ended the call.

CHAPTER 8

Saturday, July 10 - 6:00 a.m.

Lisa poured a cup of freshly brewed coffee and sat down at her kitchen table. She looked at a weather app on her phone and mimicked the perky weather forecaster. "It's a hot, sunny morning in Miami, showers in the afternoon, temps in the mid-90's." *What else is new?* Bored with the weather, she decided to try Dorothy again. She'd already tried twice before and figured the third time would be the charm. When it wasn't, she listened to Dorothy's message again. It was short but now it sounded different to Lisa. It sounded urgent.

"There is something you should know."

Noticing the message had been left just after midnight, a detail Lisa hadn't previously focused on, she began to worry. Phone in hand, she turned her attention to her email account. *Maybe there's something from her there.* In her in-box she found a message from Roger Jensen, a name she recognized.

Dear Lisa,

I am Dorothy Jensen's nephew, Roger. Dorothy left instructions to contact you in the event of her death. There is no easy way to say this. Dorothy died a few days ago. She was murdered, and the police are still investigating. I'm about to empty her home of its contents and Dorothy wanted you to have some items of hers. Since it appears you live only a few hours away, I need you to stop by and collect whatever you want. You are welcome to have the entire lot. I'm not interested in any of it and plan to clear her things out as soon as the police are finished, so let me know if you'll be coming. I will meet you at her condo.

Sincerely,

Roger Jenkins

With tears streaming down her face, Lisa read the email again. "Murdered," she said the word aloud. "Who would murder Dorothy? She tried to let me know something was wrong, and I missed the call." She broke down, wondering if she'd ever be able to forgive herself.

I knew I'd lose her someday. But not this way. I've got to get up there before that place is torn apart. Who knows how the local cops are handling this? No way am I letting this go unsolved. Not like Scott.

Although she'd never met him, Dorothy had told Lisa a lot about her nephew so she wasn't surprised by the tone of his letter or his lack of sentiment about losing his aunt. Still, it burned her up inside.

Dear Roger,

Thank you so much for letting me know of your aunt's passing. I cannot imagine anyone wanting to harm Dorothy and am shocked by her murder as I expect you are as well. Dorothy and I were lifelong friends. She was my teacher in middle school, a mentor and a very close friend whom I'll miss terribly. Please let me know the details of her funeral arrangements as I would like to attend. I would very much like to take you up on your kind offer to look through her things. Having a remembrance of her would mean a lot to me. I can meet you at her condominium this Tuesday morning at ten o'clock if that works for you.

Kind regards,

Lisa Owens

Roger wrote back a few hours later to confirm the meeting and sent Lisa his phone number. She dabbed her eyes while adding it to her contacts list. *So much for this being just another hot, sunny day in Miami.*

"Mac, I'm taking your advice. I won't be in on Tuesday. Something came up. Try not to miss me too much." She left the message on her boss' voicemail. "Be careful what you ask for, boss," she said after hanging up.

CHAPTER 9

Tuesday, July 13 - 7:30 a.m.

Lisa hoped the two-hour drive to Stypman Island would be cathartic and a time for reflection. Searching for Etta James on her playlist, a favorite of Dorothy's, she settled in behind the wheel and '*Something's Got a Hold on Me*' filled the car. Just as she cranked up the volume, her phone rang.

"Hello, this is Maggie Sherlock, I'm a reporter at Treasure Coast Magazine. I'm calling for Lisa Owens."

"This is Lisa."

"Ms. Owens, I hope I'm not calling too early."

"This is fine. How can I help you?"

"I'm writing an article on Dorothy Jensen. Her nephew Roger gave me your number. He said you'd be the best person to speak with me about her. I'm writing a cover story about her life and the work she did to protect the environment."

Lisa was suspicious. "What did you say the name of the magazine is? I don't think I've heard of it."

"Treasure Coast Magazine. It's a quarterly lifestyle magazine."

A lightbulb went off. Dorothy had been a subscriber. "Of course, I remember seeing it in Dorothy's place."

"Roger said you were close with Dorothy. I'm very familiar with her environmental work and the River Guardians, but I feel certain she was more than that. I want to write a story about the person, not just the work. Do you think you can help with that?"

"I'm in the car and have a long drive ahead of me, so if this is a good time for you..."

"Perfect."

"Dorothy was my middle school teacher, my mentor and my very best friend. She was like an adopted grandmother to me, so yes, I can help you."

"Did Dorothy have a career, a family? Let's start with that."

"Dorothy was a teacher for forty-five years at Southlake Middle School in Miami. She told me children are especially vulnerable in the middle school years. Peer pressure and bullying are at their worst, puberty, body changes, all that stuff. Although her students thought they were rather grown up, Dorothy knew they were just children trying to figure out the world. She had a rewarding career helping kids make a good start."

What a difference she made. I wish I could say the same thing. The thought filled Lisa's head and her mood hit a new low as she cruised up the on-ramp for 95 North.

"She never married or had children of her own, but Dorothy was beloved by the many hundreds of students she'd touched over the years. I often wonder how she managed that." Lisa pushed a strand of hair away from her face and adjusted her sunglasses. "My circle of friends seems tiny compared to hers."

"You make her sound like a very special person."

"She was, Maggie, she was. Although she retired quite a while ago, several of her students remain in touch with her. Every year, at Christmas, her mailbox is packed with holiday cards."

Next Christmas those cards will be marked return to sender. Lisa slid into a full-blown funk at the thought.

"Could you tell me about your friendship with her? How did that come to be?"

"I'm not sure what she saw in me but looking back, I think she could tell that I needed her, and I guess she needed me too. Whatever the reason, we kept in close contact throughout the years, and a deep and lasting friendship formed."

"Can you give me an example of a time when she was there for you?"

A smile came to Lisa's face. "There are so many but here's a good one. I was a volleyball player at the University of Miami and was obsessive about the game. I played on a full scholarship and let me tell you, I took the word 'serious' to a new level. Anyway, there was this game we were expected to lose. I was freaking out over it. That sweet woman knew how worried I was and drove two hours in pouring rain to show up for me. I still remember how surprised I was to see her in the bleachers. It wasn't a good night for the Hurricanes, we got our butts kicked, but I played for her that night and had one of the best games of my career."

"Do you still play?"

"Not anymore, these days kickboxing is more my thing. Dorothy was fascinated with kickboxing; I remember her saying she wished she could have been a kickboxer too." Memories washed over Lisa like waves in the ocean. She looked through the windscreen up at the sky. *Maybe they have kickboxing in heaven.*

"What advice did Dorothy give you? She was your mentor, right?"

"After I graduated with a degree in psychology, Dorothy encouraged me to leave Florida. She thought I should have an experience living somewhere else. I took a job in Washington, DC as a policy aide for a manufacturing association. The work was dull and unrewarding. Dorothy and I had a lot of late-night phone calls where she pointed out my job was not as important as experiencing life somewhere new. She was right, of course, the DC social scene was amazing, like nothing I'd ever seen before. Those were some days. To think I was about to quit and get out of there. I would have missed so much if it weren't for Dorothy encouraging me to stay."

"Lisa, this article is going to be so rich thanks to you. I'd like to ask something personal now, you don't have to answer but I think it would add to the story. Is there a time you can recall, when you had to lean on Dorothy, or when she leaned on you?"

Lisa's eyes filled. "This is hard for me to talk about, and I'm not sure I'd want you to include it in your story, but you'll understand the person Dorothy was if I share it with you.

"When I lived in DC, I met a congressional aide at a co-ed volleyball game in Rock Creek Park. His name was Scott Diaz. We fell in love and a year later, he proposed. I called Dorothy that night and told her every detail. We were on the phone for hours, it's my happiest memory of her. Soon after,

Scott was gunned-down and killed while walking to his apartment from a nearby Metro station."

"Oh my God, I'm so sorry, and now you've lost Dorothy in a similar way."

"Maggie, my world shattered when Scott died. It was as if the bullet had hit me, too. The memorial service was a shit show thanks to the press. No offense, but they showed up in force with their cameras, hoping for photos of Scott's grieving parents and me, his young fiancée. They wouldn't give us a break and camped out in front of the place where we were staying. It was awful. Dorothy made the trip from Florida to be with me. I remember her running out of the house with a fly swatter, shooing them away. It was so funny; we all had a much-needed laugh."

Yes, Dorothy was with me for all of it. What am I going to do without her?

"Out of curiosity Lisa, did you ever find out what happened? Who killed Scott?"

"They said it was a robbery gone wrong. But then, questions started coming up." Lisa's shoulders tensed and she gripped the steering wheel so tight, her knuckles whitened.

"In Washington, there's no shortage of conspiracy theories. Was the robbery classification a cover-up? Was Scott's death somehow tied to politics? Was the murder intended to send Scott's boss a message? Did he know something that could damage his boss? I'd put all of it out of my head until an officer in the DC Police Department asked to meet with me." Lisa paused as memories of that time came up, she became more unsettled.

"I wasn't sure I'd go through with the meeting, but Dorothy encouraged me. She told me it was time to take matters into my own hands. I learned the DC Police had received a tip from a female caller who identified herself as 'Vanessa'. The informant said Scott's death wasn't the result of a robbery and that she knew why he'd been killed. The police didn't follow up on the call for reasons that were never made clear. Here comes the part you can't print. Okay?"

"Understood."

"The questions surrounding Scott's death tortured me, a suspect was never identified, and Vanessa was never located. It led to my mistrust of the police, something I carry with me to this day and I'm a cop. After I returned to Florida, I wanted to avenge Scott's death or at least make some meaning of it, so I trained for a career in law enforcement. I was completely driven, a recurring theme for me, and graduated at the top of my class at the Police Academy. Today, I'm a homicide detective in Miami, a homicide detective with trust issues. I've worked on hundreds of cases and solved a bunch of them. Work gives me some satisfaction but I'm miserable. Losing my best friend makes it even worse."

"There's a lot of damage from losing Scott and now Dorothy. Let me guess, you put your work first and your personal life on the back burner. Right?"

"That's me, a hopeless workaholic because I don't trust my team to do the job right. I don't want the families of murder victims to go through what I did. Not knowing is the worst." Lisa shook her head and pressed her foot on the accelerator.

"Any final thoughts about Dorothy, Lisa?

"I'm an only child. My dad died when I was three. My mother remarried years ago and lives on an island off the coast of Brazil. She and her husband manage a boutique resort there. We keep in touch with email and WhatsApp, but our relationship is distant. Dorothy filled that void. She was always there when I needed her most. She couldn't solve my problems for me, but I'm grateful she was there holding my hand as I went through them. How many people can say they had a friend like that? I was so lucky; I have to think of it that way."

"That's very touching. I promise to do justice to Dorothy in my article, and I'll send you an advance copy so you can be sure I got it right. Best of luck to you, Lisa. I hope brighter days are ahead for you."

Well, I guess this was a cathartic drive after all. A sign for Stypman Island loomed up ahead. Pulling off the main highway, Lisa took the exit. Her thoughts turned to the man she'd soon be meeting - Roger Jensen, Dorothy's nephew.

Well, I know they didn't like each other and saw little of each other, even though he lives just a few hours away. Lisa made mental notes, just as she would before questioning a suspect. *I remember Dorothy telling me this guy embodies everything wrong with the world. He's greedy, he doesn't believe in climate change, he's a racist, a misogynist, and he's homophobic. Great, Dorothy, just great. He's like half the men in Florida.*

It would fall to Roger to make the arrangements for Dorothy's body to be cremated and her ashes scattered at sea. Dorothy could have asked Lisa to handle those responsibilities, but she knew her death would hit Lisa hard. Better for Roger to deal with the problems her demise would create. So, she tasked him with selling her condominium and closing out her estate. Her Will stipulated that in return for his efforts, Roger was to receive the paltry sum of $1,500 and the contents of her home although she anticipated he wouldn't want her things. The rest of her assets would go to a small children's museum in Miami, where over the years, she'd taken hundreds of students on field trips. Dorothy understood that what she bequeathed Roger was certain to irritate him. Her lawyer had even said as much when drawing up the Will, commenting she thought it didn't seem right. Dorothy had replied, "Well, dear, you've never met Roger."

CHAPTER 10

Tuesday, July 13 - 10:00 a.m.

Arriving on Stypman Island, Lisa pulled into a coffee shop and made a call. "Hi, Roger, It's Lisa Owens. I'm here on the island. I'm stopping for coffee. Can I bring you something?"

"No, thanks. When you arrive at the building, stay downstairs. I'll meet you there. There's something I need to explain before we go up to Dorothy's place."

"Is everything alright?"

"I'll explain more when you get here. Hey, did that reporter get a hold of you?"

"She did, I think she'll write a nice piece. Thanks for referring her to me."

"Just meet me downstairs when you arrive. I'll be looking for you."

Lisa pulled into the Coquina Reef parking lot and saw Roger waiting, his hands on his hips, and squinting in the bright Florida sunshine. She guessed he was in his early to mid-forties—tall, somewhat overweight, with thinning black hair. Lisa parked in a guest space and grabbed her purse and coffee.

"Hi, you must be Roger. I'm Lisa," she said as she extended her hand.

"I was expecting someone older than you." Roger shook her hand and looked her up and down.

"Well, I hope you're not too disappointed," Lisa responded, annoyed that Roger hadn't taken his eyes off her chest.

"No, not at all. You're a pleasant surprise."

Inwardly, Lisa rolled her eyes. *This jerk is everything Dorothy said he was.*

"I wanted to meet you here before going up to the condo because something happened up there that you need to be aware of. Dorothy's murder, well, it was brutal. Most of the mess is cleaned up but things are... well, out of place. We have the 'all clear' from the authorities to enter, but I didn't want you to be shocked. Okay?"

Heart pounding, Lisa's anxiety rose. A lump grew in her throat and she dry-swallowed. Her eyes watered behind her Maui Jim sunglasses. "What happened?"

"I'm not sure," said Roger. "The police told me her body was mutilated in a way that suggests the murder was gang-related. Crazy, right? What the hell could that old broad have done to piss off a gang?"

Lisa exploded, she moved toward Roger until her face was just inches from his. "That old broad was my best friend in the world. So, when you refer to her in front of me, give her the courtesy and respect she deserves, or I'll kick your ass up and down this island. Understand?"

Roger's jaw dropped. He tried to reply, but Lisa cut him off.

"Now, when you say her body was mutilated, what exactly does that mean?"

Stepping back, Roger stammered, "Her head was cut off, her eyes were gouged, and her tongue was cut out."

Adrenaline coursed through Lisa like a strong current in a stormy ocean. Desperate for answers, her police training kicked in like muscle memory. "Let's go upstairs. I want to see for myself." She headed for the elevator. Roger made no effort to move, infuriating her. "Now, Roger!"

She thought she was prepared but seeing the apartment in shambles caught Lisa off guard. Frantic to find something to ground her, something that hadn't changed, her eyes darted around the once familiar place. The furniture had been pushed around and sofa cushions were strewn about on the floor. Drawers were open and piles of books were on the floor, even Dorothy's treasured oriental rug was pulled back and shoved in a heap against a wall. *I don't think I can do this,* she thought and then, she saw something that hadn't changed; the turquoise ocean with its rolling waves just outside the windows. It was enough. Lisa steadied herself and focused.

"The police did a number on the place; they took me through when I arrived here the first time. They wanted to show me what they did and what was damaged by the crime itself."

Lisa heard him but didn't respond. Her trained eyes took it all in. Even though the murder victim was a close friend, the crime scene was not unlike many she'd seen before. She looked in the guest room and guest bathroom. *Nothing happened in here.*

"Umm, she was in there," Roger waved toward what had been Dorothy's bedroom.

The sheets, blankets, and pillows had been removed but the blood-stained mattress remained. *Not enough blood on the mattress to account for this type of killing, most of it must have ended up on the floor.* Although someone had attempted to clean it up, bloodstains, smears, and spatter were still present throughout the room. There was blood pooled on a nightstand, next to a paperback book.

Roger stood at the entrance to the bedroom. Noticing Lisa studying the nightstand, he said, "That's where they found her eyeballs."

Lisa's gaze turned toward a large blood smear on the floor in front of the chest of drawers where Dorothy kept her sweaters. Instinctively, she knew what happened there. More to herself than to Roger, she said, "And this must be where they found her severed head."

"Her tongue was over there," said Roger, pointing toward a smear that feathered out a few inches before stopping.

Lisa examined the floor. "It looks like someone slipped there."

"Can we please get out of this room?" asked Roger. "I'm not feeling so good."

They left the bedroom and went back into the living area. Fumbling with the lock, Roger opened a sliding glass door to let in the ocean breeze. Instead of a breeze, a rush of hot, humid air filled the room. Unsteady on his feet, Roger pushed the door closed.

"You okay?"

"I'm woozy. I need to get out of here. Hang around and take whatever you want. Everything needs to go. My buddy is buying the place, and it can't look like this when he sees it. A crew comes tomorrow to haul everything away, so if you want anything, take it today." He headed toward the front door.

"Your friend is buying it? The condo is already sold?"

"Yeah, I let him have it for a cheap price, I'm not getting the money so what do I care? He's using it to be with his girlfriend. You know... he's married."

Lisa thought she might be sick. *Dorothy would be so disappointed.*

"Are you sure you don't want anything of Dorothy's? Many of these things were very special to her and are valuable."

"No." Roger opened the door, ready to leave. "As you probably know, I wasn't exactly fond of my aunt. The sooner all this crap is gone, and this place is sold, the better. Oh, I almost forgot, the list of things she wanted you to take is on the kitchen table. You have my number if you need to get a hold of me."

He was about to close the door behind him when Lisa called after him. "Hey! Before you go, the last time I heard from her, Dorothy had something on her mind, something she wanted to talk with me about. Any idea what that might have been?"

"I'd be the last person that woman would have shared anything with. Knowing her, she probably wanted to make sure you voted in the next election. She was totally losing it."

"Roger, you never told me when the funeral service will be."

"Funeral? Her body's being cremated, and a guy I know who runs a fishing charter will toss the ashes in the ocean. That's more than she deserves."

Lisa's jaw sagged in shocked disbelief.

CHAPTER 11

Tuesday, July 13 - 10:30 a.m.

Lisa placed the cushions back on the sofa and sat down. There was so much to take in. Questions swirled in her head. *How on earth could something this horrible happen to Dorothy? Did she know she was in danger? Is that what she wanted to talk about?* Lisa knew all too well that terrible things happen every day. Scott had been murdered, and now Dorothy had met the same fate. *I'm like a magnet for murder. Who says lightning doesn't strike in the same place twice?* She went back into the bedroom, took out her phone and began taking photos.

When she finished, she left the condominium and went to her car. Opening her trunk, she removed a small case that contained some tools she used in her work. Back in Dorothy's bedroom, she collected several blood samples from various places throughout the room, labeling each and noting where they had been collected.

Fingerprint powder was everywhere. Noting and measuring the bloody footprints on the tiled floor, she whispered to herself. "Sloppy police work, there are multiple prints from the officers who attended the scene. There'd be hell to pay if my guys did this."

Now what? Lisa looked around. It was warm in the condo. She checked the thermostat; it was set to eighty degrees. Dorothy was always cold and kept the temperature setting at eighty. Lisa smiled at the memory and turned it down to seventy-four.

Thirsty, she opened the refrigerator, and had a small meltdown. There, on the bottom shelf, where they always were, bottles of beer stood waiting for her. Coors Light, her favorite brand. Dorothy despised the taste of beer but kept it for Lisa's visits.

The sight of the beer made Lisa's eyes moisten. She stood in front of the open refrigerator staring at it and feeling she was missing something important. It took a few more seconds before it dawned on her. *Huh, there are five bottles here.* Lisa thought back to her last visit. She recalled finishing up the last remaining beer and saying she'd buy more on her next visit. Dorothy would hear none of that and said she would re-stock Lisa's private stash. Well, apparently, she'd done that. *Beer is sold in six packs, not five. So, where's the sixth beer?* She scratched her head and closed the refrigerator door. *One thing's for certain, Dorothy didn't drink it.*

Opening the kitchen trash can, she peered inside, "Bingo!" She took a photo of the bottle in the trash and put on a rubber glove from her kit. Pulling the bottle from the trash, she held it up and examined it in the light. There was a tiny smudge of blood and what looked to be a partial fingerprint. Lisa placed the bottle in an evidence bag and labeled it.

A parade of people must have passed through here since the murder, any of them could have helped themselves to a beer. But just maybe, I'll get lucky. Severing a head isn't easy work and it was eighty degrees in here. Could be the killer was hot, thirsty and stupid.

Realizing this would be her last visit before the condo was cleared out, Lisa did what she was expected to do. She knew every item on the list Roger had mentioned, Dorothy had given her a copy of that same list a while back. First, she went to a small, porcelain jar displayed on a bookshelf in Dorothy's bedroom. Taking the lid off, she removed a set of diamond earrings. The earrings were small but made from fine white diamonds, expertly cut, and given to Dorothy as a gift from a former student who was now one of the leading jewelers in Miami Beach.

Although they weren't on the list, Lisa collected the framed photographs displayed throughout the condo: Dorothy's parents, former students and friends, and a favorite one, Lisa and Dorothy standing together on the beach with the ocean behind them. Lisa gazed at the photo and whispered, "This is going in my office." She put the photos in a reusable grocery bag she found in the kitchen pantry.

Next, she removed a painting from a wall in the living area, one she knew well. It was done by a local artist who'd made it big and now lived in Key West. As a gesture of support and encouragement, Dorothy bought the piece of art for a small amount of money years ago when the artist - a former student - was starting out and in need of cash. Now, it was valued around a hundred thousand dollars.

Last on the list was Dorothy's prized oriental rug. *There's no way I can manage this today.* Lisa pursed her lips and stared at the bulky carpet. Agonizing over it for a few minutes, she bent down and touched the soft wool. "I'm sorry, Dorothy," she whispered. Tears flooded her eyes.

Looking around the condo one last time, Lisa noticed something on the kitchen counter that she'd missed earlier. She picked up a blue file folder containing several papers and the answer to a question that had been weighing on her. The folder contained several medical documents, some with handwritten notes Dorothy had made in the margins. Lisa's eyes widened, three of Dorothy's notes catching her attention.

INOPERABLE TERMINAL SIX MONTHS AT MOST

As she continued reading through the file, a missing piece fell into place. Dorothy had been diagnosed with stage four pancreatic cancer. Lisa felt her heart would break. *This is what she wanted to tell me. It's why she wanted me to stay overnight.* At the bottom of the stack of papers was a letter-sized envelope. *It has my name on it and that's Dorothy's handwriting. I can't right now, I just can't.* Unable to bring herself to open it, she stuffed it in the pocket of her jeans and left the condo. Struggling with the bags and the large painting, she made her way to the elevator and got on. It stopped one floor below, and in walked Clara Anders with her dog. Lisa acknowledged them with a sad half-smile, her eyes red and puffy.

Clara understood. "Oh dear, are you a relative of Dorothy's?"

"She was my best friend."

"I'm so sorry," said Clara. "Can I help you carry something?"

"That's so kind of you," said Lisa. "If you could take this bag, I can manage the painting."

"I've always loved that painting," said Clara.

"Oh, you knew Dorothy?"

"Yes, I'm Clara Anders. My husband and I live right below her unit. We looked after her a bit, you know, checked on her and brought her the newspaper, things like that. We enjoyed a cup of coffee together every now and then."

"Well, it's nice to meet you, Clara. I'm Lisa Owens, and who is this?" Lisa looked down at the furry, brown dog.

"This is Marley."

Bending down to pet her, Lisa said, "Hello, Marley, what a pretty dog you are." Marley had been sniffing at Lisa since entering the elevator. She licked Lisa's hand and sniffed the painting and the bag Clara held.

"She smells Dorothy," said Lisa.

"Yes, she does. We were told she has an amazing nose. Is it still terrible up there? The reason I ask is that there was so much blood, it came through Dorothy's floor and into our place."

Shock read across Lisa's face. "How horrible! And yes, it's still bad. Dorothy's nephew wants to get it cleaned out and told me that if I wanted something of hers, I had to come this week. So here I am."

"Well, I'm glad you got that painting," said Clara. "I know from Dorothy that it's a very good one, and she wouldn't want it to go to just anyone, especially not Roger." The women shared an understanding smile.

"Listen, besides being a close friend of Dorothy's, I'm also a homicide detective. I work in Miami. I'm curious about what happened. Would it be okay if I came by one day soon to talk with you and your husband?"

"Aren't the local police investigating this?"

"They are. I just want to be sure it's being done correctly. I want to be sure there's justice for Dorothy, and sometimes a small, local police department... well, they just aren't as thorough as they should be."

"We've had similar thoughts. We moved here from New York. Although living on a small island is wonderful, the local resources aren't what we're used to. We'd be glad to help, although I'm not sure if there's much we can tell you."

"Here's my contact information," said Lisa, putting the painting on the floor to rest while pulling a business card out of her purse. "If it's okay, I'd like to take your phone number so I can reach you."

With the number in her phone contacts, Lisa loaded her bag and the painting into her car and said goodbye.

"Well, maybe they can help me find some answers," Lisa said to herself. She waved at Clara and pulled out of the parking lot.

CHAPTER 12

Tuesday, July 13 - 3:00 p.m.

On the drive back to Miami, Lisa made a phone call. She needed a favor and knew she could count on Bruce Kim. A gifted investigator, he worked in the crime lab at the Miami City Police Department. The two had collaborated on several tough cases. Without his knowledge, Lisa wrote a recommendation for Bruce that resulted in a promotion and pay raise at a time when he needed the extra income. That act of kindness cemented their friendship.

"Hi, Bruce, it's Lisa. Have a minute?"

"Sure, Lisa, what's up?"

"I need to ask a favor. A close friend of mine was murdered on Stypman Island. I'm on my way back now, and I have some evidence the local police missed. I was hoping you could help me out by checking some DNA, a few blood samples and a fingerprint. It's a long shot, but maybe there is a match in the database.

"Sorry about your friend. You okay?"

"I'm hanging in, all things considered. Bruce, if you do this it has to be on the DL. It's not my case or our jurisdiction. My confidence in the local police department is ..."

"Let me guess, slightly lacking? I get it. Drop off whatever you have at my house. I'll take it in and run everything late tonight. The lab is a lot quieter then. I should be able to get what you need on the double."

"Hey, remember that asshole we nailed in the Sylvester case? His name was Alfonse DelGrosso."

"Yeah, what about him?"

"He threatened me, said I would pay for locking him up. I'm wondering if he could have had something to do with my friend's murder, you know, to get back at me?"

"DelGrosso? He's behind bars. He's small-time. Maybe he's got some reach but to be honest, I'd be surprised if he's involved. The crew he runs with doesn't do anything for free and Alfonse doesn't have the coin."

"You're right. I just can't figure it out. Who would do this? She was a kind elderly lady, and it was brutal, she was beheaded, eyes gouged out, tongue cut."

"Holy hell!" Bruce gasped. "Classic kill for a snitch. Somebody's sending a message."

"The local cops on the island think it's gang-related."

"Did your friend have enemies? Anybody at all?"

"None that I'm aware of. Her nephew couldn't stand her but after meeting him, I'm ruling him out. He's a real dick but not a murderer. Can't stand the sight of blood." Lisa hesitated for a second, recalling a tough lesson she'd learned earlier in her career. "Although we've seen that before."

"What about adversaries? Someone who benefits from her death?"

"I've been thinking about that. There's one possibility, but it seems kind of far-fetched. Dorothy founded a group, the River Guardians. They have a pending lawsuit against the biggest water polluter in Florida, one of those big agriculture companies."

"I don't know, Lisa. Those greedy bastards piss me off, too. They're screwing with the Everglades, for God's sake. But those lawsuits go nowhere because the damn companies buy everyone off. Doesn't seem likely another lawsuit would drive them to kill your friend."

"You're probably right, Bruce. But then, who was it?"

Back in Miami, she drove to Bruce's home, a ranch-style house in a family-friendly neighborhood. Driving through the tree-lined streets, she wondered if she'd ever live in a place like this.

Millie, a precocious eight-year-old, answered the door wearing a pink shirt with a bright graphic of Dora the Explorer.

Lisa smiled at her. "Hi, Millie. It's so nice to see you. What a great shirt. I love Dora."

Millie grinned. "Hi, Lisa, wait here. I'll get my mom."

Over the years, Lisa had become friends with Bruce's wife, Aki, a part-time professor at Miami Dade College. The women enjoyed working out together on Saturday mornings at a kickboxing gym and had become close. Aki Kim hurried to the door wearing an Old Navy ball cap, dirty running shorts, and a well-used Miami Marlins t-shirt.

"Well, look who's here. Sorry I'm such a mess. I was doing some gardening in the backyard. There are always so many weeds." A tiny, two-year-old appeared, the Kims' youngest child, Chloe.

Lisa smiled at her. "Hey there, Chloe."

The little girl grinned and ran back inside.

"Ah, she is so shy. Sorry for her bad manners."

Lisa laughed. "I was shy when I was little, too. I'm sorry to stop by without calling. I have something I need to leave for Bruce. He's expecting it."

"He called me to say you'd be dropping something off, and I was to be sure to keep the girls away from it."

Lisa handed Aki the grocery bag containing the blood samples and empty beer bottle. She had secured the top of the bag with a rubber band.

"Well, this doesn't seem very official." Aki held the bag up and raised her eyebrows.

"It's the best I had to work with. Thanks so much for getting it to Bruce. We should have dinner together one day soon... or better yet, I'll babysit, and you two can enjoy a night on the town."

"That's a deal. Are you able to stay for coffee?"

"Not today... there's a lot going on. But thanks, anyway. Hey, have fun in the garden."

. . .

Later that evening, Bruce opened the shopping bag and found several items - each one marked and in an individual evidence bag. An accompanying note from Lisa contained her instructions.

Bruce took the print then swabbed the beer bottle for DNA. Next, he ran each of the blood samples Lisa had collected. Finally, everything was entered in the crime lab's various databases, including CODIS, the FBI's Combined DNA Index System. If there was a match on file, he'd find it.

CHAPTER 13

Tuesday, July 13 - 11:30 p.m.

Sleep was impossible. Lisa kept replaying the scene in Dorothy's condo, unable to bear the thought of her dear friend suffering in fear. She hoped the end had come quickly. Wide awake and flat on her back in bed, it hit her from out of the blue. She bolted from the bed and turned on the bedside light. Recalling another sleepless night not so long ago, she grabbed her phone and double-checked the calendar already knowing what she'd see there.

Goosebumps rose on her arms and her hand shook as she stared at the phone. Her friend's murder had occurred on the same night she'd been jarred out of a sound sleep. Her shaky voice barely a whisper, she spoke to a ghost. "Dorothy, it was you, wasn't it?"

Remembering the letter she'd found, the one she didn't have the courage to read earlier, she walked across her bedroom and picked her jeans up from the floor. Stuffing her hand in a pocket, she pulled out the letter and returned to her bed. Cold with fear, she pulled the covers up. After looking at her name on the envelope for several moments, she opened it, realizing this would be the last communication she'd receive from someone who'd meant everything to her.

> My dearest Lisa,
> If you're reading this letter, you already know about my cancer. Telling you I am about to leave you is the most difficult thing I've ever done. I love you so very much. I'm sure you know that. You have been one of the

brightest spots in my life, and I am so very thankful to have known you.

Looking back, I have few regrets. I see now that I should have taken more chances and embraced life more fully than I had the courage to do. Life is short and precious; it makes little sense not to spend it chasing happiness.

My heart broke for you when you lost Scott, and even more so when you put your happiness to the side to make your work your focus. I understand that choice seemed better than taking a chance on having your heart broken again. I'm writing this letter because I'm certain I could never say these words to you. After all, I am in no position to judge you, nor would I ever do so.

I've lived a long life, and there is one thing about which I'm certain. Sadness, bad things, and bad people have always been a part of life, but not the best part. Go after the best part, Lisa. Find someone to love and build a life with that person. Honor Scott's memory, and mine, with love and let go of the rest.

Lovingly, Dorothy

Reading the letter several times, Lisa dabbed at her eyes with a corner of the bedsheet. Like looking in a mirror, she'd been confronted with the truth. *Dorothy was right, I have put happiness to the side, and I gave up on what might be. How the hell do I find happiness now? I don't even know where to start.*

. . .

Wednesday, July 14 - 12:30 a.m.

When sleep finally came to Lisa, it was brief. The sound of her phone ringing woke her up. Grabbing it from her bedside table, she sat up. "Hello?"

"It's Bruce. Sorry to wake you. We have a match."

The call from Bruce ended with arrangements to meet in an hour. Lisa spoke to the framed photo of a young man on her bedside table. "Well, Scott, I guess happiness will have to wait a little longer."

An hour later, she pulled into the parking lot of a dingy Waffle House restaurant. Entering, an old man mopping the floor and the aroma of coffee, fried bacon and disinfectant greeted her. Bruce waited at a table in the back of the empty restaurant. A copper-colored plastic coffee pot sat on the table, along with mugs and spoons.

"Believe it or not, I come here because the coffee is pretty good," Bruce said, filling the mugs.

Lisa sat across the table from him; her facial expression told him she wasn't here for small talk.

Bruce got the message. His expression turned serious; his voice precise as he spoke. "I pulled out all the stops to get this done fast, it just goes to show how much quicker things can happen than what we're told. Anyway, we have a match. The guy you're looking for is in Brooklyn. He was picked up for assault and is behind bars at the Metropolitan Detention Center in South Slope. The DNA and fingerprint from the beer bottle are an exact match. There's more. I checked travel records, the guy, whose name is Angelo Scarella, was just here. Travel records show he flew to JFK from West Palm the day after your friend's murder."

Lisa felt her eyes water and dabbed at them with a paper napkin. "Why would Scarella want to kill Dorothy? Is there a connection to DelGrosso? Please tell me there isn't. I can't handle the idea that I could have been the reason for her murder."

"I don't know, but it turns out this Scarella character is no model citizen. According to his file, he's a person of interest in some terrible stuff and has documented sadistic tendencies." Bruce slid a large manilla envelope across the table. "I made copies for you."

Lisa took the envelope and placed it on the seat next to her. "I wonder what he wanted with Dorothy. Was he a former student?"

"I don't think so. From what I could find, Scarella was born in Brooklyn and stayed put. He grew up in a mob neighborhood and still has strong ties there. If I had to guess, I'd pin him as a contract killer."

Lisa's eyes widened. "You think he was hired to put a hit on Dorothy? Bruce, that just can't be."

"There's one more thing. Something I think you should be aware of."

"What's that?"

"It's about the Stypman Island police. It looks like the local police chief isn't working the case, at least not seriously."

"What do you mean?" Lisa put her mug down and leaned in closer to Bruce.

"After you asked for my help, I got interested in the case, so I did some checking. The locals haven't put anything in the crime database. The blood samples they took, any fingerprints they collected... nothing is being entered or followed up on. It seems like they're sitting on this."

"This is exactly what I was afraid of. Why would they just sit on it?" She paused, then said, "I don't want to share the match with them just yet. Are you okay with that?"

"Whatever you want to do here is okay with me. You and I are the only people who know about this right now. What's your next move?"

"I want to talk to Angelo Scarella. I need to see his face when I ask him about Dorothy."

"You can't just go to Brooklyn and say you're there to interrogate one of their perps. He's out of your jurisdiction. Hell, this whole mess is out of your jurisdiction."

"I know, but there's someone up there I'm hoping will help me."

"Well, whoever that person is, they'd better be high up the chain."

"He is."

CHAPTER 14

Wednesday, July 14 - 3:30 p.m.

After calling Mac and letting him know she'd be taking a few more days off, Lisa boarded a flight from Miami to LaGuardia Airport. Upon landing in Queens, she hopped in an Uber to Little Italy to meet an old friend, Ronnie Rutherford, and her husband for an early dinner.

Ronnie had always been a total knockout and Lisa could see her shiny auburn hair from the car window while the Uber was still a half block away. She and Lisa had become friends when they both lived in Washington, D.C. Since then, Ronnie had moved to New York and met her husband, Charles, who stood on the sidewalk next to her as Lisa exited the car and pulled her carry-on suitcase toward the striking couple. Ronnie was fair and small, while Charles was dark, broad, and imposingly tall. Already an undersheriff in the NYPD, Charles was a rising star with full responsibility for the Borough of Brooklyn.

The three exchanged hugs outside the entrance of La Luna, a tiny Italian restaurant that was no more than a hole-in-the-wall. "So, Lisa," said Ronnie, "it's great to see you and all that, but what's up? You said there's something urgent you wanted to talk about. Why did you want to see us? Or should I say, why did you want to see Charles?"

"Ronnie, you know I always want to spend time with you." Lisa gave her friend another warm hug. Linking her arm with Charles', she added, "And Charles, I could look at you all day." She winked at Ronnie.

"Well, I'm starving. Let's grab a table and order some dinner. Then we'll see what Detective Owens has on her mind." Charles raised his eyebrows at

Lisa and gestured toward the door of the restaurant. "I love this place; they have the best eggplant parm in the city."

The restaurant was anything but fancy but judging from the aromas wafting out of the kitchen, Lisa could tell it had promise. Charles had called ahead, and reserved a table in a quiet corner at the back of the cozy dining room. They ordered quickly, and Ronnie selected a bottle of Chianti. Lisa's mouth watered when the wine and a basket of garlic bread arrived at the table. She hadn't eaten anything all day but a few airline peanuts.

Forcing herself to ignore the bread, Lisa jumped into the reason for her visit, explaining about Dorothy's murder and why she was interested in talking with Angelo Scarella. Without hesitation, she posed the question she'd come to ask. "Charles, is there any chance you could open some doors for me at the Detention Center? I need to talk to Scarella."

Charles finished swallowing the bread he'd just stuffed in his mouth. "I'm always down for helping a sister officer, especially when she's one of my wife's very best friends. Here's an idea, what if I question Scarella? You can watch from the next room. I'll wear an earpiece, so if there's something you want me to get into with this guy, you can cue me. That keeps you out of it, we avoid a bunch of complications, and you'll still get to see this guy's reaction when he's confronted about your friend."

As Lisa considered Charles' proposal, a server delivered three heaping servings of eggplant parmesan to the table. "That'll work, Charles. I owe you big time." Relieved he'd agreed to help, Lisa turned her attention to the table. "Tomorrow we'll confront Scarella, but right now, I'm diving in and I'm eating all of this." She glanced up and smiled at her friend, "Don't judge me, Ronnie."

CHAPTER 15

Thursday, July 15 - 10:00 a.m.

Angelo Scarella, or Angel as he was known on the street, wasn't enjoying his stay in the South Slope Detention Center. Having grown up in Brooklyn's Fort Greene neighborhood, he was a local boy. At forty-two years of age, Angel looked like a mobster; olive complexion, dark slicked back hair, and deeply set steel-gray eyes under heavy brows. Angel killed for money; he'd even kill his own mother if there was a fat paycheck involved. After meeting Ricardo DesFuentes, he saw the potential for a big payout and hopped a flight to Florida. Now, he found himself back in Brooklyn and behind bars.

Money was everything to Angel. With no other accomplishments to his credit, flashing cash around was the only way he knew to gain the admiration of others and bolster his own self-esteem. He pursued designer clothing, flashy jewelry, and expensive women, using his money to impress his low life friends.

Back from Florida, he'd invited his neighborhood crew out for drinks at one of Park Slope's most popular bars where a drunk Wall Street trader accidentally bumped into him, spilling beer on Angel's favorite silk suit. Angel snapped and smashed the guy's face into a concrete pillar, breaking his jaw and knocking out his front teeth. When the guy's girlfriend tried to intervene, Angel punched her in the nose, knocking her out cold.

Now he was cooling his heels behind bars waiting for a shady attorney and a few thugs to scare his victims into not pressing charges. Accustomed to the finer things in life, time in the Detention Center was proving to be uncomfortable. His lawyer had promised he'd have him out by the end of the next day.

"Take a seat, Scarella," Charles Rutherford was direct in his instruction as Angel entered the brightly lit interrogation room. On the edge of her seat in the room next door, Lisa moved closer to the one-way mirror. "So, this is the guy who butchered Dorothy," she whispered to herself as she got her first look at him.

Smug, and smiling, everyone realized Angel assumed the charges against him had been dismissed. He dropped into the plastic chair on the opposite side of a metal table from Charles, leaned back and casually crossed his legs.

"Let's get into this," Charles continued. "DNA and a fingerprint were taken from a beer bottle left at a murder scene on Stypman Island in Florida. An old lady was cut to pieces in her own bed. Funny thing, the DNA and the print are an exact match to you."

Angel's smile fell.

Charles didn't mince words. "You're looking at a one-way ticket back to Florida. They still have the death penalty down there, and from what I hear, they like to use it."

Scarella's eyes became wide as saucers and the beads of sweat forming at his hairline sparkled under the bright ceiling lights. Charles saw the fear and dug in deeper, "Look man, I can make your life a little better, or I can make it much worse. I might even keep you here in New York and away from the electric chair, but you need to start talking, and you need to do it now."

It only took a few seconds for Angel to crack. "Look, man... it was a mistake. I was in the wrong apartment."

Lisa gasped.

CHAPTER 16

Friday, July 16 - 3:00 a.m.
The large jail, noisy all day, was quiet. Alone in his cell, Angel tried to rest on the metal cot, but it was no use. His mind raced with thoughts of being locked up in a place like this for the rest of his life. Wondering what death by the electric chair or lethal injection might be like, his mind wandered back to the warnings about the eternal fires of hell issued by the nuns and priests at the Catholic school he'd attended long ago. *I hope those fuckers made that shit up.*

Although Charles Rutherford had grilled him for over an hour, Angel hadn't given up DesFuentes. Not yet at least.

DesFuentes has power, he thought, *he can get to me, even in this pea-green, prison cell. And Rutherford wanted to know about somebody named Alfonse DelGrosso. Who the hell's that?* Angel's brain exploded with worry.

Rutherford has the juice in this place. He can make things better for me. But can I trust him? The lawyer says to keep quiet, but can that asshole get me out of this mess?

"Damn it!" He yelled in frustration. "Why did I take that beer? What the hell was I thinking?" Tormented by his own stupidity, he closed his eyes and rolled over. *It's too hot in here and the smell...* He punched the thin pillow, damp with his sweat. *I can't handle more nights like this.*

• • •

8:45 a.m.
Exhausted from his restless night, Angel waited at the door to his cell. His head ached, his skin was oily, and his hair, in need of a washing, stuck flat to his head. Even worse, he smelled bad; a shower would help.

A guard finally appeared, "Okay, let's go," he instructed and opened the door to the cell. Angel walked toward the shower facilities holding a thin, rough towel and a clean pair of underwear, the guard following behind. Doing his best to portray confidence, Angel walked with a swagger for the benefit of the prisoners sizing him up as he passed their cells. Angel's swagger wasn't fooling anyone. Fear had etched itself into his face.

Arriving at the showers, he hung his towel on a hook and took off his jumpsuit, leaving it on a metal bench. He only spotted two other prisoners in nearby shower stalls. *Where is everybody? No wonder this playpen stinks, these cons don't wash.*

He stepped under the warm water and lathered his head with the shampoo and body wash combination provided by the taxpayers of New York City. He was feeling better until the water temperature turned blistering hot. "What the fuck!" Angel yelped. He jumped from under the scalding stream, only to be shoved back under and held there.

Cursing and shouting, Angel tried to break free, his eyes stinging with soap. A jagged object pierced his neck and Angel writhed in pain as it ripped deep into his flesh. He saw blood... his blood... spurting out in front of him and knew he was finished. Collapsing onto the shower floor, he watched his blood circle the rusty drain on its journey to the sewers of Brooklyn.

Just before he lost consciousness, he heard his attacker say, "Greetings from Florida."

CHAPTER 17

Friday, July 16 - 12:30 p.m.

Lisa stood at the gate, waiting to board her flight back to Miami. With not a lot to do, she called Bruce Kim who picked up on the first ring.

"Hey, Lisa. Still in New York?"

"I'm at the gate right now. Bruce, the look on his face when he was confronted with the DNA and fingerprint match said it all. He's our guy alright, but he's insisting it was a mistake."

"What? Cutting an old lady's head off... that's no mistake."

"Not the murder, the victim. He said he killed the wrong person."

Bruce took a moment to consider what he'd just heard. "Well, that could answer a lot of questions. At least we know Dorothy wasn't targeted by a gang. Did you ask if DelGrosso put him up to it?"

"We did. He swore he never heard of DelGrosso, and I believe him. All we know right now is that he was in the wrong apartment that night."

"Well, then someone else who lives in that place is involved with some bad people. Did he say who put him up to it?"

"No, but my friend in the NYPD is still working on him. If Scarella was working for someone and screwed up the hit, he's scared to death. Bruce, gotta go, they're calling my flight. I'll be back tonight. I'll call again tomorrow, okay?"

"Okay, Lisa. Safe travels."

. . .

8:00 p.m.

Back in Miami, Lisa was dog-tired. She showered, put on an oversized college t-shirt, and climbed into bed. A few minutes later, her phone buzzed. Seeing the number on the caller ID, she picked up.

"Lisa, it's Charles. I've got something to tell you that you aren't going to like."

"Go on."

"Scarella is dead."

"Shit, what happened?"

"He was shanked in the shower. Hit the jugular... he bled out fast. I'm sorry, Lisa."

"Any idea who did it?" Now out of bed, Lisa paced the floor as she asked the question.

"Not yet. There aren't any cameras in the showers, and the guard who was on duty is MIA. Guessing he was paid off to look the other way. We're doing our best to track him down, and I'll let you know if we find him. We're also looking at all the inmates who could have gotten to Scarella. That will take some time, though." Charles paused, then said, "Not long before he was killed, Scarella sent a message asking to meet with me. I'm pretty certain he was about to talk."

"Do you think whoever Scarella was working for is behind this, Charles?"

"If I were a betting man, I'd put money on it. We found a burner phone in his apartment, and I've got our tech people working on opening it up. Assuming we can get into it, we'll be able to see who he was calling or who was calling him. We might even get a lead on who he was working with in your neck of the woods. Obviously, I'll pursue this and keep you informed of any developments."

"Charles, I appreciate the call and everything you're doing to help. Sorry to have dragged you into this."

"You didn't drag me in, Lisa. Hey, be careful, okay? Whoever's behind this is dangerous. If they get wind of what you've been up to, they might come after you too and if something happens to you, Ronnie will never forgive me... hell, I'll never forgive me."

"I promise I'll be careful, but there's no way I'm letting this go. Ronnie knows better than anyone what I went through when Scott's case went cold. That's not happening again."

. . .

8:30 p.m.

As tired as she was, Lisa couldn't sleep now. After a quick search of the contacts list on her phone, she selected a number she'd added on the day she'd met with Dorothy's nephew at Coquina Reef.

"Hello, Clara, this is Lisa Owens. We met the other day when I was taking some things out of Dorothy Jensen's apartment."

"I remember. How are you, Lisa?"

"I'm good. How is Marley?"

"Oh, she's fine." Clara's voice warmed a bit. "Jason has her out on an evening walk on the beach."

"Sounds like heaven." Lisa smiled at the normalcy of Clara's description, something missing in her own life. "Clara, I have a question I thought you might be able to answer."

"Um, okay. What's up?" Clara sounded hesitant and cautious to Lisa.

"I hope my asking this doesn't upset you, Clara. I'm continuing to look into Dorothy's murder, and I'm wondering if there have been any other deaths at Coquina Reef since she was killed."

"Other murders?" responded Clara. "Thank heavens, no."

"Not just murders," said Lisa. "Have there been any other deaths?"

"There have been two, both older women." Lisa held her breath and waited for Clara to finish.

"One died in her condo of a heart attack, and the other had an accident. The poor thing slipped in the shower at our community pool. She hit her head and died right there. It's very upsetting for all of us."

"I'm so sorry, that's just terrible. Umm, could I ask you something else?"

"Okay, although you're making me a little nervous."

"Which condos did these women live in?"

"Lisa, please don't tell me you think those deaths are related to Dorothy's. I'm not sure I could handle that kind of news."

"I don't know what to think. Right now, I'm just collecting information. There may be no reason to worry. Now, which apartments did those women live in?"

"Well, the woman who died at the pool, her name was Mary Dillard. She lived in the building next to ours on the top floor, the center unit facing the beach. The other woman, Josephine Paulsen, the one who had a heart attack, also lived in that building in the corner apartment next to Mary Dillard - the same corner apartment as Dorothy's - just in the other building."

Lisa remained quiet. The silence between the two women seemed to last forever. "Lisa, is everything okay?"

"Oh, sorry, Clara. Yes, everything's fine. Thanks for the information."

"Well, it's clear you know more than you are free to say, so I won't press you. But I have another question. Do you remember that gorgeous rug of Dorothy's? The one she had in her living room?"

"Sure, I remember," said Lisa, still recovering from what she'd just learned. "It was beautiful. Dorothy was so proud of it."

"Well, Jason and I couldn't bear to see it thrown away with everything else. When they were clearing out Dorothy's things, we pulled it out before it went in the dumpster with everything else. We had it cleaned, and I think you should have it. We can take a drive down to Miami and bring it to you if you'd like."

"That's so kind of you." Lisa's heart warmed; the rug hadn't been lost after all. "If you and Jason would like it, please keep it."

"We have a lovely silk rug we bought in Turkey," said Clara, "one that is very special to us. I hope you can use Dorothy's."

"Well, I'd love to have it. I wanted to take it when I was there, but I couldn't manage it alone. I can't tell you how touched I am that you and Jason did this for me."

"Think nothing of it; it's our pleasure. Dorothy would be ecstatic to know it's with you."

"I'll be making another trip back to Stypman Island in a few days. I can pick it up then if that would be okay."

"Perfect, we'll just hold it for you until you can get back here. We'd love to have you to our place for lunch or dinner if your schedule permits. Jason wants to meet you, and I know a dog that will be very excited to see you again."

"That sounds nice, thank you for the invitation. I'll call as soon as I know when I'll be up there."

CHAPTER 18

Friday, July 16 - 4:00 p.m.

After a long week in Washington, Congressman Wallace "Wally" Wallingford was glad to be back in Florida and on his way to a motel room to indulge his proclivity. It wasn't sex that he found exciting; it was what came after - inflicting unimaginable pain. He enjoyed the tears, the trembling lips, and the look on his victims' faces when they lost hope, wishing death would replace the horror they'd endured at his hands.

Brutalizing women wasn't a new thing for Wally. It started on his sixteenth birthday when his father and his older brother took him to a motel to experience his first sexual encounter, a rite of passage among the Wallingford men. With his father and brother yelling crude comments through the doorway of an adjacent room, young Wally found himself nervous and unable to perform.

When he emerged with the woman who'd been hired for the occasion, his father's face said it all. Disgusted and ashamed, his father placed some cash in the woman's hand. "Thanks for trying, honey. I guess he didn't inherit much from my side of the family." Once she was out the door, Wally got a slug in the stomach and a warning. "Never embarrass me like that again."

His brother joined in with insults, remarking that Wally's dick was too little to fuck with anyway. "Tiny Wally," he called him. The nickname caught on fast at the prep school the boys attended.

The trauma of that night, and the ongoing abuse at school, left Wally with profound feelings of inadequacy. When those feelings took over, he found he could make himself feel better by beating the hell out of a woman.

Wally's brutality wasn't limited to women; it became the basis for his career. Re-elected three times over, his political career was not about improving the lives of his constituents on the Treasure Coast. It wasn't about making a name for himself in the history books, either. Had he been interested in those things; he had the ideal opportunity to do so. Destructive discharges of polluted water from a misconceived dam at Lake Okeechobee had plagued the Treasure Coast for decades, starving Florida Bay of the freshwater it naturally received through the Everglades.

Wally could have used his influence to correct that man-made disaster, saving the ecosystem of south Florida. Instead, like others before him, he collected massive campaign contributions from big agriculture companies, which benefited from failed water management practices that exacerbated harmful algal blooms. Blooms that resulted in serious health problems for many of Wally's constituents and poisoned the rivers of the Treasure Coast.

Wally had no interest in algal blooms. He focused on one thing only. Power. He defeated his political opponents and hung on to his seat in Congress not on the merits of his accomplishments but by working the system to his unfair advantage. Promises of lucrative contracts and federally funded projects kept the right local politicians in place. Once under his thumb, Wally demanded their endorsements and tasked them with recruiting wealthy donors. He accumulated an enormous war chest and used it not just to defeat his opponents but to crush them.

He hired the best investigators to dig up dirt on his adversaries, and if there was no mud to sling, he employed social media experts to make some up and disseminate it so convincingly that the good people of his district couldn't tell what was true and what was fiction. Anyone who ran against him would never recover. That was Wally's rule, and he was ruthless about enforcing it. It had a chilling effect on would-be opponents, making it that much easier for him to tighten his grip and stay in office.

In Washington, Wally made no bones about using his influence to help those who could benefit him the most. As the Ranking Member on the House Transportation Subcommittee on Coast Guard and Marine Transportation, Wally appeared on several people's radars. On one particular radar, he flashed bright red.

• • •

4:30 p.m.

Two months ago, the girl had just turned eighteen. To celebrate her birthday, she went partying with friends at a popular nightclub outside of Orlando. Using a fake ID, she gained access to the club and downed several sweet-tasting shooters. Drunk and succumbing to peer pressure, she was introduced to crystal meth, smoking it from a small glass pipe. From then on, living without the drug became unimaginable to her.

Severely addicted and in need of a fix, the girl now found herself in a motel room having made a terrible trade for the tiny white crystals burning in the pipe she held to her mouth.

A man with a long, scar on his face stood over her. "That's right, girlie, breathe that shit in... nice and deep. Feel better now?" He pushed the pipe to her mouth. "Take another hit." She fell back on the filthy, stained mattress.

"Do everything he says. It will be over fast." The man opened the door of the shabby motel room and stepped out. Another man, older and overweight, entered. He wore a dark suit with a white shirt and a red silk tie. His stomach bulged over his belt, and a tiny American flag was pinned to his right lapel.

. . .

7:00 p.m.

Catherine Wallingford sat alone in the living room of the large home she shared with her husband. A curled wig sat atop her head, hiding the fact that she hadn't bothered to wash her hair for several days. Slightly off-kilter, the wig made her look lop-sided and drunk, which she was. She seemed to swim in a chartreuse caftan that was far too large for her rail-thin body, the fabric billowing around her when she moved. It was the same outfit she'd worn for most of the week.

"God knows I need this," she slurred while pulling the stopper from a crystal decanter containing Blanton's Black bourbon. She poured a glass and brought it to her lips. The decanter was less than half full. Just forty minutes ago, the liquid had reached the top.

Filling her glass again, Catherine heard her husband's car pull into the driveway. Even with the liquor, her body tensed when he barreled through the front door.

"Does Marcus have dinner ready?" he asked without looking at her.

"He just put it on the table. Nice to see you, too," she slurred.

They sat at opposite ends of the long dining table, neither of them looking at the other. Catherine set her eyes on the plate in front of her. Their personal chef had made beef tenderloin tonight. She took a small bite and glanced up at her husband. Repulsed at the sight of him shoveling food in his mouth, she spit it in her napkin. *Look at him, a pig at a trough, I'm going to be sick.*

Wally finished and wiped his mouth. Seeing his wife's plate still full, he licked his lips. "Not eating again, Catherine? Give me your plate." She hadn't said a word since she sat down at the table. *I've had enough, I can't stand the sight of him.* Without acknowledging him, she walked out of the dining room and headed to her room.

Those close to the congressman knew his wife was an alcoholic. Infrequently, she'd make a public appearance with her husband, smiling, even waving if necessary, but never saying a word. On those occasions, she heard the whispers behind her back. People felt sorry for Wally and admired him for sticking with her. Alone in her room with her bourbon, Catherine cried angry tears. "They have it wrong," she told herself. "I'm the one who stuck with him, and his sins are far worse than my dependence on alcohol."

. . .

Saturday, July 17 - 4:00 p.m.

Catherine could tell something wasn't right. *He's home early,* she thought, tossing back the bourbon in her glass. Usually, he came into the living room and criticized her for drinking. Today, after spending most of the day in his local office, Wally rushed into his study, and slammed the door shut.

Holding her empty glass in front of her, Catherine spoke to it, as if it was a friend. "What a welcome change, don't you think? Why ruin a good thing?" She staggered from the sofa, then stopped. "I almost forgot about dinner," she said. She grabbed the decanter and took it with her.

At the desk in his study, Wally tapped on his phone screen to start a video he'd just received from someone he didn't know. Staring at the screen, his pulse quickened. "It's that girl from yesterday. What the fuck?" he yelled at the phone. The girl was naked and crying on the filthy, disgusting mattress. Her face swollen, bruised and smeared with blood that ran from her nose and mouth. Burns from Wally's cigarette marked her right cheek, the blisters, ugly and fluid filled.

"Oh, shit," Wally muttered, anticipating what was coming next. He saw himself step into frame. The images were crystal clear. "Damn it, there's no mistaking its me." His anxiety boiled over. He was naked, his erection apparent but looking smaller than he thought. "I'll fucking kill whoever did this!" He slammed his fist down on the desk.

Wally held his breath; his hand went to his head as he watched himself punch the girl in the face. Blood flew out of her mouth, and her head snapped back. Enraged, Wally balled his hands into fists and screamed, "This will ruin me!" He watched himself grab the girl's thin neck with both his hands and squeeze until she was gone.

Shaking, Wally turned the video off and made a phone call. "What do you want?" he demanded.

"I saw what you did to that girl, Congressman. You like it rough, don't you?" said the voice on the other end of the call.

"Who the fuck is this?"

"We will meet each other soon enough. You and I can help each other. We're going to be good friends. I will be at the Atlas Club at ten. Don't be late."

. . .

10:00 p.m.

Located just off the Florida Turnpike and forty minutes from the Wallingford home, the Atlas Club was frequented by bored men looking to stop off for a drink and a little excitement before heading home to their families in the suburbs after a hard day of work. Later in the evening the crowd was younger, rowdier, and hornier.

Wally chose a parking space away from the strip club's brightly lit entrance, where a huge orange and green neon sign advertising the name of the place hung overhead. *Fuck, I hope nobody sees me in this shithole.* Although it was dark, he put on sunglasses and stuck a Marlins ball cap on his head before leaving his car.

As Wally reached the doorway, an imposingly large, well-built African American man wearing a tight, black t-shirt with the Atlas Club's logo printed on it stepped forward. "Follow me."

So much for my bullshit disguise, Wally thought. He pulled his cap lower.

The main room of the Atlas Club held an oversized u-shaped bar at which several men gathered. Loud country music played over a sound system. On top of the bar, two young women, wearing G-strings, spiked heels, and dangling earrings, danced and collected bills. Wally gave them the once over as he walked past the bar. *They look bored. I could liven things up for them.* Spilled sour beer and disinfectant accosted Wally's nostrils. Breathing through his mouth, he followed the man to a private room at the back of the club.

"In there," said the man, indicating that Wally should enter.

The room was painted black. Mirrors lined the walls and a large sectional couch covered in purple velvet took up most of the space. In front of it were two small brass cocktail tables that looked worse for wear.

Ricardo DesFuentes sat with his legs crossed and his arm resting on the back of the couch. A bottle of Patron Gran Platinum and two shot glasses sat atop the cocktail table in front of him.

"My name is Ricardo DesFuentes. Please sit and allow me to pour you a drink, Congressman. You've had a long day."

Wally sat on the end of the purple sofa, away from DesFuentes. He accepted the tequila, downing it in one swallow. The shot burned his throat, and he stifled a cough. DesFuentes smiled and refilled the shot glass.

"What do you want?" asked the congressman after downing the second tequila shot, noticing it went down easily this time.

"It's very simple. You like girls who you can, let us say, push around. I can supply you with that which you enjoy. In return, you will do something for me."

"And what is that?"

"I have people who work for me. They travel by boat to Florida from the Bahamas. I would prefer for them not to be harassed by the Coast Guard during their voyages. I believe you can arrange that."

"I see," replied Wallingford. "And what about that video you sent me?"

"That, Congressman, I will keep as insurance should you ever decide to end our friendship."

"Friendship? That's what you call blackmailing me?" Wally feigned outrage. "You have some nerve asking me to use my influence to protect your fucking boats. What are you transporting anyway?"

"Cocaine," replied DesFuentes. "And for the record, Congressman, I am not asking you. That video could end up in the wrong place."

Wally snapped back, "You set me up. How the hell did you do it?"

"I have my methods, and I always get what I want."

Wally knew he'd been beaten, at least for now. "Pour me another drink. It looks like we're gonna be friends after all."

CHAPTER 19

Sunday, July 18 - 8:30 a.m.
The white Sea Ray L650 cut through the water about twenty-five miles off the coast. It had been purchased at the Miami Boat Show, where the boating elite went to see the newest models of expensive watercraft and to be seen by others who could afford to drop a cool million or more on a toy that would sit unused in a marina for most of its life. Onboard the impressive vessel was its owner, Ricardo DesFuentes.

This far off the coast, the ocean was a deep sapphire blue and crystal clear. DesFuentes stood at the stern with a beer in his hand looking down into the depths while waiting for one of the several lines that had been baited and cast for him to be hit. As he waited, he worried.

Everything, my wealth, my business, my very freedom, depends on people following my instructions and doing exactly what I tell them. One mistake, one error, could destroy all of it. He took a swallow of beer and wiped his mouth with his hand. *There are huge rewards in this business and enormous risks. And lately, people are making mistakes. I've been fast to correct them, but nonetheless, there have been mistakes. It's time to make changes.*

Far in the distance, DesFuentes could see what appeared to be a Coast Guard vessel cutting through the water. *My new friend will protect me from that, but I need a better way to get the cocaine on shore and to the distribution channel.*

He racked his brain for an idea. None came. As he contemplated his problem, a tuna hit his line. "Vamos!" A deckhand ran to the fighting chair where DesFuentes worked to reel in the fish. The blue and yellow tuna fought hard for its life, but soon the struggle ended. "Get it in the boat," DesFuentes yelled to the deckhand who netted the fish and pulled it onto the teak deck. Still fighting for its life, the tuna thrashed.

"Let's put this thing out of its misery." DesFuentes smiled at the deckhand. "I like this part the best." He picked up a wooden club and raised it above his head. "Lights out, fishy." The club came down hard on the magnificent animal's head. "Toss it back in," he instructed. "The sharks need to eat."

Back from his fishing trip, DesFuentes showered, poured a tumbler of Patron, and sat at his desk. In front of him lay an invitation to a fundraising ball. The invitation was addressed to Andrew Smith, one of his many aliases. Bored, he opened the envelope.

The event was to benefit the Stypman Island Institute for Marine Life Preservation. Accompanying the invitation was a brochure describing the Institute and its work. The cover featured a photo of a young man on an ATV on the beach at night. DesFuentes skimmed it. The brochure explained that one of the most important activities of the Institute was its work protecting the sea turtles that nested on Stypman Island, and in particular, the endangered leatherback sea turtle. It explained how every night during the long nesting season, Dr. Peter Guise looked for leatherbacks on the beach.

The brochure provided details about what the scientist was surveying, the process he followed, and other facts that DesFuentes could have cared less about. He was about to toss it all in the trash when a smile crossed his face.

Swallowing the tequila, he called the number on the invitation and spoke with a volunteer. "Can you tell me if Dr. Guise will be at the event? I'd like to meet him."

"Why, yes, they'll all be there, Mr. Sampson, Dr. Guise and Dr. Mercier."

"Excellent, I want to reserve your largest table, I believe that's for twelve people."

The volunteer took his information and charged him $100,000. Andrew Smith had just become a platinum-level donor to the Stypman Island Institute for Marine Life Preservation.

CHAPTER 20

Sunday, July 18 - 9:59 p.m.

Kitty Sampson sat in front of her computer, waiting for her boss to join the video call. She nervously twisted a strand of her hair and held her breath when her screen announced his arrival. The glow of the computer screen in his otherwise dark office, made Ricardo DesFuentes, look like the demon he was. Kitty flinched when his illuminated image emerged from the shadows and onto her screen. He didn't say hello or acknowledge her.

"I want to learn about the Stypman Island Institute for Marine Life Preservation. Your brother is in charge there, correct?"

"Why are you interested in *that* place?" asked Kitty, taken off guard.

"I've just become a platinum member; I want to know everything."

"Okay..." she said the word as a question. *If it gets him to leave me alone, I'll tell him whatever he wants.*

"My parents founded the Institute. The stated purpose of the place is to study and protect local marine life. Its actual purpose was to give my loser brother, Mike a job. My Dad called in some political favors to make it happen."

"Tell me about your family, Kitty."

Oh, fuck, she thought, alarm registering on her face. "What's this about? Why do you want to know about them?"

"When I ask you a question, you will answer me truthfully. If you don't, there'll be consequences not only for you but for them, too. Now, tell me everything."

"My family has lived on Stypman Island for three generations," Kitty stammered, "but my dad made his money on Bimini ... you know, the island.

He owned a construction company and speculated Bimini would become a desired destination for wealthy people looking to build secluded, oceanfront homes. When the island became known as one of Ernest Hemingway's favorites, my dad bought as much oceanfront property as he could afford. Within a few years, his investment paid off big time."

"Smart man, your father. Just about every idiot who can afford it wants to live like Hemingway." DesFuentes smiled at his joke. His white teeth glowed in the dark and Kitty thought of a shark.

"Continue."

"I have two brothers. Carl is a physician, he's two years older than me and lives in Dallas. He's twice divorced and now married again. The first wife was a cheerleader, if you can believe it. The second was a nurse he caught sucking off his neighbor." Kitty was speaking fast and out of breath, unable to believe the words spilling past her lips. *Why am I telling him this?* DesFuentes smiled, clearly enjoying the story.

"As I already said, my other brother, Mike, is a loser. He likes to fish and not much else. My Mom was concerned he wouldn't amount to much and got my dad to call in some favors. A plan was hatched to establish the Institute as a publicly funded, not-for-profit organization with Mike as its president."

DesFuentes kept looking down as Kitty spoke. *Shit, he's making notes, why would he be making notes?* A million possibilities raced through her mind, none of them good. She looked at her computer screen, waiting for DesFuentes to say something, anything.

"Continue."

Oh, fuck! Kitty took a deep breath. "Grant money got the organization up and running, and a donation of land made on behalf of the island's residents provided a home for the place. Mike wanted to walk away from all of it years ago to go live on his boat and catch bonefish in the Bahamas. With a wife, two kids, and a mortgage, that wasn't realistic, so he kept at it, eventually developing a sustainable business model that created enough cash to pay himself a good income."

"Interesting. Now, tell me Kitty, if your brother is like you, he's no boy scout. Correct?" DesFuentes looked at her, his dark eyes burning through the computer screen.

"Well, he ... oh, what the fuck! He earns a comfortable living but when he wants something more, he helps himself to funds from the Institute's donations. He's smart about it, taking a little here and there throughout the year - not enough to raise eyebrows. He inflates his expenses, empties the petty cash, and takes some of the cash donations at fundraising events. No one pays much attention to the Institute's finances, anyway."

"Your brother told you this?" DesFuentes raised his eyebrows.

"I have a degree in Accounting from Florida State. He asked me about audits because he was afraid he might get caught. I gave Mike some great tips to cover his tracks, but he ignores them. You know what he does? When the auditor raises questions about missing cash, Mike just blames the incompetence of his volunteers, and it works."

DesFuentes stopped making notes. "That's helpful information, Kitty. So, your brother is a thief. Now, tell me how the place operates."

Kitty collected her thoughts. "Besides Mike, the Institute employs two scientists, a group of unpaid interns, and a bunch of local volunteers. The interns are students with recently completed college degrees in biology or marine biology. There are no paying jobs for them anywhere; they need a master's degree for those and Mike takes advantage of that. They rotate through every six months and perform the labor that keeps the place running while working for free. The volunteers are mostly retirees looking for something to do. They do the grunt work, answer the phones, attend local fairs and festivals to ask for donations. That kind of crap." Judging from the look of approval on DesFuentes' face, Kitty could tell he was impressed. "It's a hell of a business model. Mike's proud of it, he says he should be featured in The Wall Street Journal." Kitty wiped sweat from her forehead. *God, I need a Xanax...*

"One last thing, Kitty, I want to know about the scientists who work at the Institute. Tell me about them." DesFuentes nodded, to indicate she should begin.

"Okay, but then I have to go. No more questions."

"I want to be clear about something, Kitty." DesFuentes moved his face closer to the computer screen, his enlarged features more menacing than before. "I will tell you when I have no more questions. Until then, you will sit there and answer them."

Kitty leaned back, as if to get away from him. Closing her eyes in defeat, she let out the breath she'd been holding. "One of Mike's best decisions was to hire a Ph.D. to advise him and perform the research work that gives the Institute its reputation. The guy's name is Peter Guise. Although he's young, Peter established himself as a leading expert on endangered leatherback sea turtles. On most nights, he's out on the beach. He works all night into the early morning, searching for female leatherbacks emerging from the ocean to dig their nests and lay eggs on the beach. Peter tags the turtles and marks every nest, recording the date it was made and its GPS coordinates."

DesFuentes looked confused. He cocked his head and frowned. "Why would a person choose that sort of work? It doesn't seem very attractive, up all night looking for animals that may not even be there."

"It wouldn't be for me, that's for sure," Kitty said. "The work is difficult, dirty, sweaty, and not very well-compensated. But the story of the sea turtles is..." Kitty stopped for a moment to consider her words. "Well, it's magical."

DesFuentes shifted his attention from making notes to Kitty. He looked at her and tilted his head. "Magical?"

"I know, it sounds ridiculous. After swimming thousands of miles, leatherbacks, and all sea turtles, return to the same beach area where they were born to lay their nests. Better understanding that feat of nature is a dream job for someone like Peter. It has some degree of fame, too. He's been featured on Good Morning America, CBS News, and once in a Discovery Channel documentary."

"What about the other scientist? The woman?"

"Her name is Simone Mercier. She's from Martinique, and she's gorgeous. It wasn't any surprise that my brother hired someone who looks like her. Exotic, flawless mahogany complexion, long brown legs, and a perfect body. She looks like a runway model." Kitty could see the look in DesFuentes' eyes as she described Simone. *I'll bet that pig is getting a boner.*

Kitty's thoughts turned inward for a moment and she became self-conscious. At age forty-one, she felt like a carton of milk that had reached its expiration date. Her plan had always been to find a rich husband. When that didn't happen, she took matters into her own hands. With a loan from her parents, she opened a shop. It did well, but it didn't make her rich. To her parents' delight, she paid back their loan and managed to buy several other shops and a restaurant on Stypman Island.

Kitty handled the books for her businesses and relied on locals to operate her establishments. A demanding boss, she didn't pay her employees much, given the limited employment options in the area. Along with her success came a series of young boyfriends. Kitty employed them in her businesses and invited them to her bed, amazed by what a case of beer and some weed could buy. *Fuck Simone Mercier, I can still get boys.*

"Kitty, I asked you a question!" DesFuentes appeared to be losing patience.

"Oh, sorry, I didn't hear you." Kitty refocused.

"If she looks like that, what's she doing working with turtles? The magic again?"

"Yes, the magic. I had a conversation with Simone after she started working at the Institute. She told me that ever since she was a young girl, she wanted to be a conservation scientist. An experience she had as a participant in Dr. Jane Goodall's Roots and Shoots program inspired her. Do you know what that is?"

"Enlighten me."

"The goal of the program is to help young people become the informed generation of compassionate citizens that Dr. Goodall felt the world needed. After meeting Jane Goodall in person, Simone said she was never the same. She studied hard and earned her Ph.D. in Marine Biology. She went to the Sorbonne. It's in Paris."

"I know where the Sorbonne is. Keep going."

"Back in Martinique, Simone couldn't find a job doing what she loved, just offers for modeling work and that kind of thing. She felt pressured to marry one of the wealthy Frenchmen who came to Martinique on holiday.

Just when things seemed like they would never work out for her, she saw a job posting Peter Guise had placed in a scientific journal."

"Who hired her? Dr. Guise or your brother?"

"Simone interviewed with Peter on Skype. She told me she liked him right away and could see herself working with him. No fool, she said she could tell Peter liked what he was seeing too, and figured he was wondering what the rest of her looked like. Anyway, Simone has this French accent that I'm sure Peter found charming, and her love of marine life science is obvious. He offered her the job at the end of their interview and she accepted right away. The Institute got her a work visa and the rest is history as they say."

"Fill in the history, Kitty. Leave nothing out."

"Peter sent Simone a note after the interview to say how much he was looking forward to working with her. He also wrote that he was confident they would be good friends. Simone wondered if Peter would still want to be good friends once he learned her sexual preferences didn't involve men." Kitty paused. *How's that boner, DesFuentes?*

DesFuentes sat up straight in his chair. "She's gay? She's not fucking your brother?" His question sounded urgent.

"Yeah, she's gay, and no, she is not fucking my brother. I told you, he doesn't care about much other than fishing, not even sex. He's kind of a weirdo."

"Tell me more about this woman scientist."

"Simone settled in on Stypman Island quickly. She told me her work at the Institute was everything she had hoped it would be and things with Peter have worked out fine. He shows respect for her knowledge and is complimentary of her work. Simone's job is like Peter's. She locates, records, and monitors loggerhead and green sea turtle nests. Two other species nest here too but they're very rare.

Peter does the same thing as Simone but with leatherback turtle nests. There are fewer leatherbacks because they are so endangered, but Peter's responsibilities are more extensive than what Simone's work requires. Peter takes blood samples from the leatherbacks and tags their flippers."

Does he want to know all this? He hasn't asked me to stop talking yet. Shit, DesFuentes, what the hell are you up to?

Kitty continued, guessing DesFuentes would tell her to shut up if she was talking too much. "Simone records the nests she finds and marks their location using GPS. Sometimes, she uses wood stakes, I'm not sure why. She also checks to see if the eggs have hatched. There are hundreds of loggerhead and green sea turtle nests for her to record so her workload is heavy. Peter's work has him on the beach throughout the night; Simone's duties happen in the early morning."

"How does she find the nests?" DesFuentes asked.

"Simone finds nests that were laid the previous night by looking for the tracks mother turtles make in the sand when they crawl out of the surf and back to the ocean. Loggerhead tracks are always in the shape of commas, while green sea turtle tracks look like a series of diagonal lines—almost as if the turtles had karate chopped their way up the beach."

"Tracks in the sand," DesFuentes considered this for a moment. "What about the leatherback turtles? What type of tracks do they make?"

"You *are* interested in this stuff." Kitty cocked her head, surprised at his questions. "The leatherbacks are easy. They're fucking enormous. Their tracks look like somebody drove a tractor up the beach."

"Back to Dr. Guise. Was he upset he'd hired a gay woman? It seems he wanted to have sex with her." DesFuentes was back to making notes.

"He was disappointed to learn Simone is gay, but she says it doesn't stop him from checking her out now and then. Eye candy, I guess."

"So, Dr. Guise likes the ladies. Interesting." DesFuentes was seeing another angle he could pursue. He stroked his chin with his index finger.

"Before you get the wrong idea that Peter is some Casanova, let me give you the facts. He's average looking, at best. Shaggy, unkempt hair, unremarkable brown eyes, and a face that's usually covered with dark stubble. He's in his mid-thirties. From what Mike says, he's sick of scraping together money to make ends meet. All that recently boiled over when Peter's girlfriend dumped him. It was kind of a big deal since he's only dated four women in his life, and he thought this one was the one."

"How do you know so much about him? Did he tell you?"

"Hell, no, Peter doesn't talk to me. He told Mike, screamed it at him because he was so pissed about losing his girlfriend. The chick just up and left. On the way out the door she told him she saw no future with him and wasn't okay with the lifestyle his income afforded. Told him he has a job people want and because there are so many biologists in line for it, Mike doesn't need to pay him much. She even told him he's easy to replace. What a cold bitch, right? Mike said he thought Peter was about to quit on the spot. Of course, he didn't. I mean, where would he go? So, he's back out on the beach, poor guy."

"The girlfriend was right. Guise is a sucker, and I have what I need." DesFuentes ended the video call.

CHAPTER 21

Tuesday, July 20 - 11:15 a.m.

Along with the hot summer temperatures, the murder rate in Miami was increasing by the day and breaking records. In her office, Lisa was reading a case file she'd just been assigned. She looked up when Mac appeared in her doorway. Seeing him in the corner of her eye, she stopped reading and looked at him. "Another dead kid. This one was only sixteen," she said as she raked her fingers through her hair.

"It pisses me off," said Mac. "And it won't stop until the damned guns are off the streets. Every cop in the city knows it but the politicians don't see it that way. You'd think what happened in Parkland would have been enough."

"It makes me angry too. It doesn't have to be this way." Lisa pushed back from her desk, looking defeated.

Mac shook his head and stuck his hands in his pockets. "Sometimes I feel like we're wasting our time. Give it your best, Lisa. Let's find the killer and give that kid's parents some closure. That's about all we can do."

. . .

"Hey, Bruce, I'm on the Yang murder, you know, the sixteen-year-old." Lisa stared at a photo of the dead teenager as she spoke into the phone.

"I heard about it. That poor family, what they must be going through."

"Any idea when the ballistics report will be complete?"

"End of the day, I think."

"Hey, feel like talking something through with me? It's about the deaths on Stypman Island, something's been bothering me. It won't take long."

"You buy the coffee, and I'll swing by your office in twenty."

"Deal."

· · ·

"It could be nothing..." Lisa handed Bruce his coffee. "...but it's been bugging me. Maybe if we go through it together?"

"My curiosity is piqued. What's on your mind?"

"This is a police report from Stypman Island." It flashed up on Lisa's screen, and Bruce read over her shoulder while she pointed at the pertinent lines. "Josephine Paulsen was discovered dead in her condo by Chief Jackson. The cause of death listed is a suspected heart attack. There was no autopsy at the request of the family." Reading further, she said, "She died in a chair facing the ocean." Lisa pulled up photographs of the scene, including Josephine's body slumped over in an easy chair.

"So far, I don't see anything fishy. The victim's family is out of town so there's no way to know if something was removed from the condo. The police chief wrote that he didn't notice anything that had been disturbed."

"So, where are you going with this?" Bruce asked.

"Let's keep reading, I haven't gotten to the part that's eating at me yet. The next of kin, a daughter, was located and notified of her mother's death, and the body was sent to the morgue. The medical examiner signed the death certificate." Lisa stopped reading and pointed at the screen. "Okay, right here, this is the strange part. Do you see it?"

Bruce studied the report, re-reading it twice before he saw what Lisa was getting at. "It doesn't say how he came to discover the victim's body."

"Now let's look at this." She pulled up another page and scrolled down until she found the right file. "This is the police report on the death of Mary Dillard. She died the same day as Dorothy. Officers Witherspoon and Whitefeather investigated this one."

"Witherspoon? Wasn't she one of the first to respond at your friend's murder?"

"You're right, she was there. Okay, this report is pretty thorough and includes the details about who alerted the police to the death in the changing room."

"Last one." Lisa pulled up Dorothy's murder investigation file. "I've read this about a thousand times already. But I want to double-check something. And there it is," Lisa pushed her chair back and looked at Bruce. "The description of how Jason Anders called to notify the police about blood dripping from his bedroom ceiling. It's just as we would have expected. It's a regular practice of the Stypman Island Police Department to include the details of police notification in an investigation report."

"That's routine practice everywhere."

"It's strange, right? The chief didn't include those details in the Paulsen report. I mean, what happened? He just showed up for no reason and found her dead?"

"It's sketchy, especially since he's the boss. If a rookie cop had written that report, I wouldn't give it a second thought."

"Thanks, Bruce. I'm not sure what it means, but I think it might be something."

CHAPTER 22

Saturday, July 24 - 7:00 p.m.

Ricardo DesFuentes, aka Andrew Smith, stepped out of a black super-stretch limousine. With him, a party of five men and six women. The women, all trafficked from Eastern Europe, were prisoners in the land of the free. The men accompanying them were regional managers in a vast network organized to distribute cocaine. Tonight, they were being rewarded by their supplier.

Amped up from the lines of coke they'd snorted in the limousine, they paraded through the ornate glass entrance doors of the stately Banyan Tree Country Club. The women's tight gowns, toned bodies, and ridiculously high heels commanded attention. The men on their arms were extraordinarily fit, their muscled arms bulging under designer tuxedos. Most guests attending the black-tie event were aged, wealthy socialites in conservative attire. The 'Smith' party was hard to miss.

A photographer from a local magazine that featured society events stepped in front of the party to take their photo. Andrew Smith put up his hand and said in a calm but firm voice, "There will be none of that tonight, my friend. Do we understand each other?" The photographer nodded and received a fist full of folded new hundred-dollar bills.

Kitty Sampson and her companion made their way into the ballroom after first stopping at the bar, where she ordered a cosmopolitan for herself and a rum and coke for the young man accompanying her. Her brother, Mike came over to greet her. "Thanks for coming, Sis. Our big brother, Carl, called to say he couldn't make it again, something about wife number three."

He widened his eyes in mock surprise before leaning in and kissing Kitty's cheek.

"Poor Carl. That's what he gets for living in a place like Dallas. I mean, really Mike, look what he has to choose from there, cheerleaders and this new wife, she's what? Some kind of Jesus freak?"

"Well, to be fair, dear sister, wife number two was a nurse." Mike took a sip of his drink.

"Yeah, apparently the 'head' nurse," replied Kitty with a sly grin. Caught by a fit of laughter at his sister's crude joke, Mike spat his drink.

"Hey, at least he sent a check. And thanks for yours. Very generous of you."

"Glad to help." Kitty introduced Mike to her date, a handsome young man who was currently working as a lifeguard at one of the island's public beaches during the day and at Kitty's restaurant a few nights each week.

"Dude, awesome party. I'm Dillon." The young man extended his fist to bump knuckles with Mike.

"Thanks, man. Hey, are you old enough to drink that cocktail in your hand?"

Annoyed, Kitty interjected, "I'm in no mood for you to ruin my evening with your juvenile banter. Nice seeing you, Mike. C'mon, Dillon, let's find our table."

As they walked into the main ballroom, someone reached out and grabbed Kitty's elbow, squeezing it tightly.

She winced from the pain, turning to see Ricardo DesFuentes standing next to her. "Kitty, how surprising to see you here."

"You, too, Ricardo. You really *are* a sea turtle lover." Fear shone in her eyes.

"Tonight, my name is Andrew Smith, and I am very surprised you have the time to attend parties. Wouldn't your time be better spent at work?"

"Righteous," muttered Dillon as he admired the beautiful young woman in a red sequined gown accompanying DesFuentes.

Kitty gave him a disgusted look. "Dillon, get us another drink from the bar."

"I see you like them young, Kitty, just like me." Still gripping her elbow, he pulled her closer and whispered, "You're falling behind schedule, and a lot more is on its way to you in the weeks ahead. Catch up! Do you understand?"

Kitty could feel DesFuentes' warm breath on her ear. It made her skin crawl. "I haven't let you down yet, Ricardo. I mean Andrew. And I don't intend to."

"That's good to hear. I'm about to begin a system of transporting product into the country that will result in more regular shipments, the volume you will deal with will increase; within a short time, it will double. You'd better to be ready. I don't like to be disappointed." He released Kitty's arm and walked away.

"Fuck me," Kitty muttered under her breath. *How the hell am I supposed to launder that much dirty cash and not end up behind bars?*

Kitty and Dillon found their assigned table where a man she knew was already sitting. He stood and extended his hand. "Good evening, Kitty, you clean up well. It looks like we're seated at the same table tonight."

"So we are, Manny. Mike has it reserved for local business owners. We can have our own little Chamber of Commerce meeting. Are you single tonight?"

"I am," replied Manny, who looked as if he'd been stuffed into a tuxedo a few sizes too small for his plump body.

"Dillon, this is Manny Gonzalez. He owns Manny's Bar and Grille."

"Awesome to meet you, dude. Manny's is a great spot, one of the best on the island."

Manny Gonzalez grinned at the compliment. "It's nice to meet you, Dillon. Is that a rum and coke?"

"Sure is, man."

"We Puerto Ricans, that's our drink. Come to think of it, I'd like to have one of those with a cigar, but they make me go outside to smoke. I'll be back later. Save me a seat next to you, Kitty."

Kitty whispered to Dillon, "I can't stand that man, but he runs a great restaurant. I've been trying to get him to sell it to me. Maybe tonight's my lucky night."

"That dude needs to lose a few. His cumberbunny was about to pop."

"The word is *cummerbund,* not cumberbunny, and you're right, that thing is about to blow. Shit, here comes that couple who own the wine shop. They're fucking snobs, and they're sitting with us. Please try not to embarrass me."

. . .

"Welcome, friends, to this year's annual fundraiser. On behalf of all of us at the Institute, we are delighted you're here and we wish you a very pleasant evening." Mike Sampson stood at the podium and spoke into a microphone. "I would like to introduce the members of our Board seated throughout the room." As their names were read aloud, the Board members stood to polite applause.

"And now, please give it up for the two scientists who make it all happen... Dr. Peter Guise and Dr. Simone Mercier."

The two received a rousing ovation. As Head of the Institute, Mike learned long ago to keep his remarks short. People who could afford to attend an event like this were not interested in listening to speeches.

"And now it's my pleasure to introduce our congressman, a good friend to Stypman Island and our marine life, Wally Wallingford."

Mike's voice amplified throughout the large room. He shook hands with the congressman and then turned the microphone over to him. After light applause, the congressman made a few brief remarks about the need to protect the environment and ended by telling the crowd to enjoy their evening. Out of the corner of his eye, the congressman saw his new friend, Ricardo DesFuentes, and acknowledged him with a slight nod of his head.

Peter Guise took it all in. He was required to attend the ball and schmooze with the guests, something he dreaded. He looked across the ballroom and saw his colleague engaging a table of major donors. Simone was dressed impeccably and looked even more beautiful than usual. Chatting up the table, she appeared to be at ease in tonight's formal environment. A smiling Suzette Thawlington, Chair of the Institute's

Board and its largest donor, stood next to her. Her obvious admiration of Simone further unsettled Peter.

Peter couldn't have felt more out of place in his rented tuxedo and borrowed dress shoes that were too tight for his wide feet. It had taken him hours to figure out how to tie the bowtie that now hung crookedly around his neck. *I feel like a second-class citizen*, Peter thought as he walked through the crowded ballroom with a plastic name badge identifying him as a staff member. *My world is so far away from all this. The limousines parked outside, the thirty-piece band. Lobster entrees, fancy table settings.* Peter took in every detail. *I want this kind of life and I'll never have it.*

"How the hell do all these people have so much damned money?" he muttered as he looked longingly at a table filled with gorgeous young women and their handsome dates. Seated at that table and taking note of Peter Guise and his obvious distress was Ricardo DesFuentes. He gestured for Peter to join him.

"Oh, great," said Peter under his breath, "just when I couldn't feel any more inferior, the beautiful people want me to come over."

Peter walked over to DesFuentes, who pulled a chair from another table and asked him to sit down.

"My friends," said DesFuentes. "This is Dr. Guise. He's the lead sea turtle researcher at the Institute." DesFuentes identified himself to Peter as Andrew Smith and, using first names only, introduced Peter to the other members of his party.

"So, Dr. Guise, is that very attractive associate of yours, your date for this evening?" DesFuentes turned his attention toward Simone Mercier who caught him looking her over and abruptly turned away.

"Please call me Peter, and no, I'm single tonight. Simone is a co-worker, no more than that. I'm on duty tonight and the Institute won't even pay for my dinner, let alone a plus one." Everyone laughed at this, and for a moment, Peter felt more at ease. The band broke into a lively salsa tune and DesFuentes stood, announcing that it was time to get out on the dance floor. Peter wished everyone a good evening and turned to leave.

"Dr. Guise, you do not dance?" DesFuentes asked.

"No," said Peter, "I have two left feet, and besides, I borrowed these shoes and my dogs are barking."

DesFuentes laughed. "Well then, please be my guest and enjoy some champagne. Katrina will keep you company."

Long, dark, silky hair, perfectly tanned skin, big brown eyes, and legs that went on forever... that's how Peter would remember her. Her bright red sequined gown was skin-tight and slit to the top of her toned brown leg. Red stilettos completed her outfit. Peter sat back, looking at the vision in front of him. *I could stare at her forever.*

"Are you enjoying yourself?" asked Katrina in heavily accented English as she moved to sit next to Peter.

"It's just another work night for me," Peter replied, feeling awkward and a little nervous. Katrina's perfume intoxicated him. She poured him a glass of champagne. He downed it, and she refilled his glass.

"Well," Katrina said, "let's see if we can have some fun." Something about the way she smiled at him told Peter things were about to get interesting.

"Sure, I'm down for some fun," Peter said, unconvinced he meant it. "What do you have in mind?"

Katrina poured them both another glass of champagne, took Peter's hand, and led him out of the ballroom to a private lounge at the end of a hallway.

"What's this room?" he asked.

"The VIP area. We had a drink here when we first arrived. I was told a lot of business happens here, private conversations, things like that." She turned the lock on the wooden door and turned to face him. "It's a place to get away from everyone else."

Tugging the lapels on his tuxedo, Katrina pulled Peter close, and they sat back on an overstuffed sofa. Peter began to sweat.

"Is this really happening?" he said, more to himself than to her.

She kissed his mouth and untied the bowtie that had taken him hours to get right, pushing her body against his. He kissed her back, unsure if he should, his mouth opening just a bit, her soft tongue brushed his bottom lip. She helped him out of his tuxedo jacket and unbuttoned his white shirt.

Peter stammered, "H-Hey, why m-me? You're the most beautiful woman here. And aren't you with Mr. Smith?"

Katrina laughed, "It's okay, I like you."

Opening her evening bag, she withdrew a small gold box that contained white powder and a tiny straw. She put the straw in her right nostril, inhaling quickly. Handing the straw to Peter, she said, "Go ahead... your turn."

Inhaling through the tiny straw, Peter felt a rush and a sense of heightened alertness. Enjoying the buzz, he grinned. Katrina kissed him again, more passionately this time. Responding, Peter kissed her back, his tongue found its way into her mouth, his hands on her breasts.

Unsure where his confidence was coming from, Peter reached behind Katrina's back, his nervous fingers fumbled with the zipper on her dress. She stood and smiled seductively while allowing the shimmering gown to slide down her body where it puddled at her feet. Peter wasted no time unbuttoning his pants, pushing them to the floor. With a laugh, the beautiful young woman jumped on him, and they fell back together across the sofa.

When they finished, Katrina dressed, combed her hair, and fixed her makeup. Peter stumbled into his clothes, wondering if she'd noticed the hole in his underwear or the rental company's name sewed onto the inside pocket of his tuxedo jacket. *If she did, she doesn't seem to care.*

"Now, I want you to speak with Mr. Smith," she said.

Peter was shocked. "But we just..."

"Yes, we just fucked."

"Won't he be angry?"

Flashing her big smile at him, Katrina responded, "It was his idea."

Back in the ballroom, they approached the man known to Peter as Mr. Smith. He motioned to Peter that he should sit next to him.

As Peter complied, he stammered the words he'd been practicing in his head. "Mr. Smith, it's a real p-pleasure for m-me to thank you f-for supporting the Institute, sir."

DesFuentes smiled broadly. "As much of a pleasure as fucking my date?"

Peter froze, not knowing what to say. He felt the heat rise in his face. His mind racing, he braced for the worst. *Is this guy about to punch me? Fuck, I might lose my job over this.*

"My friend here just got caught with his pants down, and he thinks I'm going to kill him," DesFuentes announced to the table and burst into laughter. He bent over and slapped his knee. With the rest of the table doubled over enjoying the joke, Peter managed an awkward smile and wished he could crawl under the table.

DesFuentes composed himself and said, "It's okay, my friend. Katrina was my gift to you this evening... anything for the sea turtles." He put his arm around the scientist and gripped Peter's shoulder, pulling him closer, like two best friends sharing a secret. "I think you are wondering why I gave you Katrina, aren't you? Well, I am going to tell you, my friend. Earlier tonight, I saw you looking over here, and I recognized that look. It is the look of a man who wants more, a man who is hungry, a man who is greedy, a man who wants his share. Am I right?"

Peter nodded, shocked this stranger had read his mind with such accuracy.

"How much money do they pay you at the Institute, Dr. Guise?"

"Not much, sir."

"Why, Dr. Guise, have you settled for so little? I like the turtles, too, but someone with your brains and intellect, you could do so much better for yourself and your family. Do you have a family, Peter?"

"No, sir, I don't."

DesFuentes made a stern face. "Family is everything, don't forget that. I would like to help you, Dr. Guise. I will call you in the morning to arrange a time for us to discuss a proposal that will benefit you more than you can imagine." Handing Peter a shot of tequila, he added, "Let's enjoy the rest of the evening, shall we?"

The party wound down at eleven o'clock, and the guests began their exit from the ballroom. DesFuentes stood outside in a shadowy area of the large entranceway, talking privately with Congressman Wallingford while the rest of his party waited for their limousine to pull up. A few minutes later, the car arrived, and the women began to get in. As Katrina moved to enter the limousine, DesFuentes held her back.

"Not you, my dear. My friend, the congressman, has other plans for you tonight."

A look of disappointment on her face, Katrina stepped away from the limousine and headed toward a dark gray Mercedes, its front passenger door had already been opened for her. Peering inside, she could see Wally Wallingford in the driver's seat. In his right hand, out of her view, he held a syringe. The needle dripped with fentanyl.

CHAPTER 23

Sunday, July 25 - 9:00 a.m.

"Dr. Guise, I am offering you the opportunity to make a lot of money," DesFuentes explained. The two sat in DesFuentes' office. Peter appeared overwhelmed by his surroundings and by what DesFuentes said to him.

"A few times each week, a shipment will be dropped in the surf late at night by my boat. The drugs will be contained in black, waterproof packaging that floats. The packages will be marked with luminescent paint and are impossible to see at night. When a special type of flashlight that I will provide for you is shined on them, the luminescent paint will light up, making it possible for you, and only you, to locate them."

Peter sat quietly while DesFuentes explained the rest of the scheme. "Because your job is to be out on the beach looking for sea turtles, you have the perfect cover. No one will suspect you of doing anything illegal. Once you have the packages on shore, you will bury them in the turtle nests you have marked off to keep people away from them. They'll be safe there. You will send us the GPS location. It's important for the location to keep changing so that no one becomes suspicious. The packages will be picked up by my people who will appear to be fishermen trying their luck in the surf. Their appearance will change, sometimes it will be old men, other times it will be a man and his wife or young son. They will leave your payment in the same nest where you will retrieve it."

"I can't bury anything in the nests," said Peter. "That will harm the turtle eggs and compromise the viability of the hatchlings."

"I don't give a shit about turtle eggs! What's in those packages is valuable to me and must be protected. The nests provide an extra layer of protection, and you, my new friend, will do what I say."

"What do I get for doing this?" asked Peter, realizing he had little choice in the matter.

"Three and a half thousand dollars for every drop you handle. Two drops each week comes to twenty-eight grand each month, all cash and tax-free. You keep every penny. There's a drop-off scheduled for tomorrow around two in the morning. Do we have a deal?" DesFuentes extended his hand.

There was no telling what DesFuentes would do to him if he said no. Holding his breath, Peter shook DesFuentes' hand. It felt like he'd just jumped off a cliff.

"How many packages are coming?"

"There will always be three. Here's the flashlight. Be on the lookout, Dr. Guise. The boat will flash a signal. You flash back just once. When they see your light, they'll drop the packages and leave. You know the rest."

Peter frowned. "What if I miss a package or one goes missing?"

"Don't let that happen. You don't want to know the price you'll pay for mistakes."

. . .

Monday, July 26 - 1:50 a.m.

Peter was anxious. There was no sign of a boat yet. He'd had a slow night with very little sea turtle activity. Now, with all the drunks and lovers having left the beaches, he was alone in the dark night. The surf was low, and the ocean was calm with just a few small waves breaking close to shore.

Peter drove his ATV further down the beach when out of nowhere, he saw a quick flash of light about two hundred yards out. Wasting no time, he pushed the button on his flashlight, sending a beam of light in the direction of what he knew to be the boat he'd been expecting.

Unable to make out the boat, he heard its engine picking up speed as it headed back out to sea. He hopped off the ATV and ran to the surf line. Using the flashlight DesFuentes had given him, he shined the beam on the water but saw nothing.

Moving the light back and forth across the surface, Peter started to panic. *What if I can't find them? What if they float ashore and someone else finds them?* As if by magic, three bright neon blue objects appeared, bobbing in the dark water.

Keeping the flashlight directed on the objects, Peter made his way into the waves and swam out to retrieve them. One by one, he grabbed them and made his way to the shoreline. He bundled the packages together with a bungee cord and secured them to the ATV. With that accomplished, Peter drove to a secluded area of beach and headed up near the dunes and a leatherback nest he'd marked a week earlier. Avoiding the nest itself, he dug a hole and dropped the packages in. Using his GPS device, he recorded the exact coordinates of the nest. He would send the coordinates to the number DesFuentes had given him once he was off the beach. After filling in the hole, he used a palm frond to sweep the area around the hiding place, erasing his tracks. He continued to sweep as he made his way back to the ATV, making it impossible to tell that anyone had been there.

. . .

The following night, Peter returned to the same nest and dug down. He felt it before he saw it, three and a half thousand dollars wrapped in shiny, black plastic and bound with black duct tape. The same routine continued in the nights ahead. It almost seemed too easy. Never in his life had Peter expected to make so much money, so fast. There was a problem though, one he hadn't anticipated. The cash was piling up. He called DesFuentes.

"Dr. Guise, why are you calling? Is there a problem with the shipments?

"No, sir, I have a question, though. I need your...well your expertise, since you have experience with this kind of thing."

"In the future, do not bother me with requests. We are not friends. Now, what is it?"

"Where the heck am I supposed to put it all? I know I shouldn't use a bank, but I need a safe place to put the cash. What do you do with your money?"

"What I do with my money is none of your business. And I don't care what you do with yours, just don't attract any unwanted attention. If that happens and it causes me a problem, I will be very unhappy." The line went dead.

. . .

"Thanks for your business," the man behind the counter said. He handed Peter some paperwork and a receipt for one year's rent on a storage unit. Peter had paid cash. The place was called 'The Stow Away'. Selected for its location, should a fast getaway be necessary, the facility was off the island and next to an entrance to the Florida Turnpike.

Sweating and grunting, Peter dragged a long, heavy metal box from the back of his pickup truck. He'd found it at one of the area's many thrift stores. Formerly used for tool storage at an auto repair garage, Peter intended to use it as a safe. Dirty with automotive grease, and chipped and scratched from years of use, the box would accommodate a lot of cash. A new combination lock from Walmart secured the heavy steel latch. Peter stored his payments in the box except for a small amount he deposited in his bank account every other week. *I'm gonna need another box.* He grinned at the thought.

CHAPTER 24

Monday, July 26 - 9:00 a.m.

Hungover, and in her pajamas, Catherine Wallingford made her way into her kitchen. Squinting, she closed the blinds to block out the bright sunlight. Hands shaking, she mixed up a tall Bloody Mary to get the day started, switched on the television and settled in at her kitchen table to watch the morning news. A fresh-faced reporter with perfectly styled hair looked at her through the television screen.

"The remains of a young woman were found early this morning off a remote stretch of highway ten miles north of Stypman Island. The body was discovered in a retention ditch by a college student. The victim was nude, and her hands were bound behind her back. It appears she'd been tortured. The medical examiner determined the cause of death to be strangulation, pending toxicology results. Reported to be Caucasian, approximately twenty-years-old, five feet nine inches tall and weighing one hundred fifteen pounds, the victim had long dark brown hair and brown eyes. Her face was badly disfigured, making identification difficult. Anyone who has information about the victim, or this crime, should contact the police."

Catherine shuddered and gulped a mouthful of her drink. The news story was hauntingly familiar. She checked the calendar. "Wally was on Stypman Island for that fundraiser on Saturday night." She spoke the words to herself, studying the calendar, hoping she had the date wrong. "He wasn't far from where they found that woman's body." She drained the glass and tossed back a chaser. "For strength," she told herself.

Catherine went upstairs and opened the door to her husband's bedroom. The tuxedo he'd worn was in a heap on the floor. "I suppose I'm to take this to the cleaners," she mumbled. She bent over and picked up the suit, checking the pockets and finding them empty. As she shook the wrinkles from the jacket, a shiny speck of red fell to the floor. She examined the jacket further and found nothing.

Turning her attention to the tuxedo pants, Catherine noticed two things. A dried spatter of something dark brown on the side of one pant leg and some long strands of brown hair on the back of the other. Looking toward the zipper, she found something else, something she expected to see, dried semen.

Sitting on Wally's bed, she made a call. "This is Catherine Wallingford," she said to the homicide detective on the other end, "I am congressman Wallingford's wife."

"Yes, ma'am, how can I help you?"

"I saw the report about a body that was found off the highway this morning. I found that report highly disturbing."

"Yes, ma'am. It's terrible what happened to that young woman."

"I'm wondering if you've been able to identify the victim."

"No, Mrs. Wallingford. It will be some time before we know much more."

"You have no clues or suspects?"

"No, ma'am, there isn't much to go on. We aren't publicly sharing this right now, but the only thing we have, and it may be nothing, is that the victim had a couple of pieces of what looks to be red sequins caught in her hair."

Catherine looked down at the shiny round speck on the floor. A tsunami of pain and regret washed over her, taking her under. "Thank you, Detective," she managed to say. "I hope you find whomever is responsible for this."

CHAPTER 25

Saturday, July 31 - 11:00 a.m.

"It's still hundreds of miles away, Clara," Jason said. He was watching the Weather Channel while his wife stared at the ocean.

"It's somewhere out there, another hurricane, and once again we're right in its path." Clara rubbed her temples to ease the ache growing in her head.

"At least Jim Cantore isn't on the island yet," said Jason, trying to make light of the situation.

"You won't think that's so funny when he's reporting from the beach outside our windows. I want to get off this island before things get crazy."

Marley hopped up on the sofa next to Jason. "We're right in the center of the cone of uncertainty. That can't be good for us, can it, girl?" said Jason as he stroked the top of her head. A graphic display identifying a large area in which the hurricane would most likely make landfall was on the television screen. Computer-generated maps of the strengthening storm's predicted paths flashed up next. "Oh, no, girl, look at those spaghetti models." Jason sat forward in his chair, not wanting to believe what he was seeing. The colored lines showed the storm heading to South Florida, several of them passed right through tiny Stypman Island.

Clara's phone rang. It was Kim Witherspoon. Clara put the call on speaker.

"I thought I'd call to check on you two. We're expecting mandatory evacuations, and the bridge will be closed. You still have a few days before the storm hits. When are you planning to leave?"

"That's always the dilemma, Kim. If we leave too early, and the storm changes path, evacuation might not be necessary. If we leave too late, we'll be stuck in monster traffic jams. A few years ago, we were caught up in the nightmare of a last-minute rush to leave. Everybody was trying to get out of Florida at the same time. It was a category four, and the entire state was in the cone."

"I remember that. No gas and people stuck on the highways. It was terrible."

"We vowed to never have that experience again, so we bought a small house in the Blue Ridge mountains that we use as our back up place. We named it 'Plan B'. It's a long drive but with our own place, we don't have to worry about finding a hotel and we can stay as long as we want."

"Promise me you'll take this storm seriously. It's looking like the real thing this time. Climate change has altered the game and not for the better. This little island we live on is only a few feet above sea level."

"Oh, believe me, we know we're vulnerable living here. I forget which hurricane it was, but a few years back, the ocean broke through a narrow point not far from here. Part of the island was cut off from the rest of it, people had to use boats to get to their homes. I hate to even think about it. What are you doing? Are you leaving too?"

"I'm on duty so I have to stay. My girlfriend, Simone, will be off the island; she's staying with one of the Board members at the Institute where she works."

"Be careful, Kim. Everyone I've ever known who rode one of these out, swears they'd never do it again."

"I'll be careful. See you on the other side of this thing. Tell Jason and Marley I said to enjoy the mountains."

While Clara and Jason fretted about heading to the mountains, the water level in the spout of the Goethe barometer that hung beside a window in their kitchen climbed. Marley didn't need the barometer to know the pressure was dropping. She felt it in her ears. Though the coming storm was still far out to sea, her nose alerted her to something different in the air. Something dangerous.

The next day, the Anders made final preparations for their departure. Clara hummed *Carolina in My Mind* while she cleaned out the refrigerator and emptied the freezer.

"What are you doing?" Jason asked.

"I don't want to deal with spoiled food if we lose electricity so I'm cooking everything we've got. We're having a feast tonight."

"A feast? Maybe I like these storms after all. I'm getting started on loading the car. "C'mon Marley." Marley joined him as he went back and forth to the car from the condo, jumping in the back seat each time to be sure she wouldn't be left behind. "Not yet, girl," said Jason. "We'll leave early tomorrow."

The next morning, they were up before sunrise. "Jason, we should have left yesterday," said Clara, pouring coffee into travel mugs. "Google Maps is already showing that I-95 North is stop-and-go."

"Great," Jason responded with a look that said he thought the traffic news was anything but that. "I'm just hoping we can get out of Florida before lunchtime. I love our home and I hope it's still here when we return but living with these blasted hurricanes is exhausting."

The sun was just rising from an angry ocean. "Come take a last look," said Clara.

Jason stood next to her gazing at the magnificent sight. "I never tire of that. C'mon, it's time to go."

Jason and Clara locked the door and walked in silence to their car. Even at the early hour, the air was sticky and unpleasant. After a quick pee in her favorite spot, Marley hopped in the car, and the three left Coquina Reef.

"Let's hope there's something to come back to," said Jason as he steered toward the exit of the community.

Clara didn't reply. Sipping coffee from a travel mug, she swiped at a tear that had escaped down her cheek.

· · ·

Monday, August 2 - 11:00 a.m.

At the Stypman Island Institute for Marine Life Preservation, it was all-hands-on-deck. Without hurricane glass or storm shutters; volunteers, staff, and interns nailed plywood to the windows. Inside, Simone Mercier was covering computer equipment with plastic and overseeing arrangements to secure the Institute's sea life exhibits while Peter Guise backed up research data on a hard drive. The Honda Rancher ATVs they used on the beach would be moved into a garage later.

"Peter, where will you shelter during the hurricane?" asked Simone, making conversation.

"I'll be at my place," he replied, not looking up from what he was doing. "The building is concrete block, so I should be okay. What about you?"

"The entire police force is on duty, and Kim will be at the station," replied Simone. "Suzette Thawlington invited me to use a guest room at her place."

"Suzette Thawlington?" Peter looked up in surprise. "I hear she's got a freaking mansion! You'd better be on your best behavior, don't leave your dirty underwear on the floor," he teased before checking his phone.

"I know." Simone grinned. "Lots of pressure for me to represent well, but I can't think of a safer place to be during a hurricane than in that castle of hers. She told me she has multiple generators, so we'll even have air conditioning if the power goes out. She invited the interns to stay with her too but none of them have taken her up on the offer. I can't understand why."

Peter stood back from the computer and began pacing. He checked his phone again. He looked at Simone with uneasy eyes. "They're all talking about the hurricane party supplies they've gathered. From what I'm hearing, they're riding out the storm together, and it's all about liquor and the snacks. Cheetos, Doritos, and subs from Publix are on the menu along with rum drinks."

"I don't know what a Cheeto is, but it sounds like a fun party, unless things get serious. I've been through my share of these storms on Martinique. Definitely not a party."

Peter went back to the computer and waited for the backup to be completed. "Hey, by the way, that lecture you gave last week must have been fantastic."

"I thought the audience looked bored," replied Simone. "My presentation was about sand temperature and climate change and how warmer beaches make for more female hatchlings and cooler temperatures result in more males. I didn't exactly have them on the edge of their seats."

"Yup, the old 'hot chicks' and 'cool dudes' way of remembering that. Folks always laugh at that. Anyway, someone must have liked what you had to say. We collected over six grand in cash donations that night."

"I know, can you believe it? Usually, we only get a few hundred. I almost fell over when the volunteers handed me the donation box with the total."

"I heard it was mostly twenties."

"The jar was stuffed. I asked Mike to pick it up right there at the lecture and take it to the bank. I didn't want it hanging around." Simone lowered her voice. "I hope you don't mind my asking, but is everything okay? You seem worried, and you keep checking your phone."

Rattled by the question, Peter stood up and made for the door. "Yeah, I'm okay. Just checking the weather forecast. I need some fresh air. Back in a few."

Inside his pickup truck, with the windows up for privacy, Peter tried reaching DesFuentes. The call went to voicemail. He tried again. "C'mon, pick up, pick up! I need you to cancel tonight's shipment. There's a fucking hurricane. Shit! Voicemail again." He left a message, "Hey, this is Peter, call me back, it's important." He dared not mention anything about the shipment of drugs.

CHAPTER 26

Tuesday, August 3 - 2:30 a.m.

Miserable, Peter waited on shore. Soaked with rain and perspiration, he sat on the ATV, mosquitos biting his bare feet. *The ocean is so rough. I wonder if it's coming.* The flash signalled just after three a.m. The voyage from the Bahamas had taken longer than usual.

"It's about fucking time," cursed Peter, his voice drowned out by the roar of crashing breakers. He flashed his light back.

Tossed around in the rough surf, the packages were difficult to keep track of with the beam of the flashlight. The rise and fall of the waves made them disappear, only to reappear some place else. Moments later, it was clear the worst was happening. "Fuck no!" Peter screamed in disbelief as the packages were carried away in the strong current.

Peter ran into the water, jumping through small waves and diving under the larger, more powerful rollers. Fighting the undertow, he swam into deeper water. The warm ocean felt ominous. *Warm oceans make for stronger hurricanes*, he recalled.

Catching his breath and treading water, Peter scanned the surface with the beam of the flashlight. Glowing bright blue, just beyond an incoming wave, was one of the packages. Breast stroking, his head out of the water, Peter swam toward it. "Almost have it," he said to himself when something large moved beneath him, brushing his leg. Instinctively, he pulled his legs up. *What the hell was that?*

"Shit!" The thing, whatever it was, bumped his legs again. Stronger this time, it pushed Peter forward. *It's a shark, a massive one!* His mind raced and panic set in. *Think, man think! You studied sharks. You're an expert, damn* it. "Punch it in the nose," he told himself. *How the heck am I supposed to do that in the dark?*

Frantic, Peter turned in circles, shining his flashlight in every direction, looking for a splash, a fin, or anything that might tell him what to expect next.

Seeing nothing, he treaded water and hoped for the best. The floating bundle was next to him; he grabbed hold of it. The second package bobbed a little further out. As he swam to reach it, a wave crashed over him, pushing him down and sending him tumbling backward underwater. Disoriented and struggling, he found his way back to the surface. Choking on seawater, he gasped for breath.

Another wave hit, sending him below the surface again. Making his way back to the surface, Peter gulped air and kicked his feet hard, trying to stay above the surface. Crying with fear and exhaustion, he screamed, "God damn it, I fuckin' hate this shit! I fuckin' hate it! Fuck! Fuck! Fuck!" The yelling helped. He felt stronger and reached to grab the second package. Peter looked around; the third package was nowhere in sight. Exasperated, he yelled to no one, "Where the hell is it?"

Completely spent, he made his way out of the water and dropped the two packages on the soggy sand. He scanned the water with the flashlight but saw nothing. "He's gonna kill me for this." Tears filled his eyes. And then he saw it twenty yards down the beach in the piles of white foam made by the crashing waves. The wet sand sucked at his feet making every step a chore as he ran to retrieve the third package.

Worried about the possibility of high water, Peter decided to bury the packages in an area rarely used by beachgoers. *Even if they're exposed by the storm, it's less likely they'll be found by someone passing by*, he reasoned. Navigating the ATV in the driving rain squall, Peter headed to Olive Beach. Hopping off the ATV, he checked the GPS. He talked himself through the plan he'd devised earlier in the day. "Two weeks earlier, Simone marked three loggerhead nests and one green sea turtle nest here. The green sea turtle nest will work better," he decided, "it's high in the dunes, and less likely to get washed out."

Digging deeper than normal, Peter used duct tape to secure a steel washer to the packages before dropping them in the hole. If the storm interferes with GPS, he reasoned, DesFuentes' men could still find them with a metal detector. Peter knew metal detectors were especially effective for finding metals containing iron. The washers would do the trick. *I've done everything I can do*, he thought, wiping sand from his hands. *It'll have to be good enough, DesFuentes.*

Tired and wet, Peter headed back to the Institute. Intermittent gusts from the storm's outer bands had passed, giving way to howling wind and pouring rain. Peter's ride was miserable; pelted by blowing sand and sheeting rain, he struggled to find his way. Reaching the Institute's gravel parking lot, he had an unwelcome surprise. A light was on in the main building.

"Shit, somebody's here," Peter muttered.

As he entered, he saw his boss, Mike Sampson. Visibly startled, Mike slammed the top drawer of his desk closed.

Mike's words came out of his mouth fast. He blabbered non-stop, without taking a breath. "You look like a drowned rat. Rough night, buddy? You're coming in awfully late in this kind of weather. There can't be many turtles nesting with a hurricane on the way."

Not knowing what to make of the situation, Peter responded with a lie. "Tell that to one very large leatherback momma. I had a heck of a time trying to tag her and ended up in the surf. Funny thing, when I got a hold of her flipper, she was already tagged. I got the number, though. I'll check the system later to see who she was."

The lie was a good one. There would be no records to fake, nothing much to record, and no evidence Peter had just lied to his boss.

"What are you doing here, Mike? It's after four in the morning. You riding this one out?"

Mike looked uncomfortable. "Hell no, dude. I woke up an hour ago and realized I forgot to take our insurance policy paperwork with me." He stuffed some papers in the pockets of his rain slicker, Peter noticed they were already bulging.

"It looks like the storm's heading right toward us. It's a full-blown hurricane now, the name is Frieda. If things go tits up, there might not be much left but our insurance coverage. Landfall is expected around 8:00 a.m. Let's get the fuck out of here while we still can. It's gonna be a long day."

"I'm headed to my apartment," said Peter. "I probably won't have any power, but the place is up a few feet. I'm pretty safe there."

"Well, stay out of harm's way, buddy. I'm outta here. See you on the other side of this thing."

. . .

6:00 a.m.

In North Carolina, Clara and Jason read the report on the internet.

"Hurricane Frieda officially made landfall at 5:50 a.m. as a Category 3 storm. After heading straight for Stypman Island, Frieda stalled before continuing a westerly path toward land, coming ashore twenty-five miles south near Jobay inlet."

"We dodged another bullet." Jason squeezed Clara's shoulder.

"I'm not sure I have many more of these left in me," she replied. "I'm going back to bed; I didn't sleep a wink."

. . .

Stypman Island was flooded, trees were toppled, and those that remained standing were stripped of their leaves. Bushes and vegetation were brown from salt and windburn, debris was strewn everywhere and sunken boats, their topsides barely visible in the whitecaps, littered the river. The beaches, now seriously eroded, had taken a pounding from the raging surf. Several homes lost large sections of their roofs. Clean-up would take time, but the island had survived another hurricane although it continued to be cut off from the mainland, its only bridge closed because of high winds. The driving rain continued, and the lowest points on the island were now underwater. With the power out, moisture and humidity began its slow creep into residences and buildings.

Peter woke to a loud noise coming from his burner phone. His head hurt, a result of the six-pack of beer and the shots of whiskey he'd put down a few hours ago to unwind from his tortured night.

"Dr. Guise?" said DesFuentes.

"Yeah," answered Peter, his voice groggy. "I guess you're returning my call."

"What's on your mind? You said it was important."

Peter explained his concern about the hurricane and the possibility of losing the packages of cocaine, adding that the reason he'd called was to ask that the shipment be delayed until after the storm had passed.

"You called to tell me that the drop-off schedule was inconvenient because of some bad weather?" DesFuentes snarled. "Did the drop take place or not?"

Peter answered, "Yes."

"Where are the packages now?"

"I buried them on the beach and marked the GPS as usual. I taped a piece of metal to them so they can be located if there's a problem with GPS."

"You did what? You left them on the beach in a fucking hurricane?"

"That's what I am supposed to do," objected Peter.

"You idiot!" the angry voice boomed. Peter's head throbbed; he pulled the phone further from his ear. "You were supposed to use that big brain of yours and keep them with you until the damned storm passed."

"Where would I keep them?" pleaded Peter. He was shaking and felt sick to his stomach.

"I don't care where you keep them. Go get them. If they aren't where you left them, you'd better damned-well find them. That's over a million dollars you left out there."

"Didn't your guys pick them up already?"

"No! I assumed you were smart enough to keep the packages with you. No one is on the beach this morning. My men can't get on the island because the bridge is closed. Go get that shit and call me back when you have it."

Peter pulled on a pair of shorts, a t-shirt and a rain slicker. Opening the door to his apartment, he was hit with a powerful gust of wind and a wall of rain from an outer band on the back end of the storm. Frieda's eye had passed and was moving its way west across South Florida. Although the worst was over, the winds continued, and rain came down in buckets.

Running to his pickup through water that was up to his ankles, Peter was soaking wet by the time he got inside the truck. Driving was difficult, and he slowly made his way to the Institute. Once there, he walked through standing water to the garage and pulled up the heavy wood door. Hanging on the wall of the garage and blowing in the wind was a white canvas bag with the Institute's logo printed on it. He grabbed it before getting on an ATV. While backing out of the garage, his heart sank when he drove over a long black racer snake struggling to find dry ground. "Shit! Sorry, buddy." Peter looked down at the snake. "I didn't see you there."

Swerving to avoid a fallen coconut palm, Peter felt better when he reached the entrance to secluded Olive Beach and saw it empty. *Nobody's here, please let the drugs be where I left them.*

Eight inches of water filled the parking area, and Peter could hear the loud, angry surf raging just beyond the dunes. Bracing himself against the gusts of wind, he climbed the stairs to a wooden footbridge and made his way across to the beach. The wind still howling, Peter steadied himself to avoid being knocked over by the stronger gusts.

"Holy crap, the beach sure took a beating," he said to himself as he gazed at the area ahead of him. Olive Beach looked very different than it had just a few hours ago. Severely eroded, a dramatic eight-foot escarpment had formed near the dune. Hundreds of white sea turtle eggs, uncovered by the waves, blew around like ping-pong balls on the sand.

Relief washed over Peter when he saw the two stakes Simone had planted. Eying them, he struggled up the escarpment. Anxiety and adrenaline coursed through him as he dropped to his knees and began digging with his hands. Coming upon the round, leathery eggs he'd been careful to avoid disturbing the night before, Peter did something that, just a day ago, would have seemed inconceivable. He tossed the eggs out of the nest along with the sand. *Where the hell are the packages?* he thought. Scooping sand with both hands, he strained to dig even deeper. His fingertips touched them before he saw them... the packages were still there. He brushed the sand away, revealing their black protective wrapping. For a brief second, a wave of relief washed over him. Then, he panicked.

CHAPTER 27

Tuesday, August 3 - 7:10 a.m.

Peter turned; someone stood behind him. Because of the whipping wind and the crash of the surf, he hadn't heard the person approach. Now it was too late. Looking up, he recognized Officer Bill Widley.

Bill Widley was a local celebrity. A graduate of Florida State, and an ironman athlete in his early thirties, Widley was easy on the eyes and even easier to talk with. He'd been patrolling the island's beaches for ten years. He became a local hero after saving a Haitian man and his five-year-old daughter from drowning when their small boat sank off the coast while on their way to what they'd hoped was a better life.

The rescue was bittersweet. Lost at sea were the man's wife, two sons, and a friend. Bill had been photographed drenched and exhausted, kneeling on the beach, with his arms around the man and the young girl, all three of them in tears. The photograph went viral, appearing in the national press along with a story about the incident and a headline that read, "The Very Best of America."

Widley yelled over the loud surf, "Hey, Peter, what are you doing out here in this mess?"

Peter brushed sand into the hole, hoping it was enough to block Widley's view of the packages he'd just uncovered. He shouted back, "I'm testing some new technology. I want to see if it can help us understand if the nest is still viable."

Widley's response stunned Peter, "I wondered what that is you're digging up."

Fuck! He's seen them!

"It doesn't seem like it's working," yelled Peter. "This nest isn't viable." He pointed to the turtle eggs now scattered about.

"I figured as much when I saw you tossing them. Anyway, you shouldn't be out here now. Is Simone here, too?" Widley stood over Peter, looking into the hole in front of him.

"No, it's just me. She's sheltering off the island."

"Well, that's where you should be. My orders are to make sure people stay off the beach. The surfers can't resist swells like these."

"No problem, Bill, I just need to finish up. I'll be out of here in a minute, I promise."

"Okay, man, but don't let me catch you back on the beach until we give the all-clear." Bill Widley headed off into the rain.

Shaking, Peter tried to calm himself. He stashed the packages in the canvas bag he'd taken from the Institute's garage and scrambled off the beach.

. . .

Tuesday, August 3 - 1:15 p.m.

By noon the sun broke through the clouds, and an hour later it shone its brightest on the Treasure Coast, and the day became one of those amazingly clear, beautiful days that happen after a large storm has passed. The sky was an intense blue and the ocean calmed. Hurricane Frieda had crossed Florida and was now in the Gulf. The power was still out, but the bridge was open. As they had done time and time again, island residents began making their way back in order to inspect the damage done to their homes.

Peter lay asleep in his dreary apartment. He'd emptied a bottle of Cruzan rum to calm his nerves, passing out in sheets soaked through with sweat. After returning home, he'd called DesFuentes and was told to hold the packages and not let them out of his sight. Having the drugs in his apartment made him anxious. He'd pulled the blinds so no one could see inside. Without electricity, the place was dark, hot, and sticky. His damp, sandy clothing lay in a heap on the floor where he'd left it, a reminder of the previous day. Tucked behind a box of old biology textbooks on the top shelf of his closet was a million dollars of cocaine.

CHAPTER 28

Wednesday, August 4 - 2:00 p.m.

Beau Jackson smiled with anticipation. The bank statement he'd been waiting for had just popped up in the in-box of a stealth email account set up by an offshore bank in Belize. He tapped the keys on his computer and entered the passwords that would reveal not only his account balance, but how far he'd come and, how much further he had to go before reaching his goal.

He had plans, big plans, for a new life far away from Stypman Island. A life that didn't involve drug lords, murder, and the everyday headaches that came with being a police chief on a tiny island. He planned to live off the grid in Costa Rica. In his mind, he could see it clearly: cold beer, hot sex, and incredible sunsets. After bribing the right officials, he was already registered as a permanent resident. That status afforded him the right to bring his guns into the country because you never knew when your past might catch up with you.

Earning his way to paradise was proving to be easier than expected. In return for eighty thousand tax-free dollars each month he transported bundles of cash to Kitty Sampson's shops and establishments where it was laundered. Jackson provided protection for the cash, and his regular visits to Kitty's establishments went unnoticed. As a hands-on police chief, those visits were viewed as him taking an interest in the community.

A life in Coast Rica wouldn't come cheap. Jackson figured he'd need four million. His account balance showed $2,700,000. *Time to get back to work,* he thought.

. . .

3:00 p.m.

Looking up from the desk in her small office at the Blue Manatee Grille, Kitty Sampson saw she had a visitor. Of all her businesses, the Blue Manatee was the crown jewel. With sweeping ocean views, a killer wine list, and a reputation for first-rate gourmet food and impeccable service, the restaurant was always booked. The Blue Manatee had weathered the storm well, giving Kitty time to do what she needed to do. Launder her boss's money.

"Hello, Beau," Kitty said as the chief walked in and closed the door.

Jackson had a black duffle bag over his shoulder. He handed it to her, and she slid it under her desk. She handed back an identical bag filled with blank paper.

"Our boss wants you to know he isn't happy. He says you aren't keeping up."

"He's being ridiculous and sending way too much dirty cash. I can't push it through without putting up some pretty big red flags."

"That's interesting, but it's not my problem. It's not his problem, either. He wants to know how you plan to catch up. The drugs are getting on shore reliably now, that's making a huge difference. A ton more cash is coming in. It's good for all of us."

"Look, the only way I can launder more money is if I have places to process it through. I've been trying to get Manny Gonzales to sell me his place, but I'm not getting anywhere with him. His restaurant is the biggest on the island and brings in a crap load of revenue. It's perfect for what we're doing. I'd be able to put everything through with extra capacity."

"What's Manny's hang up?"

"He's being a stubborn asshole." Kitty snapped a pencil in frustration. "I've offered him a lot more than he could get from anyone else, and he knows it. He just doesn't want to sell to me. He says I own too much of the island already, and he doesn't want his business going to a gringo chick. His words, not mine."

"I don't know the guy but that doesn't sound like a reason to turn down money. What's his story, Kitty?" Jackson put his hands on his hips.

"The American dream, that's his damned story." Exasperated, she threw up her hands. "Manny is about to turn fifty-eight. He's a bald, brown, chubby little fucker. He left Puerto Rico twenty-five years ago and worked his way up from the bottom. When a former boss asked Manny to partner with him in a new restaurant, he jumped at the chance. Manny saved every damned penny he got his hands on and years later, he bought the business, named it after himself and made it into what it is today."

"He's proud of the place, Kitty. He's not going to give it up easily. But maybe I can help persuade him. In the meantime, figure out something to fix this mess you're in. The boss isn't happy, and that can only mean bad things for you."

. . .

Saturday, August 7 - 8:30 p.m.
Having survived another hurricane, the islanders were in the mood to celebrate and Manny's was hopping. A local band played top forty tunes, and the dance floor was crowded. Every table was occupied while thirsty patrons stood four-deep at the bar. Then, everything changed.

Guns out, a team of armed Immigration and Customs Enforcement officers burst into the dining area. "ICE, this is a raid!"

The place cleared out in a hurry; most guests made for the exits without bothering to pay their tabs. Wasting no time, the officers headed into the kitchen where they rounded up the staff, marching them out to a blue bus that was waiting in the parking lot. The wait staff, several in tears, were pulled aside and told to stand against a wall as their identities were checked. Standing in a corner and out of the fray, Chief Jackson watched the last of the patrons make their way to their cars.

Manny was at his home, smoking a cigar and watching baseball when the raid took place. By the time he arrived at his restaurant, the commotion was over, and his establishment was quiet.

The ICE raid had taken out over a third of the kitchen staff, and just as Manny's re-opened, inspectors from the Fire Department showed up, citing the place with multiple code violations. Manny's was shut down until the required corrections were made. Three weeks later, it was still closed.

Kitty Sampson reached out to Manny again, offering to take the place off his hands. Manny hung on, refusing her offer. With the once successful bar and restaurant closed more than it was open, Manny's clientele found other places to frequent, and most of his staff found other places to work. In a matter of weeks, Manny's was sinking fast.

Kitty kept her fingers crossed.

. . .

Sunday, August 8 - 4:00 p.m.

She was supposed to have the day off but with three fresh cases on her desk, Lisa returned home to her apartment after spending most of the day in her office. Although she was exhausted, Dorothy's murder remained forefront in her mind. Deciding to take a chance on an idea she'd had earlier in the day, Lisa placed a call to Josephine Paulsen's daughter. It had been easy enough to get the number, now she wondered if her idea would pay off. When the call went unanswered, she left a message. A short while later, her phone rang.

"Thank you for returning my call," said Lisa. "I'm a detective in Florida following up on some routine questions relating to your mother's death. First, let me express my condolences to you and your family."

"That's very kind of you," replied Rochelle, her voice soft and unsure.

"Do you have a few minutes? My questions won't take very long."

"I can only tell you what I know, which isn't very much."

"I understand," said Lisa. "These questions are more or less routine so no pressure. Okay? Now, do you recall Chief Jackson mentioning how he came to find your mother's body? He didn't include that information in his report."

Rochelle thought for a moment before answering. "No, he didn't say. He just told me he was the one who found her and that she looked peaceful."

"To your knowledge, had your mother been diagnosed with a heart condition or high blood pressure?"

"No, my mother never mentioned any medical problems. She wasn't a smoker and was in good health for her age. I called her physician just to be sure. The doctor assured me she hadn't been diagnosed with anything indicative of heart disease."

"Rochelle, have you been to Stypman Island since her mother's death?"

"No, I haven't. I feel bad about that, but my son is autistic. Travel is difficult for him, and I've been putting it off." Rochelle explained that her mother's body was flown to Chicago for burial. "It sounds a bit macabre, but her remains are still in a refrigerator at the funeral home. She won't be buried for two more weeks."

"Why is that?"

"My uncle wants to be at the funeral. He's recovering from surgery on his spine and is bed ridden. He's taking my mom's death especially hard."

"That's so sad. It sounds like they were close?"

"They were twins so... they were really close and spoke by phone every day - they told each other everything."

"Rochelle, could you tell me the name of the funeral home you are using?"

"It's the Skellinger Funeral Home in Oak Park. Billy Skellinger is the owner. My parents knew his dad."

"Again, Rochelle, my sincere condolences. Thank you for your help."

Lisa had her next lead.

After Googling the funeral home, she placed the call. When Billy Skellinger picked up, Lisa made a request. "Mr. Skellinger, I need a liver sample from the Paulsen body. Can you help me with that?"

"Liver? Her death certificate says heart disease."

"Yes, but some new questions have come up, and the liver sample would help to answer those."

"I'm happy to assist, Detective, just send me the paperwork by email. I'll personally collect the sample and send it first to your office first thing tomorrow. You'll have it Tuesday morning."

"That's great, Mr. Skellinger. It's true what they say about Midwesterners being so helpful. Hey, would you happen to know the full name of the deceased's brother?"

"Why sure, I do. I have it right here from the obituary we ran for the family. His name is Benjamin Alexander Ganley. He lives in Evanston. I have a phone number if you'd like it."

"Mr. Skellinger, you've been a great help. Could I ask you for one more favor?"

"I don't see why not. What do you need?"

"Would you keep my request for the liver sample to yourself? I'd like to avoid further upsetting the family. I'm not sure anything will come of it, and they're dealing with enough as it is right now."

"I won't say a word, that's one less uncomfortable call to make."

. . .

Tuesday, August 10 - 9:30 a.m.

Bruce Kim was waiting in his lab drumming his fingers on his desk, when Lisa arrived. He'd agreed to run toxicology screens on the sample taken from Josephine's body and was eager to get on with it. "Lisa, this investigation of yours is getting damned complicated. What have we gotten ourselves into?"

"I don't know, but maybe we're about to find out." Lisa held two large coffees and handed one to Bruce, who gratefully accepted it. The two sat in his private office just outside the main lab space. She took a cardboard box out of the brown leather tote bag that had been hanging from her shoulder. The box had been delivered an hour ago and contained an insulated container with a section of Josephine Paulsen's liver packed in dry ice.

A grin crossed his face as Bruce looked at the box. "I wonder if a part of her is happy to be back in Florida."

Lisa groaned at the lame attempt at humor and sipped her coffee. "If the Chief of Police is involved in this, things are going to get very ugly and fast."

Bruce nodded his head in agreement. "I've been thinking the same thing. And not to make things worse, I took a careful look at the other victim's file, the woman who died in the pool bathroom, Mary Dillard. That one doesn't seem right, either. From what I can see, the victim hit her head more than once, and the impact of one of those blows appears to have been much more severe than it should have been given the victim's size and the type of fall."

"What are you saying?" Alarmed and confused, Lisa stared at Bruce as if she'd seen a ghost.

"Hang on for a minute, I'm not finished yet. I also looked at photos of her clothing and saw something I didn't like."

"Her clothing? She was found in the nude, wasn't she?"

"She was, but her robe, swimsuit, and flip-flops were in the changing room where she apparently left them before getting in the shower. It's her flip-flops that worry me. I think they may have been sanded off."

"What?" Puzzled, Lisa's mouth hung open.

"Sanded off to make them smooth. And slippery."

Speechless, Lisa felt butterflies in her stomach.

"Judging from their overall condition, they appear to be new rubber sandals, but the bottoms are worn down and perfectly smooth. The bottom of a flip-flop would smooth out over time from wear but in different places depending on the owner's stride, whether they drag their feet, have a turned-in foot... you get the idea. The bottoms of these sandals appear to be evenly smooth over the entire surface."

"What are you thinking, Bruce?"

"The victim was set up to slip and fall. And somebody helped her fall again, just to be sure the job was done."

Lisa sank back in her chair. "What's next? Every time I think I'm getting a handle on this, there's more. Was any of this in the Medical Examiner's report?"

"The multiple head trauma was noted, but judging from the file, the police don't seem all that interested. And nobody appears to have noticed the flip-flops. If you think you're looking at an accident, you wouldn't even be considering something like that. Still, I don't get it. Why the hell are old ladies being targeted by a killer?"

Lisa took a deep breath. "This is only a guess but hear me out. What if all three deaths are related? Mary Dillard lived in the condo next to Josephine Paulsen. When he was interrogated, Angelo Scarella said he didn't mean to kill Dorothy. He was in the wrong place. The same thing could have happened to the Dillard woman. Maybe Scarella never told us about her because we didn't ask."

"Or she might have seen or heard something," added Bruce.

"I'm thinking Paulsen was the intended victim. Her condo was in the same location as Dorothy's, just in the other building. Three murders at one small condominium complex. It's time for me to make another trip to Stypman Island."

"No way, Lisa. You need help with this mess. Why not call in the State Police? This thing is way out of control and until we test this liver sample, we don't even know if it's three murders."

"I hear you, but Dorothy's murder is at the center of this. I owe it to her to figure it out. I don't trust cops not to cover for other cops. We both know about the blue wall of silence and all that bullshit. I saw how that came into play when Scott was killed. I'm not letting the same thing happen to Dorothy."

"Lisa, be realistic. This is bigger than what you can handle on your own."

"I need a little more time, then I'll get help. I promise."

CHAPTER 29

Wednesday, August 11 - 4:00 p.m.

The traffic on I-95 North moved slowly as it left Miami, but once Lisa passed Boca Raton, the road opened. She put on her playlist, turned the volume way up, and pressed down on the accelerator, arriving on Stypman Island just as Tom Petty finished up 'Free Fallin'. Turning off the music, she looked at the time.

"A few minutes after six, perfect. Just in time for dinner," she said as she pulled into a parking space at Coquina Reef. Taking in a deep breath and slowly releasing it, she looked in the rearview mirror, applied some lipstick, and brushed a few stray hairs into place. "Okay, calm down and get a grip, you got this."

Carrying a bottle of chardonnay, Lisa felt her nerves getting the better of her as she entered the building where her good friend had been brutally murdered. One floor below where Dorothy had met her tragic end, Lisa knocked on the door and heard Marley bark.

"You must be Lisa," Jason Anders extended his hand and introduced himself. Marley was also at the door, tail wagging. She jumped on Lisa, welcoming her. Smiling, Jason said, "I understand you've already met our ferocious dog."

"Marley, I'm glad to see you, too," Lisa bent down and stroked the dog's head. "Thank you so much for the invitation, Jason." She handed him the bottle of wine. "Something smells delicious."

Clara stepped out of the kitchen and gave Lisa a hug. "I'm so happy you could come. Sit down and make yourself comfortable. I'm just finishing up in here and need a few minutes. I'm cautiously optimistic about the meal. It's looking like a success. Jason, how about a drink?"

"Great idea. What will you have, Lisa?"

Suddenly I don't feel much like a Coors Light, Lisa thought. "Anything is fine, whatever you and Clara are having works for me," she answered as she made her way into the living room.

Rolled up in plastic, in the corner of the room, was the rug Clara and Jason had rescued. Seeing it, a lump grew in Lisa's throat. Looking out the window at the waves and thinking the view was the same, just one floor lower, Lisa's thoughts went to Dorothy and how much she missed her. Feeling very alone, maybe more so than she'd ever felt, her eyes welled up.

Jason arrived, carrying a small tray with three glasses. "I hope vodka and club soda is okay."

"Perfect." Lisa took a glass and tried to hide her emotions.

Clara joined them in the living area, and Jason offered a toast. "To our friend, Dorothy."

They raised their glasses. Lisa choked up, quickly swiping at the tears escaping down her cheeks. "I'm so sorry, I promised myself I wouldn't be like this tonight. It's just that there are so many memories here."

"Please, don't feel bad about letting a few tears loose," said Jason. "You're among kindred spirits here. Not a day goes by that Clara doesn't have a meltdown over this whole terrible thing. And if I'm being honest, I've shed a few myself."

Lisa saw Clara's watery eyes and smiled sympathetically, a look passing between two women who understood each other.

"We need to change the subject, or this evening won't be much fun for anyone. It seems you weathered the storm okay," offered Lisa.

"We were very lucky," said Clara. "We went to our home in the mountains to avoid the worst of it. Thankfully, when we returned, things were as we'd left them. No matter how long we live here, I'll never get used to hurricanes."

"Well, your home is stunning. How long have you lived here?"

"About two years," said Jason. "We used to live in New York in a town called Douglaston, just outside the city. Clara was a high school English teacher, and I worked with start-up companies. After we retired, we were looking forward to starting a new chapter. We'd vacationed on the island over the past thirty years, so we knew we wanted to be here."

"Dorothy just loved living here, I'm guessing you feel the same way."

"Being on this island is different from most places in Florida," explained Clara. There aren't any large shopping centers, big box stores, or tourist attractions. You have to go to the mainland for those things, which is fine by us. Life here is quiet and relaxed. The locals like it that way. I hope it never changes but sadly our elected officials seem to think differently."

Grateful her hosts were doing most of the talking, Lisa took a quick assessment of the evening so far. *They realize I'm shaky, they're making it easy for me.*

"When we bought this place, we only had one thing on our minds, we wanted a view of the ocean," Jason continued. "Whenever we'd vacation, the room with the best view always went to our friends, parents, or family members. So, after years of looking at the parking lot, we just wanted to see the ocean every day for the rest of our lives."

"Well, you couldn't have found a better spot," said Lisa.

"Walking in here," Clara motioned around the room, "we were so taken by the sight outside the windows, we forgot to look at the rest of the place. After we closed, we realized how much work it needed."

Jason finished the story. "Although the renovation experience was less than enjoyable, the result was worth it. At least until we found ourselves spattered in blood."

Clara glared at him. "Jason! Let's not go there tonight!"

Lisa took a long swallow of her cocktail.

"Neither of us wanted to be in a crowded place, and we're enchanted with the sea turtles that nest on the local beaches," added Clara, changing the subject. "The Gulf Stream runs close and warms the water. That attracts all kinds of fish and marine life. As a child, Jason wanted to be a veterinarian and was excited to volunteer at the local sea turtle hospital, just south of here."

"They're incredible creatures," said Jason, "and what we humans do to them is just heartbreaking. Some get hit by careless boaters and are maimed by propeller strikes. Others become entangled in fishing lines or accidentally hooked. And just about every turtle we see at the hospital has swallowed plastic, some so much it ends up killing them. The ocean is chock full of plastic. Every day on our beach walks, we pick up what the ocean has spit out. It's never-ending."

"Clara, are you involved at the sea turtle hospital, as well?" asked Lisa.

"I have an interest in marine biology, I studied up on sea turtles and the other local marine life as well. I teach tourists and school groups about sea life and what they can do to help protect it."

"So, Lisa," said Jason turning serious, "I hate to be a downer, but Clara says you're looking into what happened upstairs."

"I am. As I explained when Clara and I first met, I'm concerned that the local police may not be equipped to investigate Dorothy's murder. To be honest with you, I'm coming up with more questions than answers."

Careful not to alarm her hosts, Lisa posed the question she'd traveled two hours from Miami to ask. "So, did you know the other two women who recently died here?"

"We knew them both," answered Jason. "Not especially well, but we knew them as neighbors. Mary Dillard, who died at the pool, was a very sweet woman who kept to herself. She had a difficult hearing problem, so it was challenging to converse with her."

"But every morning, no matter what, she managed to get to the swimming pool," added Clara. "She enjoyed being there before anyone else showed up. Like a lot of older people, she kept to a strict routine. She was up early, went for her swim, and spent the rest of the day reading. She was in bed with the lights out at 7:30 in the evening."

"How do you know all that, Clara?"

"Mary told me. I spoke with her now and then at the mailbox. She seemed lonely, so whenever I saw her, I'd check to see if she had her hearing aids in. When she did, I made an effort to spend a little time with her. As Jason said, she was a sweet lady."

"What about the other woman, the one who had the heart attack? What was she like?"

"Oh, you mean Josephine Paulsen. They say it's not good to speak ill of the dead," said Jason. "She was something else, a real piece of work."

Clara piped in. "Be nice, Jason."

Lisa laughed. "I can tell there's a story coming on."

"There sure is," said Jason.

"Let's keep it for dinner," added Clara. "Anyone hungry?"

They sat at a round antique table, set with a small ceramic vase of fresh white tulips in the center. Marley found a spot underneath, near Lisa's feet.

"The table looks lovely, Clara," said Lisa while placing her napkin on her lap.

"Thanks. Jason and I found it in an antique store in Provence when we vacationed there several years back."

Jason smiled. "It cost twice as much to have it shipped as it did to buy it."

Clara placed a platter with roast chicken, grilled lemons, and asparagus on the table, along with a small bowl of roasted fingerling potatoes. Jason opened the bottle of chardonnay Lisa had brought and poured some into each of their wine glasses.

"Has anyone moved into Dorothy's place yet?" Lisa inquired, making conversation.

"They sure have," said Clara. "And we haven't traded up."

"The perils of condo living," added Jason. "You can't choose your neighbors."

"Oh, no." Lisa suspected what was coming. She remembered Roger telling her he'd sold it to his friend.

"The new owner is an obnoxious man who spends weekends here with his girlfriend. She talks on her phone outside the condo, wearing only a towel and high heels. Who does that? I can't imagine what Dorothy would have to say." Clara threw up her hands.

"Oh, I can imagine." Lisa took a bite of chicken, then changed the subject. "So, tell me about Josephine Paulsen."

Clara answered first. "Josephine was lonely. She'd lost her husband soon after moving here, and I think that changed her. I was told she was outgoing and friendly before he died. After her husband passed, she developed a reputation as a busybody, but I think that behavior was her way of getting some attention, maybe even her way of keeping us all safe."

Jason said, "Well, that's one take on her. Here's mine... that woman was a nosy, pain in the butt."

"Jason, that isn't very kind," Clara scowled.

"There is nothing kind to say about her. Ask anyone in this community. They'll all tell you she was a busybody, always peering out her window with those binoculars of hers, snooping on people, and ratting them out to the condo association, even to the police."

Lisa dropped her fork.

CHAPTER 30

Thursday, August 12 - 6:40 a.m.

Having returned to Miami from Stypman Island, Lisa was stepping out of the shower when her phone rang. It was Bruce Kim, Lisa picked up right away. "Hey, Bruce, are you in the lab already? It's not even seven yet."

Bruce spoke quickly, his voice was higher than usual, and Lisa could hear his worry. "The toxicology screen came in on the Paulsen sample. Your hunch was right... she didn't die from heart disease. She was poisoned. We have another murder."

Suddenly cold, Lisa pulled her robe tighter, she stood barefoot on the wet floor of her bathroom. "What was used on her, Bruce?"

"Strychnine. That poor lady had a nasty death."

Lisa's thoughts turned to Dorothy's murder. Which had it worse, she wondered. "I have news for you, too. Last night, I had dinner with some of Dorothy's neighbors, the ones who live below her and had the blood leak into their place."

"That must have been hell for them. Are they okay?"

"No, they're not okay, not yet at least. But get this, Bruce, they told me Josephine Paulsen was a busybody who constantly looked out her windows with binoculars. She had a reputation for reporting things she saw to the condo association and to the police. Her condo is in the same location as Dorothy's, just in the other building. It makes sense she was the one Scarella was after."

"So, she saw something she shouldn't have?"

"Or someone. She had a twin brother. She spoke with him every day. I have his number. I'll reach out to him to see if she told him something that could help."

"Sounds worthwhile. Lisa, you're one hell of a detective, but the bodies are piling up and I'm freaking out. Are you sure you don't want to bring in some reinforcements?"

"Not just yet. We're getting close now. When the time comes, I'll do what is necessary. I promise. Right now, I've got to get to work."

. . .

10:00 a.m.

With her phone on speaker, Lisa crossed her fingers. *C'mon pick up, please pick up.* "Hello," an elderly man answered the call. His voice was shaky and weak.

"I'm trying to reach Benjamin Ganley. This is Lisa Owens... I'm a police detective in Florida following up on his sister's death."

Lisa understood her call would be upsetting. She'd taken the man by surprise. Now he was distressed and stammering. "I'm Josephine's brrr-other."

"Mr. Ganley, I'm so sorry for your loss. There are some additional details I'm trying to run down regarding your sister's passing. I understand from your niece, Rochelle, that you were especially close with your sister. You're twins, right?"

"Yes, that's right," the man answered, his voice tight and high pitched.

Lisa could hear him crying. Her heart broke for him. "I understand this is difficult for you, sir, but could you please tell me if you spoke with your sister the day she died or within a few days prior to her death?"

"We were each other's best friends and talked every day since her husband passed away. I spoke with my sister the day she died; it was our birthday. As far as I know..." he paused briefly to collect himself, "I was the last person to do so."

"What did she tell you about that day?"

"She was happy. She'd just come from lunch with a friend, and that morning someone sent her a bottle of gin for her birthday. Josephine said a pretty young woman delivered it to her door."

Hearing what the man just said, Lisa sat up straighter. "Did she mention who sent her the gift?"

"That was the perplexing thing. She thought it was from me, but I didn't send it; and it wasn't from Rochelle, she doesn't approve of drinking. There was no name on it. Detective, why all the questions? My sister had a heart attack."

"I apologize for upsetting you. Since there wasn't an autopsy, we have to do some additional follow up to close things out."

"Is there something more you need?"

"Mr. Ganley, in your last conversation with her, did your sister mention if she saw anything unusual recently?" Lisa bit her bottom lip and waited for the man's reply.

"My dear sister was always looking out her windows, and if there was anything going on, she saw it. It wasn't her most endearing quality. She told me that two nights earlier she saw two men get off a boat on the beach late at night. I believe Josephine said it was around midnight. She told me they looked as if they were up to no good, dressed in dark clothing and carrying duffle bags. They ran right under her windows. She thought they were doing something illegal, so she called the police."

"Did she see their faces? Did she recognize them?"

"Funny you should ask. She said they looked right up at her. She saw them clearly but didn't recognize them. She even offered to give a description to a police sketch artist. She was a real piece of work, my sister."

"Did she say if anything happened after that?"

"Josephine told me that the police officer she spoke with said he would refer it to the chief of police. If she heard from him, she never said."

"Mr. Ganley, by any chance, do you know if your sister drank the gin she received?"

Benjamin Ganley was silent as he pondered the question. When he answered, Lisa could hear a slight change in his voice as he recalled a happier time.

"She told me she was counting the minutes until five o'clock so she could crack that bottle open. Josephine didn't love much, but by God, she loved a good martini."

CHAPTER 31

Thursday, August 12 - 5:00 p.m.

For most people in Miami it was the end of another long workday but Lisa sat alone in her office, staring at the three computer screens in front of her. Stacks of paperwork were piled everywhere. She'd be there for hours.

Exhausted, elbows on her desk, she held her head in her hands and wondered what she was doing with her life. The note from Dorothy haunted her, as did the promise she'd made to herself... a promise to chase happiness. *I haven't done a thing to make good on it. With the Stypman Island murders, my life is even more out of control.*

Lisa sucked in a deep breath and steeled herself for another long night. She was working several cases, while also overseeing the work of junior detectives. One of just two women in homicide to be promoted to her level of authority, the expectations of her were sometimes overwhelming.

She tried to focus on the screen in front of her. The case was another John Doe, shot point blank in the head and left on the street. She wondered if John Doe's family was out looking for him or if they were even aware their lives were forever changed. *Maybe they don't even care.*

Loud banter outside her office door interrupted her concentration. Five young officers - all guys - were making plans for a basketball game after work and trash-talking.

"You're gonna get your ass kicked, Garcia."

"Says who, you pussy."

"Fifty bucks says we take you losers by at least ten points."

"I'll take a piece of that."

"Don't you guys have anything better to do?" Lisa stood in her doorway, hands on her hips.

"Hey, Lisa, we're just winding up for the day," said Tony Garcia, a rookie detective who Lisa believed showed promise.

"That must be nice, Tony. Last I looked, we had something like nine hundred unsolved murders in Miami. I wonder what the good citizens of our city would say about you guys working banker's hours."

"Jeez, lighten up. We're all working hard... we need to burn off some steam, and from the looks of it, so could you." No sooner had he said it, he regretted it. Tony Garcia saw her coming at him. His pals slinked back to their desks leaving him alone to face his boss.

Lisa stood in front of the rookie and put her face in his. "Don't tell me what I need, Garcia. Get back to work and show me some progress on the Yang case. That kid's parents are still waiting for answers while you're out here fooling around." She raised her voice so the other members of her team could hear, "And if any of you use the word *pussy* in this office again, there'll be trouble. Got it?"

Lisa closed her office door and sat back at her desk. Her male colleagues played by different rules. To earn their respect, she'd learned she had to prove herself to them every day. That meant being smarter, working harder, putting in longer hours, and most importantly, solving cases. Individually, the guys in the department were great. Most were smart, professional, and good to be around. But give them strength in numbers, and their behavior deteriorated. The department could feel like a high school locker room, a place where she wasn't welcome and didn't fit in.

Pacing around her office, Lisa beat herself up. *I blew it with them. It doesn't matter how hard I work; everything just gets worse. I'm miserable. My team thinks I'm a bitch... Worst of all, Dorothy's case is getting cold.*

She stopped pacing and stood looking down at her desk when it struck her. From this vantage point, she could see the computer screens and stacks of files that surrounded her when she was at her desk. *I'm even more pathetic than I thought. I've built walls. Walls of work to keep everyone else out.*

Sinking down into her chair, Lisa surrendered. *God, I miss Dorothy. She'd know what to say right now.* Sitting with her eyes closed, her head cleared. *Dorothy already said what I need to hear. It was in the note she left me. The note I can't stop thinking about.*

Feeling down, Lisa pulled up the website for Women in Law Enforcement. Bernadette Washington, a senior FBI official established the group to foster professional networking among female law enforcement officers. Bernie Washington understood women faced unique challenges in a male-dominated profession with a testosterone-filled culture. An active member of the group, Lisa had received support and mentoring from Bernie herself. Over time, the two became friends and stayed in touch.

As the group grew, local chapters were formed. At Bernie's urging, Lisa became a founding member of the Florida chapter. She spoke at the chapter's meetings and had led a few professional development workshops at conferences.

Scrolling through the chapter's webpage, looking for anything that might offer her some encouragement at a time when she was feeling so overwhelmed, Lisa clicked on the mentorship page where members posted advice or requested it. Near the top of the page, among the most recent postings, was one from an officer whose name Lisa recognized immediately. Kim Witherspoon was looking for a mentor, specifically someone who could help her advance her career.

Wasting no time responding to the post, Lisa explained she was a senior homicide detective in Miami and that she'd be glad to help. She hesitated, then finished her reply.

> By the way, I'm very interested in a murder case on Stypman Island.

Two hours later, Lisa heard back. Kim Witherspoon was eager to connect.

CHAPTER 32

Friday, August 13 - 2:00 p.m.

With each driving about half the distance between Stypman Island and Miami, Lisa and Kim agreed to meet the next day in Boca Raton at The Yellow Parrot, a bar not far off I-95. With her playlist blaring Post Malone's *Circles,* Lisa arrived first and parked near the entrance. She'd chosen black slacks and a white blouse for the meeting. If she was to be a mentor, she figured she should look like one.

The Yellow Parrot was outfitted with tropical decor for the tourist crowd, most of which came to Boca from New York. Lisa went inside and sat at a table next to a window overlooking the parking lot. A few minutes later, a newer model Subaru Outback pulled in and Kim Witherspoon got out wearing jeans and a white tank top. When she entered, Lisa waved her over.

"You must be Kim. It's good to meet you. I'm Lisa."

"You, too. Thanks for reaching out. It means a lot."

"Have you ever been to this place?"

"No, never. Google found it. Gotta love Google."

They both smiled, and the ice was broken. With long drives ahead for both, Kim asked for a Dr. Pepper, Lisa chose black coffee.

"I grew up on this stuff," Kim explained, wrapping her fingers around the glass. "My girlfriend thinks Dr. P is the worst thing ever. She keeps it out of our house, so I grab one when I can."

"No judgment from me, I have a thing for fried pork rinds. My fiancé was addicted to them and got me started."

"I'm into those, too," said Kim laughing. "A bag of rinds, a Dr. Pepper, and I'm a happy woman."

Having found at least one thing in common, the conversation turned serious.

"Lisa, I'm at a loss. The chief who leads our department doesn't like me. I can't seem to do anything right, and he keeps information from me that could help with our cases."

"Well, you wouldn't be the first female officer to have those complaints. Why don't you think he likes you?"

"When I was first hired, he was nice to me. Too nice, if you get what I mean."

Lisa rolled her eyes. "Yeah, I get it. Boy, do I get it."

"Then he found out I'm gay, and things changed fast. I figured if I did good work and put in the hours, he'd get over it, but he hasn't."

"Does he treat you differently from the other officers?"

"I'm the only woman in the department, and if there's something unpleasant to do, something that nobody wants to do, that assignment comes to me. If there's a last-minute call that's going to end up taking all night... guess who's getting that? But what irks me the most is that when he gives credit for doing good work, it always goes to the guys, even if I'm the one who deserves it." Kim threw her hands in the air. "And the names he calls me, 'honey' and 'blondie.' It's degrading. Behind my back, he refers to me as 'the dyke.' It's hard to admit, but it's getting to me. I'm watching my back all the time, and I can't sleep." Pointing under her eyes, Kim added, "See these dark circles?"

Lisa listened, understanding Kim's need to unload. Then she leaned over the table and slid her coffee to the side. "Sounds like he's trying to push you out. I wish I could tell you something that would make this go away, but we both know it doesn't work like that. Kim, you've got to push back. Discrimination is illegal, and the law is on your side but there are ways to stand up for yourself that work better than others. I have some suggestions that can help. Before we get into all that, those dark circles you pointed out are an easy fix. Here's something I discovered years ago." She pulled a tube of concealer from her bag and handed it to Kim. "I don't sleep much either. This stuff helps."

"Thanks, but I rarely use makeup."

"Me, neither. It's not makeup, its camouflage. The first rule when dealing with an adversary is to never let him know he's getting to you." She handed the tube to Kim. "Now, onto more important things. If you'd like, I can hook you up with a networking group for gay cops, a pretty cool police captain in Orlando runs it."

Kim's mouth fell open. "I had no idea there was a group for gay cops in the 'don't say gay state.' Who would have thought?"

"Kim, can I ask you a personal question?"

"Sure."

"Are you happy? I mean everything considered; work, personal life, just life in general."

As she pondered the question, a tiny smile came to Kim's face, the stress that had been there just a second ago seemed to melt away. "Yeah, I think I am. I'm with someone I love, and we live on a beautiful island. Heck, who gets to do that, right? I'm living my truth, and my parents and friends haven't just accepted me, we're closer than ever."

"That's so great to hear." Lisa's eyes watered. "Never let go of the people in your life who make you happy. They'll get you through the tough parts. Like dealing with a bad boss."

"That's good advice, but I see tears. Everything okay?"

"Oh, sorry about that. I hardly ever cry, but lately, it seems I'm making up for lost time. To be honest, the advice isn't mine. It was recently given to me, and I suck at following it, but for the first time, in a very long time, I might be ready to."

"I thought you said you're engaged to the guy who got you into pork rinds?"

"I *was* engaged. His name was Scott, and he was killed shortly after he proposed. That was a while ago."

"I'm so sorry."

"He was shot. The police said it was a robbery. The investigation was bungled, and the cops tried to cover up their mistakes. No one was ever arrested. There are a lot of unanswered questions. He was a congressional aide, and it may have been political."

"Not knowing, that's got to be horrible for you."

"It haunts me every day, and it's why I became a cop. I thought if I worked hard enough, I could prevent the same thing from happening to other people. Catching killers was supposed to bring meaning to Scott's death, but somehow it hasn't quite worked out that way."

"Can I tell you something else that's personal?" Kim asked.

Lisa wiped her face with the back of her hand. "Sure, go ahead."

"When I first came out to my family, I had an unexpected conversation with my Meemaw. We lived in Dunnellon, real crackers... everyone had a Meemaw there." Kim opened her hands, palms up as if to apologize.

"Anyway, she was a tough old bird who had strong opinions about everything. I was afraid to come out to her and thought she'd turn me away. When I did, she told me a story. She said she had a son I'd never heard anyone in our family talk about. She told me he'd taken his own life when he was seventeen. Suicide was considered something to be ashamed of back then, and the family kept it quiet. She said the pain of losing him stayed with her and she cried every day." Kim took a sip of her soda then leaned across the table toward Lisa.

"She told me things changed for her when I was born, and that the love she felt for me saved her. Here's the thing, Lisa, she told me love is the only thing that matters, that God wants us all to be happy and to find love. She said it was her greatest wish for me."

"That's so sweet. Your Meemaw was way ahead of her time." Lisa wiped her eyes.

"That woman knew what she was talking about. She told me she thought her son, my uncle Edson, was gay and that might have been the reason he took his life. She wanted me to know I was loved, no matter what. They say grieving is the last act of love you can give someone. You'll never replace Scott, but the only way to fix a broken heart is to open yourself up to new love." Kim reached across the table and grasped Lisa's hand.

Lisa smiled a broken smile, her tear-filled eyes conveying gratitude for the empathy this stranger had shown her. She sat up in her chair and shook off her emotions. "This conversation has become about me, but I came here to help you. I have some suggestions you might want to try."

They spent the next hour talking through Kim's situation before the conversation turned to Dorothy's murder. "Kim, can I ask you a few things in confidence... about the murder that took place on Stypman Island? I know you were first on the scene."

"I was first on the scene, my boss took me off the case that same day. Why the interest?"

Lisa took a few minutes to explain her relationship with Dorothy Jensen and her visit to Dorothy's condo after the murder. Without disclosing more than she needed to, she said, "I know who Dorothy's killer is, and I know she was murdered accidentally. I think the intended victim lived in the building next door. There have been two recent deaths there. Can you tell me anything about those?"

Kim sat up straight in her chair, rattled by what she'd just heard. "Lisa, did I just hear you right?"

"I'm afraid you did."

Flummoxed by Lisa's revelation, Kim did her best to answer. "The deceased women in the next building were around the same age as your friend. But you've got to be wrong about this. One died of a heart attack, the other slipped in the shower, I investigated that one myself. What in tarnation would make you think they might have been the intended victims?"

"I think one of them saw something she shouldn't have, and the other might have been a mistake, just like my friend. Is there anything you can share with me that might be helpful?"

"As I just said, I was sent to do the write up on the death in the pool bathroom, it was typical slip and fall. That poor woman hit the back of her head on the floor. It's the worst way to fall."

"Kim, my forensics guy in Miami pulled up that file. The victim hit her head twice, once much harder than would be expected given the type of fall and the victim's size. In addition, the photographs in your report show the victim's flip-flops had been sanded smooth so they would easily slip on a wet floor."

Kim's mouth dropped open as Lisa continued. "Thinking back, was there anything about the scene in that bathroom that rang alarms? Anything that didn't add up?"

Kim composed herself and took her time before responding. "Not really. The victim swam in the pool every morning and showered afterward. That was confirmed by the other residents. The only thing that didn't make sense to us was that the bathroom floor was spotless except for a few footprints. That seemed strange because the cleaning crew hadn't been there yet. When I pointed that out to River, he was the other officer with me, he agreed. The cleaners showed up while we were doing the investigation. They confirmed they clean the bathrooms each day, around ten in the morning. The pool area is next to the beach, so you'd think there'd be sand on the floor and the regular dirt from foot traffic. But you could have eaten off that floor, Lisa. I know because we took a lot of time examining it. If you check the photographs, you'll see I'm right."

"You're smart to have noticed that. That's good work, my forensics guy missed that, and he rarely misses anything. Was there anything unique about the footprints?"

"No, not really. They were from athletic shoes, men's size eleven-and-a-half."

"Well, that's something, men's footprints in a women's bathroom, and those are some pretty large feet. What do you know about the other death, Josephine Paulsen?"

"I had nothing to do with that. Mrs. Paulsen was an annoyance to say the least. She was always calling to report all kinds of things. I've taken calls from her myself. Anyway, the chief was first on the scene there. He handled just about all of it himself. Kept us out of it."

"Does he normally do that?" Her suspicion growing, Lisa sat back in her chair.

"What do you mean?"

"Handle natural cause of death cases himself?"

"No, he doesn't go near them, but for some reason, he'd been calling her and checked in on her after he couldn't reach her by phone. He's the one who found her body."

"Do you know if Mrs. Paulsen called in to report something the night Dorothy Jensen was killed?"

"I'm not sure, but there's an activity log I can check."

"That would be a big help, but you need to be very careful. Your boss might be involved somehow. I can't share everything just yet, but as I said before, I have good reason to believe Josephine Paulsen was the intended victim the night Dorothy Jensen was murdered. Her condo is in the same location as Dorothy's but in the other building. As you pointed out, Mrs. Paulsen was known for being a busybody, keeping an eye on things and all that. I think she saw something she shouldn't have and somebody came to take her out before she could talk. That person went to the wrong building and killed Dorothy. For some reason, poor Mary Dillard got mixed up in it."

"Holy shit, if that's true, then what you're telling me is the killer murdered Dorothy, set up Mary Dillard's fall, and came back to murder Josephine Paulsen. But how could that be? Mrs. Paulsen died of a heart attack."

"There's more I haven't told you."

Kim leaned across the table. "I understand this sounds horrible, but please tell me you think my asshole boss killed her."

"I can't say that's the case, but things sure aren't adding up."

"Well, if Mrs. Paulsen was killed because of something she saw, why was Mary Dillard killed? I mean, who the hell would sand off an old lady's flip-flops, so she'd fall?"

"I have no idea, but it seems like something Dorothy's killer would do; he was that type. You know, the more twisted the killing, the better."

"You're right about that. I saw what he did to your friend. I'll never forget it."

"Or..." Lisa tilted her head and squinted her eyes.

"Or what?"

"Or, we have two killers."

"What?" Kim went pale. "Two killers? Why would you think that?"

"Because that's what I do. I consider all the possibilities. We can't rule anything out - not yet."

"Do you have anyone working with you on this? If it's okay, I'd like to help. I think I can learn a lot from you." Kim moved forward and sat on the edge of her seat.

Lisa hesitated. *This is it,* she thought. *Either I trust her or go it alone. She's inexperienced, but she's smart, and the look on her face when I told her about Mary Dillard, she cares about getting things right.*

"Kim, this could get dangerous. I don't want to bring you into it unless you're sure it's what you want."

"I'm sure, Lisa, and I promise you can count on me. I won't let you down."

Breaking the log jam that had been in her way for years, Lisa found the courage to reach across the table and shake Kim's outstretched hand. "To be honest, I could use some help. If you're game, I'd be glad to have you with me. The only condition is that we don't share what we're up to with anyone, not even your girlfriend."

"Agreed. Partners?" Kim extended her hand. Lisa shook it.

"One other thing, we need to keep our communications limited to the phone. No email, no texts."

Lisa put ten dollars on the table for the drinks, and they made their way out of the Yellow Parrot. Before getting into her car, she asked, "Any chance I can get into Josephine Paulsen's condominium to take a look around?"

"The police work is wrapped up, and I doubt there's anyone there, but the place is locked."

Lisa raised her eyebrows and smiled at Kim, "Well, that's never stopped me."

CHAPTER 33

Friday, August 13 - 7:30 p.m.

Upon returning to Stypman Island, Kim showered and dressed in her uniform. She was working the night shift and was due at the station in half an hour.

Simone stretched out on the bed with her head propped up on a pillow, a thick textbook rested on her lap. "Girl, you look way too good in that uniform, come over here and arrest me. I surrender."

Kim brushed off the comment without responding and applied the concealer from Lisa.

"Babe! You're using makeup now? Are you stepping out on me? You have a thing for Stewie, right?"

Kim smiled. "Yeah, he's just my type. Do you have any idea how smart you were to choose a career working with animals instead of people?"

Simone grinned back at her. "It's your boss again. He's why you've been in such a funk, right?"

"He's part of it." Kim checked her watch. "I've got to get going. Someone I admire told me that to get ahead in this boys' club, I need to team up with the good guys, outsmart the assholes, and outwork all of them."

"There you go," said Simone. "Great advice, you'll be running that police department before too long."

"That's the idea." Kim blew Simone a kiss and walked out the door.

· · ·

The activity log contained no entries for the night of Dorothy Jensen's murder. Kim checked the staff schedule. *Looks like River and Stewie were on duty that night...*

"Hands up, Kimbolina!" Kim jumped from her chair when the barrel of a gun touched the back of her head. It was Stewie Williamson, hired by the chief as a favor to his father, a county commissioner whose influence was always for sale and useful at election time. Stewie was twenty-one and wanted to be a cop because he liked guns. He'd been warned that an itchy trigger finger would get him in trouble one day but Stewie hadn't gotten the message.

"You're such a fucking weirdo, Stewie! Put the damned gun away." Already jumpy, Kim was pissed. *How the hell did this jerk get hired?*

"Scared ya, didn't I? Anyway, Kimbo, I'm out of here. River's covering my shift tonight."

"Too bad for me, I guess. Have a nice night, Stewie. Go play in traffic." Relieved to be rid of him, Kim sat back at her desk.

River had been on the force for two years. Quiet and introverted, he did his job without complaint. Three-quarters Seminole and proud of his heritage, River was tall and lean with neatly trimmed black hair and dark eyes that sparkled when he smiled.

Although they weren't close friends, he'd confided in Kim that he was just biding his time on Stypman Island while pursuing his dream of working with the Fish and Wildlife Conservation Commission. He wanted to help enforce the laws regarding fish and wildlife resources, something he was passionate about. Those jobs weren't easy to come by, and a strong recommendation from the chief would be important.

After some time had passed and the two officers had settled into their shift, Kim posed the question she'd been waiting to ask. "River, remember that busybody, Josephine Paulsen who was always calling here?"

"Sure, she just died. The chief found her body."

"Do you remember if she called in to report something just before that murder happened at Coquina Reef?"

River thought about it for a minute, then replied, "Yeah, she did. I took the call. It was probably the only call she ever made here that sounded like something real. She said she saw two guys jump off a boat and onto the beach in the middle of the night. She saw them run through her condo complex carrying duffle bags."

"That does sound like something. Did we follow up on it?"

"I'm not sure. I turned it over to the boss. Who knows what happened after that... you know what he's like."

"I sure do. Did Mrs. Paulsen say if she got a look at the guys? Was she using those damned binoculars like she always does?"

"She sure did and you're right, that lady gave those binoculars a work out. She actually wanted to come in and have a police artist draw the faces she saw. Can you believe that? What a character... may she rest in peace."

"Is that in your report?"

"Every word. Here, check it out." River pulled up the computer file containing incident reports for the month on his screen. After a moment, he said, "That's funny. It isn't here."

"What about the paper backup files?" suggested Kim.

River leaned over and pulled open a file drawer. He reached for a file folder containing incident reports for the month and thumbed through them. Perplexed, he looked over at Kim. "It's not here. I don't know what's going on, but I'll get the blame for that report being missing. Shit, I can't afford that. So why the interest, Kim?"

"Nothing really, just something Stewie mentioned that made me think of it, that's all."

Before leaving at the end of his shift, River left a note on Chief Jackson's desk:

Hey boss, I was looking for the report I wrote about Josephine Paulsen's last call to us before she died. It isn't on the computer, and the paper file is missing. Any idea what happened to it?

Thanks, River

CHAPTER 34

Saturday, August 14 - 8:00 a.m.

After working the night shift with Kim, River headed to his tiny apartment just off the island. He planned to grab a few hours of sleep and spend the afternoon fishing, followed by burgers and beer with his buddies. His phone rang and seeing it was his boss, he groaned, "Please don't call me back in."

"Hey, Whitefeather, it's the chief."

"Hello, sir. How are you?"

"Couldn't be better. Enjoying your day off?"

"I'm heading out to fish in a while. What can I do for you, sir?"

"Well, the question is what have I done for you?"

River wrinkled up his face, "Um, what's that?"

"You'll be happy to know that with my strong recommendation, effective today, you're employed at the FWC."

"You're kidding! Chief, are you serious?" River couldn't believe it, it had to be a joke. Frowning, he waited for the other shoe to drop.

"I sure am. I wouldn't kid you about something I know is so important to you."

"I didn't realize you were even aware of my interest in the FWC."

"Well, I am, kid. So, here's the thing. You no longer work here on Stypman Island. The new position is effective immediately. You need to report to FWC headquarters in Tallahassee first thing tomorrow for processing and training. Sorry about the last-minute notice, but this came from out of the blue. FWC is sending you an email with the necessary information."

Blown away by the unexpected news, River stammered, "I-I-I don't know what to say, sir. I've wanted this my whole life. Thank you so much."

"My pleasure, kid. The fish will have to wait; Tallahassee is a long drive from here. Get packed and gone. I'll tell everyone at the station you said goodbye. Make us proud."

"I sure will. Thanks again, Chief."

. . .

6:30 p.m.
Kim called Lisa and filled her in on the previous night at the police station.

"So, there were no copies of Whitefeather's report?"

"None," said Kim, "And there's more. This morning the chief sent out an announcement saying River is gone. He got his dream job with the Fish and Wildlife Commission. His department phone number and email are already disconnected. I don't have any way to reach him."

"Sorry for the pun but that sounds a little fishy. River might be involved in this. It could be the reason for his disappearing act."

"River? No way, Lisa. He's a total boy scout. He'd be the last one to do anything that crossed the line."

"Well this wouldn't be the first time a good cop was compromised so let's put him on the list of people to check out. Is the chief aware that you and River were looking for that report?"

"At the end of the shift, River left him a note asking about it.

"That could explain River's disappearance. I'm more and more concerned about your boss. You need to be extra careful. If he's up to something, and thinks you're onto him, he'll be after you." Lisa let her message sink in before continuing. "Kim, do you think any of the other officers in your department could be involved in this? Are any of them, you know, *shady*?"

Kim thought hard about the question. "There are only three now that River is gone. Stewie is as weird as they come, but I wouldn't call him shady. Bill Widley is as good a cop as you'll ever find, and Dan, well, he seems okay, too. So... no. If someone is shady, it's the chief."

"I'm all but certain he's involved in Josephine Paulsen's death, so stay away from that and let me handle it. He doesn't know about me yet. We still have a lot of questions about Mary Dillard's death. Do you think you can make progress with that?"

"Where do you want me to begin?"

"Well, I'd be looking for a guy who wears size eleven-and-a-half shoes. I'll check to see if the guy who killed Dorothy Jensen had big feet. You check the chief's. If neither of them match that shoe size, you can investigate other possibilities."

"Like what?"

"More than one killer. Look for a motive. There's a reason somebody wanted her dead."

CHAPTER 35

Saturday, August 14 - 7:00 p.m.

Judy Clofine was in a good mood. A realtor specializing in condominium sales, her sales pitch was printed on the back of her business card: "I've been in every condominium on Stypman Island!" The statement wasn't exactly true, but over the years, she'd been in more than her share of condos, even when the owners of those properties hadn't given her permission to be there.

About to close a sale that would net her a fat commission, she'd bought a new outfit earlier in the day to reward herself and was looking forward to showing it off tonight. She'd just hopped out of the sack with her boyfriend, Viktor Morosov. A pre-dinner quickie. Viktor had been on his game and the sex had been satisfying. Judy had put out too, she owed him that much given what he'd recently done for her. They hadn't talked about it since it happened and probably never would. Judy had blocked it out of her mind. It was like it had never happened at all.

Phone in hand, she scanned the death notices for Stypman Island, a regular practice of hers. Seeing a name she recognized, she called to Viktor, who was stepping out of the shower. "Things are going my way. I can't believe my luck, another condo with a killer ocean view just became available at Coquina Reef, the third one this month. That *never* happens."

Victor walked from the bathroom naked, drying his hair with a bath towel. "If it's already on the market, you'd better hustle. The ones with the ocean views, go fast."

Judy stood in front of him, she stroked his chest hair with her index finger. "I didn't say it's on the market, I said it just became available. Josephine Paulsen died. Remember her?"

"I remember her alright. I hated that bitch. She fired me."

Viktor owned and operated Paradise Cleaning and Home Care Services. A business Judy had helped him build by referring her real estate clients to him without disclosing their relationship and her conflict of interest.

"To be fair, didn't she catch you stealing something of hers?" Judy raised her brows and her mouth curled into a sly smile.

"So what? I still hated her. Nosey bitch that she was."

"Well, you're gonna love her when I scoop up another big commission. This one's ripe for the taking. It's mine. I'm not missing another one." Judy kissed Viktor's mouth. Turning toward the bathroom, she looked back. "Pour us a drink baby, I won't be too long."

As Judy headed to the shower, her phone buzzed, and she answered, "This is Judy Clofine, how may I help you?"

"Ms. Clofine," said a female voice. "This is Carol from Mercury Mortgage Corporation. We haven't received a payment from you in over three months. I'm calling to see if there is a problem. Our records show that we've contacted you about this several times before."

Fuck yes, Carol. The problem is that I should never have picked up. "I can't take this call right now. You'll have to try again at another time." Judy ended the call without waiting for a response and turned on the shower.

Judy had been doing well as a top producing real estate agent at Beach House Realty, a job she'd held for almost two decades. That changed after she was summarily fired. The company discovered she'd been lying to clients and enforced a non-compete agreement, blocking her from doing business with anyone on the customer lists she'd developed while in their employ. Judy tried fighting the agreement in court. Racking up six-figures in legal fees, she lost the battle. Now she was broke, and behind on her bills.

Deciding she'd had enough of working for someone else, she opened her own agency: Judy Clofine Real Estate, Inc. With no savings and mounting bills, she was forced to take a two-hundred-fifty-thousand-dollar loan from the only lender that would give her one, the Bratva, a Russian mafia organization she knew little about. Her Bratva contact was a man she knew as Zoran. If Zoran wanted to see her, she met him in the backroom of a tiny cafe in Ft. Meyers almost four hours away. Judy's loan payments were made electronically to an untraceable account. If her payment was late, Zoran called and reminded her of her obligations to him, insisting she make the drive to Ft. Meyers. Each time she met with him, Judy became increasingly frightened of Zoran, and that was the idea. With a thirty percent compounding interest rate, her loan ballooned out of control. Her financial problems made her anxious and, when she felt like that, Judy went shopping, which made her money problems even worse.

Years ago, when she was starting out, Judy had provided great service to her clients, exceeding their expectations. Now, her work habits were very different and those early clients were in their eighties and nineties. As they passed on, their heirs, remembering their parents' experience with Judy, called her for help with the sale of the newly empty property.

Keeping a list of clients cultivated in her early years, Judy checked in with them on a *social basis* endearing her further and keeping her name top of mind. That way, when the time came, the call was initiated by the client's family rendering Judy's non-compete agreement inapplicable. As Judy saw it, you never knew who was about to die and become her next meal ticket.

Tired of working hard, Judy now employed a system to ensure the sales that came her way were quick and easy. She convinced sellers to underprice their property by lying about market conditions and property values. Then, she turned those condos over to a list of buyers she had previously lined up by lying to them about properties not yet on the market but about to become available. Sales happened faster, and Judy received commission on both ends of the transaction, making for a nice return with the least amount of work. The only flaw in her system is that Judy had to wait until condos became available. With Zoran breathing down her neck in Ft. Meyers, the waiting had become a problem.

Freshly showered and dressed, Judy admired herself in the full-length mirror mounted on the center wall of her walk-in closet. She adjusted a strand of dyed blonde hair that had fallen from the pile pinned up on her head. Turning to the side to admire her figure, Judy liked what she saw. "Lookin' good, girl," she said to her reflection. "Fifty-four, no one would guess."

Viktor waited for her in the living room. Dressed in a black silk shirt, open to the chest and creased ivory trousers, he was nursing a tumbler of ice-cold Russian vodka. When he saw Judy, his eyes widened. "Wow, baby, you look hot! Is that *another* new dress?" he asked, noticing the bright pink strapless number that hugged her thin body in all the right places.

"New shoes, too!" Judy pointed toward the shiny gold sandals on her feet. "They're Stuart Weitzman, I couldn't pass them up."

Before heading out to dinner, the couple were enjoying cocktails together. They sat across from each other in the modern style living room, each looking at the other, the way two people do after sex. Viktor handed Judy a flute of Veuve Clicquot, her new favorite champagne. The characters in a novel she'd recently read were drinking it. Now, she insisted on doing the same.

"So, how'd you miss it, babe? It's unlike you," asked Viktor. He took a sip of his drink and ran his tongue over his lips.

"Miss what?"

"The other sale at Coquina Reef. You said there were three, and that you missed one."

"Oh, that," Judy rolled her eyes and a look of disgust crossed her face. "Some idiot named Roger Jensen let it go for a song; it never even hit the market. That's not going to happen again." Judy reached for the bottle and poured herself more champagne. "I'm going over to the Paulsen place tomorrow to see what shape it's in. You kept a copy of her keys, didn't you?"

"Yeah, they should be with all the others."

"Let's hope they still work. I've got buyers lined up who'll do an all-cash deal with a quick close and a decent sales price. I'll get the listing. This is a sure thing, baby."

Viktor poured himself another drink and anxiously fingered his glass having heard this from her before. Judy's real estate deals were never a sure thing. Viktor had used his Russian connections to introduce her to the Bratva. At the time, she was confident she'd be able to repay the loan with no problem. Now that wasn't looking so likely.

"Baby, I love the outfit, I really do, but we've got to cut back on expenses. That loan is due and we need that commission you're about to bank just to pay the next installment. These people, they don't play around. This is getting fucking dangerous, babe. I can't protect you."

"Stop worrying. Zoran will get his damned money." She tossed back another glassful. "I'll snap some photos at the Paulsen condo tomorrow and send them to my buyers. I'll have it under contract before anyone's the wiser. It's got a great view and if it's half as nice as I think it is, I can unload it for a *very* good price." Judy raised her hand and rubbed her thumb over the tip of her index and middle fingers. "The commission will be more than enough to keep your Russian friends off our backs." She downed her champagne. "Let's go eat. I want a lobster for dinner and you for dessert."

. . .

Sunday, August 15 - 4:30 p.m.
After working most of the day, Lisa made another trip to Stypman Island. It was late afternoon by the time she arrived at Coquina Reef. To avoid running into other people, she climbed the stairs to the fourth floor and easily located Josephine Paulsen's condo. At this time of day, the temperature outside was at its hottest, and, thanks to a tropical downpour that had lasted all of five minutes, the humidity had climbed way up.

Lisa made fast work of the old lock on the front door and bolted it after entering. The apartment was immaculately clean, its layout was the same as Dorothy's, but where Dorothy's home had been warm and inviting, this place seemed cold and sterile with its bright white walls and modern furnishings. Shiny white marble covered the floor and large artificial palms provided most of the color in the room but for a few oversized abstract paintings.

Her eyes stopping on a small, framed photograph of Josephine and her husband in happier times, Lisa whispered, "Okay, Josephine, let's see if I can figure out what happened to you." Noting the chair facing the ocean, she added, "And that must be where you died."

Lisa opened the kit she'd brought with her and took out a flashlight with a high-powered magnification device attached. She began the process of methodically examining the tabletops, counters, and floors. She walked toward a bookshelf and saw something she knew to be important. Something that had played a part in Josephine's murder and Dorothy's too. *There they are.* A pair of binoculars stood on one of the shelves.

Scanning the floor with the flashlight, she found a sliver of broken glass in a corner of the living room. Using tweezers, she picked it up and placed it in an evidence bag. Continuing the process, she discovered more tiny shards scattered about and a piece of broken glass about the size of her fingernail. She collected all of it. As she was sealing the evidence bags, the sound of a key turning the lock on the front door caught her attention.

Clicking off her flashlight, she ducked down and out of sight, waiting to see who was entering. The door opened, and a woman walked in.

"This is perfect, the kitchen and main rooms are in great shape, and I just love the polished marble on the floors. Now let's see if the bathrooms have been updated." The woman was talking to herself as if she were making a mental checklist and speaking loud enough for Lisa to hear her every word. "This will go for top price, especially if I can get them to throw the furniture in with the deal." She took her phone from her large purse and started snapping photos.

"Hello," said Lisa, surprising the woman. "I'm Detective Owens. Who might you be?"

"I-I-I'm Judy Clofine," she stammered, obviously startled. "I didn't know anyone was here. I'm a realtor," she added, regaining her composure.

"Ms. Clofine. Why are you here?"

"I came to see the property, so I can sell it."

"Have you been contracted to do that?"

"Well, not yet, but I expect to be."

"May I ask how you came to have the key to this unit?"

"Oh?" Judy looked at her right hand and seemed shocked to see she was holding the key. Recovering quickly, she added, "A friend of the owner lent it to me."

"Could you please give me the name of this friend?"

"His name is Viktor Morosov, he worked for Mrs. Paulsen."

"Until the owner of this property retains you as their realtor, you are trespassing. Please leave now and don't return until your situation changes and you have a contract with the owner."

"I'll go, thank you, Detective."

Relieved the intruder was a realtor and not Chief Jackson, Lisa let out an exasperated sigh. *What people won't do to make a buck.* Deciding she'd look into them later; she added the names Judy Clofine and Viktor Morosov to her notes with a reference that Viktor had worked for Josephine. Then she got back to work, looking for anything that might shed light on Josephine's death.

Checking the kitchen cabinets, Lisa whispered, "This woman wasn't just nosey, she was anal. Everything is immaculate and in its place." She opened the shiny white cabinets in the kitchen, taking mental stock of their contents. "Six of everything, plates, glasses, bowls. Except for the martini glasses, there are five of those. The broken bits have got to be from the missing glass. A million bucks says we'll find traces of strychnine on them."

Recalling her conversation with Josephine's brother, Lisa looked in a liquor cabinet. *Hmm...no gin. The bottle she received as a birthday gift isn't here; there's no way she could have finished it all.*

Having seen enough, Lisa prepared to leave and looked back at the chair where Josephine Paulsen had met her end. "I know what happened, Josephine. You saw what you weren't meant to see. They poisoned you to keep you quiet, and Chief Jackson did a clean-up job to cover up the truth. There's only one question. Who wanted you dead?"

CHAPTER 36

Monday, August 16 - 12:00 p.m.

Wanting to impress Lisa, Kim was doing her best with the Dillard case. She'd been able to check the chief's shoe size by measuring a footprint, it was a size nine. She was disappointed. A text message from Lisa arrived later in the afternoon. It read: 'Mine didn't have big feet - size eight and a half.'

After spending hours running into dead ends, Kim couldn't find anyone who had any sort of motive to want Mary Dillard dead. Unsure where to look next, she checked with the county clerk's office to see if the deceased woman had left a will. Finding one, she learned the sole beneficiary of Mary Dillard's estate was an organization called the Briarcliff Literary Society located in Santa Monica, California. Without other leads, she took the long shot and dialed the number for the literary society. A woman answered and identified herself as Ethel O'Brien. Kim introduced herself, explaining she was a police officer in Florida calling about a recently deceased woman named Mary Dillard.

"Well, how might I help you?" asked Ethel O'Brien in a sweet voice with a slight Irish brogue. Kim guessed she was an older woman.

"Mrs. O'Brien, with your permission, I'm going to tape this conversation. It's easier to listen if I don't have to take notes. Would that be okay?"

"Certainly, dear. I suppose that would be alright."

"Mrs. O'Brien, did you or someone at the Briarcliff Literary Society know Mary Dillard?"

"I've been the head of the society for a number of years and I've had quite a few telephone conversations with Miss Dillard. She'd call once or twice each year, that is until the poor dear began having hearing problems. After that, she didn't enjoy talking on the telephone any longer."

"What can you tell me about her?"

"Well, I came to know her reasonably well and can tell you she and her sister, as I recall her name was Olive, continued to live in their family home in the town of Meriden, Connecticut when their parents passed away. You see, Officer, neither of the two ever married."

Kim couldn't be certain, but she picked up on what she thought might be an insinuation that the sisters were gay. *I guess you did know Mary Dillard reasonably well...*

"The sisters owned and operated an office supply and stationery business their father had started and passed on to them. When they sold the business, they moved to Stypman Island." Ethel O'Brien cleared her throat and continued. "With no other family, it was quite hard on Mary when poor Olive died after a battle with ovarian cancer. I heard from her a little more often during that time."

"So, she's lived alone ever since? Did she tell you anything about how she spent her days or who she spent time with?"

"From what I could gather, there isn't much to know. Mary felt it important to remain in good physical condition. To stay that way, she made a habit of climbing the stairs to her condominium on most days instead of taking the elevator and she religiously swam laps in the pool each morning. She kept to herself and was an avid reader of biographies. Like many of our members, learning from the life journeys of those who led remarkable lives was of great interest to her. She told me that when she reflected upon it, she'd concluded her own life had been rather unremarkable. Isn't that just the saddest thing?"

"That is sad, what else can you tell me, Mrs. O'Brien?"

"Miss Dillard was among our most loyal contributors. With her very first contribution, she sent the society a lovely note saying that she attributed her love of reading to us."

"Why was that?"

"Years ago, our organization sent a small parcel of biographies to Miss Dillard's local library, and one of those books was about Mary, Queen of

Scots. Miss Dillard chose to read that book because she shared the same first name and became a devotee of all kinds of biographies from that point on. She added in her note that books had proven to be her most reliable friend. I found that a wee bit sad as well. She asked that we use her contribution to do for others what we'd done for her. Since then, she sent us a small amount of money every month. She loved her biographies... she certainly did."

Not wanting to alarm the woman she was questioning, Kim thought hard about what she'd just heard and considered the best way to position her next question. "Have you been contacted by anyone regarding Mary Dillard's gift of her estate to your organization?"

"Why, yes, I have. There have been two parties as of this point. Your call would make it three. A few days after her death, we had a phone call from Miss Dillard's attorney, an amiable woman. Have you spoken with her yet?"

"Yes, I have, she directed me to you."

"Well, then you know this already. She called to inform us Mary had passed away and that she'd named our society as the beneficiary of her estate. As you might imagine, I was most surprised to learn that bit of news."

"Who was the second party you've heard from?" asked Kim.

"That same day, a lady called me. A real estate agent who said she had a buyer for the Dillard property, one who could take it off our hands and for a good price."

"Are you sure this lady called you the very same day?" Alarm bells sounded in Kim's head.

"Yes, I'm quite certain of it."

"Mrs. O'Brien, could you please tell me the name of this real estate agent?"

"I have it here on my desk. Her name is Judy Clofine."

"Did the realtor say how she knew your organization was the beneficiary of Miss Dillard's estate?"

"No, she said nothing about that, and I must say, I found it a bit curious. After all, we'd just had that news a few hours earlier. It was rather shocking to learn Ms. Clofine already had a buyer interested in the property. I suppose news must travel fast on a small island, but poor Miss Dillard wasn't yet cold in her grave. God rest her soul."

"Mrs. O'Brien, could you please tell me if you agreed to sell Miss Dillard's property to Judy Clofine's client?"

"Despite our reservations about the timing of Ms. Clofine's call, we agreed to sell. You see, we're just a small group of people who enjoy reading. The last thing we'd ever need or want is responsibility for managing a property on the other side of the country. Glory be, the sale is scheduled to close next week."

"Would you mind sending me a copy of the sales contract?"

"I suppose I can do that. It's here in my email. I'll forward it to you if you'll kindly give me your email address."

"Mrs. O'Brien, I just have one last question. What will the society do with the proceeds of Mary Dillard's estate?"

"Well, we had quite a long chat about that. We decided those funds will be best used to sponsor scholarships for young people aspiring to teach reading at the elementary school level in underserved areas. We thought Miss Dillard would certainly approve of that."

"That's a lovely idea," said Kim, "and a wonderful tribute to Miss Dillard."

. . .

As promised, the sales contract arrived in Kim's inbox. She read it to herself out loud, making notes of the key details. "Okay, the buyers are Arthur and Reba Rose Lawson. They're in St. Louis and the sales price is $1,500,000." Kim read on. "Judy Clofine is the agent of record for both the buyer and the seller. The literary society pays six percent commission. That's ninety grand. Somebody might kill an old lady for that."

Kim placed a call to the Lawsons in St. Louis. After explaining she was interested in their purchase of a condominium on Stypman Island, she hit pay dirt. "That Judy Clofine," said Reba Rose Lawson, "she's really something."

"Why is that?" asked Kim.

"She told me she had a listing coming on the market that was just perfect for us, and she did."

"Did she describe the condo; I mean which one it was?"

"She did better than that, she sent us photographs. She promised an oceanfront unit with a spectacular view and she delivered."

Kim couldn't believe what she was hearing. "Mrs. Lawson, do you recall when she sent those photographs to you?"

"It was last month, about five weeks ago. I remember because I was in the salon waiting for a manicure. I have my nails done on the first Saturday of every month. Anyway, while I was waiting, I figured I'd call Judy to tell her I was losing confidence in her abilities. You know, ruin her day." Reba Rose chuckled at her comment. "My husband, Arthur, and I have been ready to leave Missouri for quite a while now but Judy hadn't been able to find us an acceptable property. I was *very* annoyed with her. The idea of another winter in St. Louis wasn't wearing well on us, so I called to tell her I'd be working with another realtor. After I said that, she said she had just the right place in mind."

"And that was five weeks ago? You're certain of that?"

"Yes, that's correct. Is there a problem, Officer?"

"No, Mrs. Lawson, not at this time."

CHAPTER 37

Monday, August 16 - 7:00 p.m.

"What's the name of the real estate person?" asked Lisa, surprised at what she'd just heard. Kim had called to debrief her on the conversations she'd had with Ethel O'Brien and Reba Rose Lawson.

"Judy Clofine."

"You've got to be kidding me."

"No, her name is Judy Clofine. Do you know her?"

"I just met that woman!" Lisa explained what had transpired in Josephine Paulsen's condominium.

"Clofine's dirty. She's guilty of something, I'm sure of it," said Kim.

Lisa could hear the confidence; Kim Witherspoon was blossoming. Unlike the first time they'd met, Kim's voice was urgent and fiery. Lisa could tell she was excited and feeling the rush that came when the pieces of an investigation began falling into place.

"You're onto something, Kim. Clofine might not be the killer, but she could the one behind all this." Lisa leaned back in her chair, considering the different possibilities. "We already know she didn't kill Dorothy, someone else confessed to that, but Clofine might have contracted the kill."

"What about Mary Dillard?"

"Hear me out, Kim. I saw Clofine. She's a bleached blonde with a ridiculously huge boob job and barely a muscle in her very skinny, middle-aged body. There's no way she was capable of murdering Mary Dillard. She would have had to lift the victim up in order to slam her head on the floor with enough force to cause the kind of damage that was done. If she's behind this, she had help. The guy who killed Dorothy sure fits the bill but his footprints don't match."

"And Mrs. Paulsen, how do we explain that?"

"This whole thing could be about money. You know, greedy people selling the homes of elderly people out from under them."

"Okay, but how's the chief involved?"

"Depending on how much money is involved, he could be playing a part in covering up the tracks and keeping a lid on things. He seems to be doing that with Dorothy's murder. Paulsen's too."

"Okay, so now what?"

"Keep an eye on Clofine. See what else you can find out about her."

"Do you still think there's more than one killer? I mean, it seems so unlikely. Multiple killers running around on such a small island..."

"Nothing would shock me at this point."

"I'm on Clofine. Thanks for pointing me in the right direction. Something's not making sense though. What are we missing?"

"We don't have all the pieces yet, but you're doing excellent work. Thanks to you, we have a whole new angle to consider. Just follow your instincts and the facts. You'll solve this case, you'll see."

Encouraged by Lisa's supportive words, Kim tailed Judy Clofine for the next few days, noting where she went and with whom she interacted. She learned Judy lived with Viktor Morosov, and that he operated Paradise Cleaning and Homecare Services. The same man who Judy claimed had given her the key to Josephine Paulsen's condominium. After a few more calls and some checking with Mary Dillard's neighbors, Kim uncovered an interesting connection.

CHAPTER 38

Thursday, August 19 - 8:45 a.m.

Viktor Morosov was smiling when he left Judy's house. Things were going well, and his girlfriend was happy. She was being nice to Viktor, which wasn't always her way. It had been like that ever since he'd done that thing for her. Now she was trying hard to make it up to him. Last night she was feeling generous and surprised him with a gift; a second-hand Rolex watch she'd found in a shop that specialized in estate pieces. After that, she'd been more than attentive to his needs in bed. *Funny thing,* he thought, *she didn't have to make it up to me, I didn't mind doing it, and it was no worse than other things I've done.*

Viktor looked at his wrist and the gleaming watch. "What the hell am I supposed to do with this?" he asked himself. He knew Judy couldn't afford the watch, and that worried him. "I can pawn it for cash," he muttered, "but she won't be happy about it. Guess I'll be the only person cleaning toilets with a fucking Rolex on my wrist."

As Viktor walked toward his van, which was parked in the driveway of Judy's home, he noticed a squad car on the other side of the street. A female officer got out and approached him.

"Viktor Morosov?" asked the officer.

Startled that the officer had called him by name, he replied, "Yes, I'm Viktor."

"My name is Officer Witherspoon. I'm with the Stypman Island Police and am investigating some recent deaths. If you can spare a minute, I'd like to ask you a few questions. Otherwise, we can talk at the station."

Viktor was shaken. "What can I do for you?"

"You own Paradise Cleaning and Homecare Services, is that correct?"

"Yes."

"Mary Dillard and Josephine Paulsen were clients of yours, right?"

Blood rushed from Viktor's head. "Y-Yes," he stammered.

Glancing down at his feet, Kim saw Viktor was wearing athletic shoes. *Those are some big feet; this might be the guy.*

"Ms. Dillard died in an accident that we aren't so sure was an accident. I'm interested in your whereabouts on that day. It was early Tuesday morning, four weeks ago. Could you help me with that?" Kim continued before Viktor could reply. "The details of Josephine Paulsen's death are also questionable. You gave Judy Clofine the key to Mrs. Paulsen's condominium without permission from the owner. I'm wondering if you can explain that to me."

Panic rose in Viktor's body and he fought the impulse to run. Instead, he balled his fist and threw a sucker punch. Knocked off balance by the blow, Kim found herself sitting on the driveway and tasting blood.

Viktor made a run for it. As he unlocked the door of his van, she yelled and pointed her weapon at him. "Freeze, Morosov!" Viktor glanced at her before opening the door and climbing in. Back on her feet, Kim scrambled toward the van and aimed her gun. She yelled again, "I said, freeze!" He raised his hands. "Smart move, now get out of the van."

. . .

"Hey, Witherspoon, congratulations. Nice work." Chief Jackson made a good show in front of the news reporter who'd come to the police station to cover the story. *Isn't this just great? Witherspoon's a hero, just like Widley. I'll never get rid of her now.* He had to hand it to her, though. She solved a murder that everyone else thought was an accident. He eyed her as she gave a statement to the reporter, his brain racked with questions. *How the hell did she do it, and what else is she looking into without my knowledge?* The questions bothered him, and it showed on his face.

Under pressure, Viktor Morosov confessed to killing Mary Dillard, and even though the chief insisted otherwise, he claimed he had nothing to do with Dorothy Jensen's murder.

A search of his van and some follow-up interviews cemented the Dillard case. Morosov hadn't yet confirmed his girlfriend's involvement, but that was coming. Judy was maintaining her innocence and had already lawyered up. She found it difficult to explain how she knew Mary Dillard's condo would become available weeks before she'd died, or how she'd known that the Briarcliff Literary Society was the beneficiary of Mary's estate. The District Attorney was proceeding with charges against her and Judy Clofine would have her day in court.

For now, Kim was a hero with a bruised face and a cracked tooth. Watching her talk to the news reporter, Chief Jackson fought off the impulse to punch her in the mouth a second time.

. . .

"Hey, girl! Congratulations!" Lisa was calling from her office, having seen the police report pop up in her inbox.

"Lisa, good to hear from you." Kim was at home, icing her sore jaw.

"Well, I couldn't miss the chance to congratulate Stypman Island's newest hero."

"I could never have done this without you. Thanks for trusting me."

"Nothing to thank me for. We make a good team. Besides, I know you'll pay it forward one day. How's your face? I heard you took quite a punch."

"To tell you the truth, it hurts like hell, but it's more than worth it. I'm getting my tooth fixed later today. My dentist insists on doing the work for free. Can you believe that?"

"The benefits of being a hero in a small town."

"I have to say, I've learned so much from you and from working on this case. Looking back, I feel kind of stupid I didn't recognize the Dillard case was a homicide. If it had been up to me, the bad guys would have gotten away with it."

"Don't beat yourself up. The bad guys get away with it more often than people know. Thanks to you, this time they didn't. Once you were pointed in the right direction, you figured it out fast. What you were able to do is impressive. Be proud of yourself, you slayed it."

"Thanks, Lisa, this is the best I've felt about my job in a long time. Even my boss said some nice things to me, although it was more like a public relations ploy than anything sincere. I'm interrogating Morosov later today to go over his side of the story again. We're learning a lot about him since the arrest, but we still need him to give us the goods on his girlfriend."

"This arrest is good for your career, Kim. People notice this kind of thing. Don't let anyone steal the credit from you."

"I hear you. So far, the chief is staying out of it. I guess we'll see if that changes soon enough. He hates all the attention I'm getting. By the way, he pushed Morosov hard on Dorothy Jensen's murder. Something's up with that because we know Morosov didn't do it. Anyway, Bill Widley's been helping me, and I asked him to join me in the interrogation. I thought the chief would blow a gasket; he likes Bill about as much as he likes me."

"Who's Bill Widley? Is he trustworthy?"

"You'll have to meet him one day. He's the kindest, most decent guy you'll ever meet, and yes, I trust him. He's good at his job and easy on the eyes. Coming from a gay chick, that's saying something."

"You're right. I *do* have to meet him. Well, good luck with it, and let me know if I can help."

"There is one thing, I can't ask Morosov about Josephine Paulsen. Everything's on the record now. My boss insists she died of a heart attack. He'll go ballistic if I suggest otherwise. Any ideas?"

"We know the chief is up to his neck on that one so let's stay away from it for now. Morosov might just give you something on his own. Besides, we can always circle back and press him on it later if we need to. I have a lot to catch you up on, Kim. I'll be back up there in a few days. Once I'm on the ground, I'll call you, and we can figure out a place to meet." After a pause Lisa said, "Hey, by the way, can you do me a favor?"

"Sure, anything. What do you need?"

"Keep an eye on your boss without letting him know you're watching him. Just see how he's spending his time. Pay attention to where he goes and who he's meeting with... that kind of thing."

"I can do that."

"Great. Having some recon about what he's up to will save time when I'm there. Just be careful and back off if he gets suspicious."

CHAPTER 39

Friday, August 20 - 12:00 p.m.

"Okay, Viktor, we know you killed Mary Dillard to help your girlfriend."

Viktor Morosov sat on the other side of the wooden desk from Kim Witherspoon. Yesterday he'd punched her in the face; now, with his hands cuffed and shackles on his ankles, he looked defeated. To Kim's right sat Bill Widley, who looked every part the all-American hero in contrast to the Russian killer. The interrogation was being taped; Viktor had declined to have an attorney present. He'd given a lot of thought to what he would say in this conversation. He'd tell it all, then he'd throw Judy to the wolves to save himself.

"What's in this for me?" Viktor asked.

"Well, we're willing to help you, Viktor, but it depends on how cooperative you are with us," said Bill, playing the good cop while Kim played the tough cop.

"We aren't making any promises until we hear what you have to say," said Kim. "But the District Attorney might be open to lesser charges in return for your full cooperation. So, tell us, Viktor, why kill a defenseless old lady?"

Three and a half hours later, they had his answer on tape.

. . .

Carla Weston, a politically ambitious District Attorney, would prosecute the case against Viktor Morosov and Judy Clofine. It would be her biggest case to date, and she was intent on making a name for herself by putting the two behind bars, if not in the electric chair. The case was her ticket to bigger things and an office in Tallahassee. Today she found herself in a shabby police station on tiny Stypman Island. The road to Tallahassee wasn't glamorous.

The D.A. was all business. Wearing a dark gray blazer and matching pencil skirt with a white blouse and pearls, her appearance and no-nonsense demeanor sent a powerful message; she was going places and was not someone to mess with. She sat with ramrod posture on a metal folding chair, a yellow legal pad resting on her crossed legs. The stiletto on her foot twitched, signaling her impatience. Across from her sat Kim, Bill, and Chief Jackson.

Carla Weston thought about the task at hand. *I've got my work cut out for me. Somehow, I'll have to use whatever these three small town putzes give me to secure a conviction and another feather in my cap. God help me. Let's get this circus started. At least Widley is nice to look at...*

"Okay, this is how I plan to proceed," Carla explained as she took control of the meeting. "I'll want to listen to the taped interrogation several times over. Then I'll decide the best path forward and whether Morosov gets a break in order to get to Clofine. I'll make up my mind once I've considered all the facts. Right now, I'm here to get an in-person debrief on the full investigation. Who's going to start?"

"It basically comes down to this," began Kim. "Mary Dillard was a quiet, older lady. Everyone at Coquina Reef, that's the name of the community she lived in, liked her well enough although she kept to herself because she had a hearing problem. Her neighbors will testify they remember her for her gentle demeanor and warm smile... they'll say she'll be missed. They're also going to say that, over the past few years, her increasing forgetfulness had not gone unnoticed. They were watching out for her and making sure she was alright."

"Okay," said Carla. "We have a sympathetic victim. So far, the only question I'm asking myself is which will it be for Morosov, the electric chair or lethal injection? Florida offers both options."

Chief Jackson laughed loudly at the District Attorney's crude remark. Kim widened her eyes and took a deep breath, shooting a distressed look at Bill that he didn't miss. He nodded back at her for assurance.

Kim continued. "Judy Clofine needed to sell Mary Dillard's condominium for the real estate commission. There was $90,000 at stake. In order to do that, Mary needed to be gone, and she wasn't going anywhere on her own. Her attorney will testify that Miss Dillard made her wishes clear. Staying put in that condo was important to her. The idea of life in an assisted living facility had no appeal. She arranged for her groceries to be delivered each week, she did her own laundry, and made her own meals. A taxi took her to medical appointments. One thing she didn't do for herself was clean her condominium. That gave Morosov and Clofine the opportunity they needed."

Carla Weston was busy making notes, and Kim continued. "According to Morosov, Judy Clofine was desperate to make the sale. We've confirmed she had a cash buyer lined up to buy the Dillard place weeks before Dillard died. She even sent photos of the place by email. We've got the email and date it was sent. Morosov told us that Clofine owes a lot of money to some bad people and they were coming after her for it. She made payments electronically. If we can get her bank statements, we'll have a record of those payments, and she'll have to explain them." Kim paused before adding, "Clofine had plenty of motivation to want Mary Dillard dead."

"I agree, Officer Witherspoon. Based on what I'm hearing, we can make the case that Clofine was motivated to kill. Please continue." *This must be my lucky day. This chick isn't half as dumb as I thought she'd be.*

"Judy came up with the idea that Viktor should tell Miss Dillard she was a 'priority customer' and he'd no longer send his employees to clean her place. Instead, he'd personally do the work himself. That kept everyone else out. To get her to trust him further, Viktor told Miss Dillard he'd do her windows at no charge because 'a magnificent view should not be obscured.' Those were his exact words. She fell for it and let him have the run of the place. She read books and looked out at the ocean while he worked. Viktor said a lot of times she'd fall asleep while he was there."

"So fucking devious," interjected the chief. "Carla, make sure the jury understands that."

Carla gave him a sharp look. "I know how to do my job."

Rebuked, the chief kept his mouth shut.

Kim suppressed a smile and continued. "While Mary focused on her books, or napped, Viktor went through her things. He went through her records and files and learned how much was in her bank accounts, when her social security check arrived each month, what medications she took, and where she kept her jewelry. Viktor also found Miss Dillard's will and discovered she had no heirs. He took photos of the will to share with Judy. He gave us his phone; the photos are still there."

"Excellent," said Carla while making notes. "Fucking excellent."

"The will makes it clear that upon Ms. Dillard's death her property and assets were to be donated to a literary society located in Santa Monica, California. According to Viktor, Judy did her research and concluded the organization wouldn't know much about the value of the property. She told him the literary society was run by some old biddy on the other side of the country who'd want to get her mitts on the proceeds from the sale as quickly as she could. She called it a win-win."

Kim continued, "I spoke with the head of the literary society, a very sweet woman named Ethel O'Brien. She confirmed there was a quick sale and sent me the contract."

Bill picked up from Kim. "The plan to kill Mary Dillard went off without a hitch. Viktor waited in the toilet closet in the women's bathroom at the Coquina Reef swimming pool. Familiar with her routine, he knew what Miss Dillard's every move would be. He also knew that without her hearing aids, he needn't worry about startling her. While she was in the shower, he poured a soapy solution on the floor outside the shower. The previous day, while cleaning her condominium, he used sandpaper on the bottoms of her rubber flip-flops, smoothing them down until any slip resistance they provided was eliminated.

With the floor slick with soap, Viktor maneuvered around the corner of the shower area, out of sight. Once Ms. Dillard had fallen, he slammed her head on the floor to make sure she died. Before he left the scene, he checked to make sure she didn't have a pulse."

Bill paused briefly, allowing the D.A. some time to catch up. She was filling up pages on her legal pad with lightning speed. "Satisfied his victim was dead, Viktor cleaned up the solution he'd poured on the floor, carefully wiping down everything with the same cleaning product used by Coquina Reef's maintenance crew when they tidy up the pool bathrooms. That's why the floor was so clean when Kim and her partner attended the scene of the death. He left a few footprints though, and we've been able to match them to his athletic shoes. Once he was finished, he slipped out a window and onto the beach where he walked to a nearby public parking lot used by beachgoers. Judy Clofine was waiting for him in her car."

Carla Weston's mouth hung open in disbelief. "He said all this in the interrogation? You've got this on tape?"

"We do," replied Bill.

"Unfuckingbelievable! Not only is he devious, he's also dumber than dirt. Mark my words, his Russian ass will fry."

Bill held his hands in front of him, palms out. "Hold on, Ms. Weston, there's more."

"We asked Morosov about his company, Paradise Cleaning and Homecare Services," Kim explained. "He told us that owning the company over the past several years literally put the keys of hundreds of condominiums on Stypman Island into his hands. Keys he made copies of and keeps in Judy's garage. He said most of his clients spend only a few months of the year here. As you're aware, to claim Florida residency and the tax advantages that come with it, six months and one day of residency is required. Morosov said that's too much sun and too much heat for most of his clients so they shorten their visits, believing no one will be the wiser. While they're away, they pay him to check on their homes. These home checks," Kim raised her eyebrows, "gave Morosov the chance to rifle through his clients' possessions and personal papers. Morosov told us Clofine often joined him on the home checks so she could scope out the properties for a potential sale."

Dumbfounded, the D. A. shook her head. "This is one of the most deceitful schemes I've ever encountered. Tell me more about Judy."

Bill answered. "Judy and Viktor go back a bit. They met at a bar and hit it off. Morosov told us he offered to kill Judy's former boss when she told him the guy had screwed her over. He said he was kidding, but somehow, I doubt it. Anyway, that remark must have done it for Judy, because she took him home with her that night and he's been with her ever since. She's got a nice two-bedroom place on the island, mid-century modern style. It's small but private, surrounded by palm trees with a swimming pool in the backyard."

"It sounds lovely," said Carla, "but why does it matter where she lives?"

Kim answered this time. "Judy's been struggling to hold on to the place because of her financial problems. She's way behind on her mortgage payments, and let's not forget, she owes money to some bad actors."

"Got it," replied the District Attorney. "Not only did Clofine need money to pay her debts, but she and Viktor were also at risk of losing their home. That fact ties them together." Carla uncrossed her legs and turned the page on her legal pad. "So, who the hell is Viktor Morosov, anyway?"

"Here's what we've learned so far," responded Bill. "Viktor Morosov is forty-eight years old. He immigrated to the United States after the Soviet Union collapsed. His father was a ranking member of the Soviet politburo, and the Morosov family had a good life until the U.S.S.R. broke apart. When the government fell and the privileges enjoyed by the Morosovs were gone, Viktor's father took his own life. His mother died less than a year later. After that, the decision to leave Russia was easy for Viktor. He hated the place and wanted out. The son of a politburo elite, Viktor had received a first-rate education that included learning English. Morosov knew he wanted to come to America, but to get here he needed money."

"How do you know so much about him?" asked the District Attorney.

"This all comes from the Moscow police who, it turns out, are very interested in Morosov, too," said Kim. "So interested, they want him back there."

"Maybe they'll get their wish," said Carla.

"You called Moscow?" interjected Chief Jackson, completely astonished.

"No, we called the U.S. Department of State," Bill Widley explained, "and they contacted the Russians. Apparently, we still work together on certain matters of common interest."

"Widley, for Christ's sake, why was I not included in the decision to contact the Feds?" His eyes wild, Chief Jackson looked panicked.

"Chief, you told us to solve this and give the D.A. an iron-clad case. We did what you asked."

"And admirably, I might add," said Carla. "You should be very proud of these two, Beau." Visibly dumbfounded, the chief went silent. Using his hand, he wiped the beads of sweat that had formed on his forehead, then dried his hand on his trousers. Carla Weston looked at him with disgust.

Bill continued, "Morosov was in a bar and overheard a man commiserating with his friends." Bill looked down at his notes, "I'm probably going to butcher it, but the guy's name was Nikolai Kuznetsov."

"Viktor bought him a drink, and the guy started talking about his problems. His family was about to lose their apartment because they couldn't pay their rent. The guy had a sickly wife, a thirteen-year-old daughter, and twin boys who were six years old. Morosov saw an opportunity to take advantage and got the man drunk. Then he convinced him to let him sell his daughter - her name is Mirna, by the way - as a prostitute, and the two would split the proceeds."

Carla cringed and sucked air through her clenched teeth. "I thought you said the daughter was thirteen."

"Sadly, that's correct," replied Bill. "Apparently, that kind of thing was pretty common in Moscow then; desperate times and all that. Without her mother's knowledge, Mirna was taken to Viktor that same night. Being so young, the girl was a virgin. Morosov took her for himself and then sold her to dozens of men. After two weeks, he had enough cash for a plane ticket. When Mirna's father came looking for his share of the money, Viktor had already boarded an Aeroflot jet from Moscow to Miami to start a new life. Mirna was left homeless on the streets of Moscow."

"That's got to be one of the most tragic stories since Les Miz," said the District Attorney, frantically scribbling notes on her legal pad.

"Well, Ms. Weston," said Bill, his eyes twinkling, "you've heard the saying that karma is a bitch."

Carla Weston looked up from her legal pad, eager to hear the punchline.

"It turns out that Mirna Kuznetsov is all grown up now. She's married to an oligarch, super wealthy, and a close friend of Putin himself, which explains why the Russians are so interested in getting Morosov back."

"Now that's rich," said the District Attorney. "Whether it's here in Florida or back in Russia, I promise you right now, that son of a bitch and his nightmare of a girlfriend are going down."

Kim took over from Bill and continued sharing the background information she'd collected. "Once in the U.S., Morosov worked at a hotel until he was fired for stealing from a hotel guest. He was arrested but got ahead of the police and made a deal with the victim to drop the charges. Viktor walked out of jail and headed north. He stumbled on Stypman Island and became our problem."

"Very good work, Officer Witherspoon, and you, too, Officer Widley. You make a good team," said the District Attorney.

Bill jumped in to correct her, "This was Kim's work, Ms. Weston - not mine."

Kim glanced at her boss, red-faced he was stewing.

As she prepared to leave the Police Department, Carla pulled Jackson aside. "Nice work, Beau. Let's give Morosov some time to sweat. Tell him I'm not sure his testimony is worth giving him much of anything in return. I'm going to work the channels to see if Moscow wants him. If they do, maybe there's a way of getting his testimony against Judy Clofine before I send him back to Putin and his rich girlfriend. I'll be in touch."

CHAPTER 40

Monday, August 23 - 4:00 p.m.

Judy Clofine had a lot to think about. The meeting in her lawyer's office wasn't going well. "Viktor could turn on you any minute," her attorney pointed out. "With his testimony, your case will be challenging at best. A plea deal is your best option."

"Excuse me, I need a quick break," she explained before heading off to the ladies room. Gazing at herself in the mirror, she was defiant. "A plea deal? Bullshit!" she said to herself. "I'm fighting this, no matter what. Screw the legal fees. I can deal with selling the house and the business, but I'm not going to fucking prison. I'll finger Viktor and let him take the fall." She gazed at her reflect a moment longer, then applied lipstick. *Who's a jury going to believe? A Russian with a shady past or a beautiful American woman?*

Her decision made, she lied to her attorney. "Yes, there was physical abuse. Yes, I feared for my life. Yes, Viktor took my money." Hiding a smile, she watched the attorney write his notes, eating up every word. *Yeah, I'm getting out of this. I'll figure out how to pay the bill later.*

With the meeting over, Judy strutted with confidence through the parking lot. Opening her car door, she was blasted with a wave of hot air. The seat was scorching hot, and her fingers sizzled when she touched the steering wheel. Sweating through her lavender pantsuit, an outfit chosen to make her appear like a respectable businesswoman, she started home.

"I need a beer," she muttered, making a quick turn into the parking lot of a liquor store that had seen better days. Minutes later, with the air conditioner cranked to the max and AC/DC's *"Highway to Hell"* on the radio, she cracked open a cold one for the drive home, finishing it just as she pulled into her driveway.

"Damn it! I'm so wound up I forgot to lock the door," Judy mumbled, letting herself in the house. Dropping her purse on a small entry table, she entered the kitchen and put what was left of the six-pack in the refrigerator. Taking a fresh bottle with her, she walked to her backyard and placed it at the edge of the pool. She dropped her sweaty clothing on a lounge chair and dove in. After swimming the short distance to the other side of the pool she made her way back underwater. As she broke the surface, she reached for the beer. It came hurtling at her, hitting hard against her cheek and landing with a splash. Someone had thrown the bottle at her. Someone she wasn't expecting. She screamed again when she saw who it was.

"You are late with your payment and you don't answer my calls. Where is the money?" Zoran asked in heavily accented English.

Shocked and frightened, Judy tried to hide her naked body by lowering herself in the water. Her right cheek stung; and a bright red mark blossomed where she'd been hit. "There's a problem with the police," she explained. "Viktor is in jail, and I've been arrested and charged. Until that's taken care of, I won't be able to make payments."

"We don't care about your problems; you owe the money. Where is it?"

"I've already told you, I can't pay." Thinking fast, Judy decided to offer Zoran something. It made her nauseous to think about it, but it might just work. She had a gun in her bedroom, if she could get him in there, she had a chance.

"Maybe there's something else I can do for you?" She stood up out of the water, showing Zoran her ample breasts. "I can make your afternoon a very pleasant one," she said trying her best to seduce him.

Zoran laughed at her.

Standing in the water, Judy felt stupid and unattractive. She thought it was over until the Russian said, "Come here, whore."

Hope sparked. *He's interested?* she thought. Judy did as she was told, slowly walking through the water toward the edge of the pool, where he stood looking down at her. She stuck out her chest, smiled seductively and hoped for the best. "Let's go to my bedroom, Zoran. It's cool and comfortable inside."

Straight-faced, Zoran squatted at the edge of the pool waiting. When she was near enough, he grabbed a fistful of Judy's hair. Screaming in agony and terror, she tried to free herself. Flailing her arms and kicking her feet, Judy was pulled up from the water by her hair until her face was so close to Zoran's she could smell the cigarettes on his breath. Writhing in pain, her mind flashed white.

"You will die now." Judy thrashed her arms and legs as he said the words. Using both hands, he gripped her head and pulled her body toward him, pinning her against the wall of the pool. With a powerful twist, he snapped her neck.

For an instant, there was blinding pain, then Judy felt nothing. In shock, her arms and legs no longer responding, she was silent as Zoran turned her away from him and pushed her face first into the water. Floating and unable to raise her head, she choked. Bubbles floated from her mouth and nose and her lungs filled with water. Sinking below the sparkling surface, Judy Clofine's body settled on the bottom of her swimming pool.

CHAPTER 41

Tuesday, August 24 - 5:30 p.m.

Arriving back on Stypman Island, Lisa was hopeful. She'd found someone local who was capable, worthy of her trust and willing to help her find out what had happened to Dorothy. Now, all they had to do was get lucky.

After checking into her hotel, she took a minute before calling Kim. From the windows of her hotel room, Lisa gazed at the turquoise ocean and began sinking into a familiar sadness as memories of Dorothy overwhelmed her. As if on cue, a group of pelicans flew past in perfect v-formation.

The Stypman Island Air Force. Lisa smiled. Dorothy always called the formations of pelicans that soared over the island's beaches by that name. It was one of many happy memories. "Chase happiness," she said aloud, both as an affirmation and a reminder. Then, she called Kim.

"Lisa, I was getting worried. Are you on the island yet?"

"I'm here. Sorry, I'm late. Can you meet me at the hotel?"

"I'll be there in ten minutes."

"Great, it's room 217. I'll order us Cuban coffee; they make it really well here."

Lisa saw the relief in Kim's eyes when she walked into the hotel room ten minutes later. "Lisa, thank God you're here. There's something I need to tell you about Judy Clofine."

"What happened now?" asked Lisa. "Clofine is such a charmer. Nothing involving her would surprise me." Lisa reached for one of the tiny tacitas of Cuban coffee that had been delivered minutes earlier.

"They found her dead in her swimming pool earlier today."

Turning away from the coffee, she looked at Kim with wide eyes. "I'm officially surprised. What happened?"

"According to the M.E., she must have dove into her pool and broke her neck. She drowned. The pool guy found her."

"Any sign of foul play?" asked Lisa.

"Not that I've heard. They're doing an autopsy. That should help answer some questions."

"Or raise new ones."

"There's more. I've been monitoring my boss as you asked. He's spending a good amount of time at different restaurants and shops on the island, but he isn't eating or buying anything. He goes in and out of the same places regularly, stays for a few minutes and leaves. I couldn't figure out what he could be up to, so I started looking for something that tied the places together. They're all owned by the same person, Kitty Sampson. She's a local girl done good and is kind of a big deal around here."

"That seems like it might be worth pursuing," said Lisa. She jotted down a note to herself on a message pad provided by the hotel.

"There's one more thing," added Kim. "The chief carries a duffel bag with him when he makes these visits. I don't know why."

"Is there anything else you've observed?" asked Lisa. She finished the last of her coffee and felt a caffeine buzz.

"There's one thing. He leaves the island a few nights each week, always at ten. I haven't followed him. It would be way too easy for him to know I was tailing him."

"You've been a great partner on this, Kim. Your boss still doesn't know about me yet, so let me see if I can find out where he's going on those nighttime trips."

"Well, you might have your chance tonight," added Kim. "He didn't leave the island the past two nights, so he's likely to go tonight."

"You said he typically leaves around ten, right?"

"Yes, almost on the dot."

"I'll be ready."

At a quarter to ten, Lisa parked on a side street, just beyond the bridge coming from Stypman Island. From this vantage point, she'd be able to see the chief driving across the bridge, but he wouldn't see her waiting for him.

"It's game time, here he comes," Lisa whispered. The metallic brown Chevy Silverado pickup looked exactly as Kim had described it. Lisa squinted as its bright headlights shined into her eyes. She waited for it to pass before pulling onto the road several car lengths behind. *Good, he's staying on main roads, I'm less conspicuous. Where are you headed, Chief?*

A few other cars shared the road. Lisa let them pass, putting them between her and the chief's truck. Eight miles later, the Silverado pulled onto a side street with the name Quiet Cove Lane. Lisa checked her GPS display. Quiet Cove Lane was a dead end with water on three sides. "Guess I'm doing this on foot," she whispered to herself. She made a quick U-turn and parked on the other side of the main road.

Dark and heavily wooded, there was only one house on Quiet Cove Lane and it was huge. Dressed in dark clothing and carrying a small backpack, Lisa moved fast, staying in the wooded areas and using the trees as cover.

The house was an impressive Spanish-style villa surrounded by white stucco-covered walls with heavy ornate iron gates in front of a circular driveway. A lighted fountain spraying water stood in front of the villa. *This place looks like something from a magazine.*

Keeping out of sight, she put night vision binoculars to her eyes. The binoculars, equipped with camera technology, were property of the Miami PD and ideal for nighttime surveillance. "There's his truck in the driveway," she whispered to herself. She watched him enter the house. A man with a jagged scar on his face stood at the doorway, holding a rifle. Lisa snapped photos of him.

"What's that in your hand, Chief?" Lisa took several more photographs.

Once the door closed, she released a deep breath while continuing to watch the property. Her vantage point behind a large date palm offered suitable cover, but the mosquitos and 'no-see-ums' were making her miserable. She took a small bottle of insect repellent from her backpack and doused herself. She could make out several surveillance cameras mounted in different places around the property and the top of the stucco wall appeared to be wired. *Whoever lives here is damned serious about security.*

Lisa continued to peer through the binoculars. The villa's windows were dark. To one side of the house was a large four-car garage, its doors open. Inside, were two vehicles, both parked front first. That's good, she thought, I can check the plates later. She snapped several photos.

Minutes later, the door to the villa opened and light spilled out into the darkness. The chief was leaving. Lisa could see that he had two or three bulky duffle bags with him. The man with the rifle took up his position at the entrance while Chief Jackson walked back to his truck. Lisa snapped more photos. *They're the bags Kim described. What's he got in them?*

. . .

For the next few nights, Lisa took up her post, waiting for Chief Jackson to cross the bridge from Stypman Island. Just as Kim had predicted, he didn't make the trip every night, but when he did, it was always at the same time and he always went to the villa on Quiet Cove Lane and left with duffle bags.

After an early morning run on the beach, Lisa sat at the small writing desk in her hotel room, her laptop open in front of her. Kim arrived with coffee and donuts from Sweet Paradise, Stypman Island's most popular bakery.

"Two cops eating donuts... like that's never been done before," joked Kim.

"Grab a chair, let's see what we've got." Lisa pulled up the photographs she'd taken on her stakeouts. One of the first things they wanted to take a closer look at was what the chief was holding when he entered the villa. Using a software program available through the Miami PD, Lisa zoomed in on one of the photos and achieved a clear, close-up of the chief's hand. He was holding what they could now see were rolled-up bags. "So, he brings empty bags in and leaves with them full," said Lisa.

"Those are the bags he takes to Kitty Sampson's businesses," said Kim.

"Okay, we've tied a few things together. Now, let's see if we can find out who lives at that fancy villa." Lisa pulled up the photographs of the two cars she saw in the villa's garage. One car was a black Maserati, the other a black Range Rover. Lisa zoomed in on the license plates.

"Those are Florida tags, alright," said Kim.

Lisa opened another window on the computer and entered the tag numbers. Both cars were registered to Stypman Island Enterprises. She'd previously looked at property records for Quiet Cove Lane. The entire street, including the villa, was owned by the same company.

"Now what?" asked Kim.

"It will take some digging, but I know people who may be able to help figure out who's behind Stypman Island Enterprises. I'd sure like to get a look at whoever lives in that place. There's no way we can go there during the day and not be seen, but I'm wondering if we can see into the back yard if we use a boat."

Lisa pulled up Google Earth and typed in Quiet Cove Lane. Although the villa was blurred out, they could see the backyard of the property was expansive and surrounded by the same white stucco wall that stood in front of the villa. Any view from the water would be obscured by the wall, large trees, and thick foliage. "A boat won't work," said Lisa.

"How about a drone?" suggested Kim. "That way, we don't have to get close to the house."

"It would require some luck," said Lisa. "Have you operated a drone before? I haven't."

"No, but my girlfriend has. She works at the Stypman Island Institute for Marine Life Preservation. They use drones to locate sick and injured sea turtles in the ocean."

"Really?"

"Absolutely," said Kim. "Boaters sometimes see a distressed turtle and call it in, but of course, the turtle is moving and hard to find. The drones make it easier to locate them so they can be captured and taken for the care they need. It's a pretty involved operation."

"I'm impressed," said Lisa. "And I'd like to meet your girlfriend."

CHAPTER 42

Friday, August 27 - 11:00 a.m.

Kim piloted the skiff along the wide canal that encircled Quiet Cove Lane. A brackish mixture of salt and freshwater, the canal ran brown with tannin. Birdsong and the hum of the skiff's motor filled the still air that hung heavy with summer humidity. Lisa and Simone sat together on either side of a bench seat behind Kim, who was at the center console.

"The mosquitoes are relentless." Lisa swatted one on her leg and sprayed herself with repellent before passing it to Simone.

"These cute outfits don't seem like such a good idea anymore," said Simone. "With all the bugs, we should be in long sleeves and pants." They'd dressed as tourists, wearing large sunglasses, wide-brimmed sun hats, and bikini tops with shorts.

"My bad," said Lisa. "Just remember, if we're questioned, we're dumb tourists confused and lost in the waterways."

As they approached Quiet Cove Lane, Kim killed the engine, and Simone launched the drone. "I'm flying it high, so it's less likely to be noticed," she explained. The drone hovered over the villa and Lisa and Simone stared at the video images it was sending. They could see the villa's backyard and a pool but no people.

"I'll reposition now so we can get a view of the front of the property," Simone worked the controls. Again, no one was visible.

"Let's give it some time and try again," suggested Lisa.

Simone recalled the drone, landing it back on the boat. Kim hit the gas, and the skiff took off, creating a welcome breeze and relief from the mosquitos. The canal was beautiful. Great blue herons, sandhill cranes, and several white egrets stood on long legs on the riverbank. Painted turtles slid into the canal from the rocks where they'd been warming themselves in the sun. Simone pointed out a dark shadow beneath the surface, "There's a manatee, there might be more around here. Kim, be careful, I don't want us to hit one."

"How can a place that's so beautiful have so much ugliness?" asked Lisa.

"Greedy humans," said Simone, "which is why I prefer animals."

About an hour later, they had better luck. As the drone flew over the villa, they could see someone lying on a lounge chair near the pool.

"Here we go," said Simone. "I'm going closer, so if we're spotted, we may need to make a break for it. Be ready, Kim."

"Go for it," encouraged Lisa. "Let's get a look at this mystery person."

Simone took her time with the drone, first flying it away from the villa and then coming across the backyard at a much lower height, stopping it just long enough to get the images they needed.

They studied the images on the display in real time. "It's a guy," said Lisa. He wore mirrored sunglasses and a white speedo. "He's fit, dark hair, maybe in his late thirties, early forties."

"Eeew, that's a *lot* of chest hair." Simone made a face.

The man bolted up from the lounge chair and looked up at the sky, his hand shielding his eyes.

"He heard the drone, time to bolt," instructed Lisa.

"On it." Simone worked the controls. The drone took off and was back on the boat in seconds. Kim was about to hit the gas when two enormous alligators surfaced from nowhere, blocking their way.

"Whoa!" Kim looked down at the monsters just inches away.

Simone, the biologist, was fascinated. "Those are huge! Gators that size shouldn't be in these waters."

"Screw the damned gators!" said Lisa. "Let's get the hell out of here before that dude gets on to us."

Kim allowed the boat to drift forward, gently bumping the alligators so she could maneuver past them. Once they were in the clear, the boat took off.

Lisa glanced at Simone and noticed the puzzled expression on her face. She yelled over the roar of the engine, "What is it?"

Simone looked unsettled. "I've seen him before," she replied. "I just don't remember where."

Back in Lisa's hotel room, they looked at the images they'd captured, now enhanced by the software on Lisa's computer. Visible were several scars on the man's torso and arms. "Whoever he is, he's been through a lot," said Kim. The pictures were good, but the fact that their guy was wearing mirrored sunglasses was a problem.

"Let's see if we can find out who he is." Lisa uploaded the photo of the man's face into a database. Details about his face, the size of his head, his hairline, his nose, jaw, and mouth were analyzed in mere seconds.

"If he has a record, he should be here," said Lisa.

They weren't that lucky. "Well, I'd call that a bust," Kim said, disappointed they'd hit another wall.

"Not necessarily," said Lisa. "At least we know what he looks like and Simone thinks she's seen him before, so we might just run into him."

. . .

3:00 p.m.

At Miami Police Headquarters, Bruce keyed the name 'Stypman Island Enterprises' into a special software program on his computer. He was able to learn the company was part of a complicated network of shell corporations that went offshore and involved several banks all over the globe. He picked up his phone.

"Somebody sure wants to keep Stypman Island Enterprises a secret. This is one heck of a tangle to unravel."

"I guess we need more help," Lisa said with dismay.

"Finally, reason prevails. I'll put in some calls."

"Bruce, not just yet. There are still a couple of things I need to check out first."

"C'mon, Lisa. At least promise me you'll stay away from that villa; I don't like the idea of you being there alone."

"I'll be careful. Thanks for all your help on this, Bruce. I'll be in touch."

CHAPTER 43

Friday, August 27 - 5:30 p.m.

"I saw these growing on the side of the road, wild and beautiful, just like you." Looking at the flowers her young boyfriend held in his hand, Kitty Sampson couldn't believe it. She was falling for Dillon.

My brother will never let me live this down, she thought as she kissed Dillon's cheek. "They're lovely," she said.

Pulling his head back so he could look her in the eyes, Dillon broke into a bright smile, "I love you, Kitty. You are one righteous babe."

Like those who came before him, Kitty kept Dillon around for his good looks. He was enthusiastic in bed, his main purpose, but she also enjoyed his company and that surprised her. She put the flowers in a vase and contemplated having a life with him. *What is it with him? How can anyone be that happy? That smile of his... and he's smarter than I thought.* Rather unexpectedly, she'd fallen in love.

After they'd finished a takeout dinner, she took the plunge. "Dillon, I didn't expect to say this, but I love you, too. I think we could have a future together."

Dillon beamed. "I knew it, I knew you loved me, too."

"I want you to finish college though. I'll pay the tuition."

"No way. I'm not taking money from you. I'll figure something out."

"Well, if you want to make me happy, you're going to finish school and I'm paying."

Dillon relented, "Okay, but I'm paying back every cent. And Kitty, I'll spend the rest of my life making you happy. I promise."

Late that same night, after some incredible sex, Kitty was fast asleep when she was awakened by the buzz of her phone. She checked the time; nearly two in the morning. *Who the hell?* Then, she saw who was calling.

She looked over at Dillon. *He's still asleep. That boy can sleep through anything.* Kitty held her breath and answered the call.

"Come see me now. I'll expect you in twenty minutes. Don't be late." The call disconnected.

Taking care not to wake Dillon, Kitty dressed in a hurry and left the house. She drove over the bridge to the mainland as fast as she dared, approaching the villa with only a few minutes to spare. Passing through the iron gates, she felt her stomach go sour. Her intuition screamed for her to turn around and run. Ignoring the alarm bells going off in her head, she walked to the front door. *Where's the goon with the scar and the rifle?* she wondered. *He's always here.*

"Come in. I'm in the office," DesFuentes' voice sounded through an intercom. Kitty had been to this place before and knew where to go. She entered and silently walked down the long hallway that led to a carved mahogany door, the only thing that separated her from whatever was to come next. She hesitated before grabbing the handle with her shaking hand. When she pulled the door open, he was waiting for her, his expression cold and blank, giving nothing away.

"Where's the guy who's usually at the front door?" she asked, trying to sound relaxed.

"Alex is doing an errand for me." DesFuentes approached her and said four words that she'd been warned about, words she dreaded. "You've let me down." He was angry, Kitty could see that now. She could hear it in his voice too. Her entire body began to shake.

"I warned you, didn't I?" Enraged, DesFuentes' dark eyes seemed to bore through Kitty's skull. His nostrils flared, his face reddened, and he balled his fists in frustrated rage. Gripped by fury, he looked around the room before deciding on his weapon. Grabbing the lamp from his desk, he ripped its plug from a socket in the wall. The room darkened. In the shadows, Kitty saw pure evil moving toward her. She stood frozen with fear.

He's going to kill me. Her eyes stung with tears, and her heart pounded against her chest. She held her breath and her head swam from lack of oxygen.

The questions, each dripping with sarcasm, came in rapid fire. "Tell me, Kitty, when I bought those businesses for you when you were first starting out, did you think I did that because I liked you? Maybe you thought I did that because I thought you were pretty? Is that it? Was it unclear to you that those businesses were for my purposes, and you were to do exactly what you were told?"

Terrified, Kitty remained frozen, unable to respond. Thoughts tumbled in her head and her self-esteem crumbled. *It's true. His money made it possible for me to pay my parents back and buy my businesses. Everyone was so proud of me. Even my brothers thought I was something special. I'm not special, I'm a fool who made a deal with the devil.*

DesFuentes waited for Kitty to reply, but she remained silent. *It won't matter what I say. He'll kill me, anyway.*

Provoked by her silence, DesFuentes swung the lamp in his hand, catching Kitty in the jaw. Knocked over by the force of the blow, she fell to the floor. The lamp crashed onto the floor next to her, its glass shade shattering. In shock and dazed from the blow, Kitty could barely think. Noticing something in her bloody mouth; she spit it out. Broken teeth.

"Get up, you pathetic bitch, before I hit you again," DesFuentes seethed.

Kitty struggled to her feet. Stepping on broken glass, she noticed the blood dripping from her chin onto her pink t-shirt.

"Now, listen carefully. I will not repeat myself. If I have to call you here again, I will kill you. Do you understand?"

Trembling, Kitty nodded.

"You will keep up with production from now on without exception. No more fucking excuses. I will make certain that Manny's Bar and Grill is sold to you this week. Other than that, I afford you no further conveniences. Those who disappoint me pay a terrible price. That will soon be clear to you. Now, leave me."

Kitty turned and ran from the villa, crying and terrified. Her drive back home seemed to go by in a flash. The entire time, she kept thinking about one thing. *What did that animal mean about paying a terrible price? That it would soon be clear to me?*

She entered her house and was relieved to see things were as she'd left them. After checking the locks on the doors and windows, she went into the bedroom and was relieved to see Dillon still fast asleep on his side of the bed.

Flinching, she splashed cold water on her face and took in the image looking back at her in the bathroom mirror. Her face was bruised and badly swollen and her bottom lip was cut and blowing up. Opening her mouth, she could see the broken teeth - three of them. She took some painkillers and sleeping pills. *With any luck, I won't wake up.*

The next morning, in a fog from the pills, her mouth and face aching, the horror of the previous night came back to her. Her eyes were open, but they weren't focusing clearly.

Kitty had the taste of blood in her mouth and needed water. She went into the bathroom, leaned down and drank from the faucet. When she stood, she winced at the sight of her battered image in the mirror.

She left the bathroom and walked to the side of the bed to where Dillon lay sleeping. *It's time to tell him what's going on - no more lying. If we leave now, we can make a run for it.* She opened the blinds and bright sunlight flooded the room. Turning away from the window, she shrieked in horror.

Dillon's handsome face was pale, his blue eyes wide open, lifeless, and staring at nothing. Kitty touched his cheek; it was ice cold.

She noticed a hypodermic needle along with a rubber tourniquet on the nightstand next to Dillon's body. Recalling DesFuentes' words, she bent over and vomited on the floor. Devastated, she began to cry. Her wailing continued until she heard someone pounding on her door. Nervously, she peeked out the front door window. It was Beau Jackson.

"Fuck, Kitty, you look like shit." The chief pushed past her and walked into the living room. "Where is he?"

"You know?" asked Kitty, surprised.

"He sent me here, told me your boyfriend overdosed. I'm supposed to help you keep it on the down low. Too much attention isn't good for business."

"Beau, this wasn't an overdose. Dillon never used drugs, not even aspirin. DesFuentes did this to punish me - he had him killed." Kitty described the events of the past night and the warning she'd received.

"All the more reason why neither of us is going to disappoint the boss again. Here's the plan. I'm going to handle this as an overdose. You're going to say you called me when you found Dillon. You're also going to say that boy was experimenting with drugs and you tried to get him to stop. You'll also say that last night he hit you in the mouth for trying to interfere with what he was doing."

"Beau, I loved him, he wanted to marry me." Kitty wiped her runny nose with her sleeve.

"Oh, please." The chief waved his hand in exasperation. "Don't be more of a damned fool than you already are. That boy was fucking you for your money, and you kept him around because you liked the size of his pecker. Now, let's get straight on this thing. We need to move beyond this and get back to work before DesFuentes sticks a needle in our arms, too. I'm keeping a tight lid on this. We'll make it go away without attracting attention. Got it?"

Giving up, Kitty nodded.

"Now, get dressed. The M.E. will be here any minute."

Two days later, walking out of the periodontist's office with three new crowns, Kitty's cell phone rang. Her mouth was numbed with Novocain. She answered, anyway.

"Ms. Sampson, this is Bryce Novak, Manny Gonzalez's attorney."

"How can I help you?" slurred Kitty.

"Is this a bad time, Ms. Sampson?" asked the attorney, inferring she'd been drinking.

"This is fine. I just left the dentist's office; my mouth is numb. What can I do for you?"

"Well, Ms. Sampson, I wanted to let you know that Mr. Gonzalez would like to take you up on your offer to buy Manny's. Is that something you're still interested in?"

"Yes, I'm still interested, but with a few conditions. The sale must be immediate and closed within seven days. It's an all-cash offer, so that shouldn't be a problem."

"I think we can do that," said the attorney.

"Manny is to sell me the liquor license with the business, and since the restaurant has gone to hell in the past month, tell him I'm paying him a hundred grand less. Got that? Oh, and Mr. Novak..."

"Yes, Ms. Sampson."

"Tell Manny I'll take good care of the place. I know how much that restaurant means to him."

"I'll do that, Ms. Sampson. I'll do that."

CHAPTER 44

Monday, August 30 - 9:00 a.m.

Deep in thought, DesFuentes tapped his finger on the desk while he studied the spreadsheet on his laptop. After reorganizing the numbers on the screen, he pressed the sum function, grunted and nodded his approval. Numbers didn't lie. His improvements were working. The cash was adding up and his wealth was increasing along with the stream of cocaine making its way into American cities. Peter Guise was having no trouble keeping up, and now that Kitty had been motivated to accelerate her end of things, Des Fuentes liked what he was seeing.

The spreadsheet tracked hundreds of accounts, money that moved among banks and financial houses around the globe. Money used to buy multiple properties and businesses throughout the U.S. and South America. Money that would enable him to leave the drug trade alive. Drug lords rarely lived to enjoy their wealth. Ricardo DesFuentes intended to be the exception.

• • •

11:50 a.m.

The staff at the Blue Heron Restaurant, formerly Manny's, was busy preparing for the lunch rush. The sun shone brightly, an ocean breeze was blowing, and the humidity level had dropped enough to make being outside enjoyable. The restaurant would be slammed with hungry customers. Kitty Sampson was in her office, paperwork spread out in front of her when Eileen

McNeil, a shift lead, knocked lightly on the door. Kitty looked up and waved her in.

Stick thin, short, jet-black hair and dark eyes, Eileen's pale skin looked as though it had never seen the Florida sun. A colorful mermaid tattoo ran up her arm, and a silver wire ring adorned her right nostril. More than competent at her work, Eileen had little confidence in herself or her capabilities, making her the perfect person to run the Blue Heron in Kitty's absence without asking too many questions.

"Here's today's mail. How about some coffee, Kitty?"

"Sure," said Kitty, dismissing her assistant without looking up.

"I'll be back in a jiff." She returned with a mug of steaming coffee with cream and one teaspoon of sugar, just the way her boss preferred.

Kitty took the mug and put it to her lips. "Last night's receipts are impressive. Keep it up, Eileen." Leaving Eileen standing at the door, Kitty went back to her paperwork.

Eileen backed out of the office mumbling to herself. "Keep it up? Why don't you see if you can keep it up without me?" She'd been working in the restaurant for the past five years, first for Manny and now for Kitty. Having started as a hostess and working her way up to a shift lead, Eileen had also filled the role of Manny's assistant. With Manny, she faced groping hands and his Neanderthalic unwillingness to give a "skirt" a management position. When Kitty bought the place, Eileen felt sure she had a good chance of becoming a manager with a woman now at the helm.

But there was no named manager at the Blue Heron. The restaurant was already making an impressive comeback and although Eileen was largely responsible for its success, Kitty hadn't rewarded her for her contribution.

The bulk of the day's mail still on the desk, Kitty stared in disbelief at a letter she'd just opened. Her hand shook as she read an audit notice from the Internal Revenue Service informing her that the parent company, under which all her businesses were held together, was coming under the scrutiny of the US government. Kitty's pulse raced as she read further.

The audit will commence at a date yet to be determined, sometime in the next few months. Basic instructions about how to prepare and the name of the auditor to whom the case has been assigned are attached.

Shit! I've been careful, but sometimes the amounts increased so quickly, I did things I would have normally avoided. Things that might be discovered. The entire operation could be exposed. If that happens, I'm as good as dead.

As she absorbed the bad news, Kitty felt a headache coming on. Eyes closed; she was massaging her temples when Eileen opened the door without knocking. She stood in the doorway.

"Kitty, I've been meaning to talk to you about something. I deserve a promotion and a raise. I'd like you to consider me for both."

Kitty's response was curt. "This isn't a good time. Please leave."

"Well, when would be a better time?"

"I'll let you know. Now, please leave. I have a headache."

Eileen raised her voice. "I can see you're very busy, and I hate to push on this, but you're leaving me no choice."

Kitty snapped, her voice was loud and her tone angry. "Eileen! You *are* pushing, and frankly, it's pissing me off. Now, get out of my office so I can concentrate!"

"You're being unfair," insisted Eileen, tears forming in her eyes. "I've been running this place, and you know it."

"Unfair?" Kitty stood up from her desk and approached Eileen. "You're a spoiled brat with a stupid wire in her fucking nose who thinks the world is owed to her. Well, you're not owed anything! I'm not raising your pay, and there is no way in hell I'm promoting you!"

Eileen stood back but Kitty was going in for the kill. She moved in front of Eileen, stopping just a few inches away. "Go do your damned job or find another one. And don't forget, I own all the decent restaurants around here, so unless you want to sling pancakes at IHOP, you'd better adjust your attitude. Are we clear?"

"We're clear." Her face flushed; Eileen held back her tears and hurried out the door.

With twenty minutes left before her shift ended, Eileen did her best to keep it together. She wanted to go home, crawl into bed, and hide under the covers.

"Eileen, bad news," said Louise, a hostess at the restaurant.

"Jack just called; he's supposed to be on the next shift at the bar, but that antique Pontiac of his broke down again. He won't be in. You'll have to cover unless you can find someone to fill in."

With no time to find a replacement, wiping tears and smeared mascara from her reddened face, Eileen stepped behind the bar just as three women sat down. Seeing her teary eyes, one of the women asked, "Is everything alright? You look upset." The voice was kind, triggering Eileen's tears to come faster. She didn't want to cry, and she did her best to control herself, but they were coming in buckets now.

"Oh, I've upset you. What can I do to help?" asked the woman.

"I'm okay," Eileen answered.

"No, you aren't," said one of the others.

"Hey, excuse me!" called the third, a gorgeous dark-skinned woman with a French accent. She caught the attention of the bartender at the opposite end of the long bar.

"What can I do for you ladies?" The bartender asked, giving a once-over to the exotic woman who'd called him over.

"Could you please do us a favor?"

"Sure," said the bartender, his name tag identified him as Frank.

"My friend here," the dark-skinned woman said, nodding toward Eileen, "needs to step away for a moment. Could you cover for her, please?"

"No worries," said Frank. "Take your time, Eileen."

"Thanks, Frank. I'll be right back." The four women went to a table where they could talk without being overheard.

"Thank you for being so kind." Eileen wiped her eyes with a paper napkin. "I'm Eileen."

"Nice to meet you, Eileen. I'm Lisa, this is Kim, and that's Simone. Now, what's going on? Maybe we can help."

Eileen explained she'd just had an argument with her boss and that she was trapped in a job that wasn't going anywhere. She went on to explain that money was tight.

"Maybe you just caught your boss at the wrong time," offered Lisa. "Good employees aren't easy to find. Your boss might have a change of heart."

"I don't think so," said Eileen. "Do you know who she is? She owns just about everything on this island, and she's vindictive. Ask anyone, you don't get on the wrong side of Kitty."

"Your boss is Kitty Sampson?" asked Lisa, although she already knew that. They'd come to the Blue Heron to scope out the place.

"Yes, that's her."

"Can I ask you a question?" said Lisa.

"Sure." Eileen blew her nose in a napkin.

"The Chief of Police comes in here pretty regularly. Right? Why do you think that is?"

"He meets with her; I think they're friends or something."

"They're friends?"

"Well, I'm not sure if they're friends, but when he comes in he goes right to Kitty's office. He doesn't knock or anything. He just goes in. Sometimes, she isn't even there."

"That's odd," said Kim.

"He always has a duffel bag with him."

"Any idea what's in it?" asked Kim.

"I don't know," said Eileen, "but once, when I was in Kitty's office leaving some receipts on her desk, I noticed what looked like the same bag sticking out from under her desk."

"So, he left it there?"

"No, he always has it with him, when he comes in and when he leaves. Um, I'd better get back to the bar," said Eileen. "It was nice meeting you. Thanks again for getting me out of there. I feel a little better."

After Eileen left, the three leaned in over the table and continued their conversation.

"So, what's in those bags?" asked Lisa.

"I don't know," said Kim, "but I'd sure like to find out."

"I have a pretty good guess," said Simone. "It's cash. It happens all the time on Martinique. Cash is moving through this place. The chief is either taking it out of here, so it doesn't have to be counted for tax reasons, or he's bringing it in."

"Bringing it in?" asked Kim. "Why would that be?"

"She's laundering it," said Lisa.

CHAPTER 45

Tuesday, August 31 - 3:30 p.m.

Kim was on duty at the police station when her cell phone rang. Seeing it was Lisa, she picked up. "Hey there, I'm at work right now." Standing nearby was the chief, he moved closer to Kim's desk and eavesdropped on her conversation.

"Is he there?" asked Lisa.

"Yes."

"Okay, I'll talk to you soon."

As Kim hung up, the chief sneered. "Was that your girlfriend?"

Keep cool, don't answer.

"I asked you a question, Witherspoon." He was leering at her and making her uncomfortable.

"Yeah, that was her," Kim looked her boss in the eye. "She wanted to tell me that she's all wet and waiting for me."

The grin disappeared from the chief's face and his mouth dropped open. Without another word, he left the station, got into his squad car, and pulled out of the parking lot.

With the station to herself and no time to gloat over her small victory, Kim moved fast. Grabbing the station's lockpick set, she tried several picks before the short hook worked its magic. Wasting no time, Kim walked behind the desk and looked in the knee hole. Her heart pounded when she saw the two black duffel bags resting on the floor. She pulled one out, opened it, and gasped.

Unzipping the second bag, she saw its contents were the same as the first and began snapping photos. She froze when she heard the door to the station opening. She held her breath and waited to be discovered.

"Hello, is anyone here?" said a voice Kim didn't recognize at first.

Scrambling to get the bags back under the desk, she called out, "Just a moment." Stepping out of the office, she saw a face she knew. "Oh, hello, Ms. Sampson, what can I do for you?"

"I'm looking for your boss. Is he here?"

"You just missed him. Is there something I can help with?"

"I just wanted to ask him a question. I'll catch up with him another time."

"Okay, I'll let him know you stopped by."

Kim watched the woman get into her car and put a phone to her ear.

Kim sent a quick text.

AT THE STATION. SAW WHAT'S IN THE BAGS.
   HE'S ON TO ME.

Moments later, the squad car made a sharp turn into the parking lot and screeched to a stop in front of the station. Chief Jackson stormed inside to find Kim at her desk with her head down. He walked past her and stood in front of his office. He turned the door handle. It was locked.

"Witherspoon, did you break into my office?"

"What did you say?" Kim feigned surprise and prepared for the fallout.

"You heard me, you sneaky bitch! I know you were in my office. What the hell were you doing in there?" The chief's face was red and an ugly vein throbbed by his left temple.

When Kim didn't respond, the chief came from behind and gripped her shoulder. He pulled her around to face him. "Answer me, Witherspoon. What the hell are you up to?"

The door to the station flew open. A young woman ran in, out of breath and clearly distressed. "Can somebody please help me? A car just ran me off the road. It almost killed me!"

"Ma'am, calm down. Are you alright? You weren't hurt, were you?" The chief asked.

Breathless, the young woman replied, "I wasn't hurt, just frightened,"

"Where's your car, ma'am?" asked Kim.

"It's in a ditch, down the road a bit. I ran here. I think the other driver might have been under the influence. Could you come with me to look at my car? It's damaged and may need to be towed."

"Certainly, ma'am. You're sure you're okay?" Kim was out of her chair on her way toward the door.

"I'm worried about the car, it's my mother's."

"Let's go take a look," said Kim, turning back to glance at her boss. "I'll let you know if we need anything, Chief."

"Holy shit," said Kim as she raced down the block with Lisa to the place where she'd parked her Prius. "I think he was about to hit me; you got there just in time."

"I saw your text and sped over here. Luckily, I was only a few minutes away. What does he know?"

"He knows I was in his office, which he keeps locked. And guess what, there are two duffel bags chock full of hundred-dollar bills under his desk right now. Look!" Kim handed Lisa her phone. Displayed on the screen were photographs of the open duffel bags, including some close-ups.

"Great work, it's time for you to disappear."

CHAPTER 46

Wednesday, September 1 - 6:15 a.m.

The turquoise ocean sparkled in the early morning sunlight and the surf line was decorated with colorful shells that had washed in with the evening tide. The beach, lined with fresh sea turtle tracks, was empty but for a few fishermen. Officer Bill Widley was heading north on his regular morning patrol when he saw Simone Mercier and decided to say hello. "Hey, Simone, what do you have there?"

"Hey there, Bill," she was on her knees in the sand, a turtle nest in front of her." A huge green was here. I just did some excavation; she left a huge clutch of eggs. Want to take a look before I cover it up?"

He kneeled next to her, and she pointed toward the clutch of eggs. "That's a lot of eggs, seems like the greens are having a great nesting year."

Simone began replacing the sand she'd removed. "They are, even with the hurricane, their numbers are up this season."

"Well, let's not count our chickens, hurricane season is far from over."

"Count our chickens?" said Simone with a confused look. "What does that mean?"

Bill stood up and laughed. "I guess they don't use that phrase where you come from. It means... don't count on something good happening before it does."

"You Americans," Simone shook her head and smiled. "You are very strange people."

"We sure are," said Bill. "Hey, I've been meaning to ask you about the new technology you guys are testing. How's it working out?"

"What technology?" Simone cocked her head.

"I saw Peter over on Olive Beach the morning of the hurricane. He was trying out some new technology in the nests. He said it could help determine if the nest was viable. It sounded pretty cool."

"I don't know what you're talking about. We'd never put anything in the nests."

"Well, Peter definitely had something in a nest. I saw it with my own eyes."

"I'll have to ask him about that. He hasn't said anything to me about new technology."

"Well, I'd better let you get back to it," said Bill. "New tracks are everywhere this morning. Looks like you're going to have a busy day."

. . .

The chief was livid. Worried, too. He sat in his office, drumming his fingers on his desk, while pondering his situation. *Witherspoon was snooping around in here and saw the bags under my desk,* he thought. *No doubt, she opened them too. Now she's dropped out of sight.* He slammed his fist on the desk. *Witherspoon, where are you? You've become a serious problem.*

The chief drove to the house where Kim lived with her girlfriend and pounded on the front door. "Witherspoon, you in there?" Making his way around the house, he looked in the windows. No one was there. Remembering her girlfriend worked at the Stypman Island Marine Life Institute, he placed a call.

"This is Chief Jackson. I'd like to speak with Simone Mercier. Is she available?"

"I'm sorry, Simone is out on the beach recording nesting activity."

The girlfriend should be easy to pick up on the beach, he thought. *If Witherspoon is hiding, I'll coax her out by grabbing Simone Mercier.*

. . .

Stewie Williamson, the youngest officer on the island's police force, was busy checking the parking areas at the public beach access points on the island. They were places notorious for drunks and vagrants spending the night. He walked up to a white Kia parked under a stand of sabal palms.

Inside the car and passed out in the back seat was a teenage boy. Stewie grinned. *This will be fun,* he thought, then he rapped on the window with his gun. The confused and sleepy occupant opened the car door.

"Yeah?"

"Get out of the car!" Stewie pointed the gun, his finger on the trigger.

The boy squealed, "Don't shoot!" Scrambling from the Kia, he raised his hands, a look of terror on his youthful face.

Stewie smirked. His day was made, he'd scared the kid to death. "Up against the car and spread 'em," he commanded, still pointing the gun.

The kid did as he was told and shook all over when Stewie frisked him. "I'm sorry, I was just sleeping here. Please don't arrest me. My father will..."

Stewie's radio crackled, and he heard the chief calling for him. "Williamson? You there?"

"Yeah, I'm here, Chief."

"Call me back on your cell. I don't want to broadcast this."

Stewie turned to the boy. "This is your lucky day. Get the hell out of here. If I catch you here again, your ass is mine." The Kia pulled out fast, kicking up dust and sand as it left. Stewie called his boss.

"Stewie, this is important. I need you to pick up a woman named Simone Mercier and bring her in."

"I know who she is. She's a hottie. What'd she do?"

"Never mind that, just pick her up. Do whatever you need to do but get her in my office now! Don't come back without her, understand? She's on the beach marking turtle nests or some bullshit like that. One more thing, Stewie. If you hear from Witherspoon, don't tell her what you're doing, and whatever you do, don't let her get to Simone Mercier first."

"Got it, boss. You can count on me."

. . .

Lisa could see the worry on Kim's face. She sat on the side of the bed and checked her voice messages. They'd been hiding out in Lisa's hotel room since the previous day.

"His messages are becoming increasingly deranged," Kim said after listening to the latest in a series of voicemails from her boss.

Lisa sat down next to her. "Any luck reaching Simone?"

"I've been trying to get a hold of her but at this time of day, she's on the beach and isn't picking up. The chief is going apeshit. What if he goes after her?"

Lisa reached over and held Kim's hand. "I'd go find her but he can recognize me now and if he follows me, we risk leading him to you. We need another way and I think I know how to do it."

Kim turned at looked at Lisa. "What is it? I'll do anything."

"You don't have to do a thing. What if we ask Clara and Jason Anders to help? They live on the beach; they can get to her fast."

"It's worth a try," Kim stood and started pacing, "and Simone knows them. She sees them on the beach all the time with their dog. Let's call, we've got to do something."

Clara and Jason agreed to help. "We saw her go by on her ATV this morning," said Jason. "If she's following her regular route, we should be able to catch up with her without much trouble."

"Keep an eye out for the chief, Jason," warned Lisa. "There's no telling what he may do."

. . .

Having finished her morning rounds, Simone drove her ATV toward the dunes and the access point connecting the beach to a small pathway that led to the Institute. Ahead of her, Clara and Jason were frantically waving in her direction.

As she drove closer, Simone could see that Marley, who was usually calm, was pulling at her leash and barking. Simone pulled up and hopped off the ATV. "You guys are out here early," she said in a cheerful voice. Noticing the expression on their faces, she lost her smile. "What's wrong? And what's with Marley, she seems agitated."

"Simone, stay right here with us. There's a cop over there, and we think he's waiting for you," Jason said in a hushed voice.

"We had a call just a few minutes ago," Clara explained. "Kim is with Lisa Owens. They asked us to tell you that Chief Jackson might be looking for you. They think he may try to use you to get to Kim. Apparently, she discovered something damaging to him and has been hiding."

Without fully comprehending what was happening, Simone glanced over at the police officer. "That's Stewie Williamson," she whispered. "Kim says he's got a reputation for being quick with his gun but when it comes down to it, he doesn't have the guts to pull the trigger." She looked at Clara and Jason, "Merde! He's coming over here."

As the officer came closer, Marley became more aggressive, pulling at her leash, growling and baring her teeth. Using her phone's video camera, Clara began recording. Jason gripped his dog's leash. "Marley, cool it, would you?"

"She's never like this," said Clara.

"She senses something's wrong," whispered Simone.

Stewie Williamson came as close as he dared given Marley's growls and snarls. "Simone Mercier, come with me."

Simone's heart beat out of her chest. "Why should I, Stewie?" she replied. "Am I under arrest?"

"I have instructions to take you to the station for questioning. Let's go."

Snarling, Marley dug her paws in the sand and pulled hard at her leash, trying to get to Stewie.

Stewie stared at Jason, "You better control that animal," he warned.

"Simone's not going with you, Officer," said Jason.

Stewie raised his voice and put his hands on his hips. "Look old man, if I say she's coming with me, then she's coming with me!"

"Simone has done nothing wrong," insisted Clara. She held her phone up in Stewie's view. "People of color don't always fare so well with white police officers, particularly those who appear to be overly aggressive. So, unless you'd like to find yourself all over social media, leave her alone. She's doing important work that our community greatly values."

Stewie's face reddened, "I've had enough of this crap," he shouted. "Mercier, you're coming with me!" He pulled his Glock from its holster and pointed it at them. Shocked, the three of them stood back. Marley continued to growl and pull at her leash.

"You," Stewie screamed at Clara, "give me that phone!" He stepped forward and grabbed Clara's wrist, knocking the phone into the sand.

"You're hurting me!" Clara yelled, yanking her wrist from Stewie's grip. Marley lunged, her teeth grazing Stewie's wrist as they caught hold of his sleeve and a shot rang out.

CHAPTER 47

Wednesday, September 1 - 7:30 a.m.

Clara screamed when Jason collapsed. She knelt beside him and held his head in her hands. "Hold on, Jason, please hold on," she whispered. Simone watched frozen in fear, her hand covering her mouth.

Scared by the unexpected bang of the gun, Marley had released Stewie's sleeve but when the bullet hit him, Jason had dropped her leash. Free of her restraint, she went after Stewie with unexpected ferocity, her teeth gripping onto the flesh of his forearm. Stewie let out a howl and dropped his gun. Stumbling backward and falling, he struggled to get away from the dog who continued to go after him.

"Simone, go! Get away now!" urged Jason in a labored voice, his face was grimaced in pain. "Take this," he reached for Clara's cell phone. "The video footage, give it to Kim."

Simone hesitated at first, then jumped on her ATV. With her own phone in hand, she called 911 and sped down the beach.

"Call the dog off! Call it off!" Stewie screamed. He was rolling around in the sand with Marley jumping at him. Her snarls filling his ears.

"Marley, come here!" Clara commanded through tears.

The dog obeyed but continued her growling. They heard a siren drawing closer. Shortly thereafter, two EMTs came running onto the beach, carrying a stretcher and other equipment. Seeing them, Clara broke down weeping. Marley turned her attention to Jason and licked his face. He was still. His shirt and the surrounding sand were red with his blood. The dog began to whimper. Jason had lost consciousness.

. . .

8:45 a.m.

Lisa raced into the emergency room waiting area, dark sunglasses and a sun hat covered most of her face. Embracing Clara, she said, "I never should have gotten you involved in this. How is he?"

Tears streaming, Clara held the embrace. "This is such a horrible nightmare. I'm so worried. Jason is in surgery; he lost so much blood."

Clara's white t-shirt and pale blue shorts were blood-stained. She'd been barefoot, having come from the beach in the ambulance. A hospital worker had taken pity on her and gave her the paper slippers she wore on her feet.

"I feel awful," said Lisa. "This is my fault."

"No, it isn't, Lisa. You're trying to put an end to whatever's going on here. Why would anyone give that idiot a gun? For the life of me, I have no idea what that officer was thinking."

"What happened to Jason should never have happened," insisted Lisa. "I promise you, Clara, I'll get to the bottom of this."

"You're right. It shouldn't have happened, but it did. Now we have to face up to it." Clara stepped in front of Lisa. Locking eyes with her, she put her hands on Lisa's shoulders. "Solve this, Lisa, whatever it is. No one is safe until you do." She removed her hands and asked, "Poor Simone, the look on her face... is she alright?

"Simone is okay. She's with Kim and worried sick about Jason."

"The doctor told me Jason will be in surgery for a while longer. He expects a good outcome unless something unexpected happens."

"I'll keep you company while you wait," Lisa offered.

"I would love for you to stay with me, but there's someone who needs you more than I do right now."

"There is?"

"Yes, can you please pick up Marley from the fire station? She wasn't permitted in the ambulance. A very kind EMT took her off the beach so I could come here with Jason. I'm sure she's upset and would be a lot happier back in our condo. There's a spare key under the mat."

"Say no more."

. . .

2:00 p.m.

Back with Kim in a hotel room adjacent to Lisa's, Simone stared at the view of the ocean while waiting for an update on Jason's condition. It had been hours and still there was no word. Her thoughts wandered, and she recalled something Bill Widley said, something that had troubled her. She'd put it out of her mind, but now it was back to bother her. *New technology in sea turtle nests?* Simone couldn't get the thought out of her mind. *There's nothing about new technology in any of the scientific literature,* she thought. *And no one has said a word about this at the Institute. Could Peter be doing something on his own?*

Using an iPad, Simone checked the previous night's GPS records. She could see that Peter had just marked two new leatherback nests in more remote areas of the beach.

While Kim and Lisa plotted their next move in the room next door, Simone sent a text and then she wrote a quick note.

• • •

"Lisa!" Kim called out. "Come over here!"

Lisa stuck her head through the door opening connecting Kim's room to hers. Seeing the worried expression on Kim's face, she asked, "What's wrong?"

"Simone is gone. She left a note." Kim handed it to her.

Hey, guys, there is something I need to check out on the beach. Bill Widley has agreed to keep me company. I feel safe with him, so please don't worry. I have my phone with me, and I'll keep a lookout for you know who.
See you shortly, Simone

"After what just happened, I can't believe she'd do that. What the hell is she thinking?" Upset and annoyed, Kim began to pace. "If I tell her to get back here, she'll accuse me of having control issues."

"Well, from what you told me about Bill, at least she's in good hands," said Lisa.

Twenty minutes later, there was a phone call from Bill, his voice cool and direct. "Kim, we're on the beach, about a mile south of where you are. You need to get over here fast, and bring your friend, Lisa."

Racing down the beach on foot, Lisa and Kim reached Simone and Bill in a matter of minutes. Simone was upset and crying. Bill stood next to her, his arm around her shoulder.

"Simone, what's wrong? Are you okay? We came as fast as we could." Kim was sweating and out of breath. She hugged her girlfriend and looked at Bill with panicked eyes.

"You must be Bill, I'm Lisa. What's going on?"

"I found something terrible," Simone said through tears. "Look at this." She walked over to a freshly dug hole in a section of sand roped off with yellow tape.

Kim peered into the hole and saw rectangular blocks wrapped in black plastic. The wrapping on one of the blocks had been cut open, exposing what looked to be a white brick. Kim backed away so Lisa could see. They both knew what it was.

"Bill scraped it with his knife. It's cocaine, the others are just like it." Simone struggled to get the words out.

"Someone put cocaine in a turtle nest?" Kim tried to process what she was seeing.

"Not someone," said Simone. "Peter did this."

"How do you know it was him?" asked Lisa.

"I saw him," said Bill, "and he lied about it."

CHAPTER 48

Wednesday, September 1 - 2:00 p.m.

Standing in her kitchen, Catherine Wallingford swallowed hard, then she poured four bottles of bourbon into the sink. She inhaled the aroma and watched as the drain swallowed up the amber liquid. *Lucky drain,* she thought. Determined to stop drinking and do something about her treacherous husband, she picked up the phone.

It was almost two years ago that Catherine first suspected Wally was sleeping around. Soon after, using her husband's Apple ID, which she found in a notebook he kept in a desk drawer, she activated 'Find My Phone,' a feature Wally didn't know existed. Tracking his whereabouts, she began to discover the full extent of her husband's perversion.

Following up on police reports, she learned of the beatings and murders. With time and patience, she'd uncovered an unmistakable trail. Afraid and unsure of what she should do, she'd hidden her husband's terrible secret, and it had ruined her life. Women had been victimized and killed, and Catherine realized her silence was to blame. Staying in her marriage while drinking away her terrible secret, she was no more than a cover for Wally, and that made her sick. Catherine made a phone call and set her plan in motion.

"Congressman Wallingford's office, this is Marjorie."

Catherine did her best to sound pleasant. "Hello, Marjorie, this is Catherine. How are you?"

Wally's executive assistant, Marjorie, worked in his office on Capitol Hill and was more than familiar with Catherine's usual state of inebriation.

She said the same thing whenever her boss' wife called. "Why, Catherine, so nice to hear from you. I'm sorry, but the congressman isn't in the office just now. Can I have him call you back?"

"Marjorie, I'm not calling for Wally. I just wanted to check something on his calendar. Could you do that for me?"

"Sure thing, Mrs. Wallingford."

"I recall Wally saying he had a black-tie event a few days ago, someplace on Stypman Island. Wally seems to have lost a cufflink. It was a special one, I thought I'd call to see if it was found."

"Let's see," said Marjorie. "The event took place at the Banyan Tree Country Club. It was a benefit for the Stypman Island Institute for Marine Life Preservation. I can text you the phone numbers of the country club and the Institute if you'd like."

"That would be most helpful, Marjorie. Thank you."

A few phone calls later, Catherine received electronic copies of the professional photographs taken at the fundraiser. She pulled them up on her iPad. Most were red carpet photos taken as the guests arrived. Although her husband appeared in several of them, she didn't see any photos of a young woman with a dress, purse, or any other item with red sequins.

Catherine next came upon a series of different photographs. Groups of well-dressed people sat at tables, arms around each other and smiling for the camera. There were also several images of couples clutching each other on the dance floor, groups dancing together, and multiple candid shots of various people holding up their cocktails at the bar.

And then, she saw her standing in the background with a champagne glass in her hand. She seemed to be talking with a young man wearing a name badge. An extraordinarily beautiful young woman with long brown hair, clad in a stunning red sequined gown.

. . .

Friday, September 3 - 4:30 p.m.

Wally Wallingford sat at the desk in his study and opened a large envelope that had been delivered in the morning's mail. Inside, he found a photo of a young woman holding a glass of champagne and wearing a shiny red sequined dress. Written on the photo in bold letters was one word.

MURDERER

Wally slid the photograph back into the envelope and shoved it into his desk drawer.

Three days later, another envelope arrived. This time, delivered to Wally's apartment in Washington, DC. Suspecting what it was, he held his breath and opened it. It was the same photograph, with different words.

I KNOW YOU KILLED HER

Rattled, he called Ricardo DesFuentes.

"The only person who knows about this is you, DesFuentes!" Wally yelled into the phone. "Why are you doing this? I'm keeping your damned boats off the Coast Guard's radar, for God's sake. What more do you want from me?"

"I'm sorry, Congressman," said DesFuentes. "I'm not sending these photographs of Katrina. You have an enemy, I suggest you find out who it is, and fast."

"Help me, damn it!" Wally continued to yell. "You need me to keep your boats safe and your damned cocaine flowing. I can't do that if I'm in jail. Find out who's behind this!"

"I make no promises, Congressman," replied DesFuentes, "but let me assure you of this; if you allow this problem of yours to interfere with your ability to protect my shipments, you will have far more serious things to worry about."

Three days passed before a mailing tube arrived at Wallingford's congressional office on Capitol Hill. Marjorie opened it and pulled out a poster-sized copy of the photo. This time there were no words written on it. Her boss was at lunch. Not knowing who the woman was, and thinking it was a gift from an admirer, she put the poster on the conference table in her boss' office. To prevent the poster from curling up, she placed a book on each corner.

Marjorie was in a lunchroom making plans for a baby shower with a group of other Executive Assistants when Wally returned from lunch with Niles Ralfs, a congressional representative from Kentucky. The two were making plans for a golf outing at Congressional Country Club later in the week.

"Wow! Who's the babe?" Congressman Ralfs walked over to the poster on the conference table to get a better look.

Wally didn't know what to do or say. His face turned a bright red, his cheeks felt hot, and his mind went blank with fear. "I-I-I don't know who that is, or why it's there," he stammered. "Umm, I just remembered I have a call in a minute. Can we figure out golf at another time?"

"Sure," replied Niles Ralfs with a wink. "I'll bet you have a call to make. Tell her I said, nice dress."

Half an hour later, Marjorie was upset and crying. After more than six years of devoted service, she'd been fired without explanation. A security guard escorted her out of the Congressional Building. With a cardboard box containing her belongings in her arms, Marjorie struggled to understand what had just happened.

. . .

"You fired Marjorie?" Catherine was surprised. "Whatever did she do to deserve that?"

"I don't want to get into it, Catherine but I have reason to question her loyalty." He'd returned from Washington, and the two were having dinner.

Noticing the glass of water in front of his wife, he asked, "You're not drinking? And you're eating the food on your plate? What gives?"

"I've turned over a new leaf, Wally. No more drinking. There are other things for me to be doing. Oh, by the way, something came in the mail for you today. It's on the desk in your study."

"Dear God! When is this going to stop?" Wally slammed his fist on the table, rattling the plates and silverware.

Catherine gave him a harsh look. "When is *what* going to stop?"

"Someone's trying to blackmail me. I think it may be Marjorie."

"Blackmail? Whatever could someone blackmail you for?" Catherine took a small bite of food.

"I'm a congressman. People make up shit and try to extort us for money. It happens all the time."

"Well, if it's Marjorie, I suppose it's for the best that you fired her," said Catherine. As an afterthought, she added, "Funny, I always liked that woman, I would never have thought she'd blackmail anyone. I hope you notified the police."

Wally didn't answer. Instead, he left the table and went to his study. Inside the latest envelope he found a series of instructions.

Congressman Wallingford: I know about the pretty young woman who attended the fundraising event on Stypman Island and what you did to her. I also know she was not your first. I am in possession of evidence that directly implicates you in several of your crimes. I will make this information available to the police and will ensure it goes public. You will be forced to resign from Congress, you will be convicted of murder, and you will spend the rest of your life in a jail cell and face execution. If this does not appeal to you, you will follow these instructions and wire $7,000,000 to the account indicated below by tomorrow evening at 7:00 p.m.

Wally's hands shook, and beads of sweat formed on his forehead. He read the instructions a second time, trying to absorb what he was reading. "Seven million dollars," he silently mouthed the words. He had that much in an offshore account, but that was it, there'd be nothing left. He'd kept that money hidden from everyone, including his wife.

"Shit!" Wally slammed his fist on his desk. "How the hell do I get out of this?" He tried calling DesFuentes, but there was no answer. Then, he had a moment of clarity. *There's a reason he isn't offering to help. He's behind this.*

CHAPTER 49

Friday, September 10 - 10:00 p.m.

The fast boat pulled away from Grand Bahama Island on its regular route to Stypman Island. With only a sliver of moon, the night was dark and calm seas made it possible for the narrow V-shaped boat made of fiberglass, Kevlar, and carbon fiber to move at speeds exceeding eighty knots, ensuring it would reach its destination in record time. As it sped into U.S. waters, its operator stared into the darkness, the two crew members with him sat close by and dozed. All three wore earplugs to dull the roar of the three powerful engines behind them. Having made this voyage several times, the trip had become routine. There were no patrol boats in these waters. Protection had been arranged.

The searchlight seemed to come out of nowhere. It pierced the darkness and blinded them. Using their hands to shield their eyes from its glare, the men froze when they heard directions being shouted at them in English and Spanish through a bullhorn. "This is the U.S. Coast Guard. Turn off your engines and prepare to be boarded!" A patrol boat pulled directly aside. Four armed men jumped aboard.

"This is boat eight-nine-seven," the captain of the patrol boat spoke into a radio. "That tip-off was good. We have a fast boat, three hombres who need a change of underwear, and a big haul of coke. We're bringing it in now."

"Good work, Captain," came the reply. "Tell your crew the beer is on me."

. . .

Peter stood on the dark beach for several hours, waiting for a signal that never came. That meant trouble. He pulled the burner phone from his pocket.

. . .

Wally Wallingford was at his home when his calls were finally returned. "Nice of you to call me back, DesFuentes."

"I am not happy, Congressman. My boat was picked up. My men are being held, and my shipment and my vessel were confiscated. It was a very expensive evening. Care to explain?"

"I have no idea what you're talking about," replied Wally. "And, for the record, it wasn't as expensive as mine. I've been forced to wire seven-million dollars to an offshore account. But you knew that already. You screwed me, DesFuentes. Nobody does that and gets away with it. I was a fool for not seeing this sooner. Our arrangement is over."

"It was not me who blackmailed you. I told you that already. But you've betrayed me. You are correct; our arrangement is over. There will be consequences." DesFuentes ended the call.

CHAPTER 50

Saturday, September 11 - 11:30 a.m.

On edge, Wally spent the morning looking over his shoulder and checking his home alarm system. Stationed outside were two private security officers. He was peeking out the window to make sure they were still there when Catherine entered his study.

"Wally, there's something I want to speak with you about." She was dressed in a white pantsuit and a large pink hat that was perched at a stylish angle on her head.

"I'm busy, Catherine. Can it wait?"

"No, it can't."

He remained at the window and watched as she made herself comfortable in a leather armchair. "So, what is it, Catherine? What's so damned urgent?"

"I'm leaving you, Wally," she said with resolve in her voice. There was no trace of emotion and no wavering as she continued. "I don't love you, I don't even like you." She locked her eyes on his. "This has been coming for a long time now."

Wally was dumbfounded. He'd considered his wife to be a weak, pathetic character, and here she was dumping him. "And where will you go, Catherine? You have no family, and you don't have a single friend. You drank them all away. I'm all you have left."

"You're right, I don't have anyone, and that sorry fact makes this very easy for me. For starters, I'm taking a cruise. I need to get away from here and from you. It leaves out of Miami later this evening. I have a car waiting out front."

"I was wondering where you're headed dressed in that get-up. You look like a fucking tourist."

She ignored the insult. "Goodbye, Wally."

Resolute, Catherine Wallingford walked out the door of her large suburban home and didn't look back.

. . .

Sunday, September 12 - 1:52 a.m.

Catherine counted the minutes in her stateroom waiting for her iPad to signal that she had a new email message. Having changed from her white pantsuit, she was dressed in black to avoid detection later. The luxury cruise liner had served a seven-course gourmet dinner, followed by an evening of dancing, cocktails, and a Las Vegas-type show. She attended none of it. After suffering through the mandatory mustering drill, she'd hung a *do not disturb* card on the door of her stateroom and stayed put. Most of the ship's passengers were now asleep in their beds. Catherine was wide awake.

Having pulled out of the Port of Miami hours earlier, the ship was headed toward the island of Curacao, not far from Venezuela. As it departed, Catherine had sent wiring instructions to a bank in the Caymans that operated around the clock to accommodate its international clientele. She was waiting for confirmation that her instructions had been received and the transaction she'd requested had been executed.

The iPad finally signaled and Catherine checked the email. It was done. There was no going back. She gulped the large tumbler of bourbon she'd ordered when she first boarded the ship. She'd been eyeing it for hours. The bourbon was warming, and it gave her resolve for what would come next.

She picked up the iPad and stood, feeling the rise and fall of the ship beneath her she walked to a sliding door that opened to a private balcony. Now on the open sea, the cruise liner had picked up speed and was moving fast. When she stepped out into the night, a warm gust of moist sea air greeted her. Gazing up, she smiled. Millions of twinkling stars blanketed the heavens, their visibility enhanced in the absence of light, something she'd always enjoyed about sea voyages.

She tossed the iPad into the ocean. Being several stories above the water, she didn't see a splash. After struggling to pull herself up on the railing of the balcony, Catherine swung her legs over, one at a time. Sitting precariously, her legs dangling above the fast-moving water, she made the sign of the cross with her right hand. Letting go of the railing, she fell forward into darkness.

CHAPTER 51

Sunday, September 12 - 9:00 a.m.

DesFuentes was fuming. His boat, along with his cocaine, had been confiscated and his men arrested. *That fat pervert screwed me,* he thought. Nothing could be traced to DesFuentes himself, but Wallingford's betrayal had cost him a lot of money. His blood boiling, he made a resolution; Wallingford would pay with his life.

. . .

Monday, September 13 - 1:00 a.m.

Wally Wallingford lay awake, terrified in his own home. With Catherine gone, the massive house seemed much too large and far too quiet. Although he and his wife hadn't shared much of a relationship, their home hadn't felt this way when she was there. He'd been alone for just a day and already he'd come to hate the place. With DesFuentes out there, Wally couldn't leave.

Having spent most of the day pacing and peering out the windows, Wally had been drinking to calm his nerves. *Is this how it started for Catherine?* he wondered. *Fuck, what did she have to worry about?* He glanced at the clock beside his bed, groaned at the time and rolled over, his head pounding from too much scotch. He needed aspirin and was about to get up when he heard a welcome noise. The tension in his shoulders eased and his headache subsided. "So, you're back already?" he called out. When there was no answer, Wally sat up in bed. "Catherine?"

"Damn it, Catherine." Wally got up and walked to the door of the spacious bedroom and pulled it open.

Ricardo DesFuentes was on him in a flash, grabbing him by the neck of his pajamas and forcing him down on the bed. A punch in the mouth silenced Wally's screams. With his hands and ankles bound with zip ties, Wally wriggled on the bed like a worm on a hot sidewalk.

"It's a shame we could not be friends, Congressman," said DesFuentes, glowering. "We have so much in common. Like you, I also enjoy inflicting pain. Do you know what they call me in Colombia?"

Too afraid to respond, Wally whimpered.

"La llama." DesFuentes' words dripped with venom. "You do not speak Spanish, so I will tell you what it means. La llama means the flame.

Wally's whimpers grew louder. To no avail, he squirmed on the bed trying to get away from his attacker.

"Now you will learn why I came to be known in this way." DesFuentes took a metal flask from his pocket and began drizzling its contents. A little on Wally's face, and small amounts on his crotch and feet. The rest he splashed on the sheets and blankets.

The pungent odor of benzene irritated Wally's nose and throat. Realizing he'd been doused with gasoline and dizzy with fear of what would come next, he screamed and struggled to break free of his restraints.

"I think you are beginning to understand, Congressman. I am going to enjoy lighting the fire that will take your life. It's a very painful way to die. Let's start with what got you in all this trouble." He lit a match and held it up so Wally could see it. Delirious and thrashing on the bed, Wally's animalistic screams intensified. DesFuentes tossed the match on Wally's crotch.

His silk pajama bottoms ignited, lighting up the darkness. Seeing the flames, Wally shrieked in horror. Agony followed. A second match landed just below his feet. Wally's screams continued as the soles of his feet were scorched and flames grew around him. In shock, Wally's body began to shut down by the time the third match landed on his forehead. With flames licking at his face, Wally Wallingford succumbed to death.

DesFuentes moved fast. He grabbed a can of gasoline he'd left outside the door and emptied its contents throughout the room. With seconds to go before the blast, he ran down the home's impressive stairway to the main floor. A loud whooshing sound filled the house when the fire exploded in the bedroom, blowing out windows and incinerating what was left of Wally Wallingford.

About to step outside the front door, DesFuentes froze when heard the sirens and saw flashing lights headed up in the circular driveway. *How the hell did they get here so fast,* he wondered. Racing toward the back of the house, he exited through French doors that led to the expansive backyard. He sprinted through the yard and reached an eight-foot iron fence that lined the property. Pulling himself up to climb over it, he shrieked when an electric shock pulsed through his body, burning his hands. *"Mierde!"* he yelled. Fighting through the pain, he managed to pull himself over and dropped to the ground. Lying on his back and writhing in agony, DesFuentes blew on his singed hands. He gritted his teeth and struggled to his feet.

After stumbling into an area of dense foliage, he found his way to the next block where he'd left his Maserati. As he pulled the car onto the road, he could see the bright glow of the inferno that had been the Wallingford home. The sight brought a momentary smile. Quietly, he said his last goodbye, "I'll see you in hell, Congressman."

. . .

7:00 a.m.

"God damn it!" yelled Bernie Washington, upon hearing the news that Congressman Wallingford was dead.

"We were pulling into the driveway when the whole place exploded," said the agent standing before her.

The FBI had received a tip from a credible source that Wallingford was involved in the murder of several young women and had been compromised by a drug smuggling operation. The same source provided details leading to the capture of a fast boat carrying a million dollars of cocaine. The FBI had been on its way to take Wallingford in for questioning when the fire happened. Bernie was leading the investigation and wanted to question the congressman. Now that wouldn't happen.

"Was Mrs. Wallingford in the house?" she asked the agent.

"If she was there, we haven't found her remains yet."

"If she wasn't," said Bernie, "we have to find her and fast. Everything seems to be pointed toward her. If I'm right and she's our source, that woman is in terrible danger."

CHAPTER 52

Tuesday, September 14 - 12:00 a.m.

Although his boats were no longer protected by the Coast Guard, DesFuentes was already back in business. Peter had just picked up a drop and was toweling himself off when he heard the words come from behind him. "Peter Guise, you are under arrest for trafficking illegal drugs. Put your hands over your head."

Peter did as he was told. As Kim Witherspoon cuffed him, Lisa took photos of the packages of cocaine before bagging them and placing them in a satchel. The women had been tracking Peter for several nights and had become familiar with his routine. Tonight, with the help of night vision binoculars and a camera, they watched him signal the boat, swim out to collect the packages, and carry them back to his ATV.

All but one of the pieces had now come together. Lisa and Kim knew Peter was receiving the drug shipments and burying them in the turtle nests and that he was receiving payments in those same nests. They understood that Josephine Paulsen must have seen the smuggling operation on the beach and that Dorothy's killer had intended to murder her. They also knew the Chief of Police was transporting drug money from the villa on Quiet Harbor Lane to Kitty Sampson's various establishments to be laundered. The identity of the person who lived in that villa, the person behind the operation, remained the last missing piece of the puzzle.

As the policewomen walked Peter from the beach, it wasn't lost on Lisa that where they were now standing was where it had all begun. Her thoughts turned to Dorothy before they were suddenly interrupted.

"Evening, ladies, and Dr. Guise," said a familiar voice. From out of the darkness stepped Chief Jackson, pointing a rifle. "It looks like tonight is my lucky night. You two ladies have been difficult to find."

Caught flatfooted, Lisa and Kim froze.

"It's about time, Chief. I was beginning to think you wouldn't make it," said Peter.

"What did you just say?" asked Lisa.

"You heard him," interjected the chief. "Peter was aware you two have been watching him. So, we planned to trap you, and now here you are. Throw the keys to the cuffs over here, Witherspoon."

Kim did as she was told. They landed about a foot in front of the chief. Peter walked backward toward the chief; neither dared to take their eyes off Kim and Lisa. Chief Jackson bent over to pick up the keys in the sand. When he stood up, the barrel of a gun pressed against the back of his head.

"Drop your weapon, or I'll pull this trigger."

"What the fuck? Widley? You don't know what you're doing."

"Oh, I know what I'm doing. Now drop the damned rifle."

Chief Jackson hesitated, then dropped his weapon. Kim bolted forward to grab it, she emptied the chamber. Bill handed Lisa a pair of handcuffs from his belt. She used them to bind the chief's hands behind his back. Still cuffed, Peter broke down in tears. The chief glanced at him and shook his head in disgust.

"Let's move," directed Lisa and the five made their way off the beach to Bill's waiting squad car, the tension among them thicker than the humidity.

Lisa parted ways with them in the parking lot. "You guys take them in, I'll follow in my car. I'm parked behind that lifeguard station over there."

. . .

Glaring at Lisa through the bars of the jail cell, Chief Jackson sat on a metal bench bolted to the floor. In the next cell, Peter Guise sat on the floor, his head in his hands.

"Who the hell are you, anyway?" Jackson sneered.

"I'm your worst nightmare," Lisa responded, her eyes piercing through the chief.

He looked away. "I still don't get it. How'd you get on to Guise and how did Widley end up on the beach just when you needed him?"

"I don't need to tell you shit," Lisa responded.

"Humor me."

"The day the hurricane hit; Bill saw Peter had hidden something in a turtle nest when they ran into each other on the beach. It didn't make sense for Peter to be on the beach in the storm. Peter told Bill he was testing new technology. When Bill told Simone Mercier about his conversation with Peter, she knew something was up. She checked the nests he'd recently marked and discovered the buried drugs. She showed us what she'd found. We figured out the rest from there."

"It figures fuckin' Widley would have his fingers in the pot."

Lisa continued, "Bill is a friend of Simone's, and we let him in on what we've been up to, he was more than happy to provide backup in case you showed up."

"Two birds, one stone," said Bill as he approached the chief's cell. "I've suspected you were up to some nasty shit for a long time now, so I was only too glad to help put your ass in jail. You're a disgrace to the uniform. The people of this island put their trust in you, and you sold them out. Pieces of shit, like you, give the rest of us a bad rep. No wonder folks don't trust us the way they should."

Chief Jackson looked up, "Watch it, Widley."

"So," said Lisa, impatient to get to the bottom of things and learn who was behind Dorothy's murder, "how do you want to play this out, Chief?" She stood in front of his cell with her hands on her hips. "Are you going to cooperate and maybe catch a break or are you going down the hard way? We know about your trips to Quiet Harbor Lane. You transport dirty money so Kitty Sampson can launder it. What we don't know is who you're working for. You can give it up or leave it to Dr. Guise over there." Lisa glanced in Peter's direction.

Startled, Peter looked up at the mention of his name, then dropped his head back down to study the floor. Unlike Chief Jackson, who was still in his uniform, Peter wore a red and white striped jumpsuit, having soiled himself on the beach. Defeated and depressed, he sat cross-legged on the floor in a corner of his cell and hadn't uttered a single word since his arrest.

The chief stood and walked to the wall of bars at the front of his cell. He gripped two of the bars in his fists and positioned his face so it was mere inches from Lisa's, close enough she could feel the warmth of his breath on her. She understood the brazen act was meant to intimidate and that he'd expected her to step back. Lisa held her ground.

The chief issued a warning. "You fools have no idea who you're dealing with."

CHAPTER 53

Tuesday, September 14 - 1:30 a.m.

Dan Collins had just arrived at the station. When he was called in, he'd been told there was an emergency and he was needed at work. After being introduced to Lisa and informed that his boss and Peter Guise were behind bars, he stood with his hands in his pockets looking like a fish out of water. Unsure what he should do, he wandered around the station, his eyes glancing at the door to the jail.

"I feel sorry for him," Lisa whispered to Kim. "He's been caught off guard, a real bag-over-the-head. I can't imagine what he's thinking right now."

"He's wondering about his future. He was pretty close to the chief, maybe even his favorite."

"Be sure to keep an eye on him and don't let him in the jail. We don't know what kind of influence the chief has over him."

"No worries, Lisa. Nobody's going in there without Bill and me."

With neither suspect talking, the late hour took its toll on all of them.

"You guys seem to have things covered. Now that Dan is here, I might head back to the hotel. I need to think, and I'll do that better with some sleep and a shower."

"No problem, Lisa. Thanks for all your help tonight," Bill answered. Kim nodded in agreement.

"I'll be back first thing in the morning. Call if you need anything." Frustrated that she still didn't know who was behind Dorothy's murder, Lisa made her way to the parking lot and opened the door to her Prius. The interior light came on and she settled in. Throwing her handbag on the passenger seat, she pressed the ignition button. She chose a few songs from her playlist for the quick trip back to the hotel. Adele belted out *Hello* through the car's speakers.

The entrance to the hotel was just off the main road. Lisa made the turn and drove through a wooded area that provided the privacy and seclusion the hotel was known for. The Prius' headlights pierced the darkness and provided the only light on the entrance road which was empty at this time of night. Completely spent and looking forward to much needed rest, Lisa had just stifled a yawn when she saw something that caused her foot to slam down on the brake. She braced herself for the sudden stop. The car lurched and Lisa pressed her hands hard on the steering wheel to prevent herself from being thrown forward. Her handbag flew off the passenger seat, its contents spilling onto the floor.

Shaken, she peered through the windshield. In the beams of the headlights, a mother bobcat, her tiny baby dangling from her mouth, looked at her before continuing across the road and into the bushes. Lisa smiled at the sight, the tension in her shoulders eased and Adele sang about what she'd do to *Make You Feel My Love.*

. . .

"Oh, come on! Where the hell is my phone?" Lisa muttered as she dug through her handbag without success. She'd checked the pockets of her jeans, the floor, and under the bed. "Well, isn't this just great?"

She threw up her hands in frustration, exhausted from the night's events. "I give up," she announced to herself, deciding she'd have better luck looking for the phone after a few hours of sleep.

. . .

Operating with a skeleton crew due to the absence of the chief, River Whitefeather and Stewie Williamson, who was on administrative leave and back to living with his parents, the night shift at the police department turned out to be busier than usual.

Bill had been called out to deal with an automobile accident, a DUI, which had resulted in some serious injuries. That left Dan Collins on duty with Kim.

The phone rang and Collins took the call. Kim could hear him asking questions of the caller. After a few minutes on the phone, he walked over to Kim's desk. "I need to go take a look at this, a lady says her house was broken into and there are things missing. I should be back in an hour. You okay here on your own?"

"No problem, Dan. I'll radio you if I need anything. Be safe out there."

Kim had her work cut out for her and was grateful for the quiet. Tomorrow would be an important day. The department would be turned over to the State police along with the two prisoners being held in the small jail. Carla Weston had already been in touch. She was salivating at the thought of prosecuting the Chief of Police and the scientist. Kim had a lengthy report to write for her.

. . .

2:00 a.m.

An enraged DesFuentes threw a crystal tumbler of tequila, smashing it against the mahogany paneled wall of his office. Standing nearby, Dan Collins winced when the glass crashed and shattered. He'd just delivered the news that Peter Guise and the chief had been arrested. Collins, still in his police uniform, feared what the man would do next. It was looking like his drug smuggling enterprise might be shut down for good.

"There's something else you should know, Mr. DesFuentes," said Collins, trying to hide his nerves. "Now that the chief's behind bars, the State police have been called in. They'll be taking over the department in the morning."

"Who's in charge now?" demanded DesFuentes. He balled his fists and Dan stepped back moving closer to the door.

"Widley and Witherspoon."

"And they're the ones who caused these problems, correct?" asked DesFuentes.

"They're the ones, sir, along with a lady cop from Miami by the name of Lisa Owens. It turns out she's a friend of the old lady Scarella cut up by mistake. She's hunting you."

"And none of them know you're with me?"

"No, sir. They have no idea. I'm not gonna tell them, and neither is the chief. Peter Guise, he may be another story."

"Who's on duty with you at the police station tonight?"

"Witherspoon. Widley's on duty, too, but he's out dealing with a car accident."

"And where is this... Lisa Owens?" asked DesFuentes.

"She said she was going back to her hotel room at the Blue Azure. It's on the island."

"Describe her to me, please."

Dan described Lisa, adding that she was driving a white Prius. DesFuentes closed his eyes and clinched his jaw. Pressing his fingers against his temples, he winced. "My head is killing me." He looked at Collins. "What do you suggest I do about this?"

Dan's eyes widened in surprise. "Me? What do I think you should do? Umm...the chief makes those kinds of decisions."

"Call damned the hotel, make sure she's there!" DesFuentes went back to rubbing his temples.

Collins nodded. He put his phone on speaker and made the call. "This is Officer Collins with the Stypman Island police. I understand you have a guest there by the name of Lisa Owens. We're working with her on a case. Can you tell me if she's still on property? She said she might checkout tonight, but something's come up. We may need her help."

Dan was asked to wait while his call was transferred to the night manager.

"This is LaTisha Wilson. I'm the night manager. Is this Officer Collins?"

"Hey, LaTisha, this is Collins. We've met before, remember?"

"How could I forget? You left me with the tab for your drinks. What do you want?" Dan cringed seeing the disgust on DesFuentes' face. It wasn't manly to stick a woman with the check.

"You have a guest there named Lisa Owens. Can you tell me if she's still there, or did she checkout?"

"Let me see... she's here, room 217. Want me to put you through to her?"

"No, thanks. I just needed to know where we could find her. Thanks for your help. Have a good night."

"She's there." Collins stuffed his phone in his pocket and looked at DesFuentes.

"Alex! Come in here," shouted DesFuentes.

Alejandro Suarez, DesFuentes' bodyguard and most trusted associate entered the room with the AK-47 that never left his side. DesFuentes and Suarez had been friends since childhood. Raped by a cartel underboss and cut with a piece of broken glass to keep him silent, Alex's face and mental health had been ruined when he was only twelve. The long, jagged scar that ran down the side of his face had defined him ever since. His friend, Ricardo, had made good on a promise to make the attacker pay with his life, and Alex had been loyal to him ever since. Although Alex's loyalty went unquestioned, his ability to operate on his own was questionable. DesFuentes had learned to accommodate his friend's limitations by providing specific instruction. Alex had come through with Kitty Sampson's boyfriend, now DesFuentes would have to rely on him again.

"Alex, there is a woman police officer who's a threat to us. I want you to eliminate her. You'll find her at the Blue Azure Hotel, room 217. Her name is Lisa Owens."

DesFuentes looked into Alex's eyes. "Follow my instructions carefully. Do you understand?"

A nodding head gave DesFuentes his answer.

"Drive to the hotel and look for her car. It's a white Prius. She'll be asleep now, but do not kill her in her room. There is too much risk getting out of a place like that. Wait for her to leave the hotel and shoot from behind as she's walking to her car. I don't want her to see it coming. A rifle is out of the question so you'll need to use a handgun. Get close and blow her fucking head off."

Alex nodded. He understood the instructions and would do as he was told.

"One more thing," DesFuentes added. "Alex, make sure you park somewhere that will allow you a fast departure. Now go. Call me as soon as it's finished."

Collins stood silently as DesFuentes arranged the hit on Lisa Owens. Afraid to move or even breathe lest DesFuentes decide that he too had become a serious problem, Collins felt a chill run up his spine when DesFuentes' sinister eyes focused on him.

"Dan," DesFuentes' voice was barely audible, "what's the one thing you want more than anything?"

Surprised and confused by the question, Collins wasn't sure what to say. He wasn't even sure he'd heard correctly. "What?" he answered.

"I asked you a simple question. What do you want more than anything?"

Collins racked his brain, certain there must be a right answer to the unexpected question. With his voice an octave higher than usual, he said, "Right now, what I want more than anything is to get the hell away from here with a shitload of money."

"Anything else?" DesFuentes asked.

Oh fuck, I was right. He's looking for something else. Collins' mind raced before he decided on an answer he thought DesFuentes would appreciate, something an alpha male would say. "I'd like a really hot babe; one who'd have to do everything I want."

"I like the way you think, Dan. If you could pick any girl you wanted, who would that be?"

A smug smile came to Collins' face. "There's this French chick who works with the sea turtles... that's who I'd pick."

DesFuentes remembered the woman. Kitty had told him about her and he'd seen her at the fundraising ball. She was a good choice. He leaned over his desk; his dark eyes locked on Collins. "Granted. I like a man who knows what he wants."

Collins looked confused. *What the hell just happened?*

• • •

Back at the police station, Dan remained quiet and focused his attention on writing up a bogus incident report about a burglary that never happened. As the night progressed, the police station became quiet, and the officers did what they normally did; they found ways to stay awake.

When Kim's phone buzzed, she picked up.

"Kim, its Bill. Everything okay there?"

"So far, so good, on your way back?"

"I'm still at the hospital. It was a nasty accident; the victim is in the ICU. I'll hang around until he's able to give a statement. I could be here for a while. That work for you?"

Collins got up from his desk and went to the coffee station to make a fresh pot. He poured two mugs of the steaming brew, handing one to Kim who was still on the phone.

"Thanks Dan."

"What's Collins doing?" asked Bill.

"He's behaving himself, just made me coffee," whispered Kim.

"Good. Call if you need anything."

The smell of the freshly brewed coffee was a welcome aroma for two people who were coming to the end of a long night. Kim swallowed a mouthful and continued working everything that had transpired over the past twenty-four hours into a time log for her report. After a while, she broke the silence. "Dan, I don't feel well, I'm dizzy."

There was no reply. Kim realized she was in trouble and reached for her phone. She felt the room spin then passed out, her head hitting the desk with a thud.

"She's out," Collins said into the burner phone he'd taken from his pocket.

DesFuentes had been waiting in the parking lot. He entered the station, wearing dark Gucci sunglasses and a black ball cap. His t-shirt and jeans were also black, as were his athletic shoes. Gloves covered his hands. Ignoring Kim, out cold at her desk, he asked, "Where's the jail?"

Giddy with anticipation, Collins opened the door to the jail stepping out of the way so DesFuentes could enter first. There were just three cells. Asleep on a bench, was the chief. Peter Guise, still sitting in a corner on the floor, occupied the cell next to the chief's. The third cell was empty.

"Chief Jackson!" said DesFuentes, his voice loud and commanding, "Get up... you have work to do!"

Opening his eyes, an expression of relief came to the chief's face. As Collins unlocked his cell, the chief sat up. His expression changed. No longer relieved, his face was red with anger. His eyes darted around the jail.

"Sorry not to have sprung you earlier, boss," said Collins, "but we had this plan." The chief nodded, wary of what was taking place, unsure who he could trust. He stood and walked out of the cell.

"Where's that bitch, Witherspoon?" Chief Jackson demanded. "And the other two? I'm gonna fuckin' kill them all."

"You will leave them to me," replied DesFuentes. "Give him his gun and get him out of here," DesFuentes instructed Collins. "And Dan, don't forget. When I text you, call Widley and tell him he's needed here. They'll be a surprise waiting for him when he arrives."

"C'mon, Chief. Time to get out of Dodge," said Dan, leaving DesFuentes alone with Peter Guise, who'd been cowering on the floor and listening to everything.

. . .

DesFuentes walked to Peter's cell. "Dr. Guise, how unfortunate we are to be meeting here." He opened the cell and removed the key from the lock. Looking at Peter sitting on the floor with eyes red and swollen from crying, he saw what he despised the most. Weakness. Although Peter's eyes were red from tears, they also held something else, a burning hatred.

Since his arrest, things had become clear to Peter where they hadn't been before. As he now saw it, his reputation, his career, and his life were over. His work had been his true calling, and he'd been fortunate to have found it. A life on the beach, working to save endangered animals wasn't a bad way to spend his time. So what if it didn't pay well? It wasn't as if the money he'd been making in the drug trade had made him any happier. His conscience bothered him too. The drugs he'd been helping to put on the street led to misery, pain, and death for those who became addicted. He'd been a fool, and it made him furious.

Peter stood and took a few steps toward the man who had ruined his life.

"Dr. Guise, I must tell you, you look like crap, and I am disappointed to learn you are so weak," said DesFuentes. "I heard you shit yourself when you were arrested. You're a poor excuse of a man."

Peter's voice started off unsteady. "You're the one who's pathetic." Gaining confidence, he inched toward DesFuentes, his voice growing louder until Peter found himself shouting. "You and your low-life drug business, you're disgusting! You ruined my life and I doubt I'm the first, you piece of shit!"

Not expecting defiance and seeing Peter's rage, DesFuentes reached for the handgun tucked in his jeans. His eyes on the gun, and with nothing left to lose, Peter didn't hold back. The pent-up rage he felt toward DesFuentes exploded at once. He sprang forward crashing into DesFuentes with the full force of his body, knocking him backward onto the floor. DesFuentes' sunglasses flew off his face and slid across the jail cell, along with his gun and the keys he'd been holding.

On all fours and recovering quickly, DesFuentes dove for the gun but Peter was closer and kicked it away. He lunged at DesFuentes a second time. Strong from his work wrangling enormous sea turtles, and consumed with anger, Peter wrestled DesFuentes for control. In the scuffle, he saw the keys on the floor and reached for them. Manipulating them between his fingers, he created a rake-like weapon that he swiped across DesFuentes' cheek.

Blood dripping from his damaged face, DesFuentes wrapped his arm around Peter's neck cutting off his windpipe. Gasping for air, Peter reached back over his shoulder and took wild jabs at DesFuentes' face with the keys, causing him to release the headlock. Blood ran into DesFuentes' mouth. Furious, he spit it on the floor. "Get ready to die!" he screamed. Peter hung onto his makeshift weapon, his fingers sticky with blood.

DesFuentes attacked with body punches, each landing hard, taking Peter's breath from him. Peter continued to hit back. With his fist full of keys, he went at DesFuentes again, this time catching his right eye with one of them, slicing it. DesFuentes saw white. Crazed, he threw a wild right hook.

The punch landed, sending Peter crashing onto the concrete floor. Head spinning and ears ringing, his broken nose gushed blood. He struggled to get back up on his feet. Through blurry eyes, he saw DesFuentes pick up his gun.

The bullet blasted through Peter's forehead and exited out the back of his skull.

CHAPTER 54

Tuesday, September 14 - 5:30 a.m.

Up early, Lisa slipped out the sliding glass door of her hotel room and went for a run on the beach. The sun was just beginning to illuminate the horizon, and a slight breeze blew off the ocean. She ran along the water's edge, thinking through the day ahead of her.

She was close to learning who was behind Dorothy's murder, but she was also out of time. *The state police are taking over today. I've got to get Jackson or Guise to talk this morning or the case gets turned over and loses momentum. I could end up empty-handed. And where the hell is my phone?* She pumped her arms and legs harder and hoped like hell for a better day.

Back in her hotel room and in the shower, it dawned on her. *It must have fallen out of my bag when I hit the brakes to avoid that bobcat. I'll be it's under the under the seat.*

She threw on some clothes and walked from her room to the hotel lobby. On her way to the parking lot, she noticed a black Maserati backed into a parking spot close to the hotel entrance. *I recognize that plate...*

She moved behind a huge potted plant, scoped out the lobby and spotted him in the hotel coffee shop across from where she stood. He held a newspaper in front of him. Lisa continued to watch. When he lowered the paper, she saw the scar on his face and her heart raced. Lisa held her breath and watched.

Alex Suarez laid his newspaper on the table and looked out at the parking lot. He turned toward the very spot where Lisa had been standing. He tossed his newspaper in a trash can and went to look around the lobby.

Lisa wasted no time making her way back to her room and out the sliding glass door. Running down the beach for the second time that morning, she looked back over her shoulder every ten yards. Leaving the beach at a public parking area, she found her way onto the main road and waved down a passing car.

"Thank you so much for stopping," she said to the driver, doing her best to appear calm. "I lost my car keys on the beach, and my phone is locked inside. Could you please give me a lift into town?"

"Well, that's right where I'm headed," said the driver, a middle-aged man wearing a loud Hawaiian print shirt and flashing a smile. "I'd be happy to rescue a damsel in distress."

"Well, I guess chivalry isn't dead after all," responded Lisa. *And if you try anything, this damsel in distress will give you an ass-kicking you'll never forget.* "Hey, can I borrow your phone? I need to call someone to pick me up."

Back at the hotel, Alex Suarez yawned and stretched before returning to his seat at the coffee shop. "The bitch must be sleeping in," he mumbled.

CHAPTER 55

Tuesday, September 14 - 7:00 a.m.

Bruce Kim was anxious to get to work. He'd received an alarming email in the middle of the night. One that had shaken him to his core. After a lot of digging by the Special Investigations Unit of the Miami Police Department's Economic Crimes Bureau, the individual behind Stypman Island Enterprises had been identified. The name was buried deep among dozens of shell corporations. Lisa's person of interest was a criminal of the very worst kind and wanted by Interpol and the FBI.

Lisa had been tracking a brutal drug lord, she was in terrible danger and if the killer learned of his involvement, so was Bruce and his family. Bruce had left multiple messages on Lisa's phone to warn her about who she was dealing with. She wasn't answering her phone or returning his messages.

Fearing it might already be too late, Bruce made up his mind. This morning, he'd tell the top brass everything. He'd rehearsed what he'd say while shaving and showering. There might well be consequences, but it was their best chance of getting out of this mess alive.

His wife, Aki, was already up and in the kitchen with his two young children when Bruce finished dressing. He was tying his shoes when she rushed into the bedroom.

"Bruce, a black car just pulled up in front of the house. Four scary-looking dudes with guns are on their way up our driveway."

Alarm registered on Bruce's face, frightening his wife. "Where are the girls?"

"They're in the kitchen eating breakfast."

"Grab them and get out the back door now. Go!"

"Bruce, what's going on?" Aki asked, the fear in her eyes apparent.

"Just do it, Aki, and be fast!"

As Aki ran to the kitchen, there was a loud knock at the door. When Bruce was sure she and the girls had made it outside, he opened it. One of the men held out a badge. "Bruce Kim, I'm Agent Wilson from the FBI. We need you to come with us."

Bruce studied the badge, relief washing across his face. "How did you know I need help?"

"The inquiries you've been making about Stypman Island Enterprises have us interested in what you've been up to. There's someone high up the ranks who's eager to talk to you."

"Glad to cooperate, fellas, but first let me get my wife. She's hiding in the bushes with our kids."

CHAPTER 56

Tuesday, September 14 - 8:00 a.m.

The rohypnol wore off and Kim Witherspoon regained consciousness. Still groggy, the first thing she noticed was her pounding head. As she came around, she smelled and tasted smoke and something else; something familiar. Blinking to clear her eyes, it came to her. The familiar odor was gasoline.

Locked in the cell formerly occupied by Chief Jackson, she pulled her shirt up to cover her mouth and nose and looked around. In the cell next to hers, face down in a pool of blood, was a body. "Peter? What the hell happened?" she yelled for help. Minutes passed without an answer to her calls and the smoke that was filling the jail was making it difficult to breathe. She gripped the bars separating the cells to steady herself and stared helplessly at the gaping hole in the back of Peter's head. Realizing there was nothing she could do, she looked away and tried not to cry.

The glow of the growing fire seemed to be the only thing able to pierce through the ever-thickening black smoke that Kim felt certain would kill her. Sweating from the fire's heat, her eyes stung and watered and her thoughts turned dark. *What's worse? Suffocation or burning to death?*

She noticed a gas can on the floor, emptied of its contents and lying on its side. Bright orange flames reflected in the shiny puddles that were scattered throughout the jail. She threw her body against the door to her cell. It didn't budge, and she resigned herself to what would come.

With tears running down her cheeks, Kim said a quick prayer, "Dear God in heaven, forgive my sins, watch over my family and friends, and please help Simone move on with her life. Amen."

With her thoughts on death, she looked out from the cell. Something caught her eye that she hadn't noticed before. Something menacing. Just a few feet away, teetering on the edge of a metal file cabinet was a second container with a wire attached to it. Kim's eyes followed the wire to the door of the jail and she understood. If someone came to her rescue and opened the door to the jail, the container, which in all likelihood, was filled with gasoline, would topple and a fireball would follow. Her body shook, and she closed her eyes. Resigned to her fate, she sat with her face buried in her shirt waiting to die.

· · ·

Unable to reach Kim at the station, Lisa called Bill Widley who was on his way back from the hospital. She explained that a Good Samaritan had picked her up, and that she was using a borrowed phone. "I'll swing by and get you. I'm just around the corner. I got a call from Dan. He said the State police are on their way."

Back together and driving to the station, Lisa told Bill about the man waiting for her at her hotel.

"And you're sure it was the same guy you saw at the villa?" he asked.

"No question about it. Same Maserati, too. Whoever we're chasing knows what we're up to. I might not be here if I'd gone out to my car."

"I don't know about you, but I'll be glad to turn this over to the State police. They can't show up soon enough." Bill made the turn into the parking lot of the station.

"I'm still hoping for one more crack at Jackson and Guise before they take over."

"You don't trust them. I mean the State police. Do you?"

"I know it sounds wrong, but no, I don't. You know how it can be, Bill. Cops protect cops. Stuff gets covered up for all kinds of reasons. The Blue Wall. It happened to me once before when someone I cared about was murdered. Somebody dropped the ball, and an informant fell through the cracks, never to be heard from again. There was a cover-up, and the case went cold. I've been living without answers ever since. I can't risk letting that happen again."

"I get that but there are a lot of good cops, too. Look at us."

"It's not always about good cops and bad ones. It's about a lack of training, a lack of concern, or just not knowing what to look for. I've seen more than my share of killers who got away with it because the people investigating weren't on top of their game."

Bill parked the cruiser, and they walked toward the station. "I hear you Lisa and I don't doubt what you've seen, I know law enforcement has a long way to go. But if cops can't trust other cops to do their jobs, well, what does that say?"

They entered the station and the smell of smoke accosted them. Bill turned to Lisa. "Do you smell that? Where are Kim and Dan?"

"Kim!" Lisa called out.

"Where's the smoke coming from?" Bill looked around the station.

Examining the floor, Lisa called him over to check it out. "Bill, there's some blood over here." Turning her attention to the jail, she tried to open the door. "It's locked and the smoke's coming from in there."

"We keep the keys over here." Bill opened a gray metal box on the wall. It was empty.

"We need to break the lock," insisted Lisa, her anxiety spiking.

"Hold on. For years we've kept a second set hidden as a backup, they're over here." Hanging from a hook behind the coffee station was the second set of keys to the jail and each of the cells.

"You gotta love a small town." Lisa mumbled as she waited for him to open the door.

"The door's warm, not a good sign," Bill said as he turned the key.

"Open it, anyway, Kim and Dan might be in there."

"Stand back," Bill cracked the door just enough so they could see inside. A wave of heat and black smoke greeted them and they could see flames.

"Bill, look!" Lisa pointed to the wire. "The door's booby-trapped."

"What? Are you sure?" He moved closer to see what Lisa was pointing at.

"See? That wire is attached to something. I might be able to squeeze in," she moved in front of Bill and put her leg inside.

"Oh, no, you don't." He put his arm out to block her way in. "How about we cut it and move fast? I've got wire cutters in my locker."

Lisa peered into the jail while Bill retrieved the wire cutters, her eyes stung from the smoke. "I smell gasoline."

"Here, put this on." Bill handed her a fisherman's gaiter. "It might help with the smoke."

"It looks like the wire leads to that container right there," she said while pulling the gaiter over her mouth and nose. "Basic but effective, if you're not expecting it." As Bill put on his own gaiter, she grabbed the cutters and snipped the wire.

"I'll go. You stay here," said Bill. Before Lisa could object, he darted inside.

As soon as he'd entered the jail, Bill saw Kim waving him away. No longer able to scream, she was doing what she could to warn him. The container of gasoline, now surrounded by flames, was dangerously close to exploding. Locating the correct key, Bill opened the cell. When he bent down to help Kim up, she mouthed one word. "Run!"

. . .

The erupting fireball sent flames everywhere, consuming the station. "You guys okay?" Lisa coughed and gasped for breath. She, Bill, and Kim were in a heap, piled on top of each other behind Bill's squad car. Bill had thrown himself on top of the two women to protect them from the blast and flying debris.

"What the hell, Lisa?" Bill choked the words out. "Are you out of your mind? What were you thinking? Dragging around ten gallons of gas in the middle of a fire?" He sounded angry and looked astonished.

"I'm a badass, get used to it," Lisa said with a tiny smile that grew into a full blown grin. "Now, get your butt off me. You had your hands full getting Kim out of that cell. The least I could do was get the gas a little further from the fire."

Bill hacked up black mucus and spit it on the ground. He wiped his mouth with the gaiter hanging on his neck and his voice softened. "Well, it's a good thing you did. We had just enough time to get out of there before the blast. You saved our asses." He looked at Lisa as if he was seeing her for the first time. Covered in soot, nose running, she was smiling at him. He smiled back.

Kim blinked her teary eyes, willing them to focus. Between fits of coughing, she asked, "How - do I ever - thank you?"

. . .

Defeated but alive, they sat together on a patch of grass watching the Fire Department put out the blaze. Kim borrowed Bill's phone and tried to reach Simone. Several tries later, she still hadn't had any luck. As her head cleared, she came to the realization that Dan Collins must have drugged her coffee. "It never even occurred to me that Dan might be working with the chief. Some cop I am," she said miserably. "I can't even recognize a bad guy after working with him for months."

"Don't sweat it, Kim. I didn't see it coming either," said Bill, "or I would never have left you alone with him last night. And it looks like he was luring me back to the station, so I'd open that door and burn right there with you."

"Well, look on the bright side, you two," said Lisa. "There isn't much to turn over to the State police now, and here they come." As Lisa spoke, three Florida State Police cars pulled in front of the burning building.

Then Bill's phone rang. Seeing it was Simone, Kim picked up.

CHAPTER 57

Tuesday, September 14 - 8:30 a.m.

DesFuentes' right eye was oozing blood, and he couldn't see much out of it. With no time to spend in an emergency room, he'd have to take his chances. He called Collins and arranged a meeting place. It was time to make good on his promise to him, not that he cared about that. He needed Collins to cover his tracks and wanted to use the girl as a potential hostage, should one be necessary. DesFuentes needed collateral. He figured Simone Mercier would do just fine. And, if she wasn't needed, he'd feed her to the sharks.

. . .

Simone slept better than she had in the past several nights. Kim had called last night to share the news that Chief Jackson was behind bars and Peter's criminal role had been exposed. He was in jail too and Simone felt she could finally relax. Sitting up in bed, she stretched her arms and yawned. A crack of sunlight shone through the small gap between the curtains. All that was missing was Kim and a cup of strong coffee.

Simone picked up her cell phone and took it off silent mode, she saw several calls she'd missed, all from Bill Widley's number. Glancing at the time, she wondered why Kim wasn't home by now. *Something's wrong,* she thought, and she pressed the button to return Widley's calls. Then a crashing noise filled the small house.

Before she could react to her front door being kicked in, Dan Collins and the chief burst into her bedroom. They stood at the foot of her bed; guns pointed. Simone screamed and slid her cell phone under the covers.

"Don't move, honey," said the chief. "Do everything I tell you, or you're dead. Get up slowly and keep your hands where I can see them."

Terrified, Simone followed his orders.

"That's a good girl," the chief snarled, motioning with his gun.

Simone stood before the intruders, shaking in fear and wearing nothing more than a baggy old t-shirt.

"Tie her up, Dan. We need to move fast... the boss is waiting outside."

Collins slapped a piece of duct tape over Simone's mouth. He was rougher than he needed to be, causing her teeth to cut into her upper lip. He bound her hands together and then did the same to her feet. Picking her up, he carried her over his shoulder. The loose t-shirt rode up, exposing her body.

He didn't bother to cover my eyes. Simone tried to recall the conversations she'd had with Kim about abductions. *Not a good sign.* Kim had explained that in the case of abduction, if the perpetrator wore a mask or the victim was blindfolded, it was more likely that the victim would be released. That hadn't happened. *I've got to fight back, or I won't survive this*, she thought. Pounding on Dan's back with her bound hands and kicking her feet made no difference and Simone began to lose hope.

Waiting in the Range Rover, DesFuentes sat in the driver's seat behind dark tinted windows. His injured eye throbbed and watered behind his sunglasses. Blood dripped from his damaged cheek. With the press of a button, he popped the hatchback, and Collins dumped Simone into the rear of the vehicle.

This is it, my last chance. Simone readied herself. She kicked her feet up at Collins, slamming him hard in the stomach. He fell backward, landing in the street.

Embarrassed, he got up fast and slapped her hard across the face. He flipped her over and held her face down. "My, oh my, would you look at that ass." He licked his upper lip.

Chief Jackson grunted in agreement. He jabbed a needle into Simone's left buttock and pushed the plunger. Almost immediately she felt woozy, then closed her eyes.

"Rest well. I'll see you soon, baby." Dan pressed a button and the hatchback door closed and locked.

The driver's side window slid down. "You know what to do next. I'll meet you both at the marina. And Dan, I'll have her ready for you when you arrive, so hurry. We need to leave as soon as possible." DesFuentes raised the window and hit the gas. The Range Rover shot forward and disappeared down the street.

. . .

Kim held Bill's phone close to her ear, shocked at what she was hearing. She heard it all - the loud crash, Simone's scream, and the scratch of the sheets. Worse than that, she heard everything the chief had said. Now she knew for certain, Dan Collins was with him.

. . .

With Simone drugged and unconscious in the back of his car, and Jackson and Collins collecting cash, guns, and computers from his home, DesFuentes could attend to his injuries. His pain was excruciating, and his damaged eye continued to bleed. He pulled into a parking space on Stypman Boulevard, the island's main shopping area. It was a hot summer morning, and the shopping area was all but empty, except for a few locals who went in and out of a coffee shop. As he turned off the engine, he glanced at the thermometer. It read ninety-two degrees, and he realized the temperature inside the car would climb rapidly in the Florida heat. *She might not survive locked inside a hot car but she's lucky I haven't already burned her alive like her girlfriend.* About to leave Simone alone in the car, he hesitated. *No one can see through the tinted windows.* He checked from outside just to be sure. Simone was invisible.

DesFuentes made his way into a walk-in clinic. At the height of tourist season, the place would be filled with snowbirds seeking medical attention for any number of ailments. This morning, the waiting room was empty. He walked up to the reception desk and took off his sunglasses. The receptionist gasped when she saw his injured face and damaged eye. Forgoing the paperwork, she rushed him into a treatment room.

. . .

Assuming responsibility for what remained of the Stypman Island Police Department, the State Police took full charge making no secret of their belief that they hadn't arrived a moment too soon. The locals had made a complete mess of things.

"This is a shit show, you two," said Dorchester Moore, dressing down Kim and Bill.

Moore, a fifty-two-year-old, highly experienced, African American law enforcement professional, was the team captain. Suffering no fools, Chester, as he was better known, made it clear he wasn't happy. "So, let's just take stock of where we are," he said. "The two suspects are no longer available for questioning, one of them is dead, and the other broke out of this playpen you call a jail, and the entire police station has burned to ashes. Sound about right?"

Bill interjected, trying to set the record straight. "Look, sir, we're dealing with something that's bigger than all of us know."

"No, you look, Officer Widley! The drug smuggling case that you folks put together has fallen apart. To be blunt, it's down the crapper, and the mastermind behind it is still on the loose and unidentified. To top it off, you tell me Officer Witherspoon's girlfriend has been abducted. What's next? Is this island paradise of yours about to blow up and sink into the fucking ocean? Well, not on my watch!" Chester wasn't finished. "Officers Witherspoon and Widley, I'm instructing both of you to stand down on this investigation. We will take it from here, do you understand?"

Both nodded.

"Good." Chester appeared calmer now. "Now, take some time off and stay near your phones. Don't even think about going anywhere near what's left of that police station."

"And you, Detective Owens, we will go to your hotel. If that guy with the scar is there, we'll take him in. But for now, it's time you return to

Miami, where you belong. Your intentions may be noble, but you're out of your jurisdiction. I just spoke with Lieutenant MacKenzie. He's your boss, correct?"

Lisa nodded.

"He told me you're one of the good ones and filled me in on your background. I'm giving you a pass. You're lucky I'm not insisting on disciplinary action."

Shifting his attention to Kim, Chester placed his hand on her shoulder. "I promise you, Officer Witherspoon, we're doing everything possible to find your girlfriend. Now, the three of you, get out of here and let us get to work."

CHAPTER 58

Tuesday, September 14 - 12:00 p.m.

Alone at a small table at the Blue Heron, Kitty Sampson gazed out at the beach. She sipped cold rosé while waiting for her lunch. Her eyes fixed on two young men doing push-ups in the sand, Kitty sighed and swallowed a mouthful of wine.

The crowd of vacationing tourists and hungry locals was keeping the kitchen and bar staff hopping. Recorded reggae music interwoven with the hum of blenders turning rum, pineapple, and coconut into pina coladas created a festive atmosphere. Busy wait staff delivered orders as quickly as the cooks and bartenders turned them out. From behind the bar, Eileen McNeil kept one eye on Kitty and the other on the rest of the place.

The lively and fun vibe changed when two uniformed State police officers entered the dining room. They made their way toward the table where Kitty sat with her back to them. Seeing them, Eileen shut off the music. Kitty's face fell when she turned around to see what was happening.

"Kitty Sampson, you're under arrest for money laundering and participating in the illegal transport, sale, and distribution of narcotics," said one of the officers in a commanding voice. "Stand and put your hands behind your back." With the entire restaurant watching, he read Kitty her Miranda rights. She winced when the handcuffs locked around her wrists. As she was frog marched out of the dining room, she glanced at the bar. Eileen McNeil wore a smirk on her face.

Once the police had departed with Kitty, Eileen turned the music back on, and the restaurant continued to serve its customers. Deciding to take a chance, she slipped into Kitty's office and looked under the desk, finding a duffel bag like the ones she'd seen before. She'd heard the officers arrest Kitty for money laundering. *Could it be?* she wondered.

Dragging the bag out from under the desk, Eileen unzipped it. "Holy shit," she gasped. "It's filled with stacks of hundred-dollar bills!" Eileen didn't think twice. Grunting, she picked up the heavy bag and shoved it out the office window into a bed of bromeliads. She left the restaurant, using the front door, making sure she was seen empty-handed. Outside, she moved fast, making her way to the spot where she'd dropped the bag.

Careful there was no one to see what she did next, Eileen hoisted the bag into the trunk of her old car, and slammed it shut. Once back inside the Blue Heron, she carried on as normal until the police arrived with an order to close the restaurant. Leaving the Blue Heron with her co-workers, Eileen drove across the bridge and off the island. And then, she kept going.

CHAPTER 59

Tuesday September 14 - 12:00 p.m.

Distraught, Kim was eager to return home after leaving the police station. Hoping to find a clue about Simone's whereabouts, she wanted to see the place for herself. Lisa and Bill joined her. They found the front door had been broken in and quickly located Simone's phone where she'd left it under the bed sheet.

"She attempted to conceal it before she was taken," said Lisa. "She's smart. She wanted us to hear what was going down."

They searched the house for anything that might lead them to Simone but turned up nothing. Kim sat on the bed, worrying. "Guys," she said, "it was important for me to see this for myself, but now that I have, we need to go. The State police will be showing up any minute now and our new friend, Chester, won't be too happy if he finds us here."

· · ·

Back on Stypman Boulevard, exhausted and disheartened, the three sat outside a coffee shop at a table under a pink umbrella, deciding what to do next.

"Well, look who's here," remarked Clara Anders as she, Jason, and Marley approached the table. Marley tugged on her leash, excited to see people she knew.

"Hey there," said Lisa half-heartedly, "and hello to you, Marley." Lisa bent down to greet the dog who was up on her hind legs. Tail wagging, she licked Lisa's cheek. Jason, still recovering from his gunshot wound, looked frail from his hospital stay. His tanned face now appeared pale, and he'd lost some weight. Clara stood next to him, holding his arm.

"Why do the three of you look as if you just walked out of a funeral home?" asked Jason. "And you smell like a campfire."

"Have a seat," said Lisa, "we'll catch you up."

As they talked, Marley sniffed the air. The island's shopping area was a paradise for her nose; food cooking in the restaurants, the smell of waffle cones baking in the ice cream shop, and fresh bread coming out of the oven at the bakery. But it was something else that had caught her interest. Sitting up straight, her nose twitching, she took time to absorb it fully before jumping to her feet and bounding forward.

Surprised by the sudden yank, Clara lost her grip on the dog's leash and Marley took off. All five at the table jumped up, giving chase. They didn't go far. Marley ran down the sidewalk to the curb, where a man with an eye patch and a bandaged face was getting into a black Range Rover. The door to the driver's side was open, and as the man stepped up to get in the car, Marley jumped up grabbing onto the back pocket of his jeans with her teeth. Cursing in Spanish, he swatted at the dog, hitting her hard. She held on.

Clara and Jason, horrified at what they were witnessing, yelled for Marley to let go but the dog ignored them. She was in the front seat on the man's lap, trying to get past him when he hit her again. She yelped from the blow but continued climbing over his shoulder working her way further into the car. As Marley struggled to get past him, her back paw sunk into the man's eye patch, her nails scratching his face and pushing into his damaged eye. Unhinged, the man screamed something in Spanish and protected his face with his hands while Marley hopped over the front seat and disappeared.

Bill was a few steps ahead of Lisa and Kim and reached the car first. Recognizing the Range Rover, Lisa called out a warning, "Careful Bill, this is our guy!"

Trapped and desperate, Ricardo DesFuentes reached for a handgun he kept between the front seats. Before he had his fingers on the grip, Bill clocked him in his bandaged face. Reeling from the punch, DesFuentes grabbed the gun and aimed. Bill moved back from the car, bracing for the bullet. In a flash, a foot crashed into DesFuentes' chest, hitting him hard enough to take his breath and knock him backward. His body bounced off the center armrest, and his arm flew back. A gun blast filled the air.

The bullet blew through the windshield, shattering it. DesFuentes sat forward, preparing to shoot again, but another kick exploded in his face, landing on his chin and snapping his head back. It knocked him out cold.

Astounded by what he'd just witnessed, Bill stared at Lisa, his eyes wide and his mouth open.

"What?" Lisa asked.

"What the hell just happened? I was sure I was done for. Those kicks..."

Lisa raised her shoulders and shrugged. "Hook kicks, I've been practicing them for years, so fast he never saw 'em coming."

. . .

"How could she have known Simone was in the car?" asked Kim.

The group sat in the waiting room of the local hospital. Simone had been rushed there by ambulance. DesFuentes was taken there too. Now handcuffed to a hospital bed, he was guarded by two State police officers. An emergency room physician had re-set his broken nose and treated his re-injured eye.

"She could smell her," said Lisa. "Dogs have incredibly sensitive noses. Simone had been in that car for some time while that creep was in the emergency clinic. When he opened the car door, her scent was released and Marley picked up on it."

"We know Marley's sense of smell is astounding, and she just loves Simone, so she went looking for her," added Jason.

"Well, however she did it, she's my hero," said Kim.

Marley sat on the floor between her owners and Jason scratched behind her ear.

"So, that's the second time she saved Simone," remarked Bill. "Impressive."

"There's more to this little dog than we ever would have thought," said Jason. "That day on the beach when Stewie Williamson pulled out his gun, I would never have thought Marley would be so brave and ferocious."

Clara shook her head and threw up her hands. "Go figure. She's deathly afraid of garbage trucks but doesn't think twice about attacking bad guys with guns."

"Well, she's a very special dog," said Lisa. "If she'd ever like to give up her cushy life on the beach, there's a job waiting for her in the canine unit of the Miami P.D."

"You can see her now," said a nurse with a Jamaican accent who had just entered the waiting room.

"Would it be okay if we brought our dog in?" asked Clara. "I'm sure it's against policy, but there's a special circumstance here."

The nurse smiled. "That adorable little dog is the only one of the bunch of you that Ms. Mercier asked for."

The group laughed and gathered to see their friend when someone else entered the waiting room and called out Lisa's name.

"Bernie!" exclaimed Lisa. "What are you doing here? Guys, this is Bernie Washington, she's a friend of mine."

Bernie nodded at the group, her expression said she was in no mood for pleasantries. "Lisa, could I have a minute with you? Alone."

"You guys go ahead; I'll catch up."

"What are you doing here, Bernie?"

"Lisa, a better question might be, what are *you* doing here? You're in the middle of a very serious situation. The person you've been pursuing is Ricardo DesFuentes, one of the most dangerous criminals in the United States, maybe in the world. When I realized you were getting close to him, I came to warn you. This guy's a cold-blooded killer. He is beyond wealthy, extremely powerful, and absolutely ruthless. He operates a drug route that comes up from Colombia. The FBI has been hunting him for years."

Astonished, Lisa tried to absorb what she was hearing. "How did you know what I was doing... and that I was even here?"

"Your friend, Bruce Kim, made some inquiries on the system that tipped us off. We brought him in, and he explained what you've been up to. He's worried sick about you, by the way. When I heard you were involved, I decided to come and warn you myself. Now that you've uncovered DesFuentes here, we can figure out a plan to pick him up and put him behind bars. I suppose I should say thanks for that."

"Well, there is something else you can say thank you for, but not to me. You'll have to thank Marley."

"Marley?" asked Bernie, confusion on her face. "Who's Marley?"

"A brave little dog with one hell of a nose."

"I don't understand," said Bernie.

"Come with me," said Lisa. "I'll take you to Ricardo DesFuentes. He's here in this hospital."

CHAPTER 60

Tuesday, September 14 - 12:15 p.m.

The chief and Dan Collins stood on the dock beside DesFuentes' Sea Ray L60. After a brief cloudburst, droplets of rainwater sparkled on the chrome railings and trim of the impressive vessel.

They'd been careful to gather everything from DesFuentes' villa that he'd instructed them to take. Mistakes were not forgiven, especially now that so much was on the line. Several canvas bags containing nine million in cash, five hard drives, two laptops, several passports with different identities, two assault rifles, four handguns, and enough ammunition to start a war lay on the dock ready to be loaded as soon as their owner arrived.

"This is where we part ways, Danny," said the chief.

"You're not coming with us?"

"I'm not a Bahamas kind of guy. It's time for me to head my own way. Tell the boss I said thanks and good luck."

"He won't like this. He's used to getting what he wants."

"No, I don't reckon he will," replied the chief, "but that's too damned bad. Besides, I'm of no use to him in the Bahamas."

"What will you do?"

"I'm going to disappear, Danny boy. Have fun with that girl, fuck her good for me." The chief winked. "Gotta hand it to Witherspoon, she has good taste." He slapped Dan on the back and walked to his pickup truck. He drove away without so much as a wave.

An hour later, Collins still waited on the dock in the hot Florida sun. His t-shirt was soaked through with sweat and his face and arms had blossomed pink with sunburn. He could have gone aboard the boat and enjoyed the air-conditioned cabin. He could have had a cold beer, but he wanted to be standing on the dock when DesFuentes pulled up. Simone was his, and he wanted to be the one to carry her aboard. Hot and bothered, Collins pulled at his sweaty jeans.

As Dan daydreamed about Simone, two black cars sped into the marina and pulled in front of the slip where he stood waiting. Six armed men wearing SWAT team apparel jumped out, guns pointed.

"Lie down face first on the dock, keep your hands where I can see them!"

Dan did as he was told, dropping to his knees before lying down. A few minutes later, he was in handcuffs, seated between two large, sweaty FBI agents in the back of a car. He should have been concerned about his arrest and everything that was about to happen to him, but all he could think about was Simone.

CHAPTER 61

Wednesday, September 15 - 5:30 p.m.

"So, who is Ricardo DesFuentes?" asked Lisa. She was with Bill and Bernie at Clara and Jason Anders' condominium. Lisa and Bill sat next to each other on the sofa with Marley snuggled in between them. Kim hadn't joined the rest of the group, opting to stay with Simone, who'd been admitted to the hospital, awaiting test results to determine what substance had been injected into her.

Lisa stroked Marley's head. Whenever she stopped, the dog nuzzled her, indicating she should continue. Bernie sat across from them in a turquoise easy chair. She smiled, watching Marley soak up the affection she'd so rightfully earned. Jason and Clara entered the room with tall glasses filled with ice, vodka, and seltzer water. On each rim was a slice of lime.

With everyone settled in, Bernie answered Lisa's question. "The intelligence we've been able to gather over the past few years is fairly thorough. Ricardo DesFuentes comes from Buenaventura, a port city in Colombia. He was born there to Luciana and Miguel DesFuentes. Luciana mended clothing and Miguel worked as a construction laborer. Both were murdered when they tried to prevent their son from being recruited as a spotter."

"What's a spotter?" asked Jason.

"The cartels use spotters, most of whom are young children, to alert them about police activity. Simply put, they help the bad guys stay one step ahead of the cops. In all likelihood, Ricardo's parents were killed in front of him, a common practice to break children down and make them fearless so they'll do whatever they're told."

"Fearless?" asked Bill. "Wouldn't that make them fearful?"

"You would think so," said Bernie, "but it has the opposite effect. Watching their parents killed is the most horrible thing kids can imagine, so they've already seen and experienced the very worst. After going through that, there isn't much of anything that could be more frightening to a child. They're left alone in the world with nothing to lose."

"Making them fearless," muttered Bill.

"With his parents gone," Bernie continued, "DesFuentes was probably living on the street and sleeping in abandoned buildings with other kids in the same situation. That's where he was likely recruited to the drug trade with promises of food and a place to sleep. Once in the cartel, he would have undergone torture and regular beatings. His body still bears the scars."

"This is heartbreaking," interjected Clara. "He never had a chance; I almost feel sorry for him."

Bernie shook her head. "As disturbing as it is, Clara, this story isn't unique to DesFuentes."

"This is a very cruel world we live in." Jason sighed and took a sip of his drink.

"And we've just seen how very cruel it can be right here on Stypman Island," said Bill, draining his glass.

Jason took his empty glass. On his way to the kitchen to make another drink, he said, "Something tells me we'll all need a few of these."

"As he grew older, DesFuentes excelled at the work and advanced among the ranks of the cartel," explained Bernie. "He developed a reputation as someone who delivered results no matter what. By the time he reached early adulthood, he'd become a ruthless authoritarian. As early as age eighteen, he was making examples of those who made mistakes or let him down. Not only would he kill people in cold blood, but he'd also have them strung up on poles before burning them alive in the street as a public display. He murdered the wives and children of people he no longer liked or needed, very often carrying out the acts in front of the offending husbands and fathers before taking their lives, too. His signature way of murdering his adversaries was to burn them alive. We're pretty sure that's what happened to Congressman Wallingford. It's awful and its something your friend, Kim Witherspoon, now knows about firsthand."

"I think I need another drink," said Clara, handing her glass to Jason. As he took it, she whispered, "Make it a strong one."

Bernie went on, "Stories about his cruelty spread, and before long DesFuentes was feared throughout all of Colombia. When the government took down the cartels, it created an opportunity for new players to take over their former territory. DesFuentes was at the head of that line. He was an experienced operator, trained by the best, and he understood the details of successful drug smuggling. He had strong relationships with the suppliers and more than enough men to staff his operation, men who feared him and wouldn't get sloppy. Most importantly, he was willing to do whatever it took to build his business and capture an impressive share of the Colombian cocaine market. We don't know how many people have died at his hands over the years, but we believe the number to be in the thousands."

"How did his operation work, Bernie?" asked Lisa.

"DesFuentes built his empire smuggling cocaine on ships leaving Buenaventura. From there, the cocaine was transferred by boat or airplane, even narco subs, and sent to his facilities on Grand Bahama Island. He kidnapped people out of Colombia to work in the Bahamas."

"Why did he work out of the Bahamas?" asked Bill.

"A couple of reasons. First, its proximity to the United States makes it an ideal location to route drugs into Florida, and from there, elsewhere in the U.S. But mostly, because he could easily bribe local officials and police."

"If so much is known about him, why hadn't he been apprehended?" Lisa asked.

"Ricardo DesFuentes is like a ghost. He appears in one place and then disappears. Money isn't a barrier for him, and that enables him to stay hidden and move freely across borders. We had a good shot at taking him in Mexico about a year ago, then he vanished. We hadn't been able to locate him until you uncovered him here."

"Any idea why he chose our little island as his hideaway?" asked Jason.

Bernie shook her head, "I couldn't say, but it suits him. It's quiet here, way off the radar, and it's beautiful. We know that's important to him.

DesFuentes worked hard for his wealth, and he likes to live a certain way. This location offered that. The State police and the FBI raided his home earlier today. I wasn't part of the raid, but I saw photos of the house and property. You wouldn't believe that place, its stunning."

"Still, it must have been a lonely life for him," said Lisa.

"From what we can tell, he never married," said Bernie. "But that doesn't mean there weren't women in his life, a lot of women. And there's at least one child. In his bedroom was a photograph of a little girl. It was in a silver frame that had an inscription that read, '*Yo amo a mi Papa.*'

"I love my daddy," said Lisa.

"Yes," said Bernie.

"As it turns out, the little girl lives nearby with her mother. A woman named Bethany Goodson. We brought her in for questioning. She was very nervous about talking to us. We think she may be more than just the mother of DesFeuntes' child; she's somehow involved. We got a warrant and went through her home and her car. The address for the Coquina Reef condominiums was entered in her GPS. She played a part in what happened here; but we aren't sure what her role was just yet."

"I think I know," said Lisa. Bernie Washington raised her eyebrows in surprise. "Josephine Paulsen's brother told me a young woman, who I'm guessing might be Bethany Goodson, delivered a gift to her on the day she died. The gift was a bottle of gin and Mrs. Paulsen's cocktail of choice was a gin martini. I have evidence the gin was laced with strychnine. Mrs. Paulsen didn't die of a heart attack. She was poisoned. Chief Jackson cleaned up the evidence before calling the M.E."

"Holy shit!" exclaimed Jason. "Just when you thought things couldn't get any worse."

Clara looked like she might faint and gulped her cocktail.

"Lisa, I'm going to need you to give us a statement about that and turn over your evidence. If you're correct, and I'm sure you are, I want to do this right and tie that murder to DesFuentes, Bethany Goodson and the police chief."

"What about Dorothy's murder?" asked Bill. "Angelo Scarella killed her, but have you been able to connect him to DesFuentes?"

"Bruce Kim connected us with Charles Rutherford earlier today. His tech team in New York was able to get into Scarella's burner phone. There are calls to and from Ricardo DesFuentes and even a few voice messages. There's no question the two were connected. We've also been able to tie DesFuentes to the prison guard who was on duty when Scarella was killed. We tracked him down without too much trouble. He wasn't the sharpest tool in the shed, to say the least. It turns out he was hiding out in a cheap motel in a place called Peekskill, about an hour or so from the city. He was out of money and called his girlfriend. We tracked his phone and now he's spending some quality time with Charles."

"Closer to home, DesFuentes had Peter Guise's blood and DNA on his clothing when we picked him up at the hospital. Judging from the damage to his face and eye, and what Officer Witherspoon told us about what she saw in the jail cell, it appears Dr. Guise put up a good fight before DesFuentes got the best of him. And thanks to Dan Collins, DesFuentes' most sensitive computer files were waiting for us when we picked up Collins on the dock. By the time we're finished, I'm confident we'll be able to convince a jury to convict DesFuentes on just about everything. As we get more into his bank accounts and financial records, we'll learn a lot more, too."

"Don't forget," said Lisa, "Kitty Sampson is behind bars, and from what we're hearing, she's talking a blue streak. She's insisting DesFuentes killed her boyfriend, a guy by the name of Dillon Callers. Chester Moore and his team are running that one down. The District Attorney is going to be a very busy woman."

"Speaking of Chester," Bernie squeezed her hands together and leaned forward, "his team picked up Alejandro Suarez. He's the guy Lisa saw waiting for her at the hotel."

Lisa sat straighter. "He was armed, wasn't he?"

"Yes, I'm afraid he was. You are *very* lucky you saw him first, Lisa. His mind seems to be damaged, but he's said enough to incriminate himself and his boss. If we can make it stick, there's an attempted murder charge to add to the pile."

"I finally connected with River Whitefeather," added Bill. "Talk about a guy who's happy with his work. It turns out the Fish and Wildlife Commission is everything he was hoping it would be. Just as Kim said, River confirmed he took a report from Josephine Paulsen the night of Dorothy's murder and alerted the chief. He's sending a full affidavit, making for another tie to DesFuentes and a direct implication of the chief's involvement in Dorothy Jensen's death. An upstanding guy like River will make for a very solid and credible witness at trial."

Bernie sat back in her chair and folded her hands. "Lisa, you did some incredible police work here. I'm very impressed."

"I had a good team working with me," said Lisa, "but I hate that Jackson got away."

Bernie gave Lisa a knowing look. "We're tracking him."

"What? How's that possible?"

"Bruce Kim told us about quiet Cove Lane. While the chief and his sidekick, Collins, were there clearing things out for their boat trip to the Bahamas, our agents placed a tracker under his truck. He's in for a nasty surprise."

"Couldn't happen to a nicer guy," said Bill. "I'll sleep better with him behind bars."

"It sure is funny to think that a criminal as formidable as DesFuentes was finally nailed by a twenty-five-pound golden doodle," said Lisa.

"Mini-golden doodle," corrected Clara.

"Well, here's to Marley." Bernie raised her glass; the others joined her toast.

"I still don't understand how she could know what was happening in that car," said Bill. "I get that she could smell Simone, but it was as if she knew DesFuentes meant her harm. I mean the way she fought her way into that car, what was that about?"

"I think Marley could tell DesFuentes was a bad guy," said Bernie. "It's common knowledge that dogs have an incredible sense of smell, but there are dogs with abilities that go much further than we'll ever understand. From everything I've heard about her, I believe Marley is one of those dogs."

"All of this is fascinating," said Lisa, "but it's been a very long day, and I'm feeling these drinks."

"I'll walk out with you," said Bill. "Sorry, Marley, but we're going to leave you now." He gently raised the dog's head from his lap.

. . .

Beau Jackson raced down I-95 South on his way to a new life. Headed to Ft. Lauderdale, he was booked on a 7:00 p.m. flight to Liberia Airport, Costa Rica. He'd packed two bags, one with clothing and, in the other, a dismantled rifle and ammunition. He'd already prepared his handgun for travel and would stick that in the gun bag when he checked his luggage. Arriving at the airport, he pulled into the long-term lot; where he'd leave his truck. Among the thousands of other vehicles, it wouldn't be noticed for weeks. He looked around the cab to make sure he wasn't leaving anything behind. *I'll miss this baby*, he thought, then he opened the door.

"FBI. Get out of the car with your hands in the air, Jackson!" Several armed agents surrounded the truck, their guns out and trained on him.

"What the fuck?" He slammed the door shut and pressed the auto-lock button. Dumbfounded, his head swam with questions. *How the hell did they find me?*

His next thought went to Carla Weston. He recalled her comments about Viktor Morosov and how she planned to handle him. He knew the D.A. would go for the maximum sentence and was aware of what happened to bad cops in prison. *There's no way I'm putting my fate in that woman's hands.*

The lead FBI agent was yelling commands, making it hard for Jackson to think. He could see the team moving closer, penning him in. Sweating and panic-stricken, his body trembled. He tried to tune out the yelling as he considered his next move. Out of options, he reached into his pocket and gripped his pistol.

"This is the last time, Jackson. Out of the car!" He nodded to show he understood. Then, he stuck the barrel of his gun in his mouth, closed his eyes and pulled the trigger. He heard a click.

Jackson sat stunned as the team of agents broke through the windows of his truck and opened the door. They pulled him out and forced him down on the hot asphalt.

"Here's a tip, Jackson," said the agent handcuffing him. "Next time you want to blow yourself away, put some bullets in your damn gun."

CHAPTER 62

Monday, September 20 - 3:00 p.m.
The Board of Directors at the Stypman Island Institute for Marine Life Preservation convened in a stuffy meeting room that vaguely smelled of rotting sea life. Suzette Thawlington, a wealthy widow and the Institute's largest donor, had asked Mike Sampson to convene the meeting. Mike sat in his usual position at the head of the old wooden conference table, while the Board members occupied the remaining seats. No one looked happy to be there.

Suzette spoke first, her southern drawl calm and assured but not especially friendly in its tone. "Mike, I suppose you're wondering why the Board asked you for this meeting. The negative publicity the Institute is receiving because of that terrible business involving Dr. Guise is compromising our mission. The very idea that such a thing was going on under your nose has called our confidence in you into question."

Mike jumped to his feet. Pointing his finger in her face, he glowered at her. "Wait one minute, Suzette! I take offense at that!"

"Shut up and sit down, Mike," interjected Andy Jones, a Board member and Vice President of Coastline Bank. "Suzette is speaking for all of us, let her finish."

"Mike," Suzette went on, "the Board has decided to terminate your employment, effective immediately."

Mike was out of his seat again. "No fucking way! The Institute is mine. I built it and I'm not going anywhere. The five of you can go straight to hell!"

Undeterred, Suzette continued, "You should be aware that we've had the books audited and examined. It's clear there's been theft, and upon closer scrutiny, it appears you're implicated. It makes me very sad to say this." Suzette locked eyes with Mike, whose face had blossomed to a deep red.

"What theft? What the fuck are you talking about?"

"I'm losing my patience, Mike," warned Andy Jones. "So watch your mouth and sit down!"

"For a long time now, we've had our suspicions. This Board isn't as clueless as you seem to think we are." Suzette took her time; she was getting at something. Mike sat stone-faced waiting for her to spit it out.

"Just a few days before the hurricane, Simone delivered a lecture on beach temperatures and how climate change is affecting the gender of turtle hatchlings. Do you recall that?" Mike didn't respond. "I seeded the cash donation jar at that lecture with my own money. Six-thousand dollars, most of it in twenties."

Mike's fingers tightened their grip on the seat of his chair. Tiny beads of sweat glistened on his forehead.

"You were the only person to have access to that cash after it was counted with the rest of the donations that night. Simone handed you the jar. I watched that take place with my own eyes. I waited to see if that amount showed up in our account. It never did."

Suzette paused, letting her words sink in. The room was silent, all eyes on Mike. "Let's not draw this out any longer. We want you to leave immediately. Also, you'd be well-advised to hire an attorney because we're pressing charges. Stealing an amount that large is a felony, we have little choice." Suzette folded her hands and laid them on the table.

Mike was speechless. He'd taken the money the night of the hurricane. He'd gone to retrieve the insurance policy and saw it there, locked in the drawer of his desk. If the storm had hit as expected, the money would never have been missed, lost in the rubble. He'd stuffed all those bills in the pockets of his slicker and walked out with them. Once in his hands, it was hard to put it back. Peter had almost caught him in the act, but apparently he had other things on his mind that night.

Mike's mind raced as he wondered how to explain things to his family and friends. Suzette's voice brought him back to the present. "I need your keys and the Institute's credit card. Would you kindly give them to me? We can arrange to have your personal things sent to your home. But right now, you need to leave the premises and not return."

Visibly stupefied, Mike did what she asked, dropping his keys and credit card on the table. Without saying another word, he stood, looked around the room and walked out the door.

"Now, onto more pleasant business," said Suzette, punching two digits on the walkie-talkie on the table. "Simone, could you please join us in the conference room?"

• • •

When Kim arrived home that evening, she found the kitchen table set for two. Something was in the oven. It smelled French and delicious. Simone stood nearby, holding a bottle of inexpensive champagne. "Not exactly Dom Perignon, but it will do."

"What are we celebrating?"

"You're looking at the new head of the Stypman Island Institute for Marine Life Preservation." Smiling, Simone popped the cork.

"That's incredible, woman!" Kim threw her arms open and ran to give Simone a hug and a kiss. "Congratulations! When did that happen?"

"Sit down, I made us a nice dinner. There is a lot to tell you, and we're drinking every drop in this crappy bottle."

• • •

Wednesday, September 22 - 10:00 a.m.
Having just returned from her morning rounds on the beach, Simone was hosing off her ATV when a call from Andy Jones came in. She picked up.

Andy was calling from his office at Coastline Bank and he sounded excited. "Simone, as a member of the Board, I'm happy to say you've already brought the Institute good fortune."

"I've been on the job for just a couple of days, Andy, and the only thing I've done is check on more turtle nests."

"Well, I have news for you." Andy was practically giddy. "My bank received a wire for the Institute, a donation of seven million dollars! Isn't that incredible?"

"What? That's hard to believe." Simone dropped the hose and put the phone closer to her ear. "Who's the donor?"

"That's the funny thing... the wire came in from an offshore account. The directive said the donor wished to remain anonymous, but it had a note that said, 'In remembrance of a woman in red.' Crazy, right?"

"Andy, is this legitimate?" Simone frowned, her suspicion growing by the second.

"It is. I made sure the bank scrutinized it before I said anything to you or the Board. Start thinking about how you can best use that kind of cash. The Board will be excited to hear your ideas."

CHAPTER 63

Saturday, May 7 - 4:00 p.m. (eight months later)
The trade winds kicked in and a soft, warm breeze blew over the beach. The ocean was a brilliant turquoise, and small waves shimmered in the bright sunshine. Rows of rattan chairs that had been set up in the sand a few hours earlier, were now filled with friends and family members. A simple arch of tropical flowers stood on the beach with the ocean behind it.

Clara and Jason sat together, holding hands, both smartly dressed for the occasion. Next to them was Bernie Washington, who'd traded her usual black pants suit for a brightly colored dress and dark oversized sunglasses. Ronnie and Charles Rutherford sat just behind them. Charles sported a white Panama hat to cover his bald head from the strong sun. He wore a seersucker suit, and a pair of dark Wayfarers. Looking like a guy in a Corona advertisement, his arm rested on the back of his wife's chair. Ronnie gazed out at the ocean and whispered to him, "Remind me again, why do we live in New York City?"

Seated next to a pretty, young woman with a yellow flower in her long black hair was River Whitefeather. He'd been assigned by the FWC to a post just outside Orlando and had traveled with his new girlfriend at the invitation of the groom.

Arriving at the last minute, Bruce and Aki Kim, along with their daughters, filled a row further back. Bruce held hands with his wife, who was doing her best to keep Millie from kicking at the sand beneath her bare feet, sending it onto the legs of Greg Mackenzie who was just in front of them. Mac was alone and sweating through his suit.

An older Black man with gray hair and a bright smile began to play Bob Marley's *'One Love'* on a steel drum. Kim, followed by Simone, walked onto the beach and toward the guests. They wore matching dresses, each carrying a small bouquet. Marley walked next to Simone who held her leash and some dog treats. Around the dog's neck was a white bow with a small pouch dangling from it. Seeing the ocean, Marley pulled on her leash, wanting to bolt for the surf. "Not happening," said Simone, pulling back. "You have an important job, so no swimming, at least not yet."

Following them came the bride and groom, beaming and holding hands. Tears streamed down Clara's cheeks. She leaned over to Bernie and whispered, "I've never seen anyone look quite so lovely."

Jason handed Clara a tissue he'd put in his pocket for this very purpose. "I expected you'd need this," he whispered.

"Any chance you have another?" asked Bernie. "I thought these sunglasses would do the trick, but I'm a blubbering mess over here."

Jason happily obliged.

The bride and groom reached the flowered arch and turned to face each other. A young minister, who wore his long blonde hair in dreadlocks, began the simple ceremony. When he asked for the rings, Simone whispered, "Go ahead, Marley, just as we practiced it."

The dog jumped on the groom, her front paws on his legs, and he removed the pouch she carried. Once the vows were said and the rings exchanged, Bill held Lisa's face in his hands and kissed her.

The reception was held later in the evening at a small outdoor restaurant overlooking the ocean. Under a full moon, the water shimmered like polished silver. Tables were arranged on an outside patio where a three-piece band played reggae tunes. Bill nodded at the man playing the steel drums, the same man who'd played during the wedding ceremony. He nodded back. The two had known each other since the day Bill rescued him and his daughter from the waves several years earlier.

"Bill how are you adjusting to your new job?" asked Bernie, who had arrived on Stypman Island just in time for the wedding ceremony.

"I'm feeling pretty good about it. The department needs to win back the trust of the residents. That takes time, but every day we're working hard at it. We'll get there."

"Well, I think you were a perfect choice to take over the department."

"I think so, too," said Kim, joining the conversation.

"You'd better think so," said Bill with a laugh. "You're my lieutenant, second in command."

"Actually," Kim said to Bernie, "we make a really good team."

"To tell the truth, Bernie, Kim's much more than my lieutenant. We're partners, there's no way I could do the job without her."

"The people of Stypman Island are in excellent hands now," said Bernie. "And Lisa? What is she saying about her new job and, more importantly, her new boss?"

"Well, let's ask her." Bill waved to Lisa, gesturing for her to join them.

After twelve years at the Miami Department of Police, Lisa had resigned from her job and accepted a new position. She now worked with Bernie at the FBI, having excelled during the twenty weeks of training at the Academy in Quantico. Her new job enabled her to live on Stypman Island with her husband. The airport being only forty minutes away, she easily traveled when her cases required it.

Bernie had convinced Lisa the FBI needed her. "You have proven instincts for this kind of work," she'd said. "And there are many more bad actors like Ricardo DesFuentes who need to be taken down. Frankly, the FBI needs smart women, and I want you on my team." After talking it through with Bill and Mac, Lisa had accepted the new position.

"Hey there, everyone having a nice time?" asked Lisa as she joined the group.

"Bernie was just asking how you like your new boss," said Bill.

Lisa smiled at Bernie. "Well, she gave me time off for a honeymoon, so I guess she's okay. Speaking of bosses, did you guys see Mac? It was sweet of him to come, but the poor guy looks like he fell in a pool."

· · ·

Clara walked into the ladies' room as Lisa fixed her makeup. "Lisa, you look absolutely radiant."

"Thanks Clara, it's kind of you to say that. It's a bittersweet day for me. I keep thinking of Dorothy, and how much she would have enjoyed this."

"Yes, she would have. It's been a beautiful day, and Dorothy would have loved every minute of it. She'd be so pleased to see you wearing those earrings of hers on your special day."

"Oh, you recognized them?" said Lisa, beaming.

"Yes, I did. They're the perfect touch."

"Are you and Jason enjoying yourselves?"

"Yes, very much. I've been talking with your mother, Lisa. She's so proud of you."

"I'm happy she was able to be here... I haven't seen her in quite a while. And she's crazy about Bill."

"By the way, Jason and your friend, Charles, have really hit it off. They're planning a trip for us to visit New York and eat eggplant at some restaurant Charles is raving about."

Lisa smiled, remembering the dinner she'd had with Charles and Ronnie not so long ago. "Charles is a great guy. Ronnie was lucky to find him."

"And you were lucky to find Bill. He's a wonderful man. I think you'll find a lot of happiness with him."

"It's funny you'd say that. I was just thinking about a note Dorothy wrote to me before she died. She told me to chase happiness."

"Excellent advice," said Clara with an understanding smile. "I'm glad you followed it."

"It's crazy how things worked out. Who would have ever thought Dorothy's death would lead me to the person I'd marry? I'd given up on marriage, a happy life... heck, I'd given up on just about everything after Scott died. Her death brought us all together."

"That it did, and now that we've found each other, let's keep each other close."

Closing her arms around Lisa, Clara gave her a hug.

. . .

After everyone left the restaurant, Bill and Lisa went for a walk on the beach.

"The beach is beautiful late at night. Come on, it will be romantic," Bill had said, nudging his new wife to agree.

"Babe, the last time you and I were out on the beach late at night, it didn't go so well. Remember?"

Bill smiled. "That's true, but there's a new chief in town, and I hear he's got things under control. I think we'll be safe."

The newlyweds took their time strolling the moonlit beach. Bill held a flashlight pointed down in the surf line, the light illuminating the water as it lapped over their bare feet. He stopped every few feet to kiss his new bride. "I can't imagine living anywhere else. It's just so beautiful here."

"I agree. I love this island, and I love you." Turning toward her husband and hoping her words had made for a romantic moment, she saw he wasn't paying attention to her. "Did you even hear what I just said to you?"

Bill was crouched down, his hand in the shallow water. "Would you look at that!" he said, examining the object he'd just pulled out.

"What is it?" asked Lisa.

"Check this out." He extended his hand, in it was a thick coin slightly larger than a quarter. "It's a gold doubloon, likely from the Spanish Plate Fleet that sank just out there, hundreds of years ago. I've heard people still find these, but I never believed it."

"The Treasure Coast," whispered Lisa. She reflected on the stories she'd heard from Dorothy about this place. "Bill, that old coin in your hand is nice, but there's something even better than sunken treasure."

He smiled at her as he straightened from his crouched position. "What's that?"

"Let's go home, and I'll show you."

ACKNOWLEDGEMENTS

In many ways this book is a love letter to Florida, its gorgeous beaches, incredible wildlife and stunning natural beauty. Ricardo DesFuentes, Wally Wallingford and Judy Clofine are metaphors for the greed and corruption threatening this beautiful place. Until we stand together to protect the environment no matter where we live, we are all their victims.

There are so many people who were with me on this journey. To those who generously took the time to read an early version of the book, Eileen and Jack Hueter, Norma Duval, Linda Whalen, Bill Norris, Patty and Ralph Jones, Paula and Peter Sullivan, Nicolette Duong and my family; Suzanne, Chris and JJ, I sincerely appreciate your being the first eyes on my story. Those initial reads were nerve racking for me and you made me feel safe and supported even when my writing wasn't quite there yet.

To all those who provided feedback, offered suggestions or just stuck with me as I stumbled my way through this project, I'm very grateful. Your kindness and input helped bring TREASURE COAST to life. Special thanks to the Treasure Coast Writers group, especially Karen Howard and R. Todd Henrichs for launching me into the world of writing and for the first critiques. Also thanks to Leslie Downey, Jason Ferrel and Raveen Khehar, my talented critique partners in California, who always have great ideas and feedback. To my writer friends; Gina Thompson, Leslie Ferguson, Patrick Holcomb and Holly Kammier, thank you for your ongoing support and encouragement.

Thank you to Megan Hueter for guiding my publicity efforts, and to my editor, Laura Taylor who showed me the ropes and made me a better storyteller. Finally, to the team at Black Rose Writing, thank you for taking a chance on me and introducing Lisa Owens to the world.

ABOUT THE AUTHOR

James Foley has a passion for weaving intricate tales of suspense and intrigue. After trading a successful career in business for life on a barrier island working with sick and injured sea turtles, James found the inspiration for *Treasure Coast* when packages of illegal narcotics washed up on a local beach. James currently resides in San Diego, California, with his wife, Suzanne, where he has discovered the joys of tequila and live music at large venues but has yet to embrace the "icy" Pacific. He loves to explore the world, hoping to touch down next in Africa. Their beloved dog Marley, who inspired a character in *Treasure Coast,* unexpectedly passed away just prior to publication. Follow James at james-foley.com.

NOTE FROM JAMES FOLEY

Word-of-mouth is crucial for any author to succeed. If you enjoyed *Treasure Coast*, please leave a review online—anywhere you are able. Even if it's just a sentence or two. It would make all the difference and would be very much appreciated.

Thanks!
James Foley

We hope you enjoyed reading this title from:

www.blackrosewriting.com

Subscribe to our mailing list – *The Rosevine* – and receive **FREE** books, daily deals, and stay current with news about upcoming releases and our hottest authors.
Scan the QR code below to sign up.

Already a subscriber? Please accept a sincere thank you for being a fan of Black Rose Writing authors.

View other Black Rose Writing titles at
www.blackrosewriting.com/books and use promo code
PRINT to receive a **20% discount** when purchasing.

www.ingramcontent.com/pod-product-compliance
Lightning Source LLC
LaVergne TN
LVHW091332200325
806438LV00001B/104